His Wounded Heart

PROTECTOR'S OF JASPER CREEK
BOOK ONE

CAITLYN O'LEARY

To my husband John. Thank you for a wonderful 26 years together. I so appreciate you humor, your love and your support.

Synopsis

He's my soulmate. But will I be enough to heal his wounded heart?

Simon

The Navy's been my life. Being a SEAL is all I ever wanted, commanding them a dream come true. But I lost sight of everything else and missed the big things—things going on right in front of me. How could I not see how much my sister needed me? I knew her husband was off and should have checked him out. Instead, I let it go and now she's dead. I'll never forgive myself. But I'll make sure nothing like that happens again. My life doesn't fit anymore. It's time to move on to where no one knows who I am—Jasper Creek, Tennessee.

Trenda

I've lived in Jasper Creek my entire life. This small town has been my safety-net, my place of peace and my sanctuary for years, but I feel like something's missing. I've become too comfortable, allowing life to wash over me. But it's time to decide if I need to take my precocious little girl and move on. Head some place where my five sisters, and the best big brother in the world, won't be nose-deep in my life.

Their Story

Fate has its own ideas and brings Trenda and Simon together. Drawn to each other, they slowly heal their old wounds and see a future together. When spectres of the past come calling, intent on destroying all that they have built, will their budding love survive or turn to ash?

Chapter One

The dinner table looked perfect. She'd even used the good china Ned's mother had given them as a wedding present. The gravy was smooth as silk in the gravy boat right next to his plate.

Liz trembled as she returned to the kitchen and opened the oven. She checked the simmering pot roast and nodded. Using the oven mitts to pull the pan out of the oven, she placed it onto a trivet on her spacious marble island, then she carefully closed the oven door.

She selected her sharpest knife to slice off pieces that were exactly the same thickness because that was how Ned preferred his meat to be cut. Liz started when the front door slammed open and some of the roast's juice fell onto the island. She bit her lip so she didn't cuss.

"Elizabeth, why isn't dinner on the table?" Ned bellowed from the dining room.

"I wanted it to be warm for you, Honey. It's coming right out." Even when she called out, she did her best to keep her tone pleasant.

"You better not keep me waiting too long," he yelled back.

After his meat was properly cut, she added it to the plate already loaded with broccoli and cheese sauce as well as creamy garlic mashed potatoes. Liz fanned the slices out so that the food had a pleasing presentation. When she was done with that, she poured the béarnaise sauce over the meat, just as Ned liked.

Liz carefully walked his plate into the dining room and placed it in front of Ned with her version of a loving smile.

"Where's my wine?" he barked. "Don't tell me you haven't got some pinot noir open and breathing for me," he warned her.

"It's right here," she pointed to the sideboard. "I opened it a half hour ago."

"Pour me some," he pointed to his glass.

She took the bottle and brought it over. Her hand trembled when she poured. A little of the red wine spilled on the white tablecloth. It reminded her of blood.

Slowly. Ever so slowly, Ned took the bottle from her hand.

"That's one, Elizabeth." She shivered at his low growl.

He poured himself some more wine, then he handed the bottle back to her.

"Can you put it back without spilling any?"

Liz took the bottle in two hands and cradled it like one would a baby, then placed it carefully on the sideboard. She came back with a linen napkin to clean up the spot where the drop of wine had spilled. When she reached out to soak up the drop, Ned gripped her wrist and twisted.

Hard.

"You're disturbing my dinner."

Liz fought back a cry of pain. She felt perspiration gather on her upper lip and between her shoulder blades. She knew from experience that she'd be branded with bruises for weeks to come.

"*You wouldn't want to disturb my dinner, now would you, Elizabeth?*"

She shook her head, making sure to keep her eyes down.

"*Because you were trying to help, I won't count that as an infraction.*"

"*Thank you, Ned,*" she gulped.

She turned to go to the kitchen, wanting to put ice on her wrist.

"*No, don't go. I want to savor my meal with you by my side.*"

Her trembling got worse. "*That sounds lovely,*" she whispered.

She watched as he speared a piece of broccoli and brought it to his mouth. He chewed, closing his eyes. Liz could tell he was savoring it. She relaxed just a bit.

After he was done chewing, he brought his napkin to his lips, then set it back down in his lap. "*That is wonderful. You did well. I see last week's reprimand helped, just as I thought it would.*"

Liz nodded.

"*I didn't hear you,*" he coaxed.

She looked up at him. "*Yes, it helped, Ned.*" Her smile was tremulous.

Looking satisfied, he reached over his plate and picked up the delicate gravy boat, and poured some of the gravy onto his potatoes. It horrified Liz when she saw how slowly the gravy came out of the boat.

It's cold!

Ned put the container back down on the table and turned his head to look up at her. His eyes almost glowed with fury. "*I think you provided me with cold gravy. Is that true?*"

Liz couldn't answer. She was terrified.

"*Let's see, shall we?*" he asked.

He picked up his fork and filled it with potatoes and

gravy, then took a bite. She watched his face turn purple with rage as he spit the food onto her shoes.

Ned shoved up from the table, knocking his chair over. He grabbed the gravy boat and flung it across the room. Liz watched in terror as the china shattered and gravy bled down the wall. Ned backhanded her against the sideboard.

"That's two, Elizabeth. God help you if there's a third."

Liz made a mad grab for the wine, just catching it before it fell over. She didn't care about her pain. Pain was nothing new, but she knew having a third infraction was utter hell. There had been four in the last two months. That's why she'd been stealing small amounts of money out of Ned's wallet every week, so she could escape. Her friend Dora was going to help her.

Ned righted his chair and sat back down, putting his linen napkin back on his lap.

"Get over here and quit your whining."

Liz's legs were trembling, and she was dizzy from the hit. She didn't know if she could walk the four steps that would bring her next to Ned.

"Elizabeth, I'm waiting," he practically crooned.

She looked at him and did her best not to show her hatred. There he sat in his three-piece suit. A white shirt that she had taken great care to iron, and an expensive silk tie that she had bought for him on one of the few days she was allowed out of the house. With his blond hair, white teeth, green eyes, and perpetual tan, he was gorgeous. How could she have not seen the monster hidden below the surface?

"Elizabeth, this is your last warning," he whispered.

Liz walked over on shaky legs and stood beside him.

Ned picked up his fork and steak knife and cut into the bearnaise-covered pot roast and brought it to his mouth, then set the utensils back down. He pulled the partly chewed piece of meat out of his mouth and set it carefully down beside his plate. Then he used his fork to wipe off the sauce from the five pieces of meat.

"Look at the meat, Elizabeth."

"I see it," she said softly.

"Look closer. How do I like my meat cooked?"

"Medium rare, Ned."

"How is this roast cooked, Elizabeth?"

She swallowed. She knew that the meat was medium-rare, but if she said that, he would say she was lying, and it would be her third mistake. But if she agreed it wasn't medium-rare, that would be her third mistake too.

"I'm sorry, Ned," she pleaded. Praying he would show mercy. Her ribs still hadn't healed from the last time.

He placed his napkin over his diner and pushed back his chair.

"That's number three. Obviously, you don't know your way around a kitchen." He seized her sore wrist in a steely grip, and she gasped in pain. "Shut up, that's nothing." He dragged her into the kitchen.

"Look at this mess. I provide you with the most expensive home on the block, a beautiful kitchen covered in marble, decked out with high-end stainless-steel appliances, and you still fuck up my meals. How is that possible, Elizabeth? How?"

He dragged her over to the gas stove and turned on one of the burners.

"Please don't, Ned. I'll do better, I promise. Please, Ned."

He pulled on her hand, forcing her clenched fist down on the burner, and she screamed.

... and screamed.

... and screamed.

Knowing that no one would ever come to her rescue.

She must have passed out because she was in the bedroom when she woke up. She curled up in the fetal position, holding her burned hand to her chest. Ned was standing over her with his gun. How many times had he shown her his five-thousand-dollar Colt Python handgun? It was his pride and joy, and he was going to kill her with it.

Ned was crying.

"I found your money yesterday. Did you know that, Elizabeth?" He pressed the toe of one of the many dress shoes that she kept polished into her hip. "Get up," he whispered.

She couldn't. She hurt too much.

"Get on your knees, Elizabeth. You wanted to leave me. Well, I can arrange that. Get on your knees."

"Huh?" she was having trouble understanding him.

"Do it. Do you want to make me angrier? Who were you going to leave with? Tell me his name."

Liz moaned. What had he just said? The pain was excruciating. Now she couldn't understand a word he was saying.

He prodded her with his shoe again.

"I asked you a question. Tell me his name. Who is he?"

Ned fell to his knees beside her and pushed back her hair. She saw how tears ravaged his face. "Just tell me who he is, that's all I ask." He wasn't yelling. He was talking right into her face, almost crooning the words. She could understand. "If you do that. If you tell me who he is. I'll forgive you. I'll kill him, but I'll forgive you. You know you're my world. I love you. You're my everything."

Liz lurched away until her back hit the bed. Even then, she tried to move further. She tried to slide under the bed.

"Don't you dare! Tell me who he is, Elizabeth. You can't leave me. You promised me in front of my parents. You said you would hold on to me for better or for worse. You said you would love and cherish me, and only death would part us. Do you remember, Elizabeth? Do you? Do you remember your promises before God?" he screamed so loud his voice was shrill.

He yanked her from under the bed by her injured hand.

She screamed this time. It wouldn't matter, nobody lived close by. Nobody would hear her.

"I told you to kneel, Elizabeth. You need to do what you're told. Now tell me what you were going to do with that money. Who were you going away with? Tell me!"

She felt the spittle spraying her face.

"Dora. She was going to drive me to the bus station. There wasn't any man. I swear it."

He swung the gun around and pointed it at her. "You're lying to me," he croaked. Tears and snot covered his face. "You unfaithful bitch. Just tell me who he is. Tell me." He pulled her into a kneeling position. "You need to tell me. You need to confess to God and me. Tell us both your sin."

He dug the barrel of the gun so hard into her forehead.

"Please Ned, there's no one. There's only ever been you," Liz cried. "Only you. But you keep hurting me. I have to leave."

He twisted the barrel, twisting her skin so hard she thought it would rip, making her forget all about the pain in her hand.

"There's only one way you can leave this marriage, Elizabeth, remember? Til death us do part. You promised our families. You promised God. Now kneel!" He yanked her into a kneeling position, then placed the gun against her temple.

~

"Lizzy!"

"Lizzy!"

Fuck, why can't I get to her? What the fuck is wrong with me? I tear at the material tangling me up and grab my gun off the nightstand.

"Lizzy," I scream one more time. Just one more time before I realize it was the dream. The same damn fucking dream about my little sister that I'd been having for the last six months ever since that fucker killed her. I should never have bribed that Minneapolis detective to show me the police report with the pictures, and the witness statements.

I latch on the safety and put my SIG Sauer back on the nightstand and push back the sheets. They're shot, soaked through with my sweat.

Not going to sleep on those tonight.

Hell, who am I kidding? I will not sleep at all, no matter what, and it's not because of sweaty sheets. I leave the lights off in the bedroom and in the tiny little living room as I stumble to the kitchen. Pressing my fingers to the bridge of my nose, I try to fight back tears.

Not tears for my loss.

No.

Tears for the life she had been leading that I hadn't even noticed. All I deserve to feel on my behalf is rage at myself for having failed her so badly. How could I have missed the signs? How could I have let my beautiful baby sister down so badly?

Chapter Two

The bottle of Jack is staring back at me from where it sits on the coffee table. What the hell had been playing on the television all night is beyond me. I just know that it hadn't been some fucking true crime show. I wouldn't have been able to stomach it. If it had been true crime, I would have shot the TV, á la Elvis, seeing Ned's face the entire time.

It doesn't matter that Ned offed himself. Every day I dream of digging him up and killing him again, slowly... ever so slowly.

Shoving out of the recliner, I know it's oh five hundred; it doesn't matter that I haven't slept a wink, and the sun's not up. My body's just scheduled to get moving at five a.m. That's just the way it is. I wonder if I'll ever break that habit. I snag the bottle of Jack Daniels and head to the kitchen. It's an easy reach to put it back in the cabinet over the fridge. The sealed bottle will be there for me for the next time I have that goddamned nightmare. I should have never read their notes.

As I shove the heel of my hand against my temple, my stomach decides to growl. I've been hungry since yesterday.

Maybe it's time to eat. But I know before even yanking open the fridge that it will be empty.

"Not empty. There's ketchup and week-old pizza."

I kind of laugh. At least I think that's what that sound is.

Fucking wonderful. Sense of humor, still intact.

I shove harder at my temple—apparently, lying to yourself brings on pain. *Who woulda guessed?* I scan the empty counter, then my gaze lands on nirvana.

Coffee.

When I go to pour my beans into the grinder, I realize I am down to the last of the beans.

"Dammit!"

I grind the beans, then pour the granules into my pride and joy, which cost me far too much money, and wait for the elixir of life.

The espresso machine was one of eight actual things I'd bothered to pack when I'd left my life to hide out in the middle of nowhere. Max and Kostya tried to talk me into putting all my other stuff into storage, but I'd insisted I didn't want it. They'd sent me a hefty check. Someone, either on their team, or one of their women, did a bang-up job selling all my shit, so here I am in Tennessee with my eight things, and a brain that can't stop swirling down a toxic drain.

"Cut it out, Clark! No backwards thinking, focus on the now."

I shake my head, then check some of my cupboards to see if there is some oatmeal that I can eat, but all I find is a can of green olives, which I hate, and a can of black beans.

Really?

How'd I let it get this bad? I look over my shoulder and see the coffee is ready, and feel my lips turn up. I think it is called a smile.

After I suck down half a mug, I face the fact that I'm going to have to go into town for groceries... and coffee. This time, I'm going to take some time and actually buy shit, not just fill the basket with random goods and get the hell out of there. That's how I ended up with nothing but ketchup, beans, and olives. I open the fridge again and lift the lid on the pizza. I think mold might have been growing on top of the mushrooms, but aren't mushrooms basically mold? For God's sake, I'm a grown-assed man.

I have to suck down the rest of the mug of coffee before I can agree with that last statement.

Despite the coffee, my stomach growls again. I guess I have to leave, which also mandates a shower and clean clothes. The morning is just getting worse and worse.

By the time I dress and am ready to go, I'm even more pissed off when I realize the one grocery store in goddamned Jasper Creek won't be open for another hour. I get up and open the can of beans and sit down at my dining room table and start eating while staring at a month's worth of mail. I divide it into three piles. The shit that's addressed to Commander Simon L. Clark, US Navy, Retired I throw in one pile that's already an inch high. Then there's the pile that's only fit for the trash.

"Who prints this shit?"

Last, I look at the shit I really don't want to look at. It's the shit that's addressed to just plain old Simon Clark. These are the ones that hit me the hardest, especially when they come from old friends. This pile is even taller than the retired pile. I look at my watch again and see that I still have forty-five more minutes to kill. What is worse, the beans are all gone, and I've been actually enjoying them. I get up and throw the fork and the empty can in the sink, then pour myself another cup of coffee.

When I sit back down, I flip through some of the

bullshit letters from the United States Navy. I should have just fire-bombed my bridges with them, then I wouldn't be stuck getting so much damned mail.

Grimacing, I look over at the top letter on the personal pile and see it's from my old boss, Josiah Hale. He is the bastard that arranged for me to get a retirement instead of a stay in Leavenworth.

Asshole.

My mug goes down hard as I set it down on the table, but as the coffee sloshes, it doesn't wet any of the envelopes. Damned shame if you ask me. I grab Josiah's letter to see what in the hell he has to say. The words are a bit blurry, mostly because he has shitty handwriting, but also my eyes are gritty from lack of sleep.

Simon,

I figure you're still pissed that I didn't let you blow up your career and go head-to-head with the suits. Suck it up. Eventually, you'll pull your head out of your ass and admit you would have done the same thing for any one of the men under your command.

I hope like hell you've thought about counseling. You need it. But then again, the only way I would have gotten my ass on someone's couch would be if Scarlett had made me, but you don't have a woman, so I figure you haven't done it. Think about it anyway, otherwise I might send my woman down to Tennessee.

Now, the real reason I'm writing is that you've had enough time being an anti-social prick. It's been three months. That's the limit. I want you to come to Nic's wedding. We set it for mid-June, but now it's going to be the first week of April. He's a chip off the old block. He knocked up Cami before they tied the knot and she still wants to wear the same dress, so *we're moving up the date. If you miss this event, I <u>will</u> send Scarlett over there. This is not an empty threat.*

Now go get your dress whites dry cleaned and don't forget to shave.

-Josiah

It shocks me that I find myself laughing. Josiah is still a fucking nut. Only a very small circle of us understands just who Josiah really is, and I am honored to be one of those people. The rest of the world wouldn't believe me if I told them. He's one of the best men I've ever known. He'd been my lieutenant when I'd first started out. I didn't much care for male authority figures at that point in my life, but Josiah was different. He helped turn my life around. I owed the man. I owed him for damn near everything.

Looking down at my watch, I sigh with relief. It is almost oh seven hundred and the grocery store will open soon. That means I can stop with the introspection and ignore the rest of the mail.

I head out and once again consider trading my baby in for a truck with four-wheel-drive, but that would mean I have some kind of loyalty to this place, and I don't. Am I really up for any kind of commitment at this point in my life? Look where the Navy left me. And Patsy. But really, that was just as much my fault as hers, but it sure as hell had stung.

I climb into my 1960 Pontiac GTO and start warming her up. She coughs a little, and that isn't like her.

"I'm not trading you in. If anything, I'll just get you a big brother. Some kind of over-the-top truck." As soon as she hears my words, my car purrs. I continue to sip my coffee. What am I going to do? I still have a house in Virginia Beach and my townhome in La Mesa, California, but I don't want to be anywhere near either of those two Navy bases, so those aren't options.

But staying here?

I could try Wyoming, or South Dakota. I have options, what with the retirement, and the rent I'm getting off my two properties. And after three months in this cabin, I've certainly proved I don't need much.

By the time the car is warmed up, the coffee has kicked in. Last night is barely a memory. I drive the ten miles toward town and know as soon as I start hitting streets named after trees that I'm close to the center of town. Seriously, what's with the founding fathers' obsession with trees? I pull into the Roger's Supermarket. I'd met the man, Roger Clemmons. He thought he was so clever naming his store Roger's since it was close to the name of that big name-brand store. Even in my shittiest mood, I hadn't had the heart to tell the poor bastard that the twenty-stall parking lot and the seven aisles of product would never convince anybody that they were in a Kroger's. I just hope I don't run into him today because all bets are off. Dreaming about my sister's death always guarantees to make me off-the-charts ugly, *and* I need an antacid. The beans aren't sitting well.

As I climb out of my car, I lament the fact that I quit smoking twenty years ago. Fucking Liam McAllister—why'd I listen to him? I could really use a cigarette about now.

Leaning against the cold steel of my car door, I watch some of the women of Jasper Creek enter the store. Looks like I wasn't the only one who got up early. Damn, I'd really hoped I could just go in and get out, all without having someone saying something nice to me that required some kind pleasantry spoken in return.

"Suck it up, Clark. The only easy day was yesterday," I mutter as I grab a wheeled cart from the parking lot and head in. Produce and dairy are on the right, meat and bakery on the left. If I manage this right, I'll be out of here in twelve minutes.

I go left and immediately run into a problem. Should have seen it coming. Of course, the bakery is a hotbed of activity first thing in the morning.

Donuts.

Total bad planning on my part, and now here I am, boxed in. There are two shopping carts and one stroller. If I make a move to back up, the women will notice, apologize, and it will initiate conversation.

Dammit!

I have no choice but to keep my head down and move forward. For God's sake, I just need some wheat bread. I'd even forgo the organic kind if it will get me out of the line of fire.

As I snatch my brand off the shelf, I know I just need to keep close to the racks and away from the bakery case and I'm home free.

"Can I help you find anything?"

Don't engage.

I kept going.

"Sir? Did you find what you needed?"

Not looking back, I just nod and wave over my shoulder as I head to the back wall of the meat department.

Made it.

When I get to the butcher shop, I zero in on the lean meats and make my selections, then turn to the first aisle, which contains the elixir of life.

Coffee.

Now here, I have no other option. I have to slow down. I have to take my time and make wise decisions. If you pick the wrong type of coffee, you're screwed for the entire week. At least Roger understands the need to have a good assortment of coffees. It almost, not quite, but almost reminds me of my days in California.

First, there are the esoteric brands. These are nothing but packaging hype. The beans are all the same selection of overcooked burned beans, but they make it sound like you're getting something unique. Yeah, sure, the only thing unique is the name like Matt's Mission to Mars. I swear pot shops and coffee shops both compete to see who can come up with the craziest names for their product.

Then I see something interesting. A whole-bean from Kona; now this has possibilities, and then another bag from Costa Rica that I'm really partial to. Just picking up the bag and squeezing and smelling it brings a momentary smile to my heart. I savor the good feeling, knowing it won't last long.

Enough of that. I've just wasted a good minute. I hit the canned goods. I need juices, spaghetti sauce and beans. Then I make my way to the dairy section. I pick up the smallest carton of whole milk for sautéing, then go to the oat milk and grab some half-gallons.

"Is oat milk any good? Is it better than coconut milk?"

Fuck me.

I turn and attempt a smile. By the way the grandmotherly type rears backward, my attempt has failed. Words are necessary to smooth things over.

"Do you like coconut milk?" I ask gently.

She gives me a timid smile. "No, I like milk-milk. My granddaughter likes coconut water. I saw there is coconut milk. I thought I would buy that for her while she visits."

That is really sweet. Really sweet. It reminds me of the type of thing my mother used to do for Lizzy and me before she passed away.

I look in her cart and see that she's selected mostly generic items and the cuffs on her coat are worn. She doesn't look like she can afford to be buying expensive coconut milk and have her granddaughter not like it.

"How old is your granddaughter?" I ask her.

"Fourteen. This is probably the last year she's going to want to come and visit and make cookies with her gran."

"Don't be so sure," I smile. "My mom and my sister baked cookies every holiday before she got married. And Lizzy didn't get married until she was twenty-five."

"You think she'll still bake with me that long?" the older woman asks hopefully.

"Sure," I choke out. I need to leave.

Now.

But first I need to finish up what I'd started. "I would take your granddaughter shopping with you and make sure she likes coconut milk before spending money on something she doesn't like."

The woman gave me a warm smile. "That's great advice. Thank you."

I nod and turn away. It's all I can do. Why hadn't I ever noticed that Lizzy stopped doing things with Mom after she married Ned?

That had been a serious red fucking flag!

Chapter Three

The produce section is next. I don't give a shit what I get. There's green stuff, some red stuff, and some orange stuff. I just throw it in the cart and make a beeline to the check-out lane.

Out.

I need the fuck out of here.

How could I not have seen the signs?

How?

There are none of the self-checkout lines in this Podunk town, and only one lane is open, so I'm stuck behind the lady with the stroller and her friend. Now I have another one of the bakery women behind me.

Patience, Clark. Just breathe.

"Honey, he's doing fine. It's just teething."

"Can we buy this?" she asks as she hands her mom a magazine.

Shit, how did I miss the kid? I mean, I saw the stroller, but how did I miss the fact there was a little girl floating around? I glance behind me and I don't see the little girl until she meanders over from the other check-out aisle.

"And why do we need a gossip magazine?" The woman who must be her mother asks.

"Why can't we buy it?"

"I will if you want, but I want you to think for a moment. Is that how you want us to spend part of our joy money this month?"

Joy money?

I put the divider on the conveyor belt, and that allows me to sneak another peek at the girl and her mother. The girl has her forefinger against her lip and a little frown on her face.

"You make a good point," she says.

Jesus, how old is she? She sounds like an adult.

"But I need to consider how much joy I will get from reading this magazine," she explains to her mother as she flips through the pages.

"Can you show me what article or articles have you so fascinated?" the pretty brunette asks her daughter.

"It's all about this actress and her kids. I've never read about them before." The daughter holds up the magazine for her mother to view.

"Do you think you could find out the same information online?" her mother asks.

Damned if the little girl's eyes don't light up. That girl might be all kinds of smart, but her mom sure knows how to handle her kid.

"I bet I could," she practically squeals. "Then I could use the joy money for something even better. Maybe something to give to the Owees for their birthday."

"Honey, that comes from a different pot. We save up for birthdays and Christmas in different ways. Your joy money is just that. It's money for you to spend on things that give you joy."

"But spending money on Aunt Chloe and Aunt Zoe on their birthday gives me joy, Mama."

I watch as she scrambles over to the other aisle and puts back the magazine and I almost feel a grin hit my face.

"Now, if you let me babysit, I could earn a whole boatload of money for joy, birthday, and Christmas."

"You're my baby girl. You are too young to be babysitting."

"I'm not a baby. I'm seven years old."

"Like I said, my baby."

"Mooooommmmm."

Who would have guessed it, but the little rugrat's whine doesn't get on my nerves.

"Sir? Can you put your things on the conveyor belt?"

I look up and realize that I'm holding things up. "Right."

I place things in order, exactly how I want them to be put in the bags so they will be evenly distributed and nothing will get crushed. I have the cart unloaded before the clerk has the second item scanned, but then she starts taking things out of order. Of course, she grabs the bread with the bottles of juice.

Down the line it goes, and the bored bagger puts them both in the flimsy plastic bag, and shoves them into my cart, and I watch as the bag tips over with the three bottles of juice landing on the loaf of bread.

"I'm going to need a new loaf of bread," I say to the cashier.

"What?"

"New bread, that one's crushed," I point to the first bag in my cart.

"What?"

I have to work really hard to understand her, since she had a huge wad of gum in her mouth, which is another thing that doesn't help keep me calm. I motion over to the cart. "Take that sack out of the cart," I command the young bagger.

"What?" he asks.

Really? Is that the only word Roger has taught his employees to use with customers?

"Young man, take the bag out of the shopping cart." He looks at me with a deer in the headlights look, his arms hanging at his sides. "Now!" I bark.

Still nothing.

I refuse to do it for him. He needs to learn.

I look at his name tag. He is obviously new since there's masking tape over the old name, and written in Sharpie is the name Dennis.

"Dennis. You're the bagger, correct?"

"Yeah," he mumbles.

Of course he mumbles.

I carefully enunciate. "Take the bag that you just put into my cart, out of the cart, and put it back onto the conveyor belt."

"Why?"

I consider him. It isn't insubordination; it is curiosity. Someone has trained him to do only one thing, and anything new in his repertoire is confusing. But I don't have the patience.

"I'll show you why after you do exactly what I told you to do."

He shrugs his skinny shoulders and swings the bag out and drops it onto the belt. I wince. Naturally, the bottle of juice slams on top of the bread.

"Ooops." I hear the word being whispered behind me. It's the brunette with the big brown eyes.

"Dennis, take everything out of the bag," I order the boy.

"Mister, you're holding up the line," the cashier says.

Who would have guessed it? I can actually understand her around the wad of gum.

"I'm the customer, and right now I need you or your bagger to procure me a new loaf of bread."

"Procure?" Dennis tilts his head to the side.

"You're making this more difficult than it has to be," the brunette whispers as she moves closer to me. "You might as well have said 'acquire.'"

"Might as well make it an overall teaching moment," I whisper back.

I turn back to Dennis. "Procure, as in retrieving or getting me another loaf of bread."

"Why?"

This time, the question comes from the cashier.

"Dennis, take the contents out of the sack," I slowly enunciate my order to the kid.

As if his life's dream is to imitate a tortoise, Dennis pulls the orange, cranberry, and carrot juice bottles out of the bag and finally he holds up the mashed loaf of bread. Neither the cashier nor Dennis say anything.

"Do you notice anything wrong with the loaf of bread?" I prompt.

They both look at me. I truly don't think anyone is home behind their blank stares. If I say 'Bueller' it'll just age me more than my gray hair and they won't get the reference anyway.

"Do you notice how the loaf of bread is almost flat?" I ask.

Dennis finally nods. The checker blows a bubble.

That's it. Now I finally want to go off. I really do. But the cashier looks like she's still in high school, and the bagger is even younger. He is at least three years younger than enlistment age, and I just can't do it. Even so, it would be so damned satisfying.

I close my eyes, trying to think how to get through to them.

"You squished his bread 'cause you put heavy stuff on it. That was stupid," a high-pitched voice pipes up. It's the daughter of the pretty mother.

I look down at the kid.

Dennis frowns at her. "He wasn't talking to you," he protests.

"Well, she's the one who understands the situation, so I'm talking to her now. What's your name, sweetheart?"

"I'm Bella. My mom says she always has to tell people here how to put things in the bags she brings, especially the eggs. It used to be that they'd be broken. There's this one girl who bags that Mama just shoos away and does it herself. Maybe you should shoo him away, Mister."

"That's enough, Bellatrix Star." Her mother's voice is stern.

"But he said that I understood things, and he's talking to me."

I look from daughter to mother and I see the consternation on the woman's face. It's clear that her daughter has relayed too much information, but the kid's a kick. Best medicine I could have asked for this morning.

"You know, if you brought in your own bags, like my Mama does, you could probably arrange things easier. Plus, it's better for the 'vironment."

I look back up at her mother. She gives me a weary smile. "You wanna play? You're going to pay." It takes a minute for me to figure out what the pretty woman is saying to me, but then I catch on. Apparently, I was going to have a hard time stopping the kid once she got going.

"He only has to pay if he swears, Mama." The little

munchkin looks back at me. "It's a dollar a swear, Mister. That's what Uncle Drake and all of his friends pay me."

"We've started a savings account," her mother says. "If she attends in-state, she already has her first year of college paid for," the woman sighs as she tucks her long, brunette hair behind her ear. She looks down at her daughter. "What's the rule?"

"We don't demand money from strangers." Bella pouts. "But all of Uncle Drake's friends were strangers before I was introduced." She swings her head toward me and pushes out her hand. "I'm Bella Avery. What's your name?"

What a fucking riot.

"I'm Co—" I stop myself. I take a breath, then shake her tiny hand. "My name is Simon Clark."

She twists her head and looks back at her mom. "See, we're not strangers anymore."

"Can you speed things along?"

I look behind the woman who has to be Drake Avery's sister and see that two more customers have queued up.

"Sorry." I wave to them.

I look at the bagger. "Get me another loaf of bread." He stares at me like I'm speaking a foreign language.

"*Now*," I say, using my command voice.

"But... but... I'm supposed to bag," he stuttered.

"I'll bag my own groceries, and the next customers', until you get back with a loaf of bread to replace the one you ruined. Hurry it up."

Dennis looks over at the checker, who just shrugs. She rings up the rest of my items, and I move along to bag my groceries. When she's done, she announces the total and I give her cash to cover it. She looks at the bills like she's never seen them before.

"Can't you use a credit or debit card?" she asks.

"Why?" I ask.

"It's a pain to make change."

"For the love of God. Are you kidding me?" Yep, I'm hanging on by a thread. Drake's sister puts her hand on my arm.

"Amanda, you owe him five dollars and eighty-five cents,"

"Thanks, Mizz Trenda."

"Yeah, thanks." I give Trenda Drake the best smile I can muster. After all, she's just saved me from a prison sentence. She nods her head with a mischievous smile. She knows that she's just saved Amanda's life.

"Mr. Clark, can I help you bag groceries?" Bella asks.

"Do you know how?" I ask the little cutie.

"Nope, but I know not to squish things, and you can teach me everything else, right?"

Her mother rolls her eyes. God help Trenda when this girl hits her teens.

"Ask your mom."

"Mama, please?"

Trenda gives me a head tilt as she finishes emptying her basket onto the conveyor belt. I nod.

"Sure, but make sure you listen to everything Mr. Clark tells you to do and move fast. We don't want to keep people waiting."

"Got it." She gives her mom a thumbs up.

"Since you can't reach, your job is to identify what items are coming our way, then tell me what kinds of things go together in a bag. Like all the canned food would go together, then all the soft items would go together, and all the produce would go together."

"Got it." She gives me a thumbs up this time.

They use both paper and plastic bags, so I choose paper. I get four bags ready, and double-bag two.

"Cans coming for bag one. Apples in bag two."

I grab them, loving the look of concentration on the kid's face.

"Should all cold stuff go together?" she asked me.

"Yep."

"Ice cream, frozen juice in bag three. Carrots in bag two."

She nails every item as it comes down the conveyor belt. She could own the store before she turns sixteen at this rate.

"Got your bread," Dennis says. "It's even wheat bread," he says proudly. Is it organic? No.

"Thanks, Dennis," I sigh. "Just put it in the bag on top of the eggs." I point to my cart.

"Should I start bagging again?" he asks.

I nod. We are done anyway. I drop off my cart and take my groceries, then follow Bella and her mom to their vehicle.

"Are you coming with us?" Bella asks.

"Just thought I would help your mom put her groceries into her car."

"She doesn't need help. She does it all the time. Don't you, Mama?"

Trenda stops at an older model SUV and pulls open the back hatch. She turns and looks at me.

"Bella's right, I can do this myself." She looks flustered.

"I don't doubt it. But I owe you one, so let me help."

"What do you owe me for?" She frowns.

"You stopped me from going off in the store. I really didn't want to do that, and you stopped me, so I'm grateful."

"I don't think you would have." She smiles up at me, and it blows me away. She isn't pretty, she's a freakin' knockout. "I always regret it when I speak in anger. What's more, you wouldn't have fixed the situation. Sadly, that was the A-Team for the morning shift."

"Are you shitting me?"

"Uh-hmm." Bella loudly clears her throat.

I look down at her, then look back up at her beautiful mother.

"You told her your name." She shrugs with a mischievous grin.

I reach for my wallet and take out my cash. I only have twenties and the five-dollar bill the clerk has given me.

"You can just give me the five dollars, and then you get to swear four more times, cause you'll have an account with me. That's what Uncle Drake and a lot of his friends do. Not Uncle Mason. He doesn't swear as much."

"Sweet Pea, we don't know how often we'll be seeing the commander, so let's give him a free pass. How about that?"

I squeeze the back of my neck. "So, you know who I am?"

She turns to her daughter. "Bella, get into your car seat. You've got some screen time on my iPad while I talk to Mr. Clark, okay?"

"Yippee!" The girl shoots into the backseat and buckles herself in.

Trenda gives me an apologetic look.

"I didn't want Bella to hear what I'm about to say. She's the biggest gossip in Jasper Creek. I'm sorry, Mr. Clark. I didn't mean to call you commander, it's just that you came off all commanderish in the store and I knew that was your title in the Navy, so out it popped. Don't think that Drake, Mason, Aiden, or anybody else just popped out with the info. Mr. Faulks owns the cabin that you're staying in. When he did the normal background check on you and saw you were Navy, he asked me if you were somebody he could trust." Trenda sighs.

I squeeze my neck even harder. Nosy landlords and gossip are not what I need.

She must have seen my expression.

"I called Drake to find out if I should give you a reference, and he explained you had recently retired as a Commander of the SEALs, and he would trust you with his life. All I told Bernie Faulks is that I verified you had retired from the Navy and you were extremely trustworthy. I figured since you hadn't used anyone as a reference, that you wanted to keep things low key, so I asked Mr. Faulks not to talk about you. Trust me, he understands that. He'll respect your privacy. He kind of lives off the grid himself, except for his business ventures and being a landlord. I promise not to tell anyone as well."

"Don't you have a bunch of sisters who live around here? One who's married to Aiden O'Malley?"

"Look, I figure that Drake probably suggested this is a friendly town to stay for a while. It is. But I haven't said anything to Aiden's wife, Evie, or any of my other sisters. I'm actually kicking myself in the ass for having called you commander, if you want to know the truth."

I hate myself for doubting her. She seems sincere, but I am gun shy. There have just been too many people who have been duplicitous in my world for the last year.

She reaches out like she's going to touch my arm, then she draws back. "I realize you don't know me," she starts. "Sometimes it's hard to trust. I don't know what else I can say, Simon." Her smile disappears, and I miss it.

"I know I'm being a suspicious asshole. It's been a shitty year. I trust the men who were under my command, so of course I trust you."

Her expression doesn't change. "It'll take time. But you will," she sighs again. She reaches into her purse and pulls out a business card holder. "I design and create websites as well as brand new businesses. Here's my business card. You can get ahold of me at this number if you need somebody here in town."

I look at the card. I'm impressed that it isn't all flowery, instead it looks sleek and professional, like someone I would take seriously.

"Thanks, Trenda."

Her smile is dim when I get it, but at least it is a smile. "You're welcome, Simon. I better get home before the ice cream melts."

I nod and grab the cart and roll it back to the entrance, then plop my groceries into my trunk and take off with Trenda's card carefully placed in my wallet.

Chapter Four

"Go to sleep, Sweet Pea. You've had your allotment of screen time for the day. You've had your Mama time, and what's more, you got to talk to Aunt Maddie. It's beddy-bye time for you. You hear me?"

"Yeah, but—"

"No more buts. You're tucked in. The nightlight's on. Do the meditation technique that Uncle Drake taught you, and... Go. To. Sleep."

"But we haven't even discussed the Commander." Bella whines.

I wince. Seriously, my kid didn't miss a trick. "What have I said about whining?"

"That it probably won't get me anywhere, and it will annoy the shit out of people."

"That'll be a dollar," I say as I hold out my hand.

"Fifty cents. I was repeating what you said." Her eyes twinkle.

"We'll debate this tomorrow." I press a kiss against her forehead and pull up her blanket. "Sleepy time, my love."

"I love you, Mama."

"Love you more, baby girl."

She gives me a sleepy grin and closes her eyes. I have the best kid in the known universe. If I thought she was really money hungry, I would have stopped her demanding money for swear words a long time ago, but now it's a fun game. What's more, the way my brother and his teammates swear, they need somebody holding them accountable, and if it pays for her freshman year in college, all the better.

I leave her bedroom door open a smidge and head toward my office. It's really the breakfast nook, so it doesn't even have a door, but I want to keep the third bedroom available as a guest room. Therefore, I have to go through the kitchen to get to my Mac, and that's the problem. Bella and I had had some of the toffee chocolate chip ice cream after her favorite fish stick dinner, but now I can literally hear that ice cream calling my name.

Trenda.

Trenda.

I'll expire tomorrow, eat me tonight.

Trenda, you'll get so much more work done with a sugar high.

Trenda!

I open up the silverware drawer and pull out a teaspoon instead of a tablespoon so I won't finish the entire pint, then grab the pint of ice cream and sit down in front of my computer with a happy smile.

First, I check my business emails, and my smile gets even bigger. One of my old clients has recommended me to one of their friends who wants a brand-new website. I love it when that happens. If you'd told me a year ago that I'd be working on websites, I would have laughed, but Maddie finally convinced me I'd enjoy doing it. I'm usually not a techie person, but when it comes to websites, I like the challenge. Besides, I outsource the ongoing technical support so that I'm not always on-call.

The email from the potential client is the first email I respond to. I ask what their availability would be and if they have three or four websites that they currently like so that I can get a sense of their style before our first meeting. That always gives me a good starting point for our initial conversation, besides just getting to know one another better.

There are a bunch of emails from different vendors after my big Christmas shopping binge. Seriously, I had totally over-bought for Christmas, and now I'm in every company's newsletter. I can't help clicking on the ones for purses and shoes. A girl needs to dream.

It is the third email on the second page that makes my blood run cold. A metal film coats my tongue, as if I'm sucking on a penny when I see the subject line. It's titled Old Sins. The sender is "Nashville" followed by non-sequential numbers from an AOL account. Who in the hell has an AOL email anymore?

Nashville?

I never want to think about my time in Nashville. That is behind me. I might be considering leaving Jasper Creek, but there's not a chance in hell that I'd ever end up in that city, or any other city in the state of Tennessee. Maybe the Pacific Northwest. That is far from Tennessee and far from a Navy SEAL base.

I swallow, and thoughts of Nashville swirl in my head.

Cold drops hit my boobs, and I jump up. Grabbing the tissues out of the box, I try to wipe up the melted ice cream off my chest and sweater. I'm a mess, both literally and figuratively. The ice cream is melted all over, but that doesn't stop me from throwing the tissues in the garbage and taking a spoonful of the melted gooey mess so that I can banish the taste of fear from my mouth.

I push back from my makeshift desk and go to the kitchen to clean things up and pour the melted ice cream down the sink, then think better of it. I sip the melted cream from the container and look out the kitchen window, thinking back to one of my last days in Nashville.

∼

I'd let myself into Brantley's apartment.

He'd only just given me a key a week ago. It was the night he told me he wanted me in his life forever. I'd made such a fool of myself, because I'd burst into tears. He'd chuckled, and sent me to the bathroom to mop up. I was always making a fool of myself around Brantley. He was so much older and sophisticated, I couldn't believe he'd chosen someone like me to marry.

Before I even had a chance to lock the door behind me, someone knocked quietly on the door. If it had been before last week, I wouldn't have answered it, but because I was going to be Brantley's wife, I knew it would be okay. I looked through the peephole and there was a middle-aged man in a suit outside. He was Brantley's age, but not nearly as handsome.

I dropped my purse and overnight case beside the door, then put the security chain in place and opened the door.

"Can I help you?"

He looked me up and down. "Nice," he drawled. "Brant sure can coax in the honey."

I started to close the door.

"Wait," he barked out. "I need you to give this to Brant. He needs to look at this as soon as he gets back from downtown. You got it? You can follow orders, can't you?" He shoved a thick file at me through the opening and I took it.

"I'll see that he gets it."

"You do that, Honey. Tell Brant to bring you around to the club sometime. He needs to show you off."

"Can I tell Brantley your name?"

"Tell him Jim from Rykers stopped by. Let him know he now has all the originals, and everybody has lost their memories, so he's good to go, and I'll send him my bill." He turned and walked down the hallway. I still didn't understand how he could have gotten past the security in the lobby. Brantley owned this building, and this apartment was on the top floor. I had to use a special code to get the elevator to even get up to this floor. I unhooked the chain and stepped into the hall.

"What's your last name?" I called to his retreating back. He didn't answer, he just pushed the button to the elevator and disappeared as soon as the elevator arrived. I shut the door and looked down at the file.

What in the heck was that?

The file was huge, and I needed both hands to keep the papers, blueprints, assay and inspection reports as well as perk tests all together, so best to put it on Brantley's desk, even though he didn't like for me to go into his study. Needs must.

His desk was an absolute horror. I would never have let my Mr. Fortnum's desk get to such a point. Maybe they did things differently here than they did in Jasper Creek. Biting my lip, I put the file on Brantley's office chair.

It slid off the smooth leather and hit the floor.

"Shoot!"

Kneeling down, I tried to put it into some semblance of order. It was for a fancy new development on the outskirts of Nashville. I'd heard Brantley and my new Nashville boss bragging about how they'd gotten the land for a song. Looking at the documents, I saw why. Most of this land rested over an old landfill that had been covered over in the late seventies.

That was the reason for all the tests to see if the landfill would be safe to build on. Four reports from four different labs came back stating that the amount of dangerous gasses wafting off the landfill made the land unusable, or highly expensive to treat before construction could begin.

Brantley had already purchased the materials for construction, even after receiving the lab results, and his crews had already started fabricating the foundation. How was that even possible?

"Trenda?"

I took a deep breath and sucked back a wave of nausea. I shuffled all the pages together and shoved them into the file and plopped it onto Brantley's disorganized desk.

"In here," I called out.

"Darlin' what are you doing in my office?" he asked with an indulgent smile.

"Somebody named Jim from Rykers stopped by. He said this contains all the originals and everybody has lost their memories?" That doesn't sound right, but that's what he said.

"Anything else?" Brantley asks.

"Yes, he said you're good to go and he'll send you his bill."

"That's really good news. Come here." He held his arms wide, and I stepped into his embrace. Being held in his arms made me feel good. A man actually cared about me.

"Did you have time to fix me dinner?" he asked.

I shook my head against his chest. He sighed.

"Leo has a lot to answer for, doesn't he know you're mine now?" He crushed me closer.

"I still have to work. I need the money for my classes and apartment," I protested.

"You need to quit work and quit school and move in here. I'll take care of you."

I sucked in a deep breath. Did that mean he was proposing?

"Now why don't you go into the kitchen and whip something up. I'm tired, I'll take a shower, and you can wow me with a grilled cheese."

He was so thoughtful.

∾

"Mama, can I have a glass of water?"

I shake my head. It takes a moment to come out of my trance and realize I am here in Jasper Creek and Bella is in the kitchen with me.

"Sure, Sweet Pea, let me get you one."

I grab a glass out of the cupboard and get some water out of the fridge dispenser, then hand the small glass to Bella.

"Anything else waking you up?" I ask.

She shakes her head, her eyes sleepy. I take the empty glass from her, then follow her back to her bedroom. She crawls into bed.

"'Night, Mama."

"Sweet dreams." I press a kiss against her forehead. She is asleep by the time I'm at her door.

I go back to my little office. I finally work up the nerve to open the email, and there are just four words.

STAY AWAY, OR ELSE.

And for this I let perfectly good ice cream melt? What the hell? Like I'm ever going back to Nashville. I don't care if my sisters offer me two years of free babysitting, which they already have. I still would never go back to that feather-fluffing city!

My hands are over my keyboard, ready to respond when it occurs to me I have no idea who sent this email.

Who?

And why now?

My fingers itch to ask who they are, but the logical side of my brain tells me not to touch it. Hell, I probably shouldn't have opened it. It hadn't gone through an email server that tags me to tell them if I opened it.

Shoot!

I stare at it. My mind wanders to the contents of my freezer. It would be so much easier to decide if I need more ice cream.

I highlight the damn thing and press delete.

Enough is enough.

I start to scroll down through my other emails, but it's no use. My work brain is shot for the night. I shut down my computer and head for bed, checking on Bella on my way to my room.

Doing my normal nightly prep, I scowl in the mirror after I wash my face and slather on my moisturizer. According to Maddie, the stuff from the drugstore was just as good as the department store, but I'm not too sure. I lean in closer to the mirror and I definitely see crow's feet. Why did they always look so good on a man, but not so good on a woman?

Now the commander? The lines on his face are sexy as hell. You can tell that he's walked through the fire.

Haven't you?

I think about growing up in the Avery household with my sperm and egg donors, which is how I think of my parents. Yeah, there had been more than a bit of brimstone in that house. I lean in even closer and examine my eyes. They're Norville Avery's eyes. All of us kids have them, of course. Having our mother's blue eyes would have been just as bad.

How could I have been a product of such evil people? Will I one day turn on Bella? I drop my forehead against the mirror and suck down tears. No, I would never hurt my baby, but God knows I've proven to be dumber than a box of rocks, just like Wanda. Yep, trusting the wrong man, believing his lies. But then again, Wanda was an evil liar herself, so why am I worrying? I realize that email shook me more than I thought.

Pushing against the sink top, I pull myself upright. I take another look in the mirror.

Cut yourself some slack, Trenda. You were young. Starving for male attention.

Brantley Harris saw me coming a mile away. Heck, it was probably tattooed on my forehead in special ink for men like him to see. I had been ripe for the picking. I so desperately wanted the happily ever after that I used to read about.

Turning away from the mirror, I go down the hall to my bedroom and slip into my oversized Bon Jovi t-shirt and climb into bed. I try desperately to think of something else besides Nashville. Anything else besides my f-up'd past.

Then there he is. The Commander. My last thought is of gray eyes.

Chapter Five

If I hadn't talked to my landlord, Bernie Faulks, twice on the phone already, I'd swear he was a ghost. I've been trying for the last week to get ahold of him, but he doesn't pick up his phone, and he doesn't have it set up to take voicemail. At no time have I been given an email address for the man, and I don't know where he lives. But there is one housekeeping item I want to discuss with him, and another thing I think he can help me out with—finding a Navy SEAL's little brother. The way it has been explained to me over at the gas station, Bernie, is one of the mountain folk, and they all stuck together. Therefore, he'll know if Renzo is up on the mountain.

Because this is a favor to one of Kostya's men, and Kostya and his woman did me a solid by helping pack up my things, I need to get some answers, even if it means dealing with people. I'd gone into town and had a couple of beers at the tavern, and asked if anyone had noticed a new guy in town. When that didn't garner any results, I went to Pearl's diner, which was apparently gossip central. I'd even talked to Pearl herself to find out if she'd heard anything, and she hadn't. Hell, I'd even asked Roger at the grocery store if he knew about anyone new who'd come to town, and I'd come up with another big 'no.'"

But all of them had said that he was probably up in the mountains, which were really just hills. Mountains are what you see in Afghanistan or the Rockies, not these low, forested, rolling hills. All of them said to talk to Bernie. Which I would gladly do, except he doesn't answer his damned phone.

Finally, I remember that Bernie called Trenda Avery when he'd wanted a reference. Maybe she would know how to track down the slippery old bastard. Her card is resting on the windowsill above my kitchen sink, so I take it down and made the call.

"Hello, this is Trenda Avery."

She answers so smoothly, it takes a moment for me to realize it is actually her and not her voicemail greeting.

"Hi Trenda, this is Simon Clark. I'm wondering if you might be able to help me."

"If you need a website built, I'm your girl. When do you need it by?" she teased. I can hear the laughter in her voice; it is almost lyrical and it makes me smile.

"So, you're a smartass, huh?"

"Yep, one smartass at your service. Now I can only say that word while Bella's at school, you understand that, right?"

I laughed. "Your kid is a stick of dynamite. It must be tough to ride herd on her."

"The toughest times are when she tries to be the mother, then we get into some sticky situations."

"I can imagine." The girl was the spitting image of her mother. I would love to see her bossing her mother around.

"Now, what can I help you with, Simon?"

"I need to get in touch with Bernie Faulks and he isn't answering his phone."

"Is there something wrong at the cabin? I know Bernie can be hard to reach even though he has a satellite phone. Maybe one of the men in town, or my brother-in-law can help you."

"From what I understand, it's Bernie I need to talk to. One of my men's brothers is likely staying up in the mountain area, and I was told that Bernie would know where to find him, or would know somebody who could."

Trenda laughs and I enjoy hearing it. "Yeah, Bernie's one of a kind. None of the old guard thought he could come back from Chicago and fit back into life here in Jasper Creek, but he did. Now he's one of the go-to people in the area."

"If you can get ahold of him," I mutter.

"Sounds like he's in his anti-social mode. It happens."

"It'd be nice if I could text him, or leave him a voicemail."

"Yeah, he sets up his satellite phone to only take voicemails and texts from numbers he has stored. He's an ornery old bug batter."

I laugh. "Bug batter?"

"It's something I came up with early when I didn't want my daughter to have a potty mouth."

"It stands for bastard, right?"

"Yep. I do try to keep my swear words as limited as possible. I live with her, and I still need to buy groceries."

I start chuckling again.

"Anyway, the best thing you can do is drive up to his place. My sister Evie is in town, maybe I could ask to borrow Aiden's Range Rover so that you could drive that up to see him."

"How far away does he live from my cabin?"

"About twenty miles if you take the mountain roads. I'd say about ten miles as the crow flies. I could draw you a map and email it to you, or..."

"Or?"

"I don't know what I was thinking. One of the last times Drake was in town, he and I took Maddie on a run up the mountain so she could do wellness checks on everyone for a paper for school. He wrote down everyone's coordinates that they visited and gave all of us copies, in case we couldn't remember the way to their homes."

"Do you go up the mountain often?"

"Not as often as I'd like to. I do help Bernie when he's gathering supplies for the folks up there. Hold on and I'll get you Bernie's coordinates."

I hear clicking and I know she is at her computer. In short order she's back on the phone with me giving me the longitude and latitude to find Bernie Faulks. "Make noise as you're coming up to his place. If you sneak up you might get shot."

I can't stifle my snort of laughter. Then I heard Trenda's rueful laughter. "Oh yeah, I forgot who I was talking to. Did you start out as a SEAL?"

"Yep. Enlisted when I was eighteen, didn't become an officer until I was twenty-five."

I could hear her thinking.

"How long did you serve?"

"In total, twenty-nine years."

"I wonder if Drake will stay in the Navy that long," she ponders out loud. I'm impressed; she didn't ask why I didn't retire at thirty years so I could take advantage of a better retirement. Not only is she funny and smart, she's compassionate enough not to broach delicate topics. There's a lot to like about Trenda Avery.

"Thanks a lot for the information, Trenda, I really appreciate it. I hope I'll see you in the grocery store again."

"Simon?"

"Yes?" I ask before hanging up.

"Can you call me and let me know how your friend's brother is doing? Now you have me concerned."

"Sure I will. Good-bye."

It does my body good to hike the twelve miles to Bernie Faulks' cabin.

When I get to Bernie's place, I can see why he rents out the shack and lives in this place. It sure doesn't look like any off-the-grid house that I've ever seen. It's a two-story A-frame with a deck out front. The man even has a decent grill on his deck, along with chairs. Looks like he isn't as much of a loner as I had thought. I hope he has the information that I need.

"You must be my renter," an old guy shouts as he limps onto the deck.

"You must be my landlord," I call back.

There's no need for us to introduce ourselves more than that since we've talked to one another on the phone twice. I walk up the stairs to his deck and nod my head at his leg.

"Gout," he says.

I wince.

"Come on in for a beer. But keep in mind, I don't have any of the fancy shit."

"Do I look fancy?" I ask.

"Your watch sure does."

I look down at my watch and grin.

"Will you take me out of the doghouse if I tell you I know and actually use every feature on the watch?"

"Do you?" Bernie asks as he opens his refrigerator.

"Yep, every last feature."

"Then you're not fancy, you're prepared. I like that. I'll give you a bottle instead of a can." He pulls two bottles of Miller, and I follow him back out onto the deck.

Once we settle and I have a few swallows of beer my gaze turns back to the inside of his house. "Did you make that furniture inside?"

He tilts his head and nods. "Sometimes I just can't abide being around people, so I needed a hobby."

"I can see that." I nod solemnly. "And the rugs? I've never seen anything like them. I felt like I was walking on works of art."

"Two sisters up the mountain make 'em. Judy and Janice. They gave them to me after I upgraded their solar panels. They used to make 'em for their family, but not much of them is left, so I took the rugs into town and talked to the gal who owns the coffee and gift shop. Before you know it, my mountain ladies are making some money selling those rugs in a shop out there in Pigeon Forge. Cost quite a pretty penny, too."

"You're a good neighbor."

"Used to be, before the gout. Shoulda gone in sooner for treatment, now it's gotten out of hand and I'm on my third round of drugs." Bernie frowns. "Can't get done everything that needs doing." He takes a long swallow of beer, then looks me up and down. "So, why you here?"

"Couple of reasons. First, there's a couple of trees that are dying on your property. One of them is really close to the cabin. Before I cut them down, I wanted your permission." I watch him scratch his chin as his brow furrows.

"It needs doing, doesn't it?" he asks.

I shrug. "To my mind, yes."

"So why are you asking permission, just get 'er done."

I chuckle and take another swallow of my cold beer. "I like your style, Bernie. I guess I've been dealing with the Brass and Suits so long, that I forgot the first rule of being in the field—it's easier to ask for forgiveness than permission."

"So, you were high up in the Navy?"

I tilt the top of my beer his way and nod. "What about you?"

"I worked for a big manufacturing company. Worked my way up, got to the point I could see how the sausage was made. Wanna know how?"

I actually did. Bernie had not struck me as someone who'd worked his way into upper management for any company, so now I was curious.

"They make their money off the blood, sweat, and tears of their employees. These are the employees who damn near killed themselves getting new technology out to market before anyone else, but do they get a pat on the back when they're done?"

I lean forward in my chair. "I'm assuming the answer is no."

"You'd be right. As soon as the profits come rolling in, they slash R&D, automate production and do massive lay-offs, all so the suits in the corner offices can get their bonuses for not only rolling out a great product early, but for having saved money by laying off people. When I saw that is how things worked, I asked for my early retirement and got the hell out of there." He stretches his bad leg out in front of him and stretches his arms toward the sky. "Before I left, I made sure to triple check that this here piece of property that I inherited from my uncle had a stream running through it like I remembered. It did. Then I sent out the company's top-of-the-line mini hydroelectric power energy generator to myself as a retirement gift. Better than a gold watch."

Bernie lets out a cackle that makes him sound like he's auditioning for the part of the Wicked Witch of the West.

We got to talking about how little electricity his home needs, and how he stores the extra in an electric battery bank. "I might want to live life off the grid, but I like my creature comforts." He grins at me. "How 'bout you? Have you needed to use the generator I left you, or has city electricity worked out for you?"

"I've been fine on the grid," I smile.

"You ain't showed your face in town much, 'cepting for gas and groceries. That cabin of mine doesn't have cable; aren't you a might bored now?"

I stretch back in his surprisingly comfortable deck chair and watch as he pulls a pipe pouch out of his jacket and starts stuffing it full of tobacco, then takes his time lighting it up.

"Well?" he asks after he takes a deep draw from his pipe.

"There's only so many runs or calisthenics a man can do before he does want something that will stimulate his brain."

"Yeah, it had to have gotten rough if you sussed me out." He cackles again, then follows it up by coughing out smoke. His eyes water, but finishing off his beer seems to set everything to rights.

"I reckon you're needing some people to watch over."

I frown, and he sees it.

"Seriously, Simon, you were in the Navy how long?"

"Almost thirty years. Went in when I was eighteen, got my degree in mechanical engineering while I was enlisted. Rose through the ranks."

"No wonder you can handle such a fancy watch. But tell me, how many years did you command men?"

"Twenty-four."

"You seem to be on the bright side, so I'm gonna assume that you know that being in charge of someone doesn't just mean you boss them around, you have to take care of them. You have to teach, guide, and provide moral support. Am I right?"

"You're right," I respond slowly. "But what's with all the philosophizing?"

"I just think while you're staying here in Jasper Creek, you need a bit of a purpose, and if part of that purpose is helping others it would work even better for you." The last bit is said as he points the stem of his pipe at me.

I get up from my chair. "I'm going to grab another bottle of beer. It seems to me before you try to sucker me into something, I might as well be compensated by two bottles of beer."

"Get one for me, too," Bernie calls after me.

"That's not good for the gout, is it?"

"Fuck that noise and get me my beer," Bernie chuckles.

I stopped with one foot in and one foot out of the A-frame. "Seriously, should you be drinking beer with gout? From what I remember you shouldn't be drinking alcohol."

I wait to see what he will say.

"What are you, my mother? You're only entitled to another beer if I get one too." He twists in his chair so he can look me in the eye.

"Bernie, I can't help it. It's all these years of leadership in the Navy, I just want to provide you with good guidance."

I leave Bernie cackling on the front porch as I let myself into his home. I grab the beer out of his fridge and think about what he's said. Bernie is a cagey bastard. His presentation style reminds me of Josiah; you'll be talking to the man about one thing and by the end of the conversation you'll find out you'd just volunteered for something completely different. I can't wait to find out what Bernie has in mind.

I twist off the top of one of the bottles and hand it to Bernie and he nods his thanks. I settle back down in my chair. "So, whatcha got?"

"Before I get into that, tell me the other thing that brings you up here."

"I'm looking for a man. He's thirty-one, half-Peruvian, half-Caucasian, six feet, two inches tall, dark brown hair, he's heavily muscled. His name is Renzo Drakos. His brother sent him this way when he was having some issues. Told him this would be a good place to wind down."

"Not another damned Navy SEAL," Bernie grouses.

"No, he's in construction. He's done well for himself. That's about all I know, except Jase is worried because Renzo hasn't called their mom in four months, and that's not like him. So, I said I would go and check on him."

"Well, that dovetails nicely with what I want to talk to you about."

"The thing you're going to try to sucker me into?"

He points his pipe stem at me again, and sparks fly. "That'd be it." He grins.

"It's not a lot. I need you to be my driver and the muscle as I make the rounds to all the mountain folk. I haven't visited them in five weeks, what with the gout and all, and I know some of them are getting real low on supplies. Now some of them just need to get off their asses and get it them damn selves, but some of them have really gotten on up there in years and need my help, and that's where you come in."

I vaguely remember a conversation I'd heard at the grocery store, something about one of the mountain people coming in and expecting a hand-out. It was yet another conversation that I'd dismissed. I did not, and do not, want to get involved in Jasper Creek politics.

"How do you know what they need?"

"It's the twenty-first century, they all have satellite phones, excepting for Junior. He knows the government is listening, so he won't use them."

I close my eyes. Hell, I know some of the special forces operators in the Navy who will use nothing but satellite phones because they feel like every other phone out there is being monitored. "What happens if he injures himself and he needs a doctor?"

"Doesn't care. You kind of have to admire his thinking. It wasn't so long ago that people were crossing the country in wagon trains, a lot of them survived and thrived without today's technology."

I shrug. He's right. There are times out in the field when technology doesn't mean shit; you have to depend on your physical and mental abilities as you literally fight to survive. Still doesn't mean that you can't worry about a man named Junior or two nice old ladies who hand-stitch rugs.

"While we're out, we can see if anyone has spotted Renzo."

Bernie shakes his head and gives me a condescending look. "Nothing goes on in these mountains that these folks don't know about. I've been getting calls and reports about this boy since almost the day he arrived."

I should have figured that.

"The tent he's living in is first class, he obviously came to stay for a while. According to Azariah, he's a better hunter with a longbow than anybody he's ever seen. Doubt he has a hunting license, though."

Bernie starts in with that cackle again, then it turns into such a terrible cough that I think he might hack out a lung. Doesn't stop him from firing up his pipe again.

"Has anyone talked to him?" I ask.

"Nah. It's clear he wants to be left alone, so none of us bother him. But Bertha won't last much longer. She can't abide someone living in the cold all alone. She's going to push her nose into his business, you just wait and see."

"Who's Bertha?"

"You'll meet her when we do our run. She's the furthest out, even further than Junior."

"Who lives with Bertha?"

"Ain't nobody lives with Bertha. Her husband passed thirty years ago, and nobody's brave enough to court her."

"How old is she?"

Bernie sucked on his pipe. "Upwards of seventy, maybe eighty."

This did not sound like a good set-up, but who was I to judge? Plenty of people in war-torn countries have it a lot worse.

Bernie chuckles and pointed his pipe at me. "Don't worry, she can take care of herself and twelve others. She's just fine, and if you go at her like she needs help, she'll throw you out on your ass."

"What's her house like?"

"It's been years since I've been in it, but Eddie built her something solid. That cabin will be standing long after you and I are gone. She's got a well, and he set her up with indoor plumbing and a septic. No electricity of course, but she has a generator. The thing that bothers all of us is that she's blind out of one eye, and she insists on driving Eddie's old truck on those backroads into town every so often."

"Well, you've caught me nicely in your net." I give him a wry grin. "Next time I'll want a six-pack."

"Sold. Just not any of those IPAs or that foreign shit. I had to drink enough of that swill while I was in the corporate world. It was nice coming home to the hills of Tennessee."

"Do you need a ride into the doctor to have them look at your leg?"

"Nah, I've got my lady friend who helps me out for those rides. Like I said, I'm on my third round of meds, the doc thinks that will clear it up."

"What about your cough?"

He coughs. And coughs. "This?" he asks. "I've had it for six months. It's just a cold."

"What did the doc say?"

"Wants me to waste my money on a damned x-ray. I said no to that in an instant."

"To each his own. So what day do you want me here, Saturday or Sunday?"

"Saturday. By the time you get here this weekend, I'll have my lists, and we'll head into town and then I'll show you how to get to everyone. If you pull your thumb outta your butt and figure out that you are settling here, which you are, then after a couple of runs with me, you can do some on your own. Course that'll be after you buy a decent vehicle."

He puts his beer down on the deck beside him, his pipe and fixings on the chair's arm, then pushes himself up. I get up too.

"Good finally meeting you. Come early on Saturday morning, don't want to be burning daylight." Bernie holds out his hand and I shake it. I watch him damn near drag his leg behind him as he makes his way back into his house.

Stubborn old bugger. I have to figure out a way for him to get that chest x-ray.

~

When I get back to my cabin, I feel energized after the walk in the forest. I can now report back to Kostya's man and tell him that his brother is doing fine. Talking to Jase Drakos the first time had grated on my nerves. I hadn't wanted to communicate with anyone from my past, but Jase was blunt and straightforward; I could see how he was friends with that tough bastard, Drake Avery.

After mixing up a large protein and fruit smoothie, I pick up my phone and call the man from the Omega Sky Navy SEAL team.

"This is Drakos."

"Drakos, this is Simon Clark. I have info on your brother."

I hear the long sigh that the man lets out. "And?"

"He's holed up in a tent up the mountain from Jasper Creek. I haven't talked to him yet, but I might see him on Saturday. All of the locals who've had sightings of him say he's in good shape. Also, word is, he's lethal with a longbow."

"Yep, that's him. When you see him, tell him I'm going to sic our sister Polly on him if he doesn't give our mom a call."

"That's the threat?" I ask.

"Trust me, it's the only threat that will scare any Drakos."

I laugh. "I'll tell him."

"Thanks, Commander."

"It's just Simon these days. And you're welcome, Jase."

I hang up the phone and start the process of unloading my backpack. I want everything precisely put away this time, instead of just keeping everything in my two big duffels. Bernie was right, I was going to be here a while, and it was time I did some things to make it more my home.

I sit down on the ottoman and rifle through the second

duffel bag for the photo. The first week when I'd arrived and found the framed picture of Mom and Liz in there, I was shocked as shit. It was the one I'd had on my mantel back home. None of the guys or their women would have packed that, so it had to have been me, but I'll be damned if I remember doing it.

I look at it and use the corner of my flannel shirt to wipe away the smudges on the glass. Mom and Liz look so damn happy in this picture. It was before Mom had gotten the cancer diagnosis, and I know it was before Liz got engaged to Ned. Mom had begged me to take leave for my birthday and come home, so I did. The two days leading up to my birthday were great. I remember them cooking for me. God, those two women could cook. Liz was supposed to stay for a week, but Ned had finagled it so she had to go home early.

The day before Liz left, I'd insisted on taking a picture of them. Mom was beaming, and Liz, well she looked happy. Happier than normal, now that I thought about it. I looked closely. She was wearing a turtleneck and Mom was wearing a short sleeve blouse. Was the turtleneck to hide bruises? My birthday falls in mid-September, too early for a turtleneck. When I'd mentioned it to Mom, she'd insisted that Ned was a great guy and that I had turned cynical since I'd joined the Navy.

Just how many signs did I miss? My finger traced over Liz's smile. I pushed up from the ottoman and put the photo on the coffee table. The same table where I usually put the bottle of Jack Daniels after one of my nightmares.

It was time for a new habit.

Chapter Six

When I get home after dropping Bella off at school I'm pumped. A new customer, a chance at making an interesting friend, and I was going to see Evie one more time before she left town. Life couldn't be any better! I'd only seen her once in the week she'd been here looking over the repairs on her home here in Jasper Creek. I grab the mail from the box, and then juggle that with the three bags of groceries that I'd purchased.

Not for the first time I thank my lucky stars that I have these bulletproof burlap grocery totes that can handle everything I need to carry without giving way under the strain. I plop the mail and the bags onto the kitchen counter, then start putting the groceries away. As I'm folding up the bags to put them back in the car, I find the mail. Most of it's going straight into the recycle bin, but I'm really hoping for a letter from Piper for Bella. She loves getting letters from her aunt in California.

"Ah-ha!" My little sister came through again. "This is going to make Bella's week!"

It's a thick envelope too, so Piper probably spent too

much on a pretty 3-D card. Heck, this might even make Bella's month.

I leave that on the kitchen counter, then rifle through the rest. Yep, medical bill summaries from when Bella had strep throat, bill, bill, letter from my congressman, time for my annual check-up. Ah, sugar foot, another letter from one of those lawyers. Dang it, when will they realize that I'm not going to be part of that class action suit? The company's data wall was breached, they hadn't sold my personal data. What's more, the whole thing was just putting money into the lawyer's pockets and each claimant will probably get a nickel in the end. I put that envelope along with the others on my little desk. This time I'm going to write back to the lawyer and tell them to stop sending me letters.

I am done!

I go back to the kitchen and start whipping up the batter for cinnamon streusel coffee cake. I'd picked up a new thing of sour cream because I hadn't been sure that the tin I had was still fresh, but it was. I use the sour cream instead of milk to give the cake a little bit of a tangy taste. It's a recipe I perfected while I lived at the family homestead. Mom had never been big on either parenting or cooking, so I'd stepped up. This is Evie's favorite.

I'm pulling the cake out of the oven just as Evie is letting herself into the house.

"Hey! You are the best big sister in the world," Evie calls out as she saunters into the kitchen with a huge grin on her face. She gives me a hug from behind as I start the coffee. "Do I see my favorite creamer?" The hug gets tighter. I glance over at the almond-flavored coffee creamer that I just took out of the fridge to go with her coffee.

"It sure is," I say as I turn on the coffee maker, then I turn around and give her a proper hug. "It's so good to see you, Evalyn Lavender, I've missed you." My breath feathers the top of Evie's hair.

"Normally I would give you hell for at least five minutes for calling me that atrocious name even though there is homemade coffee cake, but I've got bigger fish to fry with you. Why in the hell are you thinking of moving?" Evie demands to know as she pushes her way out of my arms. God, she's a strong little thing. *Wait a dog-gone minute—*

"What gives you the idea that I'm thinking about moving?"

"When Aiden and I came back here two months ago and were supervising the re-build of the house after the explosion, you were asking a lot of questions about the cost of not just the materials and labor, but of the land too. Aiden figured it out. He knows that you're sitting on a couple of acres out back, and must be thinking about selling. He's right, isn't he?"

Oh shit. What do I say?

"Yeah, you're taking too long to answer. You never could lie worth a shit. Why, Trenda? Why? This is where you grew up. This is where your family is."

"Really? Drake doesn't live here, he's in Southern California, and so are you. Piper's with you both. Zoe is away at school and so is Maddie. All you do is seagull."

"What in the hell are you talking about? What does seagull mean?"

"All you guys do is basically swoop in and demand to know what I'm doing, shit on it while telling me how I *should* live my life, and then swoop back out again. That's what I mean by seagull."

"Whoa, Sis, that's pretty harsh, don't you think?" Evie stares at me and I can tell I've hurt her feelings.

"Didn't you just do that, by telling me I'm doing the wrong thing by moving?"

"Well, yeah," she reluctantly admits.

"Then there's Mom and Dad whiling away in the state penitentiaries. You tell me, Evie, what in the hell is keeping me here in Jasper Creek?"

"Bella loves her teachers, she has a lot of friends here, this is where your customers are."

I snorted. "Evie, my customers are all over the US, and I've been doing websites for people in Canada and the UK for the last two years. I can work from anywhere. As for Bella, she is the most outgoing child I know, she can make friends anywhere we land."

"Yeah, but who is she going to con out of money? She only has enough for two years of college," Evie teases. But under the teasing I hear hurt.

"Evie, you don't even live here anymore. Almost all of your time is spent in Southern California."

"Yeah, but Aiden and I have talked. This is where we eventually want to raise our kids. Aiden already has fifteen years in, so he's talking about retiring. People are already trying to recruit him."

My heart clenches. "For real? You'd raise your kids here?"

"I'm not getting any younger. I'm twenty-seven, I need to get a move on. I already told the Senior Chief that I was getting a head start on the program. I've got too many of the other Midnight Delta wives leaving me in the dust."

I don't know what to say, and Evie catches on. "Trenda? What's really going on with you? A year ago you would have been ecstatic."

"I wish I knew."

Evie gives me a deep look, trying to delve deep into my psyche, but she just finds confusion.

"Let's have coffee cake," I suggest.

"Do you have chocolate sauce?"

"Am I your big sister?"

Evie grins and sits down while I get out everything we need and put it all on the table.

"So, fill me in on the gossip," Evie commands after she takes a mammoth bite of chocolate-covered coffee cake. "How are Chloe and Zarek?"

"You really go in for the kill, don't you?"

I take a small bite of the cake, but chew slowly so I can think about my answer. "They're still as in love as the day they got married."

"But...?" Evie prompts.

"I'm worried about Chloe. The miscarriage hit her hard. Zarek has been a rock and he's tried to get her into counselling, but she insists she doesn't need it. With her history she knows better than that. The hell of it is, I think Zarek needs some help too. Not just because of them losing their baby, but Chloe's depression is bringing back old memories for him on top of what's going on today. But he's too busy trying to be strong for Chloe and he's not seeing the forest for the trees. Damned firefighters."

"Just as bad as special forces operators," Evie nods. "Would it help if I drop by and try to talk to Chloe?"

"Couldn't hurt."

"How about Zoe? I'm surprised she hasn't plowed in on her twin's business."

"She's killing it at school. She's already been accepted into a doctorate program. She has her eye on a victim's advocacy job working for the state."

Evie winces, just like I did when Zoe first told me.

"That's a tough row to hoe."

"She's committed. You know Drake finally got his degree in psychology." I couldn't help the grin on my face. I am so damn proud of him. He's worked so damned hard for this. Taking online and night courses and accomplishing this even with his erratic schedule.

"He took the ten-year plan," Evie giggles.

"Who cares, he did it."

"Yeah, he did. Aiden finished his degree the third year he was in. I've asked him if it bothered him that he came in as a noncom, and his answer has always been, 'no'. I think he liked being down in the dirt and mud, learning from the ground up. Plus, his family down in Mexico was still kind of..."

"Yeah." I don't say anything more and neither does Evie. Aiden's family down in Mexico had been involved in some nefarious stuff fifteen years ago, but his uncle has worked hard to turn the family business legitimate over the years.

"So why do you want to leave? Do you want to go back to Nashville?"

"God no!"

"You never have talked about what happened..."

"And I'm not going to start now. As far as I'm concerned that door is closed and double locked. It's in the past. I like to live in the present with an eye on the future. That includes Evie O'Malley wanting to have children in the near future."

"Aiden really wants me to wait until he retires. He wants to make sure that he's home for the entire process. He's not thinking straight. The opportunities that he's been offered aren't exactly desk jobs. I figure he'd be away just as much then as he is now," Evie laughs.

"I can't imagine that."

"What, having your guy being gone so long?"

"No, just having a guy." I shudder.

"Trenda, are you sure you don't want to talk about Bella's father? I know that's always been a forbidden area, but, Sister, it sounds like you were really hurt, and you're painting all men with the same brush."

I laugh. "You're funny. You've got it all wrong. I know there are good men out there, Evie. I see you with Aiden, and Chloe with Zarek. Then Drake, despite his Neanderthal tendencies is one of the most caring and supportive men I've ever seen. I adore our big brother."

I fight back tears. God, when I think of everything Drake went through, the shit that his life had been like, and he came out on the side of angels? It is a miracle.

Evie reaches out and covers my hands with both of hers. "That's exactly what I'm saying, Honey. You can't close off. You have to look. Someone is out there for you."

I turn my hand over so we are palm to palm. "Evie, you don't understand. It's not the men that I don't trust, it's me. Growing up having Norville as a father, and being surrounded by such filth like his friends and our uncles, my barometer is beyond screwed up."

"You can't know that for sure."

"I know it now, but I didn't know it when I went to Nashville. Back then I was sure I knew what I was doing."

"But—"

I cut her off. "I'd been certain. Evie, there wasn't a doubt in my mind that I knew the man who fathered Bella. Sure, I knew him inside and out. He was perfect for me, in my eyes. Not a perfect man; I knew his bad points, but I knew he loved me unconditionally. I knew we were destined to be together, just like you knew Aiden and you were."

This time I can't stop a tear from escaping.

"Oh, Honey, everybody makes mistakes."

"Not like mine. You'll never know, Evie. But no mistake, no man, could have been worse than mine."

"Did he hurt you? Physically I mean."

"It needs to stay dead and buried, Evie. It's for the best."

I get up from the kitchen table, picking up our empty plates and taking them to the sink. I grab the edge of the counter for all it's worth, trying to put that moment back into the box deep in my mind where it normally stays. A place that I never look at. Never think about.

I didn't notice Evie coming up behind me, so I jump when she wraps her arms around me and rests her head against my shoulder.

"Do you know how much I love you?" she asks.

I nod. It is all I can do. Words are beyond me.

"You were what, nineteen?"

"Nineteen and a half."

"You were a baby, Trenda."

"Not really. Not living in our hellhole of a house. Not after watching Wanda and Norville. We all were decades older than we should have been. Nobody had a childhood in that house."

"You're wrong. Maddie, Chloe, Zoe, Piper, and me all had childhoods. That was because of you and Drake."

I grasp her hands that had snuck around my waist. I turn around to look into her eyes. "And you. It was the three of us, remember? Then when Drake left for the Navy, it was you and me, we were like the two musketeers, then I left you in the lurch for those six months I was in Nashville."

This time I can't stop the tears.

"I left you," I whisper.

"You were trying to better yourself so you could earn more money, remember? You were bound and determined to make our situation better."

"Yeah, and instead I came back broke and pregnant."

"You gave us all Bella. She was a shining light."

"Another mouth to feed."

"Hush up. She was the best thing that ever happened to this family and you know it."

I suck down the tears that are ready to fall. I can't lay my past on Evie; I've said enough.

"Trenda, you might not be willing to tell me everything, but now I know, this man needs to die."

I can see the feral look in my sister's eyes and don't doubt her words.

"He's in my past. I never want to think of him again."

"Give me a name."

My laugh is weak. Evie is serious. "Nope, not going to happen. No matter what, he fathered Bella, and that's a gift. He's done. Over. Never to be thought of again."

"That's not true. He's holding you back from living a happy life. It's killing me that you won't open yourself up to happiness."

I frown. "What are you talking about? I am happy. I have my daughter and all of you. I don't need a man to complete me. What's more, I know for a fact I would choose a loser. So this topic is closed. Got it?"

"Trenda, I absolutely fucking agree that you don't need a man to complete you. You are perfect the way you are. All I'm saying is that opening up your heart, just a little bit so that you might find someone special would be a good thing."

"You lucked out with Aiden."

"Yeah, I did. God knows I wasn't open to love, but that bastard just steamrollered right on past every single fence, gate, and barrier I had. I didn't stand a chance."

"Well, there you go. You didn't have your heart open to love, to get your one and only, why are you feeding me this garbage that I need to open mine? Especially when we know that my heart and brain are flawed and they pick assholes."

"Ass*hole*. You've picked one asshole, not plural. You were young and stupid. You're my big sister. Who do I come to for advice? You. Why? Because you're wise, and these days you would see through an asshole like the one in Nashville."

I reach out and take my little sister's hand. She grasps it and holds it tight.

"I appreciate everything you just had to say. I do. But a man just isn't in the cards for me," I whisper.

Now Evie looks as sad as I must have just a minute ago.

"Okay," she says softly. "But I'm going to say one more thing, and then I won't bring this up ever again, okay?"

I sigh, then nod.

"Kids watch their parents. They emulate their parents. Pushing men away, and never being open to a relationship with a man, are those the traits you want Bella to emulate?"

I bite my lip and look over at the fridge where school pictures of Bella and all of her artwork are hanging. I can't deal with what Evie is saying. I just can't. Not after thinking about Brantley and what really happened the night I left him. I turn back to her and paste a smile on my face.

"So, you want a baby, huh?" I ask.

Evie sighs, then smiles. "Oh, yeah. I want a little girl just like Bella."

"I want to hear more." I smile as I guide her back to the table.

Evie hadn't left much of the coffee cake. Just two slices left, one for Bella and one for me. We will have them for dessert tonight. I'll never know where Evie puts away all that food in her tiny body, and never gains weight. It must be how fast her mind spins.

I look at the clock on the microwave. I have three and a half hours before I need to leave to pick up Bella. That's plenty of time to get in a little work for my new client. I eye the dishes in the sink, then think about the fun work.

Dishes.

Computer.

Dishes.

Computer.

The dishes really need time to soak.

I plug up the sink and turn on the hot water so they can soak. That will surely help get them clean before I put them into the dishwasher. One day I'm going to have to look into upgrading the damn thing, considering the fact I almost have to completely wash the dishes before putting them in the dishwasher.

After the sink is full, I turn off the water and dry my hands then head to my teeny, tiny office. I pull up my Photoshop program and grin. Seriously, this is really coming together. I really like how the background looks against their logo, especially the way I'd made the logo pop with a three-dimensional effect.

I need to find some stock photos to depict just the right image that the client is going for, so I hit the icon for the web. As soon as I do that I can start working on the back end, which is another part I love doing.

How lucky am I?

I totally adore all parts of making websites. When I go to click on the stock photo gallery website I see I have more email, and I shudder.

When that second email came two days ago, it put me in a bad place. It had been titled *You Sinner* and cut me to the core. When I thought about what had happened the second to the last day I was in Nashville, that is exactly how I'd felt. But when I opened it, the message didn't make any sense. STAY AWAY, OR YOU'LL REGRET IT. Who could possibly think that I would ever want to go back to Nashville?

After deleting that email and deleting my trash, I had unsubscribed from every mailing list I'd ever signed up for. I would have changed my email address except it was on all my business cards. So now the incoming email was either business, friends and family, or from the evil AOL address.

Don't be a wimp!

I have to open my email server and look at it. It might be Piper needing something or my current client requiring an update. I click.

You Whore

Another title that stabs me in the heart. Even when I was a nineteen-year-old virgin, living at home, trying to take care of my younger siblings, how often had my mother, Wanda, called me a whore? How many times?

Then there was that day in Nashville when I'd heard it again. That hideous, that monstrous, that devastating day when my world fell apart.

~

I looked down at the cookbook again. I had to use Brantley's paperweight from his office to keep it open, because I'd just bought the cookbook yesterday, and it was stiff so it wouldn't stay open to the page I needed.

I was trying to cook him chateaubriand; according to the butcher at the high-end market I'd gone to yesterday, it was the best piece of meat I could purchase. I'd purchased the tarragon and demi-glace at the store, and knew that Brantley had good bottles of red wine at the condominium that I could use for the sauce.

According to the cookbook it said I needed to cook it with chateau potatoes. It took me over fifteen minutes to figure out they were just baby new potatoes sauteed in oodles of butter and some garlic, then popped in the oven and served with some herbs on top. My mouth was already watering.

I opened the oven to put them in when I heard Brantley come in. Damn, he was early. I hadn't had a chance to dress up yet. I wanted tonight to be special. I got the feeling that this might be the night he was finally going to propose.

"Darling, I'll be right out." I always liked using that word, it sounded so sophisticated.

I closed the oven and wiped my hands with the kitchen towel.

He didn't say anything so I went down the hall to see him. I always liked seeing him in his suits.

"Brantley?" He wasn't standing in the foyer or the living room. I would have noticed if he'd passed me to go to our bedroom.

The acrid scent of cigarette smoke made me turn to the window.

"Who are you?" I asked the skinny woman in a very pretty lavender suit and sky-high lavender heels.

"I think the better question is who are you?"

"I'm Trenda Avery. I live here. How did you get in here?"

"With my key. I have keys to all of my residences."

She took a long inhale of her cigarette then blew it out as I tried to understand what she meant.

"This condominium belongs to Brantley Harris."

"And I'm Brantley's wife."

I took a step backward, and I thought I might fall. "You can't be. She's dead."

"That was his first wife, Eloise. I'm his second wife, Carla. Brantley and I have been married for five years, didn't he tell you about me?"

I kept taking steps backwards until I hit the credenza and I leaned against it.

"That's not right, you can't be. Brantley can't be married," I whispered.

"Sure he can."

"But-t-t he's my b-b-boyfriend."

The woman started to laugh, and she kept laughing. "That is so delicious. I can't believe that one of Brantley's whores just called him her boyfriend. Have you ever called him that to his face?"

I shook my head.

"For fuck's sake. He's fifty-four years old, and what are you? Legal I hope. Tell me you're at least eighteen."

It was so cold, my teeth began to chatter. I nodded my head.

"Do you think you're the first whore he's shacked up with here in his little love nest?"

It was like she stuck a knife in my gut.

Whore?

"I didn't know," I struggled to get the words out. "He was married. I swear."

"You dumb cow, one little internet search would have told you. Are you telling me you didn't look him up? I don't believe you."

She crushed her cigarette out on the glass coffee table. Would it scar?

She sauntered over toward me.

"You're past your sell-by date, Trenda. I want you to pack your happy ass up and crawl back under whatever rock you came from. Do you understand me?"

She was in my face as she said those last words. I couldn't say anything. I was in too much pain.

"Fine, don't talk. Nod your head."

I nodded my head.

She reached up and patted my cheek. "What a good little whore."

. . .

I click on the email. *You and your daughter need to stay in Jasper Creek.* My glass of water topples off the table as I jerk back in my chair and yelp.

I clamp my hand over my mouth, thanking God that Bella isn't home. I go to the kitchen and get two towels to sop up the water. At least the glass isn't broken; luckily it had hit the rug, not the linoleum.

Why would Carla or Brantley be doing this to me? Carla was the one who called me a whore and Brantley knew I was from Jasper Creek.

Why is this happening?

Do an internet search. It's what you should have done eight years ago, remember?

I call up my search engine and type in Brantley Harris Nashville and the first thing that pops up is a huge picture of him, filling my screen. I scroll down just a bit and gasp.

It's an obituary.

Brantley died three weeks ago. It doesn't seem possible. He might have been old, but he was always bigger than life.

I read further. He'd died in bed of a massive heart attack. He is survived by his loving wife Carla Harris and his three sons, Brantley Harris, Jr., Richard Harris, and Kevin Harris.

He has sons?

So, it has to be Carla sending me those emails. But why? She has to know I will never step foot in Nashville ever again, but how did she know about Bella?

I shut down my computer. I can't think, and I need to get my shit together before I see my baby. Chloe has tried to teach me yoga, but my body doesn't bend as well as hers, so squats, crunches, and lunges for me. Maybe the exercises will stop my mind from whirling around. I put down the mat in the living room and do rep after rep of each exercise and after my limbs are trembling, my mind is still going a million miles a second. I look at the clock. I still have an hour and a half before I need to pick up Bella. I decide to go take a shower.

When I get out of the shower I'm a little calmer, but my mind keeps twirling around, like it's in a blender. Somehow, I have to turn my mind off, and the only thing I can think of that will do the trick is to read. I grab my reading device and pull up one of my favorite books, then sit on the side of my bed. I pick up my phone and set my alarm, then I slip under the covers and snuggle down under my duvet. I go to the seventy-five percent mark, so I can read where everything is close to being resolved and the hero and heroine are going to fall into one another's arms. I need this. Even though I know this will never happen for me, a girl can still dream.

When the page comes up I find I'm right, he is holding her in his arms. They're going to kiss. I let myself be transported. Time has no meaning, I'm in the story.

Chapter Seven

After talking to Bernie, I realize it's time to get off my ass. I've been doing some searches on Jeeps, Range Rovers, and trucks. I hate to pay for a brand-new vehicle since it loses its value as soon as I drive it off the lot. Dalton Sullivan has the perfect truck, that old, dilapidated thing that the man had tricked out to the nines on the inside. Nobody ever expects it.

Problem is, the only good connections I have to find me a truck that runs worth a damn are from the Navy, and I really don't want to tap one of them. Maybe in another few months.

Maybe.

I think about calling Trenda again. I think about it real hard; after all, I need to start making friends in this town if I'm going to stay.

Sell it to someone else, Clark.

I rub the back of my neck as I take my thermal mug of hot coffee and get into my cold Pontiac GTO and start her. The reason I can't call her is that if I spend much more time talking to her, I'm going to want to see her, and then I'm going to want to *really* see her. See *all* of her. And Trenda Avery strikes me as the forever kind of woman, and that is *not* what I'm looking for.

As I start getting closer to town, I drive by the gas station and it's jam-packed, not conductive to having a conversation to find out if they could recommend where I might find a used truck or something like it. I slowly drive into the center of town. I like it here. I'd driven through the town square when I'd first come to Jasper Creek, and it was like I was stepping back in time. It has the county courthouse with a big clock overlooking the square. In the middle of the square is a park with a bronze statue of somebody, probably a man named Jasper. On the other three sides of the square are small businesses and I will bet my bottom dollar that one of them will be a good restaurant or diner.

I am not wrong. I see a little sandwich board out front with the words *biscuits and gravy special* written in chalk on the front. I am sold. I park my car in front of a storefront on the left and head that way. When I push open the door a cowbell rings and everybody in the whole place looks up to see who has come in to join them. When they realize it's a stranger, they stare longer, sizing me up.

"Seat yourself, and I'll be with you in just a minute," a middle-aged woman shouts from the cash register. She has a great smile and I can see why people flock to her restaurant, even if the food is only average.

I look around and see that there are no tables available. A big guy pushes back from his seat and picks up his plate, utensils, and everything else from the table, and takes it over to the woman who looks like she's doing everything by herself.

"George, you don't have to bus your own table. I would have done it," the woman protests.

"It's fine, Lettie. Here's a twenty. Keep the change." As the man walks past me toward the door, he does a chin tilt toward the table. "Now you have someplace to sit."

Lettie rushes over to the table with a washcloth and has it washed clean before I can even get to the table. She hands me a menu. "Everything's good on the menu, but Ma's outdone herself with the cheesy grits and bacon casserole this morning." Lettie leans closer to my ear. "She serves it with avocado slices," she said softly.

"Well then I'm sold," I say handing the menu back to her.

"That's just the side dish. Can I get you biscuits and sausage gravy? Or, Mama makes some mean brown sugar oatmeal pancakes, with a rasher of bacon, of course. Course a man your size might want both."

"If I was twenty years younger I might have gone for it, but I can't work off that much food as easily."

"Yeah, and them there doctors are constantly harping on cholesterol and all them other diseases. I tell you what, my Mama and her Ma, we call her Little Grandma, they are both fitter than fiddles, and they sure as sugar haven't changed their diets none."

"How old is Little Grandma?"

"She's having a birthday this month, so she'll be one hundred and three then. My daughter will be bringing her in during the lunch crowd. We put her up on a stool near the door and she hands out menus. She and my great granddad started this place, so there's no keeping Little Grandma away. Most of the food we cook here is based on Little Grandma's recipes."

"Then I'll tell you what, Lettie, hook me up. I'll go for the biscuits and gravy, the pancakes, bacon, and the casserole."

"Coffee and orange juice, right?"

I nod.

"Okay Sug, I'll have that right out to you. In the meantime, make some friends." She taps on the table next to me where two women her age are talking. "Alice, Florence, start talking to the new boy. I'm expecting to know everything about him by the time he's done with breakfast, got it?"

"Leave it to us," the one with the purple hair says, then she shoves their table next to mine.

"Hi, I'm Florence, I'm not the shy one." She fluffs her purple hair. "Alice is the shy one. I've been working on her for forty years to come out of her shell, maybe today will be the day."

I watch as Alice calmly takes a sip of her coffee and gives a little shrug as she looks at me. She's clearly saying, *what are you going to do?* I have to choke back a laugh. Seems to me that Alice can communicate just fine.

"Are you the hermit that's renting Bernie's cabin?" Florence asks. It's fascinating to watch just how much sugar and cream she stirs into her coffee.

"Yeah, I'm that hermit, but I thought I would come down off my mountain today."

"Why?" Florence asks. "Are you just here for the good food, or are you a bigwig from one of them big box chain stores, looking to put all of our neighbors out of business?"

"Florence, drink your coffee and let me handle this a different way, okay?" Alice says softly.

"But get some information from him. Lettie's going to want to know something when she gets back."

Alice rolls her eyes. Then she extends her hand. "Hello, I'm Alice Draper, my son runs the hardware store here in town and when I have free time from watching my grandkids, I do some volunteer work around town."

I take her hand and shake it. I like her.

"My name is Simon Clark. I recently retired from the Navy and a friend of a friend of mine suggested Jasper Creek as a place to unwind for a while before I decide on my next move."

"Stagnate is more like it," Florence says as she sets down her cup of creamy sugar. The whole mug looks like a pool of white.

"I don't know about that. Jasper Creek has been growing now that they built the John Deere manufacturing plant in Knoxville," Alice gently disagrees. "We've got that new housing development out where the Lally's old farm was, and you know that they're putting up some apartments right at the end of Chestnut."

"Apartments. That just brings in a bunch of transients if you ask me." Florence sniffs and turns her attention back to me. "You're not part of the John Deere folks. My nephew works there as a supervisor, he hasn't mentioned any Navy men. He would too, since we've been inundated with the likes of that Avery boy and his accomplices."

Interesting.

Alice frowns. "Florence, you need to dial it back. You know perfectly well that every one of those Avery children have turned out wonderfully. Someone upstairs must have been watching over all seven of them, because with Wanda and Norville as their parents they were dealt a raw deal."

"All I'm saying is that after Drake and those other Navy types showed up, poor Delmar ended up in jail."

Alice rolls her eyes again. "Florence, I realize you dated him in high school, but he was a bully back then and he turned into a bully with a badge thirty years later. You read the papers, he belonged behind bars."

"I still say it was a set-up. You heard what the others had to say."

"Those are the same people who get drunk at Chucky's

Friday and Saturday night but sit in the front pew on Sunday morning. You need to be listening to a new group of people."

"But Delmar was a really good kisser," Florence whines.

Thank God Lettie finally arrives with my mountain of food. I didn't hear all of the details of what had gone down here in Jasper Creek five years ago when Mason brought his team here to back up Drake. The less I knew, the better. I did know that Drake's parents ended up in the state pen.

"I brought catsup, hot sauce, maple and boysenberry syrup and fresh butter made at Shivley's farm. Is there anything else you need?"

I'm going to have a stroke just looking at the food, but there isn't a chance in hell that I'm not going to try to eat it all.

"No, Ma'am, you've set me up good."

She pats my shoulder, then turns to Alice and Florence. "Did you get his details?"

I start shoveling in the cheesy grits so that I don't have to answer questions.

"Florence was too busy complaining about Delmar and Drake Avery for Simon to get a word in edgewise," Alice says with a twist of her lips.

Lettie laughs. "Sounds about right." She turns her attention to Florence. "You should have given up on that bully senior year when he beat-up that sophomore and got suspended for a week. What you ever saw in him, I'll never know."

"He was a—"

"Good kisser." Alice and Lettie say simultaneously.

"Good Lord, Florence, if that's all you're looking for in a man, go buy a date up in Nashville for a night and be done with it."

Thank God I'd just swallowed my bite of pancake,

otherwise I'd be choking on my food. Did Alice just suggest that Florence purchase a man for a night? I make a grab for my glass of orange juice and take a hasty sip, again not wanting to be dragged into the conversation.

"You're just lucky you have Dave. You don't know what it's like to be a single woman in a small town," Florence pouts. Then as sure as the sun sets in the west, Florence turns to me. "Are you single, Simon?"

"Yeah, but I've been told on multiple occasions that I'm not a good kisser."

Alice starts coughing, but I know she is really laughing.

"You're not?" Florence clarifies.

"No, ma'am. You're going to have to look elsewhere. It sounds like new men are being hired at the John Deere plant, maybe you should start having breakfast at a diner closer to Knoxville."

Florence turns to Alice. "What do you think of that idea?" she asks her friend.

"Couldn't hurt."

"I'll go pay the check," Florence says as she gets up from her chair. Alice turns to look at me.

"Damn shame."

"What?" I ask with a smile.

"You being a bad kisser, and all. You do realize that piece of information is going to be all over Jasper Creek by the end of the day, don't you?"

I take a sip of my coffee. It's good. This place sure knows how to put together a good breakfast. "I figured so. I'll just have to live with a ruined reputation."

"I think some of the ladies might be willing to overlook the drawback," Alice says as she fishes out some bills from her wallet and lays them beside her plate. "If you need anything, don't forget to stop by the hardware store. If Dave doesn't have what you need, he'll know where you can get it."

"Is the store open today?"

She nods. "Eight to six, Monday through Saturday."

"I'll stop by. I have a couple of questions about buying something more suitable if I want to drive some of the backroads."

"Talk to Dave. He might be able to point you in the right direction on that."

"Sounds like your son is plugged in."

"He inherited the hardware shop from his dad, who inherited it from his father. It's almost an institution around here, so yeah, he's plugged in."

"Are you coming, Alice?" Florence asks from the diner's entry.

Alice smiles. "It was nice meeting you, Simon," she says as she gets up.

I stand up and smile. "Same here, Alice."

"You might be a lousy kisser, but you are a gentleman."

"Need to make up for my deficiencies somehow," I grin.

I watch as the two ladies walk out of the diner, then sit back down to finish the best breakfast I have ever eaten.

Chapter Eight

I look up from the kitchen table as I hear the rumble of a large engine. I might have gone a little over the top, but what the hell; if you're going to have a mid-life-crisis, you might as well go all out. Fred drives the Silver Dodge RAM 3500 to the front, right beside my GTO, his son Arnold pulls up behind him in his red Dodge RAM 1500. I'm happy to see that he's gotten rid of the bronze nut sack off the trailer hitch like I had requested. I go out and greet them.

Fred works for the county utility company and his son is still in high school. He's selling his truck because he needs something smaller since he isn't hauling horses anymore, and what's more, he wants to buy Arnold and his daughter used cars when they graduate high school.

"Simon, here she is. Arnold detailed her for you."

I shake Ned's hand, then turn to the young man. "Thank you, Arnold." The kid stands up straighter.

"You're welcome, Mr. Clark."

"Do you want to come in for a cup of coffee?" I ask.

"Nope, we want to get home and make sure everything

is hauled inside the barn and that the barn is closed up tight," Ned says.

"Why?"

"Don't trust the weatherman. He's saying we're in for a snowstorm, but I think we're in for an ice and windstorm like the one we got a couple of years back. It took out more than few roofs, and it decimated the trailer park."

I look up at the sky. The clouds look dark, but I've just put it down to the predicted snowstorm. After they leave, I go inside and call up NOAA on my computer; damned if Ned isn't right. It looks like there's an ice storm that is going to hit eastern Tennessee tomorrow. They're predicting high winds and freezing rain.

It doesn't seem that cold outside. Maybe forty-five degrees, not enough to put on a coat. Well, NOAA usually didn't steer me wrong, so I better get my ass up to Bernie's and arrange supplies for everybody today.

My truck isn't exactly quiet so I would have thought that the old man would be bundled up and out on the deck to greet me. I jump out of the truck, climb the stairs, and knock on his sliding glass window. Nothing. Of course, his door isn't locked. Trenda had mentioned how nobody in this town locked their doors. If you ask me that was plain stupid, but what did I know about small town life?

I step inside.

"Bernie?" I call out. Still nothing.

I do a quick search of all of his rooms. His bedroom is a mess, which I really didn't expect. Things are knocked over, his bed isn't made. That isn't what I'm expecting of this man. I'm surprised to find a walker.

You mean to tell me in just a week his gout had deteriorated that badly?

Then I see it, a damn satellite phone is peeking out from under a sheet on the floor. I pick it up to see who his last call was to, but his phone is locked.

Great, he didn't lock his doors, but he locks his phone.

I pull out my satellite phone, which is going to come in handy up in these hills. I always keep one with me for emergencies. I've memorized Trenda's number, so I call her, since she seems to have a handle on what goes on in this town. Once again I get her business voice answering the phone. I head outside.

"Hello, Trenda, it's me, Simon."

"Hey. How can I help you?" I am halfway around his house.

"I'm up here at Bernie's house and he's not here. His satellite phone is here, but it's locked so I can find out his last call."

"That's really odd, that thing is glued to his hip. Not that he actually answers many calls," she laughs softly. Even as I worry about Bernie, I still find her laugh smooth as honey.

"His truck is still here, but I see recent tracks of a big vehicle out front."

"Let me call you right back. He might have called someone from the fire department if he was hurt or really sick. Zarek and his team have been up to Bernie's house a few times. They've been trying to get him to reveal where everybody lives up in the mountains, but he hasn't. I'm going to give them a call. Hang on while I put you on hold."

I jog back to my truck, waiting for Trenda to get back to me.

"I've got it," she says as she gets back on the line. "It was the fire department that got up to Bernie's place yesterday.

Turns out that his foot was turning gangrene, and he realized he was in trouble, so he called. They took him to the hospital in Pigeon Forge, then he was transferred to Knoxville. According to my brother-in-law, Zarek, they're not sure if he'll be able to save his foot."

"Ah, dammit." I take a moment to absorb the news. "Trenda, I have a problem. There's a significant ice storm coming our way within the next twenty-four hours. It sounds vicious. I need to get supplies up to the people that Bernie normally cared for."

"I knew Bernie was taking care of people, but I didn't even think about the fact that with his gout he hadn't been making his normal deliveries. Are you sure about the weather?" she asks me.

"Yep."

"Let me call my sister, and I'll call you right back." The line goes dead.

Well, okay then. I start my truck and head down what someone might call a road, back to civilization.

Three minutes later, Trenda calls me back.

"Okay, that's settled. Chloe will pick up Bella from school and watch her. She'll tag Zarek and he'll hit the food pantry and see what they have available, and I'll head to the store. Whatever he doesn't get, I'll buy. You need to get to the hardware store; Dave will know what Bernie usually gets when it comes to propane tanks and you can get those. I'll reimburse you."

"Like hell you will."

"We'll discuss it when we meet at the fire station."

"You forgot one thing; we don't know where these people live."

"Oh yeah, I forgot to tell you. I'm sure that Zarek will let us use his Jeep, so have Dave deliver the propane tanks to the fire station."

"I have a truck, but—"

"Oh, and I have the coordinates for everyone, it won't be a problem finding them."

"I should have known. Are you sure you weren't an officer in the Navy?" I ask.

She laughs again, and this time I feel it below my belt.

What the hell?

"Worse than that—I'm a single mother."

This time I laugh. "Yeah, I can see where wrangling Bella would keep you on your toes."

"You have no idea. So, are you good with my plan?"

"A couple of things. I just bought Fred Sanderson's big truck, so we don't need Zarek's Jeep, and *I'll* reimburse *you* for what you spend at the grocery store."

"You can try. I'll meet you at the fire station." Again, the line goes dead.

∼

As I get to the grocery store I find out that Trenda has already called Roger and notified him of the situation. Roger, unlike his employees, has taken intelligent initiative and called over to the food bank before Zarek has had a chance to even get there. So, he was filling in the foodstuff that the foodbank couldn't supply.

"Is there anything I can do to help?" I ask the man as he fills up a box with canned goods.

"Yeah, you can carry this to the front, and then load it when Trenda gets here."

"Don't we need to check out first?"

"Simon, I never charge Bernie, so why would I start charging now?" As I take the box of canned goods to my truck I mull over what Roger had to say. I have to admit, his attitude says a hell of a lot about this town and the people in it. This might be someplace to hang my hat for more than just a little while.

"Mr. Clark, where do you want me to put this?"

I turn around and see Dennis behind me. He's carrying a smaller box. When I look inside I see it is full of frozen meat. Not just ground chuck, but rib-eyes, roasts, and chicken breasts. Yep, this is definitely someplace I could come to like.

"Just put it into the back of my truck, Dennis."

"Yes, Sir."

I take out my regular phone and text Trenda to say she could skip the store, since I was already here picking up the food. I get a thumbs up emoji in reply. I turn to go back in the store and I meet Roger with two more boxes in his arms. He can't see over the top; he's peeking around the side.

I pluck the top box out of his arms before it falls over. It's light as air.

"What's in here?" I ask.

"Stuff from our bakery. The stuff at the food pantry was stale. The last box is inside. It's from the dairy department. Then you're good to go. Zarek has a lot of produce and boxed goods coming."

He stops short. "Did you buy Fred Sanderson's truck?"

I nod, and we set the boxes in the back. He looks down then looks at me. He smiles and puts out his hand. I don't know why, but I shake his hand anyway.

"What's that for?" I ask.

"For getting rid of that atrocious set of balls that Fred had hanging from the back of his truck. I always shuddered when I saw that."

"It wasn't my style."

"Thank God." He pats me on the shoulder. "So is Zarek going up the mountain?"

"No, Bernie had asked me to do it while he was down

with the gout, so I'll do it. Trenda said she has the coordinates for everyone, so this shouldn't be a problem."

Roger looks up. "You don't have much time; the storm is closing in fast."

NOAA said I had at least twenty-four more hours, so I wasn't worrying...much.

"Thanks again," I say to Roger as I get into my truck. I head to the hardware store and I see all the propane tanks sitting on the sidewalk. As I get closer I see Dave leaning against the 'Pick-up/Drop-Off Zone' sign as I pull up.

"Let's get them loaded," he says as I turn off the truck's engine.

After we're done loading them I ask what I owe.

"Just get the empty tanks back, and we're square."

"That's a bunch of bullshit," I argue.

"I could just unload them all," Dave says with a grin.

Bastard.

I grin back. I could learn to fucking love this town!

"If you're going up the mountain in this coming storm, you're going to need to load up with other gear. Do you have a chainsaw, shovel, winch? You know what I mean."

"Bernie left me a chainsaw up at the cabin. It works fine. I'm not sure I saw a shovel, and yeah, this truck has a winch, but I need a heavy-duty tarp. Do you have one?"

"Sure. I can set you up with the tarp and the shovel," Dave says.

I follow him into his store; this time he is going to take my money.

After I have everything paid for and battened down, I head to the fire station, which is easy enough to find since I pass it almost every single time I come to town. When I pull into their parking lot, Trenda pulls in behind me.

As soon as we both get out of our vehicles, she marches

over to me and thrusts her fists on her hips. "You realize you're an aggravating man, don't you?"

"I'm happy to know that I've been downgraded to aggravating in the eyes of womankind. According to my ex-wife I was a hell of a lot worse than aggravating."

Her lip twitches and I can see she's holding back a laugh.

"So, tell me what she called you so I can use those terms to let you know what I think of your high-handedness of going to the store and packing up all those boxes and paying for them."

"I like high-handedness. I like it a lot. Makes me sound like royalty."

This time it wasn't just a lip twitch, it was a smile.

"Anyway, Roger didn't charge me a dime. Turns out he never charges Bernie, either."

That smile turns almost dreamy. I watch as she practically melts in front of me. "That is the sweetest thing I ever heard. I won't think bad thoughts about his employees for an entire month."

"It really is sweet. But *I* can't make a promise like that." I grin.

"Well, let's get the groceries loaded into Zarek's Jeep. It's right over there." She points to the big black Jeep parked in the corner of the lot. I could tell Zarek didn't want anybody to park near him so his baby didn't get a scratch.

"Nope, it's going to be the other way around. We'll take the food pantry items and put them into my truck. The main reason I bought it was so I could help Bernie out with his runs up in the hills."

"Mountains," Trenda corrected me.

"Honey, those aren't mountains. Those are hills."

Her eyes twinkled. "Mountains."

"You poor thing, you haven't even seen a picture on the

internet of mountains. Have Bella look up the Rockies for you, and then you'll see what a mountain is."

This time I get a full-blown laugh out of her. Watching and hearing her laugh is more than a treat, it is a warm caramel and chocolate dessert.

"We call them mountain folk, not hill folk, so it's mountains."

I just shake my head. "Let's head into the fire station and get the keys to Zarek's Jeep."

"I highly doubt Zarek has locked his Jeep."

"Why wouldn't he?"

"Everybody in town knows it's Zarek's and nobody would want to get on his bad side. Plus there are security cameras here in the fire station."

"Yeah, I saw those, but somebody just needs to wear a hoodie and a mask."

"I go back to my first point—nobody would want to mess with Zarek, just like they won't want to mess with you. Once they find out it's you and not Fred Sanderson's truck, you'll be able to keep it unlocked." She smiles.

"Good to know."

"Let's go talk to Zarek. He's probably already asked for time off to make the run with me."

"With you?"

"Yeah, even though he's met a couple of the people, he hasn't met all of them. The ones he hasn't met won't feel comfortable having him show up at their door. Even if he is bringing them provisions."

"So, you think you're going?" I look up. The sky is getting darker fast and it's just noon. What's more, the temperature's dropped at least ten degrees since this morning. When I go back to my cabin for my winter gear I'll go to check NOAA again; maybe they'd updated when the ice storm was going to hit eastern Tennessee.

"There's also a kid up there living in a tent. I really want to get his ass down here to town. But I'm not sure where he is. Apparently, there's a man named Azariah and a woman named Bertha who know where he's hunkered down. So, I want to talk to them."

When we enter the firehouse, everybody shouts a welcome to Trenda.

"Hey. guys. Let me introduce you to Simon Clark. He's renting Bernie Faulks' cabin for a while." She looks around the large space that houses two fire engines. "Where's Zarek?"

"Right here, Sis." A big man comes around one of the trucks, wiping his hands off on a blue rag that he then pockets. He goes to Trenda and gives her a big hug. He looks her up and down. "Please tell me that you have a warmer jacket, gloves, and hat in your vehicle."

Her mouth twists as she shakes her head. "No, Zarek, it never occurred to me to bring winter clothes when we're going up the mountain during a snowstorm," she says sarcastically.

I laugh.

Zarek holds up his hands, palms out. "Sorry, I get to be a bit of a mother hen sometimes."

"Sometimes?" I watch Trenda's eyebrows lift so high that they're hidden by her bangs.

"Okay, just call me overprotective of the women in my life. Of course you have everything you need, you're Trenda."

"Exactly. I'm the oldest Avery girl, and don't you forget it."

Zarek grins. "How could I when you don't let me? And here I always think that Evie is the scary sister."

"So now that we know I have the right clothes, I want to tell you about a change of plans. You're going to move the food you got from the pantry from your Jeep into Simon's truck, because he's going to be the one who goes with me up the mountain."

"Whoa," I say. "From what everybody is saying about this ice storm, I don't think it's wise for you to be coming with me."

"Simon, let's not waste time." She looks over at Zarek and gives him a pointed stare. "Simon's truck is Fred Sanderson's without that godawful ornament hanging off the back." She shudders. "Just pack the supplies in the back."

"Yes, Ma'am." He gives her another hug then hustles out of the fire house.

"Trenda," I start patiently.

"Give it up, Commander," she whispers. "You might be used to giving orders, but that's not going to work with me. I know what's right in this situation, you don't. Now we're just wasting time having an argument about something that eventually you're going to agree with, so let's just stop the nonsense now."

"You can follow me to my cabin. I drove straight from Bernie's into town, so I need to get kitted out for this mission. While I'm there, I'm going to check NOAA and see what it has to say about the weather. If it's going to be awhile before the storm hits, you can come with me."

She lets me lead her out of the fire station. I know damn good and well she's *letting* me. I take it as a win, and touch her lower back as we walk.

Chapter Nine

I have to admit, I've been very interested to see if Simon's made any changes to Bernie's cabin since he moved in. My guess had been, 'no.' He opens the door for me to precede him. I look around. I see three mugs that have been purchased from the coffee shop in town hanging down from underneath the cabinet, those are new.

There is a lot of mail strewn all over the little dining room table, and wedged in between all of the unopened envelopes is a sleek silver laptop. I recognize the brand, and based on the dimensions of the thing, and how thin it is, I know it cost a pretty penny.

I do one more sweep of the room to see if there is anything else that proves he has settled in, and I see a picture on the mantle. It is of two women; one is older, and the other, younger woman looks just as beautiful as her mother. Both of them have the same gray eyes as Simon. I would guess they're his sister and mother.

"Take a seat, Trenda. I'm just going to check NOAA."

"What's NOAA?"

"It stands for National Oceanic and Atmospheric

Administration. When I want accurate weather forecasts, that's where I go."

"So, what does it say?"

"This morning it said that the storm wasn't going to hit for twenty-four hours, but after having everybody in Jasper Creek look up into the sky and tell me it's coming today, I want to check again."

I giggle. "You're learning."

"Trenda, I try to always listen to the locals. They've saved my ass and my team's asses hundreds of times while we were out in the field."

I watch as he boots up his computer.

"How are you getting a connection out here?"

"I'm using my satellite phone as a hotspot."

"Fancy."

Simon gives a resigned sigh as he starts typing.

"What was that for?"

"You're the second person who has called me fancy since I've been here in Jasper Creek. That is not the honorific I really want."

"Well, if you keep using words like honorific instead of title, you're going to continue to be called fancy."

He turns his head to give me a long look. "And I stand by my assertion that you are a smartass." His voice is all growly.

"I can live with that. Actually, it's an honorific that I'm proud of."

I watch as his eyes begin to sparkle, then he turns back to his computer screen. "Yep, NOAA changed their projections. The ice storm is due to hit tonight. They're predicting high winds and icy rain at five o'clock tonight." He snaps his laptop closed and shoots out of his chair. I watch as he prowls across the room toward me, ending up standing over me with his hands on his hips.

"There is no way you're going with me this afternoon."

"If you want to accomplish your mission," I say, speaking SEAL, "then you have no choice but to take me with you." I keep my voice calm and reasonable, the same way I do with Drake when he gets all He-Man.

"I'm getting my gear." He turns and goes to his bedroom. I've already peeked in, not surprised to see his bed made up, and not just having the comforter pulled up. It was like a hotel maid had done it. The man has some true OCD tendencies.

He comes back zipping up a thin down jacket over a tight, long-sleeved thin shirt. It's a shame he's putting on the jacket, because I like how the shirt molds to his abs. Forty-seven looks damned good on him.

Then he holds out what looks like a windbreaker.

"A windbreaker?"

"Do you have anything that's waterproof to wear?" he asks me.

"My poofy parka is waterproof. Kind of." I answer.

He frowns.

"You're going to take this. I know it's going to be too big for you, but when we're out in the freezing rain, it'll keep you dry. If you're not wet, then you won't get as cold. Stand up."

"Please," I say.

"Please what?"

"Trenda, will you please stand up?" I say in my Bella-teaching voice. "That is the proper phrase if you want me to stand up, Commander."

He doesn't roll his eyes, but I can tell he wants to. "Trenda, my dear, will you please, with sugar on top, stand up?"

"And you call me the smartass," I say as I stand up.

"You should quit pushing your luck seeing as how I'm taking you with me."

"You finally see the logic in my argument, you mean."

He sucks in a deep breath, then lets it out. "Are you wearing anything underneath that sweater? What's it made of?"

I don't bother flipping him anymore guff. I choose to answer him instead. "I'm wearing a bra, and it's made of cotton."

"Hold on." He goes back into his bedroom and comes back out with a long-sleeved shirt similar to the one he's wearing underneath his down jacket. "Go put this on under your sweater. Chances are we're going to be working up a sweat as we go from house to house, so you're going to want to wear something that wicks away the moisture when you perspire, and cotton doesn't get the job done. This is polyester and Lycra; it *will* get the job done."

I take the shirt and head for the other door that I assume is the bathroom. When I go in and turn on the light, I find a room that's in perfect condition. Nothing's on the counter except a dop kit. All towels are folded and hanging up. What would Simon think about how Bella and I live? It certainly would be a shock to his system. I grin at my reflection in the mirror. Simon would probably say a bad word and Bella would make some money off of him.

I quickly put on the Lycra shirt, which isn't as big as I thought it was going to be. Actually, it's big in the waist, but tight in the boobs. I would have thought with his wide chest that it wouldn't have been. I throw my sweater on over it and hustle out to join him before he tries to leave without me. Which is why I haven't given him the coordinates yet.

The cabin is empty.

"What the hell?"

The door opens and Simon is holding all my gear from

my car. "You won't need to put any of this on until we get to the first house, if then. We should have at least four hours before the snow or sleet or icy rain starts. Where are we going first?"

"How do you want to do this?" I ask him. "Do you want to start with Bertha? She's the one who lives the furthest out; that way we drive the furthest up while the weather is still stable, and we start down the mountain before the icy rain hits."

"I think that's an excellent idea."

The look of admiration on Simon's face shouldn't make me this happy. So what if he's impressed? It shouldn't matter.

But it does.

"Thanks. Hopefully we can find that friend of a friend too, and get him in out of the cold."

"That is the hope." He smiles. "Let's get going."

I grab my things from him, which includes my purse containing the coordinates for each person's home, along with the satellite GPS tracker that Drake left for me.

When I get outside and stand in front of his passenger side door I realize it's even higher than Zarek's Jeep.

"Need a little help?"

I shiver as he whispers the question into my ear.

I turn my head and find us eye to eye, damn near lip to lip. "Are you absolutely sure you want to go, Trenda? This might not go well."

My mouth is dry, so I nod.

He reaches around me and opens the door, then boosts me into the passenger seat. "Buckle up." He closes the door and in a flash he's in the driver seat starting the engine. "Okay, Miss Navigator, where to?"

We've been on the backroads for almost an hour before I see Bertha's cabin. Smoke is coming out of her chimney, and she still has a Christmas wreath on her front door. Somebody has recently loaded her up—there are at least two cords of wood underneath her lean-to next to the house.

We're about a hundred yards from her front door when it opens, and there stands Bertha with a shotgun. I can't hear what she's saying.

"Better stop the truck," I tell Simon, but he's already in the process of doing it.

When we stop, I push open the passenger door. "Let me go talk to her."

"And how are you going to get out of the truck? A parachute?" He opens his door. "Hold on while I help you down."

I can hear Bertha now.

"State your name and your business."

"My name is Simon Clark. Trenda Avery is with me," he says as he rounds the front of the truck to get to my side. "Bernie Faulks is in the hospital."

"Are you sure this woman really needs help?" He whispers the question as his big hands wrap around my waist and lift me out of the truck. He immediately pushes back my seat and pulls my poofy jacket out of the backseat. "Put this on. It's not raining yet, so you don't need the windbreaker."

He was right, it was freezing cold at this elevation. I'm pretty sure my nose is frozen enough it's going to break off if I touch it. After he helps me on with the coat, he grabs my gloves, scarf, and hat.

"What's taking y'all so long?" Bertha yells.

I realize we're out of Bertha's sight behind the open passenger door. I step away, pulling Simon with me. He catches on and closes the door.

"Just dressing Trenda for the cold," he calls out. I glare at him for making me sound like a child.

"That's mighty nice of you. Do you mean to tell me she finally found herself a man?"

I shove his hands away as he's wrapping the scarf around my neck and start marching toward the cabin. "What do you mean finally found a man? If you don't need one, I don't need one," I call out to Bertha.

She lowers her gun and smiles. "There's a difference, Girly. I had the best of men when I married Brian Conners. No need trying to replace a man like that after he died. Is Bernie okay? Did the gout get him?"

I tromp up to her porch, and she rests the shotgun against her house and opens her arms to give me a hug. Bertha gives the best hugs.

"You're looking good, Girly. I like seeing you smiling like you are." She releases me and looks over my shoulder at Simon. "See that you keep making her smile, you hear?"

"Yes, Ma'am."

I don't bother protesting; it will just result in a verbal knot of confusion and take up more time that we really don't have. "We brought supplies." I say.

"Who chopped the wood for you?" Simon asks.

"A nice boy named Renzo," Bertha answers Simon.

I turn in time to see Simon nodding. "I thought it might have been him."

"Yeah, he's been helping me and a couple of the others with chores around our places. It's kind of nice to have some young blood up here on the mountain."

I was going to jab him in the stomach if he made some snarky remark about this not being a mountain. He glances over at me, his eyes gleaming. I know he's read my mind.

"How's Renzo doing?" Simon asks.

"He's doing a lot better than when he first arrived.

Whatever it was that was ailing him has lifted. I suspect that he'll be leaving the mountain in the next few weeks. Don't know where he'll end up, but he'll pack up his tent and go."

"You're due for a nasty ice storm, high winds and icy rain," Simon tells her.

She grins. "So, are you going to tell me something that I don't know? I can tell something like that is coming by looking in the sky. Then checking up on NOAA with my satellite phone tells me the rest."

"Shoot, Bertha, I should take Bella out of school and just have you teach her from now on. I just learned about NOAA today."

"You should bring that little darlin' up here. I've only met her three times, and I fell in love with the little sprite. Reminded me of you when you were little. How God seen fit to bless Wanda and Norville with such beautiful children that they did nothing but berate and neglect when Brian and I couldn't have any is beyond me."

I take a deep breath. "You would have made a great mama."

"Darn tootin' I would have." She turns her attention back to Simon. "Now what kind of goodies do you have for me?"

~

"She's something else. I swear to God, we left with more than we came with." I shake my head in wonder.

"Let's not go overboard," Trenda says as she fiddles with her handheld satellite GPS. "I'm just thankful she made us promise to take some of the strawberry preserves for ourselves. I think I would have cried if I had to give them all away today."

"Are they really that good?"

"She puts rhubarb in them. So yeah, they're that good."

"There's a fork in the road coming up. Which way?" We're moving at a snail's pace, but I didn't want to miss any of the dirt tracks that they call roads.

"The one on the left. I'm not sure I'm reading this right, but it looks like two kilometers and we'll get to Azariah's place. He's a Vietnam vet, and he doesn't like visitors. To tell you the truth, I think he has PTSD. I tried to talk to Bernie about that, but he shut me down. Said it was all mumbo jumbo, and that I just needed to take Azariah as he was, and not try to put a label on him."

I hear the hurt in Trenda's voice.

"You weren't trying to do that. You were trying to understand him, and knowing you, trying to find a way to help him."

She's silent. I take just a second to look over at her. Her head is bowed.

"What is it?" I ask.

"In a way, Azariah scares me a bit. Our father, he was rattlesnake mean. I try not to let the years I lived with him color the way I see and interact with men, but it does sometimes," she admits softly.

I ponder what she says. "Did it make it easier to deal with Azariah's temperament when you could put it down to PTSD?"

"Yeah," she says quietly. "At least then there was a reason. There never was one for my father or his brother."

"Why not?" I let my question drift off into silence, seeing whether she would answer.

"There's a sharp bend in the road coming up," she warns me. The cab of the truck is silent for another five minutes.

"It was bad growing up with Norville. Our mother did nothing but support him. She always took his side. Why they continued to have children considering how they seemed to hate us, I'll never know."

I reach out and put my hand on her knee. I need to do something to show her a little bit of comfort. After a minute, she covers her hand with mine.

"Anyway, we're going to have to tread softly with Azariah. I'll need to go in first, I think he'll remember me."

"Trenda, let me handle this."

"But—"

"I've dealt with a lot of vets who have suffered from PTSD. I know what I'm doing."

I hear her let out a deep breath and feel her muscles relax under my hand.

"All right." Two minutes pass. "Actually, that would be great. I wish I could say I was over my phobia about men who are angry and shout at me, but I'm not."

I turned my hand over so we were palm to palm, then I twine our fingers together. "Thank you for sharing that with me."

"Thanks for not thinking I'm a wimp."

"Honey, you're the furthest thing from a wimp that I could imagine."

More silence.

"Thank you," she finally whispers. I feel those words down deep in my bones. Before I can respond she's talking again. "On the next right turn we'll be on top of Azariah's cabin."

Before that turn the first splat of rain hits my windshield. It is a splat, no little drizzle of rain for us. I immediately see the cabin when I turn, and it is a whole different animal from what Bertha's cabin had looked like. Nope, I never imagined a wreath on the door of this house.

There are windows, but as I drive closer, I watch as each window slowly closes with interior shutters. The door has a five inch by five-inch square hole that eventually opens as I park the truck. It is no big surprise as the barrel of a gun pushes out the opening. I park the truck sideways so that he'll see the full bed of the truck and the driver's side door. I don't want him to be able to have a shot at Trenda.

I roll down my window and hold up both hands.

"I have news about Bernie Faulks. Can I get out and tell you, and if you okay it, maybe give you some supplies?"

"I can hear you just fine from where you are."

I sigh. "My name is Simon Clark. I just retired from the Navy after twenty-nine years. I'm here with Trenda Avery."

"You didn't bring those bastards Harmon or Huey, did you?"

"They're both in prison," Trenda whispers.

"They're both in prison," I yell out to Azariah. "It's just me and Trenda. She's the oldest Avery daughter, and she works with Bernie to help gather supplies. We just left Bertha's place. We have some of her strawberry rhubarb preserves to give you."

"Oh, you're smooth," Trenda whispers to me.

"You do?" the old man asks.

"Yep. She even made something special up for you. She said since you're such an ornery bastard that you deserved some hot and spicey apple chutney. She said to tell you that she put in extra vinegar."

I watch as the barrel of the gun draws back into the house, the shutter on the door closes and the actual door opens. An extremely tall and thin man with a long gray beard steps out onto the porch without any kind of weapon.

"Navy, huh?"

"Yeah. What about you?" I ask. I know enough not to get out of the truck until I'm invited.

"Fifth Marine Regiment," he answers.

Shivers go down my spine. I'd met some men who'd

served in the fifth during Vietnam. They were the most highly decorated regiment. Jesus, the battles they'd fought were unbelievable. When I'd been stuck in the middle of the Afghan mountains I'd sometimes think about the men who'd fought battles like the Tet Offensive, and here I was talking to one of those men.

"I'd like to shake your hand," I say.

"I'd like it more if you'd come inside and share some of the chutney with me, if there's some kind of bread in that truck for me."

"There's definitely bread. Trenda made sure to get you loaded up."

"All those kids turned out good. None of us could figure out how, but they did." He turns around and walks back into his cabin, leaving the door open.

"That's not the same man I talked to last year," Trenda says. "I hate that about PTSD. It makes people's loved ones feel like they're walking in a minefield, never knowing when a bomb is going to go off."

I look over at her. "You know about that?"

"Yeah, one of the men that Drake serves with has struggled with PTSD. Another had a TBI. Both of them are doing well now, but I've talked to both of their wives. It wasn't an easy path. I doubt I could have handled it."

"I'm positive you could have. Now don't try to jump down yourself, wait for me to come get you."

She rolls her eyes. "Yes, Sir."

Before I get out of the truck I pull my windbreaker from the backseat and hand it to her. "Put this on so you don't get wet on the trip into Azariah's cabin."

"What about you?"

"I'll be fine."

Chapter Ten

I jump at the sharp bite of thunder that rattles the cabin. Simon doesn't even flinch.

"I don't know why Bertha didn't just call Renzo," Azariah says right before he takes another big bite of a chutney-covered roll. "He answers his sat phone when it's either one of us. He told me outright that he's not answering it for anyone else."

I wanted to ask why, but that has nothing to do with finding the man and making sure he gets to safety before this storm really gets bad. I watch as Azariah's hand shakes when he pulls his satellite phone out of his pocket. His tremors have gotten a lot more noticeable since the last time I was here. He needs to get in and see a doctor.

It's painful watching him scroll through his phone before he finds Renzo's number. I want to help him. Simon must have seen my inner debate because he catches my eye and gives a slight shake of his head. He is probably right; trying to help Azariah will be a hit to his pride.

"Renzo," Azariah starts the call. "I'm sending two people your way."

The older man frowns. "Hold on. Hold on." He looks at Simon and me. "You can make it so both of you can hear him talk, too. Right?"

Simon nods, and Azariah hands him the phone. Simon presses a button and the phone goes on speaker.

"I don't want any damned visitors, Aza."

"Don't care if you want 'em or not. I'm sending them your way. Today the tremors are bad so I can't get to you, so I'm sending a Navy man your way to drag your sorry ass to my house."

"If I wanted to go to your house, I would already be there. What do you mean your tremors are bad? I told you, we need to get you in to see a doctor." I can't tell if the man is annoyed or concerned. Maybe he's both.

"I've seen enough doctors to last three lifetimes. I ain't going." Azariah complains.

"And I ain't going to your house, and if you send visitors, I won't be here. We clear?"

"Are you two related?" I ask the old man.

Azariah chuckles.

"Who's that?" Renzo asks belligerently.

"That'd be one of your rescuers. She's really pretty. I think you should let yourself be rescued. If I was your age, I'd definitely let her play at being my nurse."

This was *definitely* not the same man I'd met last year.

Simon and Renzo were both laughing.

"Did my brother send you?" Renzo demands to know.

"I'm Navy, aren't I?" Simon asks.

"Damned Jace. He can never just keep his nose out of anyone's business."

"Look, I'm fine with leaving grown men to take care of themselves," Simon says. "NOAA is saying that there's going to be an ice storm with fifty-mile-an-hour winds. Is your tent up for that? If not, then instead of snowflakes, you're going to be getting icy rain."

"I don't know what kind of pussy Jace thinks I am, but until I was ten, I was living in the Andes. I'm not talking the foothills; I'm talking up in the Andes. Occasionally it was cold, wet, and windy. I'm thinking no matter how bad someone in Tennessee thinks it can get, these hills have nothing on the Andes Mountains."

Simon grins and looks over at me.

"Don't be calling the mountains of Tennessee hills," Azariah admonishes.

"Then don't be sending strangers to where I'm staying."

"Normally I wouldn't, but I have to admit to being a might worried. You were looking a little stringy to me the last time I saw you."

"Stringy?" Simon and I both ask at the same time.

"Scrawny," Azariah clarifies. "You been eating, boy?"

"I've been eating fine. Seriously Aza, you send them to my place and I'm going to be pissed."

"My duty was to tell you that you better contact your mother, otherwise Jase was going to sic Polly on you," Simon said seriously.

"Aw, fuck, he seriously said that?" Renzo asks.

"That's a direct quote," Simon answers.

"Tell Jace I'll call Mom real soon."

"How soon?" Simon wants to know.

"This is a family thing. But since you seem to be so interested, yes, I'll call her in the next seventy-two hours."

"That's all he was asking, man. That's all he was asking."

"Well I'm asking for a little bit more," I interrupt. "She's your mother, it seems to me your brother shouldn't have to send out a rescue party to get you to call her. Shame on you. If she's a good one, send her some flowers, for God's sake. Mine's not, so treasure a woman who's been good to you."

I looked around when nobody says anything. "What?" I finally ask.

"Nothing," Azariah said. "I was just thinking you were right." He leans over and puts his mouth close to the phone. "You got that? Send flowers."

"Yeah, I heard the woman. Who are you again?" Renzo asks. "I'll look you up when I get to Jasper Creek."

"No need for that," Simon says. "She's going to be busy."

Renzo and Azariah laugh. "I'm not going to be too busy. I'll leave my card with Azariah."

"I think it's time we made some more deliveries. The storm's picking up." Simon tells me.

"Aza, you going to be all right?" Renzo asks.

"I'm going to be doing a damn sight better than you since I'm surrounded by four wooden walls, but who's keeping track?"

This time when they start laughing, I join in. "I'll bring more wood for you after the storm," Renzo promises, then he hangs up.

Simon gets up from the table and picks up my poofy jacket, scarf, gloves, hat, and his windbreaker. He helps me get everything on before we head for the door.

"Be careful when you get to the sisters' place. They have that gulley about fifty yards before you get to the front of their house, and in this weather it could start to fill up. Keep your eye out for it."

"Thanks, Azariah," Simon says. "I appreciate the tip."

"Call me Aza." He turns and looks at me. "You too, little girl. Hope to see you again. You tell that old coot Bernie that he better get well fast. I'm still pissed about losing that buck fifty on our last game of backgammon."

"I'll do that." Then, because I can't help it, I go over to

the man and give him a hug. He freezes for a minute, but then he returns it twofold.

"You turned out all right, Trenda Avery," he whispers into my hair.

That means a lot coming from someone who knows the history of this town and this county.

"Next time I come, I'll bring some chocolate chip cookies. I know it won't be as good as Bertha's chutney, but you might like them."

"Absolutely. Bring your daughter too. I've heard tell about her. I'd like to meet her."

I nod. I didn't want to commit until I had a better feel on how he would greet her.

"Enough flirting, Aza. We've got to go," Simon calls out. I head for the door and Simon goes over to Azariah and shakes hands with him. They speak for a moment, but too quietly for me to hear what they're saying. Azariah ends up slapping Simon's shoulder. Then Simon comes to the door and opens it for me.

The rain is really coming down, and the front yard is now mostly mud. Thank goodness I'm wearing my work boots.

Damn!

I feel myself slipping and know I'm going to land on my butt, when I suddenly feel Simon's arms surrounding me.

"I've got you."

I hear his calming voice above the rain. I take a moment to gather myself as he rights me onto my feet. "You okay?" he asks me.

"Yes."

Lightning bursts across the sky. Simon slips his arm around my waist and takes most of my weight as he guides me across the muddy field to his truck. Before I can even think, he's got the door open and me planted in the passenger seat. I fumble getting to my purse from the floor so I can get the handheld GPS.

"How many more stops?" he asks as soon as he has the truck started.

"Seven."

"Okay, Trenda, it's going to get a little hairy."

Aza hadn't been kidding about that gulley getting full. The only good thing is that Judy and Janice is our next stop. If they'd been our fourth or fifth stop it would have been game over, even with me driving this monster of a truck.

"I still say we were rude to the sisters," Trenda says for the third time as we leave Loren's place.

"They were the ones who said we needed to leave, Trenda. How was us leaving being rude?" I don't understand why she's being so insistent.

"Simon, didn't you hear Judy say that I was the first woman visitor they'd had in a year? Janice still wanted to show me two more of the rugs they'd made. They might have agreed with you when you said we should get going, but they really wanted us to stay."

Ah, that's what's going on, Trenda's tender heart is at play. "I tell you what, when we're not in the middle of a storm, I'll take you back. How does that sound?"

There is silence. "That would be great. I never want to bother Zarek, and I have to say, driving these roads intimidates me, especially since Zarek's truck is manual transmission. Bernie mostly likes to make these trips by himself," she says wistfully.

"I'll take you, problem solved." Except it isn't. We have three more stops, and now the rain has turned to sleet, and even with my all-weather tires, and driving this truck in the lowest gear, the damn thing is still trying to slip.

"Simon, in three hundred meters, you're going to be veering left and up a hill."

It's like she's read my mind. I can't see shit, so I am going to need constant navigation. As soon as I veer left she starts talking.

"Slow down even more; there's going to be another fork in the road. It's going to divide into two tiny trails and you're going to want to take the right one."

"Do you have that on terrain mode?" I ask.

"Yeah, that's how I can see that the trails are tiny. But after that it's covered with trees, so I'm just showing that you follow that direction for another thousand meters but then there's a clearing and you reach the Randolphs' cabin."

"Got it," I say as I grit my teeth. The Navy should use these trails in the rain when they do their tactical driving courses. *Fuck*, I can barely see a thing.

"Two hundred meters to fork." Her voice is soothing and steady.

"One hundred meters."

"Got it," I say as I take the trail to the right. At least the trail is pretty level. The trees have been cut away just enough so that a truck my size can get through.

Just.

I hear Trenda quietly laugh.

"What?"

"You're driving this as well as Bernie does, and you're having to deal with the storm from hell."

"I've taken driving classes, and I've been in firefights when I've had men shooting at me while I've been driving. If this is what's going to do me in, I've totally lost my edge."

Her laughter is a little louder, a little smokier.

"You sound like my brother. He doesn't have any ego issues, either."

"Please God, say you don't see me as your brother."

"No, I definitely have you and Drake separated in my mind."

"Good," I say as I pull into a clearing that actually has a roundabout, surrounded by grass. "Who are we visiting again?" I ask.

"This is Violet and Luther Randolph. They're a lovely couple, but they shouldn't be up here. It always breaks my heart to see them."

"Why?"

"You'll see. You're going to need to take everything in yourself, and you're going to need to swap out the propane tanks."

I shrug. "Okay."

I park the truck so that Trenda's side will be close to the porch. I'll be able to lift her right onto it.

When we get out, she seems anxious. She knocks, but nobody answers.

"The storm's too loud. They can't hear."

"Then you bang on it, they'll hear that."

I use my fist and bang on the door and we wait a good two minutes, but still nobody answers. Trenda goes for the handle and opens it.

"Hello? Violet? Luther? It's me, Trenda Avery."

Still no response. When she takes a step into the house, I stop her. "I'm going in first. We don't know what we'll find."

"You'll scare them. Luther has dementia, you need to be gentle with him," she hisses.

"I'll be gentle with him. But we don't know what the situation is, and I'm not letting you go in until I've checked things out, so you stay here."

I pull out my pistol and she squeaks. "Put that away," she yelps.

"Stay outside," I order.

I take two steps into the house, and call out their names. Nothing. Dammit, it is just as cold in the house as it is outside.

The kitchen is a mess. I see three cans of soup that are partially opened, and a soup pan that's tipped over with what looks like pea soup dripping onto the floor. But there isn't a trace of a fire in the fireplace. I touch the ashes, and they're stone cold.

"Mr. and Mrs. Randolph, I'm a friend of Bernie Faulks. He sent me to check on you. Are you in the bedroom? Do you need help? Can I come in?"

"Bernie sent you?" a man's voice calls out weakly.

"Yes. Do you need help?"

"It's my wife. Violet. I think she needs help."

I go to the half-opened bedroom door and looked in. The couple are in bed together. I think all the blankets in Sevier County are on top of them. The man is sitting up against the headboard with the silver-haired woman's head resting against his chest. Even from where I'm standing I can hear her labored breathing. I put my pistol back in my pocket.

"How long has she been like this Luther?"

He looks up at me with rheumy eyes. "A long time."

Damn, he is totally out of it. Violet must do all of the caretaking.

She coughs and her entire body shakes. Luther puts his hand over her mouth. "Don't cough Violet. You need to stop coughing."

"Luther, I need you to get her some water, can you do that?" I ask.

He gives me a vacant stare.

"Luther," I say louder. "Can you get some water for Violet?"

Trenda touches my waist. "Simon, I can get the water."

I turn my head a little so I can look at her. "First, you should have stayed where I put you, but now that you're here, I need Luther to leave the room so I can check on Violet," I whisper.

Trenda moves past me and goes to Luther.

"Luther, do you remember me? I'm Trenda Avery."

"Wanda?"

"No, Sir. I'm her daughter Trenda. Can you help me make soup for Violet?" She holds out her hand for him to take it.

He shakes his head and burrows closer to his wife. "I don't like Wanda."

Trenda crouches down next to the bed. "I'm *Tren*da. I'm a friend of Bernie's. I made cookies and he brought them to you, remember?"

I watch as Luther focuses on her. "You have cookies?"

Trenda turns to me, a question in her eye. I nod.

"Yes, we brought cookies. I need you to come out in the parlor and I'll get you some cookies, okay?"

He takes her hand and climbs out of bed. He is wearing a pair of long johns.

"Do you have a coat, Luther?"

He nods. I have my gaze pinned on Violet. She's not coughing now but I'm watching as her body shakes with chills.

"Let's go get your coat and you can put it on so you're not as cold."

"We don't wear our coats in the house," he explains to her as they walk out of the room hand in hand.

As soon as they're gone, I immediately rush to Violet

Randolph's side. When I put my hand to her forehead, I find that she is burning up.

"Violet?" I say loudly. "Can you hear me, Violet?"

"So cold," she whispers.

I pull back the covers and find her in her wet nightgown. She's sweated right through it, which is just adding to her misery. She starts to cough again, and it's the deep, bronchial cough of pneumonia. Her face is chalk white. She needs a hospital...now. I stalk into the living area.

I go up behind Trenda where she's standing next to Luther. I pull her aside. "We need to get Violet to a hospital immediately."

She nods. Her attention is focused on Luther as he slowly pours soup into a pan.

"I need you to go in there and change her clothes. Get her into something warm so we can take her into town."

She nods again.

"Luther." Her voice is calm and kind. She touches his shoulder when he doesn't respond. "Luther, can you look at me?"

He puts down the empty can, then turns to look at her.

"Who are you?" he asks me. "Why are you in my house?"

"I'm here to get you food." I answer. I can tell he isn't satisfied with my answer.

"My friend is going to be right back with some cookies, okay?" Trenda asks.

A slow grin spreads across his face. "I like cookies," he says shyly.

She turns to me and mouths, "*Go.*"

I leave the house, my mind racing. Thank God the backseat is a bench seat, so I don't have to deal with a console. Still, how in the hell am I going to buckle her in when she's lying down?

I pull up the tarp in the back and thanked God for Trenda's OCD back at the fire station. It had annoyed me at the time when she'd sorted the food into separate boxes for each delivery, I'd felt we were wasting time, but right now I could kiss her.

Kiss her.

Shut up! Focus on getting the food inside.

I heft their box up on one shoulder and open the door, Trenda has set Luther up stirring the soup on the gas stove, which I notice isn't lit. *She's good.* Luther's head whips around.

"Who are you?" he asks belligerently.

"I have cookies in this box," I say in a placating tone.

"I have to finish making soup for my wife."

I put the box down on the table and knock on the closed bedroom door.

"Come in," Trenda calls. When I open the door, I see that Violet is now wearing what looks like a nightgown over jeans. Trenda is tugging on a sweatshirt over the poor woman's listless body.

"Her pulse is thready," Trenda says. "Can you help with her socks?" She nods her head to the pair on the bed.

I scoop up the wool socks. When I touch Violet's foot, my jaw clenches. It is damn near blue and feels like an ice cube. I quickly pull them up Violet's feet.

"Trenda, keep her here. I've got to find something to wrap her bedding in so that it doesn't get wet while I transfer it into the backseat of the truck."

Trenda stands up and pulls off the windbreaker I had given her. "Use this."

"Perfect."

I scoop up the four pillows and squish them together so that they fit under the jacket. "I need you to open the doors for me, so I can get this into the backseat."

Trenda gently lays Violet back down on the bed, and I hear a crash from the living room. It doesn't matter, we have to go. Trenda rushes out of the bedroom and I follow. I stalk past the overturned box of food on the floor, ignoring Luther crawling around. I assume he's looking for cookies. Trenda has the door open, and ice-cold air whips into the house, even with the porch overhang. By the time I get outside she has the backseat door open. I shove the pillows into the backseat.

She climbs in and starts to arrange things, while I go back to get blankets. Violet is lying on the bed in the exact same position. She looks lifeless. I pray she can hang on long enough to make it to the hospital.

Chapter Eleven

"Slow down," Luther wails for the eighty-seventh time. He sounds like he's in anguish. I know he's scared, but he isn't helping. Plus, there's the fact that I don't know how Simon can see where he's going. It's a mystery to me.

"It's all right, Luther. We're going to be fine." I try to say it in a soothing manner.

"We're going to die."

He's rocking back and forth.

"Violet needs you." I rummage through my purse and finally find a napkin from the bakery. I thrust it between the seats. "Take this, Luther. You need to wipe Violet's forehead. It will help her."

"We're going to die," he moans loudly.

"Take the napkin."

"We're going too fast," he screeches.

Simon doesn't even flinch. "Turn on the defroster, Trenda," he asks me calmly. I look at the complicated dash and finally find it. I turn it on.

"We're going to die."

"Please take the napkin, Luther. Violet needs you. It will

help make her well." Luther reaches out, but he can't reach it.

"I can't." His lower lip trembles, and he starts to cry. I unbuckle my belt and kneel up on my seat.

"Goddammit, Trenda, get your ass planted back in the seat and buckle your fucking belt!" Simon roars.

Terror races through me at the sound of a man's rage. I force it down and press the napkin into Luther's hand. "Take this."

"We're going to die," Luther sobs as he looks me in the eye.

"Take care of your wife," I respond, then turn and buckle back up.

"You ever do something that goddamned foolish again, I will tan your hide." Simon's knuckles are white on the steering wheel where they hadn't been before. "Lady, you scared me to death," he breathes softly.

With those last whispered words, every bit of my fear evaporates. This is not a man who's going to abuse me. This is a man who protects people.

"I won't. I promise."

It was at that moment I realize Luther is quiet. I turn in my seat and see that he's softly wiping Violet's brow. I watch as he strokes back the thin strands of her white hair. He then kisses her forehead. "I'm taking care of you," he whispers. "You'll be better now."

I feel the truck slip, and hear Simon growl. I look up and his shoulders and arms are tense as he pulls the steering wheel to the right. "Come on, Baby. Stick with me. It's not much further," he croons.

The inside of the truck is a million degrees with the defroster on, but I'm not going to take off my hat or gloves. I don't want to do a darn thing that might interrupt Simon's concentration. I peer out the window, trying to make sense of what I'm seeing, but it just looks like sheets of rain and an occasional blur of trees up ahead. I look over at the speedometer and see we're going twenty-two miles an hour. Luther is right, it is too fast, but when I look behind me at Violet, I know it isn't fast enough. The GPS in my hand shows we still have eight miles to go before we make it back to a paved road.

Violet starts to cough.

She continues to cough. It's unending.

"Have Luther lift her head and shoulders up," Simon tells me.

"Luther, you need to lift Violet up, so that her head is resting on your shoulder."

He gives me a blank stare.

I bite my lip. How am I going to explain this? "Luther, can you pull Violet up so you're face to face?" I ask him.

"She'll cough on me."

I feel my frustration start to mount, but I have to keep calm. I know this is just part of his disease. I know his symptoms get worse when he's stressed.

"Luther, can you pull Violet up so she's sitting?"

"Like this?" He pulls her up so that she's sitting on his lap.

"Good job, Sweetheart. You did good. That will help her not cough as much."

"My name is Luther, not Sweetheart," he frowns at me.

I sigh. "Yes it is. You did a good job, Luther. Why don't you stroke her back and whisper to her. She needs you."

"Okay."

Luther starts humming.

For the first time since we started down the mountain, there is peace.

"Well done, Trenda. You pulled off a miracle."

Simon's words wrap around me like a warm hug. I look

over at him. His hands are relaxed now as they hold the steering wheel. I don't know how, considering the fact that he's basically driving blind. It must be a SEAL thing. And he also has a smile on his face. A smile for me. I feel the flicker of fireflies going off in my tummy, and we're in the middle of a disaster. How is this even possible?

"This is the last fork in the road coming up. Remember there's a tree splitting it. Veer right."

"Got it."

I know she has to be scared, but she sounds cool as a cucumber. I'm concentrating on the road ahead, so there is no way I'm going to look out of the corner of my eye at her, but I know in my gut she's monitoring Luther and Violet. She's done a hell of a job keeping Luther calm. Even though the man has propped up Violet, she still has sporadic coughing episodes that are an agony to listen to. With her body so frail, I'm worried that it is ripping her apart.

I'm at the fork, and I take the right. "Three more miles?" I ask.

"Two and a half, then we get a paved road." No excitement, just a smooth, calm delivery. This woman is fantastic in a crunch. I feel like a piece of shit for having yelled at her about her seatbelt. She'd specifically told me that she has a phobia about men yelling at her, but what do I do? I yell at her. Why? Because I'm a dumbass. When I have just a bloody minute and we're not in the middle of a shitstorm, I need to apologize and tell her I yelled because I was scared, not because I was mad.

"Trenda, there's blood," Luther yells. "There's blood. There's blood. Violet's bleeding," he screams.

I tune it out. I swear to God, the icy rain is even worse.

Fuck!

I slam on the brakes and yank the wheel to the left, barely missing the downed tree in front of us.

Shit, fuck, piss.

The airbags haven't deployed. That's a good thing; we never would have gotten off this goddamned hill, mountain, whatever the fuck it is. I look over at Trenda. "You okay?"

"Yeah."

We both turn around to look in the backseat. I had buckled Violet by using the middle seatbelt. It had grabbed her tight when I stopped, and therefore she was squished against Luther who's shellshocked. At least he's quiet now.

"Trenda," I whisper. "You deal with them. I'm going to clear the tree."

"How?"

"Don't worry, I've got it covered. You just handle those two." I could see the blood that was on Violet's chin and on the top of the blanket. It didn't look like a lot, but still, any amount of blood was just another shit sign on a really big shit sandwich.

Trenda stripped out of the windbreaker. "Take this."

"Thanks."

I pull it on before opening my door. Wind and rain whooshes in, splashing the backseat with water before I have a chance to jump out and close the door. The last thing I hear is Luther's shout. I check out the front of the truck first to see if we're stuck in the mud at the side of the trail, but it isn't too bad. The four-wheel drive had done its job and then some. We should be fine. I turn to the tree.

Jesus.

It is a big mother, but it has been dying for a while, based on the few boughs left on it. The circumference of the trunk has to be a foot and a half. I have no idea how much that will weigh, but I hope the truck's winch will pull it out of the way. I hustle back to the truck and get back in. The only sounds are Luther's soft sobs.

Trenda is in the backseat; she must have climbed over the front seat. She's mashed up against the back door on my side, Luther's leaning against her, Violet leaning against him. Trenda doesn't ask any questions when I start up the truck. I know she didn't want to do anything to agitate Luther.

I look at the trio again in the rearview mirror, trying to see if Violet is breathing. When she coughs, I breathe a sigh of relief. I start the truck and keep it in low gear as I back it up, then inch forward and position the nose of the truck to the farthest possible left end of the tree. I smile for just a moment as I remember that just this morning, I'd been shaking my head at having to pay so much for this truck because Fred had paid for every extra upgrade possible, and here I am thanking every star in the sky that he has the winch. I remember the remote control for the winch was in the center console, so I take it out, then look at my gloves. They aren't my good leather working gloves, but they will have to do.

I look in the backseat one more time. Trenda is stroking Luther's hair and humming a vaguely familiar song. His eyes are closed. I give her a thumbs up, she gives me a tired smile in response.

I leap out of the truck again and as soon as I do I'm pelted by the icy rain. I don't mind the cold so much, it's how the sleet hits my face even when I'm looking down. Why hadn't I thought of a baseball cap to somewhat shield me from the rain so I might be able to see a couple of inches in front of me without having to constantly wipe my face? I get in front of the truck and disengage the winch, then pull it to the tree. When I get to it, I pull the cable to get plenty of slack then shove as much cable as I can underneath the trunk. Thank God the limbs of the tree were still holding it up, but I'm not sure how much longer that is going to last, because the limbs don't look all that sturdy.

I look for the easiest part to climb over the trunk, then go back to where the winch cable is. When I get there I see that the trunk is even lower because some of the limbs have already broken under the weight of the trunk.

"Make this fast, Clark," I mutter to myself, as I pray no more limbs break.

I shimmy under the foliage and reach under the trunk, then grab the ring on the end of the winch and yanked the winch cord as far as I can.

"Aren't you a good tree," I croon.

Holding the end of the cable, I do my best to leap over the tree. For just a moment the SEAL team obstacle course flashes in front of me. Damn good thing I was still running that thing with the baby SEALs.

As soon as I get over the tree, more limbs crack and the trunk is mere inches from the ground. "Come on, Baby, hold on just a little longer."

I loop the winch hook around the cable and pull it as tight as I can to the trunk, knowing the truck will do the rest. I haul ass back to the truck and pull the remote control out of my pocket then press the button that slowly pulls the cable taut. I'm good to go.

I get back into the truck.

"No more cold," Luther cries out.

"It's okay, Luther. It'll get warm again," Trenda says soothingly.

I start up the truck again and put it into reverse, then slowly back up, pulling the tree with me. I grin as the top of the tree gets pulled towards the truck, giving us enough room to get past it.

"Now who's the miracle worker?" Trenda whispers.

I look over to the back seat. Luther is agitated again; he's rocking back and forth a lot faster, which can't be good for Violet.

"Luther?" I ask.

"Luther?" I say his name louder.

"Luther, Simon needs to talk to you," Trenda says gently as she turns his head towards me.

"Luther, I need to make it cold just two more times." I hold up two fingers.

"No," he says petulantly.

"Just two more, Buddy. Then we get to take Violet to the hospital. Okay?"

He shakes his head violently.

Well, I'd tried. I open the door, and hear Luther's wail, as if he's in agony. I slam the door shut. I race to the tree and unhook the winch hook and throw the end of the cable over the trunk of the tree, then pull it out from under the tree. I pull the cable out and drag all of it to the truck, careful to keep it untangled. Using the remote, I click a button and the cable starts to rewind.

Sweet.

The moment it's finished I hop back into the driver's seat.

"I have the GPS back here with me," Trenda says over Luther's sobbing.

"Isn't it a straight shot to the main road?" I ask.

"Just one sharp right in two hundred meters, then you're good," she replies.

"Got it."

Chapter Twelve

My entire body is trembling. I can't make it stop. What is wrong with me? We're done, the storm has past. Violet is alive and in the hospital. A social worker is with Luther, but I feel like I will literally shake apart.

Get it together, Avery.

I turn away from Simon and look out the passenger side window, not wanting him to see me losing it.

I don't even realize we aren't going to my house until we pull up beside my SUV at Simon's cabin. I reach down with shaky fingers to pick up my purse, then fumble to find the keys to my car. It feels like it takes hours.

"Found them," I mutter as I hold them up, still not looking at Simon. It's then I realize he hasn't shut off his truck's engine. I unbuckle my seatbelt, then pull the door handle to open the passenger side door. It's locked.

"Not so fast, Trenda."

"What?"

"I need you to look at me," Simon says softly.

"Why?"

I don't want to look at him. I really don't. Can't he catch a clue?

"Please, Honey?"

Ah, God. That voice. Those two words. He is killing me. He tentatively touches my hand which is clutching my purse. Simon doesn't do tentative. His fingers swirl a circle on the top of my hand and I start to tremble even more. The fireflies start beating in my stomach again. I gulp down a sob.

He turns off the truck and gets out. The next thing I know he's opening my door and has me in his arms.

"It's okay, Honey. You did so good. It's all going to be okay."

Even through my poofy jacket and his windbreaker, I can feel his heat. Simon's fingers thrust through my hair, cradling my head, pushing it into the crook of his neck. It is perfect. I breathe him in. It is as if his presence—his essence—gives me permission to fall apart, knowing he'll keep me safe.

I don't know what he's saying, I only know that the soft rumble of his voice is like nothing I have ever heard before, and it wraps around me, allowing me to melt even deeper into his arms.

I don't know when I realize he's picked me up. Had he even shut the door of the truck? I don't remember. When had he opened the door to the cabin? How was I standing here, with him unwinding my scarf, unzipping my jacket, and sliding my arms out of it? The room feels chilly, but somehow he's wearing just that long-sleeved shirt when he guides me to the couch and pulls me on top of his lap.

I looked down into his face. I can see that he's tired. His eyes are hooded, the brackets around his mouth a little more pronounced. I look at his hair and my hands follow. The brown and gray is soft and I bet anything, it's a little longer than he would have liked.

"You're playing with fire," he whispers. He pulls my hand away, and I put my palm flat against his chest, and push to get up. Then he slowly leans back, drawing me with him, until we're both sprawled on the couch, me lying on top of him.

Trenda, what are you doing?

I tell my mother-voice to *shut the hell up*!

It doesn't feel real, his legs stretched out beneath me on the couch.

"What are we doing, Simon?"

"We're just getting warm."

"I don't understand. The time to fall apart was earlier," I whisper. I know I must look confused.

"You need some time to unwind."

"Really?" I ask as I raise my eyebrow. "Did you fall apart when life handed you a handful of manure, or did you wait until you handled it?"

He doesn't answer. His eyes just look into mine, filled with compassion.

I shake my head. It's all so confusing, so tiring. I just want to lie here and let Simon take all of my fears away. "I didn't do enough," I finally confess. "I was so busy comforting Luther that Violet could have died, and it would have been my fault." I pause. "And even if she dies in the hospital, it will be my fault. I didn't do enough. I didn't, Simon."

Simon tilts my chin up. "That is so not true. She has a chance at survival because of you. You are the hero in this story."

I shake my head so hard my hair slaps his face. "No, you are the hero, I'm the wimpy sidekick who's there for comic relief, and I didn't even do that properly."

My attempt at humor is failing because I can feel the tears coming on again.

"Oh, Trenda. You couldn't be more wrong."

His fingers are still tangled in my hair, and now he begins to massage my scalp. I hiccup as I try to force the tears back.

"I need you to know that the decisions you made today saved Luther and Violet. Honestly? You were better under fire than most of the men that I've had under my command. One day I want to hear what things in your past have given you that backbone of steel, but left you with such a loving and compassionate heart."

"You're seeing me all wrong, Simon." My words are beginning to slur. I'm so tired, and lying on top of him feels so good. "I make the worst decisions imaginable. I've screwed up so badly in my life. Just when I think I can trust, I find out I'm wrong. I'm stupid, Simon. Just plain stupid."

"You're strong, and smart, and in just a few hours you've become someone I've come to admire. You're not stupid in the slightest."

His hand strokes down my back.

"Rest now, Honey."

"You're sho, wrong. Izz, tireds now. Shleep."

"That's it, go to sleep. I've got you."

∿

I heard Brantley unlocking the front door, so I got up from the couch so I could confront him.

"You were supposed to be home last night."

"I told you on the phone, Sweetheart, I had a last-minute business meeting in Lexington and I'd be home tonight, what's the big deal?" He sat his briefcase down and threw his suit jacket on the chair near the door.

"I made a nice dinner for us. Couldn't you have called?"

Brantley crossed the room and tried to take me into his arms, but I backed up, crossing my arms around my stomach.

"Come on, Sweetheart, don't be like this. We can have a nice dinner tomorrow night. I'll have one delivered from a really nice restaurant I know."

Of course, he wouldn't take me out to dinner, then his wife might find out about me.

It was a nightmare. Just twenty-four hours ago, before Brantley had gone on his business trip and his wife had come for a visit, telling him we're having a baby would have been the happiest moment of my life.

"I'm pregnant."

Before meeting his wife I had been so sure that he would take me in his arms and pull out the ring he'd been saving for just the right moment. Instead, I was met with a look of horror.

"I'm pregnant and I know you're married," I whispered.

"How can you be pregnant? I use a condom every goddamned time I fuck you. This has to be someone else's brat!"

Brantley swiftly walked those last three paces until he was towering over me. "Tell me, you cunt. You tell me who the fucking father is. Tell me right now."

"What are you talking about?" I gasped. I reached out and started to trail my hand down his arm to soothe him, like I had hundreds of times before, but he slapped it away. I staggered to the side.

"Tell me. Who have you been fucking, you duplicitous bitch."

"You know I've only ever been with you," I whispered.

"I might have been your first, but that doesn't mean shit. I was careful. The last thing I needed was you breeding some kind of backwoods brat."

"I'm not duplicitous, you are. You're the one who's married." Now I was getting angry.

His hands reached out and grabbed my upper arms, biting into them painfully.

"You're hurting me."

"Like I give a rat's ass. Now listen here, little girl. I'm done with this. Fuck it. I don't give a flying fuck who you spread your legs for. I want you gone. Pack your things. You're out of here."

I tried to break his hold on me as I sucked down a deep breath. Ever since I'd met his wife yesterday I'd been trying to figure out where I could stay so that I could stay in Nashville and finish my classes, but I couldn't think of anybody. Then I'd peed on a stick.

"Do you hear me?" He shook me hard. "Do you?!" he roared.

"It's your baby. This is not just my responsibility." I'd seen too many girls back in Jasper Creek with no support from deadbeat dads. That wasn't going to be me.

He shoved me away from him and I almost fell, but I kept my balance. He backed up and pulled his wallet out of his back pocket.

"You're still trying to convince me that this whelp is mine? Then here." He grabbed a wad of bills from his wallet. "This is over a thousand dollars. For a hick like you, it's like winning a jackpot. Get an abortion, a bus ticket, then buy yourself something nice. But I better not see you ever again."

He held out the cash, and all I could do was stare at it.

"Take it."

I can't move.

"Take it!"

I still can't move. He grabs my hand and shoves the money into it, then wraps my fingers around the cash. As soon as he lets go the bills drop to the floor.

"Look at you, too goddamn stupid to even hold onto your money. Then fine, pick it up off the floor. See if I care."

He stalked back to the door and picked up his suit jacket from off his chair and slipped it on. He smoothed it down and buttoned it up as he slowly walked back toward me. He looked at the money on the floor and shook his head, and then he stepped so close that we were almost nose to nose.

"Ah, Trenda. We had some good times," he said as he lightly patted my cheek. Just like his wife had yesterday.

Bam!

I was on the floor. I hadn't seen the backhand coming. I didn't make a sound. I'm the daughter of Norville Avery, I'd been trained not to make a sound after a hit.

"Now that you're on the ground, pick up the cash and leave."

I watched his shiny black shoes as he walked toward the door. They stopped. "I'll be back in three hours and one minute. I'll make you real sorry if you're still here." The door closed behind him.

I tasted blood in my mouth. I spit it out and it hit the expensive Persian carpet and some of the hundred-dollar bills.

Good.

～

I hadn't been able to get Trenda to talk about her nightmare, and that's still bugging the shit out of me three days later. I keep telling myself to let it go. Afterall, did I want someone peeking into my psyche?

Fuck no.

But that doesn't stop me from wanting to know what was going on. To help erase the dreams from her memory.

I open the door to the nursing home and smile at the woman manning the front desk. She reminds me of Violet in the sense that she could be blown over by a strong wind.

"May I help you?"

Well, her voice is sure strong. I like that, makes me feel like she can handle whatever comes through the door.

"I'm here to see Luther Randolph. His social worker should have put me on the visitor's list. My name is Simon Clark," I say as I pass her my Virginia driver's license.

She looks down at a clipboard, then squints at my driver's license and up at me. "Okay, you're approved to go up. The elevators are around the corner on your right. Go to the second floor. You'll see the nurse's station; they'll direct you to Mr. Randolph's room. I do hope he's having a better day today."

Shit.

I didn't bother asking her what she meant, I just want to get to him.

By the time I'm upstairs the nurse doesn't need to direct me to his room; I can hear him from her station.

"Where's Violet?

"Where's my wife? I want my wife.

"Why'd you take away Violet?"

"Hello, Mr. Clark," the nurse says when I introduce myself. "As you can hear, Mr. Randolph is not doing well. We've been monitoring him closely. We're discussing changing his status with his social worker and sending him to the Rolling Hills facility. But even if his status is changed, it will depend upon when a bed comes available."

"What's that?" I ask. But I know.

"It's a psychiatric hospital."

I follow the nurse down the hall to Luther's room. When she opens the door, he is sitting on the one small chair that looks over the courtyard, his head bowed. He doesn't even look up when we come into his room.

"Look, Mr. Randolph, you have a visitor."

His head whips upward. "Violet?" he yells out hopefully. When he sees it's only me he bursts into tears. The nurse quietly backs out of the room.

I walk over and crouch down in front of Luther.

"Luther," I whisper. "Do you remember me?"

"Where's Violet? She's sick. I need Violet."

I pull out my phone. I help Luther to sit up straight in the chair. "Luther, can you look at my phone?"

"I want Violet," he begs.

"Violet is here. I need you to look at my phone." I make sure the volume is all the way up, then play the video.

"Luther, Darling," the frail woman in the bed says as she looks directly into my phone's camera. "I miss you."

"Where's Violet?" Luther demands to know. He tries to shove up off the chair, but I keep my hand firmly on his shoulder, making him sit on the chair.

"Look at my phone, Luther. Violet made a video for you. She's waving to you. Do you see her? Look at my phone."

He calms down as I continue to repeat myself. Finally, he cups his hands around mine and peers into the phone.

"That's Violet," he exclaims.

"Yes it is. See, she's talking. She's feeling better."

"Violet's on television."

"Yes she is," I agree. "She's getting better, and soon you two can be together again."

He looks up at me with pleading eyes. "Now, please. Mister, I want to be with her now."

He's killing me.

"I know you do, Buddy. But she has to get better. Can you see that tube in her arm?" I point to it on my phone. Luther nods. "That tube is giving her medicine so she feels all better. She needs a lot of medicine before you can be together."

"Can I go home?"

What do I say to that? Now that the state was involved I didn't think that they would ever allow Violet to take her husband back to the mountain. And as much as I believe in free will, I don't think she should take him up there. She's too frail, and I know that sometimes dementia can lead to violence. It was an overall bad scenario.

"You can't go home. You have to wait for Violet. I'll be back tomorrow and I'll bring you some cookies, will that be good?"

He gives me a weak smile. "Cookies are good."

I stand up, but when I do, he hits my forearm. "Don't take Violet!" he shouts. I easily keep the phone out of his reach, but he makes a lunge for it. I catch him and lower him back into his chair.

"Luther, the only way I can take new pictures of Violet is if you let me take my phone."

His hand sweeps out, trying to take my phone again. I put his hand firmly back in his lap.

"Luther, did you hear me? Violet can't be on television again unless I have my phone. I need it so I can show you more TV tomorrow."

He looked so damned sad and confused. It's heartbreaking.

I put my arm around his shoulders. "It's going to be all right, big man. Tomorrow will be cookies and more Violet television. Won't that be good?"

"Trenda?"

"You want to see Trenda again?"

He nods. Then points to a spot beside his bed. I see an empty Tupperware container. Judging by the crumbs, I'd say the container used to contain brownies. "Did Trenda come and visit and bring you brownies?"

Luther smiles and nods.

"I want cookies, Violet TV, and Trenda."

I laugh. "You've got it, Buddy."

I want a beer.

Chapter Thirteen

I wish I had more women friends. Friends who aren't my sisters. Women friends who I could talk to about things like hormones and horniness without them questioning me to the nth degree. Because that's all it is with Simon, right? Hormones acting up that are causing some unwanted horniness, because in no way shape or form am I in any way liking this man. My policy is to never, ever entangle myself with a male ever again. Ever never, Amen.

But what about sex?

Shut up!

That same stupid voice has been quietly chirping away in the back of my head ever since I woke up on top of Simon. It is way worse than the *I want to have ice cream* voice. This voice is like a marching band going through my head, with mostly only the tubas and the drum section playing.

He's so kind.

Shut up, times infinity!

You'd screw up finding a nice guy if they put you in a room with a hundred and one men, fifty of them being clones of Ed Sheeran, fifty of them being clones of George Clooney and you'd still manage to find and choose the one Jeffrey Dahmer in the group.

I sit down at my tiny desk and bang my head on it.

"Mama, what are you doing?"

I give my daughter a sideways look. "Nothing, Sweet Pea, just resting my head."

"Why? It's not bedtime."

That's my girl, nothing gets by her.

"I needed to clear my head for a moment to think about the website I'm building."

"But your computer isn't turned on," she points out logically.

Lesson number seventy-nine—don't lie to your daughter, she'll catch you every time.

"I just had to figure out something in my head before I started working," I say as I smile at her. "What about you? Do you have homework you need to be working on?"

"It's Saturday."

"You're right. It is."

Good one, Trenda. You can't even remember what day it is.

"Can I see what you're working on?" Bella asked.

"Hop up on my lap." She climbs up on my lap and I realize just how much she's grown. I flip open my laptop and it starts up from sleep mode. I did not check it for mail once it starts, not wanting Bella to see anything like the last two threatening emails I'd been sent. Instead, I pull up a website for a bridal boutique that I'd made last year. They'd wanted a couple of updates, and I know Bella will enjoy seeing all the pretty dresses.

"Oooh, look at that." She presses her finger against the screen as she points to the Cinderella wedding dress. "That would look so pretty on you."

"I disagree." I tap the end of her nose. "I think that dress would look pretty on you, one day."

She gives *me* a sideways look. "You have to get married before me, silly. Do you think my daddy will ever come and you'll marry him?"

What?

I am not expecting this. Bella had never once talked about having her dad.

Not once!

"Uhmm."

"Rory's mom and dad aren't married, they just live together. Angie says it's better when they're married. She said it's good you're not just living with my dad."

Holy mother of God.

"When did you talk about this?"

"At Rory's sleepover. That's why Rory cried and Angie had to say she was sorry."

"You didn't tell me about that."

"That wasn't as important as when Rory got her own iPad for her birthday. I told you all about that. She doesn't have to share her iPad with her mom. She gets to play with her own any time she wants to."

"Well, I still say you're too young to have an iPad."

"Can I have my dad instead?"

Fuck!

I snuggle my brilliant negotiator closer. Then I tip up her chin so we can look at each other eye to eye. "If I could have given you the good and loving dad you deserve, I would have. You deserve the best daddy in the world, because you are the best daughter in the world."

She frowned. "Then why isn't he here?"

"Honey, he died," I say simply. As I watch her little face crumple, I feel like the worst person in the world because I am thankful that I get to tell Bella that Brantley is dead.

Instead of having to tell her that she is unwanted. I am cowardly pond scum.

I watch as her eyes well up with tears. "My daddy died?"

I pull her close, cradling her in my arms like I used to. "Yes, Bella, I'm so sorry, but he died."

She starts to cry quietly in my arms. "But I wanted to meet him."

He hadn't deserved a beautiful daughter like Bellatrix Star.

"I know you did, Baby." I murmur the words against her forehead.

"Is he in heaven now, like Rory's grandpa?" Big brown eyes look up at me, begging for reassurance.

"Yes, Bella. His soul has gone up to heaven."

"Will I meet him in heaven?"

I bite my lip. I believe in a just God, and part of me wants vengeance on Brantley Harris, but at the same time, I believe that every one of us is worthy of God's forgiveness. That includes Brantley. And maybe one day, I will be able to forgive him as well. Maybe.

"Mama. Will I?"

"What?"

"Will I meet my daddy in heaven?"

"Yes, Bella, you will," I assure my grieving daughter.

My precious girl continues to cry, and I continue to rock her as she mourns for something she can never have. I wish I could mourn for my nineteen-year-old self, but I can't. After having Norville and Wanda as parents, how could I have been so naïve? But I did end up with the best thing in the whole world, and I'm holding her in my arms.

Finally, Bella's crying devolves into hiccups.

I try to push up from the chair with Bella in my arms, but it doesn't work. *When did she get so big* I wonder. Slipping her out of my arms so her feet hit the floor, I get up and coax her down the hall to the bathroom. I *can* lift her up onto the counter, then I hand her a tissue, and she blows her nose.

"Are you okay, Mama?"

"Huh?"

"You look sad. Are you okay about daddy being in heaven?"

There she goes again, asking questions that hit me in my gut.

"I'm always sad when someone dies. He was special since he was your daddy."

Bella lurches forward and throws her arms around my neck. "It's okay, Mama, you didn't have to marry him. We're a good enough family."

Ahhh, damn it.

Good enough?

I never want to be just good enough for my precious baby girl.

Evie's words come back to me. Was I really teaching Bella to push away men? How badly was I confusing her?

Could I be a crappier mother?

Dropping my Bella off at school on Monday was agony. She had vacillated between smiles and crying all day yesterday, but this morning she is all smiles. She mentions four different times what a good family we are. The third time, I fight back tears. The fourth time I end up going to the bathroom so I can throw water on my face so that my tears won't show. I need to call Evie.

As soon as I get home I shut the door behind me and race to the bathroom that's connected to my bedroom. I need a long hot shower where I can cry. How did I not know what had been going on in Bella's mind? Why had I not addressed the daddy issue years ago?

When I flip the handle to hot, I know it'll take a minute or two for it to warm up. I climb over the lip of the tub and wish for some kind of relief, anything to shut my mind off. When I begin washing my hair and body, I lean against the wall, trying to get myself together. When the water finally runs cold, I turn off the faucets and get out of the tub. I avoid looking in the mirror as I dry off and drift into my bedroom.

Somehow, I end up in yoga pants and an old Tennessee Volunteers football t-shirt, sitting cross-legged on my couch. I must have scrolled through my contacts because when I look down at my phone, the picture of Evie is staring up at me, and my thumb hovering over 'dial'.

My doorbell rings.

Who the heck is at the door when I look like this? Please God, at least let it only be family. Not Zarek though; I hate him seeing me all red faced and blotchy. The doorbell rings again. Yep, that impatience has family written all over it. It's surprising they haven't just come on in. I force myself off the couch and open the door.

"Oh. Hi. I wasn't expecting you, Mr. Emory," I say to my postman.

"Hello Mizz Trenda. Have a registered letter for you." He's all smiles. "I don't get many of these. There's lots of steps to delivering one of these."

My stomach curdles. It has to be something with either Norville or Wanda. Are they getting out early? I don't want them anywhere near my baby. Another good reason to leave town.

"You have to sign right here," Mr. Emory shows me where I have to sign.

"You have to print your name too."

"Okay." I try to smile. He's so nice, but it's tough when I want him gone and I just want to read the letter.

I do what he says as fast as I can. He rips off the part I signed from the envelope. "This is what goes back to the sender, it proves you received it," he explains.

"Oh," I pretend to care.

"I hope it's good news, Mizz Trenda." He smiles and puts two fingers to his forehead in a mock salute then turns and heads down my walkway. I shut the door.

I start trembling as I see the letter has the name of a law firm on it. Now I know it has something to do with one of my parents. My legs give out just as I reach the sofa and I fall into the cushions with the letter still in my hands.

Stop looking at the damn thing and open it, you coward!

I rip open the envelope and take out the fancy piece of stationery. I start reading the letter.

Ms. Avery,

This is the second letter that we are sending you. We hope that this one you won't disregard.

It has come to my firm's attention that you have a vested interest in the estate of the late Brantley T. Harris. Unfortunately, the reading of the will has already taken place, but our due diligence on behalf of our former client compels us to reach out to you so that you and your daughter's interests are seen to as Mr. Harris wanted.

.   .   .

Please get ahold of me immediately at the following email address or telephone number listed below.

Respectfully Yours,

Horace Grant
   Attorney At Law
   Fetterman, Grant and Peterson, LLP

Everything hits me at once. No wonder I've been getting those emails—Carla Harris knew that I would be getting some kind of communication from Brantley's attorney's and she didn't want me to answer them.

I take a deep breath, and read the letter for a third time. I need to think. Was there anyone I could talk to about this? If I talk to any of my family, I'll need to explain about Brantley and everything that had happened. That will be awful.

My phone rings and I jerk up. I swivel my head a couple of times, then see it on the coffee table. I pick it up on the second ring. The number isn't familiar, so I let it continue to ring. Wait, that's a Virginia area code. It has to be Simon. My thumb hovers over the answer button, but I let the call go to voicemail.

I can't cope with him. First there was Bella this morning, now this letter from Brantley's attorney. It's too much.

"Ow!"

I yank my thumb away from my mouth. *Darn it!* I've bitten my nail down to the quick. Just how long have I been on my couch, rocking back and forth, darn near sucking my thumb?

What am I, a three-year-old?

I grab my phone and look at the time. Yep, about forty-five minutes, pissed into the wind. I see the Virginia number and hesitate, then realize it's time for me to pull up my big girl panties.

No meltdowns for this girl.

I get up off the couch, holding my phone and the letter. I need some time to think. There's no reason to do anything now. The attorneys want something from me, so I'm in the driver's seat. They can wait.

Despite the best pep talks in my repertoire, I melt down. At least it was less than an hour. I pull up Simon's voicemail and listen to it. Maybe that will make me feel better. He wants me to call him. Thank Goodness. A distraction.

"Hello?"

"Hi, Simon, it's me, Trenda."

"Hi, Trenda, I was hoping you'd be able to call back today."

I attempt to put a little bit of excitement into my voice. "Have you been doing any more rally car racing lately?"

Nope, not excited. I sound like a sad clown.

"Are you okay?"

"I'm fine," I sigh. "How are you?"

"I saw the empty Tupperware dish in Luther's room. He ate all of your brownies."

"You went to see Luther? That's so nice of you." And it was.

"It was no big deal, but I didn't see any signs of brownies when I went and saw Violet and Bernie, however Bernie told me you had been by to see him, as well. Violet's still pretty weak, so I didn't have much time with her. I was able to film a little video that I showed Luther today."

I perk up. "That's genius. How did Luther react? Did it calm him down?"

"A little. He thought Violet was on TV. So tomorrow he wants to see her on TV again. He wants cookies, and he wants Trenda. I said I could deliver on all three. I thought we could visit everybody together tomorrow, while Bella is in school. What do you think?"

That could be perfect, or it could be really bad. I'm already thinking about Simon too much, and why would I want to see him when I am darn near at rock bottom? I have to get my head together before I see any human being, especially some man that I for sure know is going to end up being bad for me.

"I'm not sure that's a good idea, Simon."

I yank my thumb away from my mouth.

No biting of the fingernails!

"If not today, maybe tomorrow?"

I realize he's coaxing me. Why does he really want me to go? The last time he had me going anywhere with him, I ended up crying all over him and he had to follow my butt home because he thought I'd drive my SUV into a tree. If I were him, I would be running in the opposite direction as fast as humanly possible.

"Like I said, I don't think us going anywhere together is a good idea."

There is a long pause. It is so long I look down at my phone to see if he's still on the line.

He is.

"Trenda, are you embarrassed about needing to cry the other day? You shouldn't be. That was a natural reaction. Damn, near anybody would have felt like it."

"Oh really? Is that why *you* were sobbing all over *me*?"

Watch out, the sarcastic bitch is in the house.

"I might not have been sobbing, but yeah, having you in my arms helped to settle me down."

"Bull pucky. I didn't notice one single moment when you didn't have everything together. You were tight as a drum. You lived up to your title, *Commander*." I say his title slowly, with as much sarcasm as possible.

There, suck on that!

"Trenda, I spent twenty-six years either working as a SEAL or leading SEALs. I have been in a lot of hairy situations. I've trained for times like the one we were in, and I've performed in similar situations, so it's not fair to compare us. What's more, with Drake as your brother, I know you know this."

I sigh, and it comes out all quivery. The bitch was gone. Instead, the awful mother and sad and confused woman are back.

"Can you tell me what's really wrong?" he asks softly.

"I don't know you well enough to lay my troubles at your doorstep. At least not again."

"Sometimes a third-party is the perfect person to talk to. Then you get an objective point of view."

"How about when it concerns my ugly past, my little girl and maybe even a little bit about a Navy commander who's moved into town?"

Again, there is silence. When it has gone on too long, I start talking again.

"See, you don't know what to say. Nobody can help me. I just need to get my shit together by myself."

As usual.

Fluffer-Bunnies! I'm crying again.

Great job, Trenda. Prove to the handsome man that you are a hormonal loser.

"How much longer before Bella gets out of school?"

"Five hours." Good, at least my voice didn't sound like I was crying.

"Can I come over?"

"Uhmm."

"Let me rephrase that. I'm coming over," Simon says in his sexy commander voice. "It'll be your choice if you open the door or not."

"Simon, don't. I'm all over the place. One instant I'm sad, and the next instant I want to throw things. If you come over, I might be laughing maniacally. Truly, I'm an ugly mess."

"It sounds to me like you're human. That's something I appreciate. Someone who doesn't hold everything in. Someone who admits when shit's gone sideways and doesn't try to hide it. I want to be there for you."

"But why?"

I'm pretty sure he isn't Jeffrey Dahmer, but the fact that I *thought* he was being nice to me because I *thought* he was a nice man means he's probably hiding a really bad side.

Stop it! Drake even told you when you called, he was a good guy. Wouldn't it be nice to lean on somebody instead of having to pick up the pieces all on your own?

Yeah, I could call Evie, but even with her, I could only tell her so much. Maybe with Simon, I could let it all hang out. Even the part where I am attracted to him, but the fact is I am not, in any known universe, going to act on it. He would understand that, right?

"Trenda? Did you hear me? You won't have to open the door. But I'll be there as soon as I can."

"Simon—"

Shoot, he's hung up.

I call him back. It just rings and rings. The butthead isn't picking up.

I scramble into my bathroom. My face looks terrible. I

try to think. It will probably take him thirty minutes to get here.

I put a washcloth under the cold water and wring it out. Then I lie down on my bed and set my phone alarm for fifteen minutes. I put the cloth over my face.

It should help.

For fourteen minutes and thirty seconds, I remember how it felt to lie on Simon's hard body. His muscles felt so good even as I sobbed.

I remember shifting a tiny bit so that my pebble hard nipples could seek the pleasurable zing of passion, which had been pretty darn impressive, since we were each wearing two layers of clothes. He'd held me through my flashback. Through my sobs. Then, as I started to settle, he continued to stroke lazy circles on my back as he hummed some pretty song to me.

I had been in heaven.

As I'd pushed up from him and he'd caught my head in his big hands and looked me in the eye, he'd given me a warm smile. "You're better now, but not good enough to drive back to town."

He'd been right, but there was no way I was going to stay with him.

"Simon," I'd said in a breathy voice. "I have to leave. Chloe and Zarek will be dropping Bella back to my house by seven o'clock tonight."

"Call your sister and tell her to keep Bella overnight. The roads will be icy. I'm not letting you drive that SUV under these conditions."

"Fiddlesticks. This is not the first time I've driven on icy roads, and it won't be the last time." I'd said. I pushed up from those hard muscles, this time pressing against his washboard abs.

"If you're so determined to go, I'm going to follow you

to make sure you get home safely, and I don't want to see you exceeding twenty miles an hour. Got it?"

I'd rolled my eyes. "Yes Sir, Commander."

He'd easily pushed us both into a sitting position.

"No more lip, Lady. My number one priority is keeping you safe."

I melted at his words.

My alarm goes off.

Urrgh! I liked that daydream!

I whip the washcloth off my face and race to the bathroom.

Better.

Much better. I don't look like the bride of Frankenstein. Now for something a little better than the college look.

The yoga pants can stay, but the Tennessee Volunteers shirt has to go. I pull it off, then throw it into the hamper.

I shoot, I score.

Rifling through my closet, I finally find a pretty, frothy, green peasant blouse. It doesn't cover my ass, but it has to do. I go and look at my phone again. I have about three more minutes. I jump to the bathroom and rummage through the top drawer of my bathroom vanity. I should use make-up more often, maybe then I'd know where my eyeliner and mascara were.

Finally!

I at least find the mascara. I pull out the wand.

Shoot!

Just how old is this? I think back to when Maddie gave me my make-up gift set. I remember it was for Christmas. Bella was still crawling. Well no wonder it's drier than dust. I throw the mascara in the trash just as I hear knocking on my door. Maybe I shouldn't answer.

Who am I kidding, of course I'm going to answer.

Simon has beautiful gray eyes, and he seems like he is at the George Clooney level of niceness.

I practically run to the door as he knocks again.

I take a moment to breathe deep. I don't want to be panting when I open the door.

Okay, I'm ready. I pull open the door.

Chapter Fourteen

Her house might be small, but it really appeals to me. She has recently planted flowers alongside her walkway, and she's trimmed back the rose bushes that are on each side of the house. I bet during springtime this place is gorgeous.

The house I'd shared with my ex-wife in La Mesa had never looked this good, and half the time she was out of a job. Here Trenda is, taking care of Bella and a home business, but she still makes time to keep her house looking good.

I knock again. She opens the door.

So pretty.

Even with a face that's still a little blotchy with tears, she's pretty as a picture.

"I wasn't sure you were going to answer the door."

"Neither was I."

I laugh. She makes me laugh a lot. It feels good.

"I suppose the nice thing would be to invite you inside."

"Hey, you don't have to be nice. If you're comfortable heating the outdoors, then we can talk while I'm on the porch."

She rolls her eyes and backs up a step. "Come in."

I do.

The first thing I see is her front room, and it looks like she's picked out some nice furniture, but the place looks comfortable. Nice, big, yellow, soft-looking couch that you could really sink into, two blue chairs on either side of the couch and a low coffee table that looks like it's been made of a real chest, not something you would buy from one of those shops at a mall. There's a low wall that has three stools facing the kitchen. Everything is in yellows and blues.

"Have a seat and can I get you something to drink?" She waves me to the couch.

I amble over and sit down. It's just as comfortable as I thought it would be.

"What would you like? I have beer, sodas, sweet tea, coffee, and water."

"How about conversation?"

Her eyes narrow. "I'm all out of that, but I can get you a nice beverage."

I can't stop the chuckle that pops out of my mouth. "Well, in that case, I would love a cup of coffee."

"How do you take it?"

"Black."

"Of course you do. I'll be right back."

I watch her heart-shaped ass as she heads to the kitchen. Yoga pants were one of the best inventions of the twenty-first century. It doesn't take her long to come back with two mugs of coffee. She bends over to place them on coasters on the coffee table in front of the couch, and now I get a peek at her pretty pink bra. Even better, I get a look at the tops of her creamy breasts.

Stop it.

This is not my plan. I'm hiding out, not looking for

some kind of relationship and Trenda has all the traits of a relationship kind of woman.

"So, wanna talk about college football?" she asks as she walks around the table to sit three feet away from me on the couch. I take it as a win that she didn't sit in one of the chairs.

"Nope. Try again."

"Professional football? The Superbowl is next weekend."

I take a sip of coffee. It's good. It's important that someone knows how to make a good cup of coffee. "Nope, not the Superbowl. Try again."

"Golf?"

"I'm disappointed. You missed on all three guesses. I expected better," I sigh. "Let's start with why you're trying to avoid me, then we can move onto why you've been crying."

"I haven't been crying," she protests.

"Your red nose says you've either been crying or you have an awful cold. Then there's the fact that you were almost in tears when we were talking on the phone. So, do you want to talk about it? I'm a good listener." I sit there looking at her, hoping she'll share.

She leans forward and rests her hand on mine and looks deep into my eyes.

"You're nuts."

I wasn't expecting that.

"Would you care to explain how you came to that conclusion?"

"You're a man, right?"

"Last I checked," I agree.

"You've been a SEAL most of your life, right?"

I nod.

"I cried all over you five days ago, right?"

"Yes, but it was totally understandable."

"I didn't ask for a dissertation. That was a simple yes or no question. Did I or did I not cry all over you five days ago?"

"Yes." *Where is she going with this?*

"Okay, based on everything that we just established, you are morally obligated to run as far and as fast away from me as possible."

I know she expects me to laugh, but I can't. Not after what happened with Lizzie.

"Are you listening to me, Simon?"

I sigh. "I hear you. I'm just not buying into what you're selling. Are you?"

She picks up her mug and takes a sip, puts it down, then leans back into her sofa. "No, I didn't think you would run, but it was worth a try."

"Why? Can't you use a friend?"

She blows out a deep breath. "I caught you looking down my blouse. Are you sure that being friends is all you have in mind?"

"Being friends is a great basis for anything else, Trenda." I say as honestly as I can.

"Simon. I'm not a good bet."

I snort. "Lady, that makes two of us."

"No, seriously. I'm not talking about me working too much and being a single mother. I'm saying my head is screwed up when it comes to men. I refuse to inflict a headcase on any man, let alone someone I like."

This beautiful and accomplished woman just said that she likes me, and I take a moment to savor it. As I look into her eyes, I can see a little more than like, and I know that if she takes a peek, she can see the same in my eyes.

"Trenda, let's just sit here awhile and get to know one another better. How about that?"

She looks at me like I've grown a third eye. When was the last time I had to work this hard with a woman? I give an inward wince. Not since I made lieutenant, so that would have been twenty-five years ago. She captivates me more than any woman I've met in the last twenty-two years, and that includes my ex-wife. I better up my game.

"Where do you see this talking ending up?" she asks.

I laugh. I can't help it. "You are going to make the best mom for a teenage girl."

She cracks a smile. "I'll probably pull out the gun that Drake taught me to shoot and clean it on the porch when the boy pulls up to take her to a movie, just like in that song."

I laugh harder. "I can picture that. Now what do I want? Yes, I'd like to be more than your friend, but I can see that you've got a wall with barbed wire up, at least today. So, for now we're going the friends route."

"Actually, I have an electrified fence with razor wire."

"Good to know what obstacles I'm facing. But this afternoon, I'm here as your friend. Did you call Chloe to go pick up Bella?"

She shakes her head.

"Did you have breakfast or lunch?"

She shakes her head.

"I had breakfast at five this morning. How about I call in a pizza order, and you call Chloe?"

"You do realize you're a darn bulldozer, right?" she asks me as she picks up her cell phone. "No pineapple, and nothing fungus-y either. Other than that, I'm good with anything."

"Got it," I say as I take out my phone.

She takes her cell phone and walks down the hall. I wonder what she's going to say to her sister. Obviously, it's something that she doesn't want me to hear. Or is she even going to mention that I am here? I think I'm the first man that she's had around her since Bella was born, and if that's true, her sisters will be all up in her grill to know what's going on. Yep, she's lying about why she wants Chloe to watch Bella.

~

I hate lying. I really do. But sometimes it's the only thing to do in a situation, and this was one of those times. I close my bedroom door so Simon can't hear what I'm saying.

"I have a hellish deadline, and one of my headaches has started."

"Dammit, Trenda, you need to get those checked out. We've all told you they're not normal. You really have migraines."

"I don't have migraines," I tell her firmly. "I've looked those up on the internet, and they're almost debilitating. I refuse to have a headache that will have me lying down in a dark room for twenty-four hours. That's just unacceptable."

"Things don't work that way. You can't just will away a migraine."

"Watch me," I say as I pace back and forth in front of my bed.

"Trenda—"

I stop pacing. "If you want me to go to a doctor so badly, then I'll make you a deal. You agree to see your old therapist, then I will go see a doctor about my headaches. What about it? Is it a deal?"

"I don't need to talk to my old therapist. I'm perfectly fine." Chloe sounds even more defensive than I do.

In my mind, I can see my little sister crossing her arms as she looks down at her cellphone that she has on speaker there in her kitchen.

"And I'm perfectly fine too," I say. "We're both perfectly fine. So, are you willing to pick up Bella and take her for the night?"

"Sure. We have everything we need over here for a sleepover. Zarek will swing by early tomorrow so she can get into her school clothes."

"That's great. And Chloe... "

"Yeah?"

"She might mention her dad. I had to tell her he was dead."

"What?" Chloe sounds floored. "Is that true, or is that something you made up?"

That question hits me hard and I sink down onto my bed. "Chloe, I thought you knew me better than that. I would never lie to my daughter about something like that. Of course, he's dead. He died recently in a car accident. Bella just asked me on Saturday about her dad, so I had to tell her he was dead."

"Oh, Sweetheart, I'm so sorry. No wonder you have a headache. Are you okay?"

"I'm just worried about Bella," I sigh.

"No, I mean you. How do you feel about him dying?"

"I don't feel much of anything. He's been dead to me since I left Nashville."

"But still—"

"I've got to go. I really have a lot of work I need to get done. Thanks so much for taking care of Bella for me. You're the best."

"You're welcome."

By the time I get back out to the living room, Simon has topped off our coffees and taken off his coat. Damn, he looks good in a sweater.

Gah!

I just got done telling him all the reasons why he doesn't

want to get involved with the crazy lady, and here I am drooling over the way the sweater hugs his chest.

See? Certifiable!

"Is everything okay with Chloe?" Simon asks.

"Yeah, just fine. We just needed a little girl-talk. You know how it is."

"Not really, but I'll take your word for it. The pizza should be here in forty minutes. I vaguely remember you saying something about your past, your girl, and me? Did I get that right?"

"Cut the bull, Commander. You know perfectly well I said my *ugly* past."

"Honey, I was married for seven years. I know when it's smart not to have a good memory."

I couldn't help but grin. "Please tell me you had a good memory when it comes to no pineapple and no mushrooms."

"That, I *did* remember."

"Good," I say as I pick up my cup of coffee and hold it in front of me like some kind of shield. Simon's eyes gleam. He knows what I'm doing.

"Until the pizza gets here, let's talk about Luther and Violet. How about that?"

I immediately relax. Talking about them will be easy.

Chapter Fifteen

Now that we've graduated to beers, and Mizz Trenda has had three slices of pizza and has just snagged one of the cinnamon twists, it's time for me to start with the real questions.

"Trenda, I really find it hard to believe that you could have an ugly past. A colorful one, maybe. An ugly one? Absolutely not."

She leans back against the sofa. We're now sitting shoulder to shoulder. I'd had to work hard to gain that closeness. Every time I get up from the couch to get a beer or napkins or something else, when I come back I sit just a little bit closer to her. Until we got to this point, her shoulder rubbing against my arm, her thigh pressing against my thigh and her heat warming me. She's relaxed.

"Trust me, it's ugly," she murmurs right before taking another ladylike sip of her beer.

"You've said that a few times. Have you ever shared this supposed ugly past with anyone, or have you let it fester to where it is a gargantuan monster hiding in your closet?"

I smiled at her ladylike snort of mirth.

"Gargantuan, huh?" She questions me as she turns her head.

"Godzilla-sized." I nod.

Her shoulders slump and she rests her beer between her legs. "I was so stupid when I was young," she whispers. I can hear the heartbreak in her voice.

"Is this about Bella's father?"

"Yeah. I can never regret him having been in my life." She looks up at me. "How could I? I wouldn't have my daughter if it weren't for him."

"She's gorgeous. You're right, you can't regret having Bella, but it seems to me that he's left some scars that you still haven't addressed."

"Addressed? That's one word for it, I guess. You're right, I haven't talked to anyone about this. If I ever mention this to Drake, he will go berserk. Of course now that he's dead, he won't have a target... Then there are my sisters. If I had told them way back when, they would have treated me like a porcelain doll and I would have hated that. What's more, I couldn't let that happen."

"Why not?" It didn't make sense.

"I'm the big sister. They need to lean on me, not the other way around."

"Even if you were hurting?"

She twists around and tucks her leg under her butt so she's facing me. "Oh really? Were you hurting after your divorce?"

I rub the back of my neck. "Yes."

"Who'd you talk to?"

"I talked a whole hell of a lot to my friend Liam McAllister. Poor bastard was sick of hearing from me."

"What about your sister or your mother? Did you talk to them about your divorce?"

"My sister, no. My mom, a little bit. I told her it was better we divorced before we brought kids into the mix."

"So, you went to Liam's house and cried on his shoulder? How much Kleenex did you go through?"

I raise my eyebrows. "Really?"

"That's my point exactly. You might have bitched about it. You might have even said it was bothering you. Did you even once say you were hurt or devastated?"

I think back to ten years ago, when Patsy left me. I'd done the typical guy thing of just emotionally shutting down until she had no other choice but to leave. I hadn't realized that until two years later when I saw one of my men pull the same stunt.

"I take your point," I tell Trenda. "No, I never said I was hurt or devastated because I wasn't. I was pissed. I felt betrayed. I tried to figure it out with Liam; being angry was the only emotion I felt comfortable talking about."

"Then why in the world do you think I would have talked about mine to my sisters? Is it because I'm a woman?"

I am so screwed.

"Yes," I slowly admit. "I guess it is." I give her a half grin. "I'm in trouble, right?"

"Since you realize you should be, you're only half a point in trouble." Her eyes have a bit of a sparkle.

"I get what you're saying, Trenda. I really do. I just have one question. Okay, two. Aren't you the woman who told me that her ugly past was biting her in the ass today? Two, don't you think it's about time you got it out into the open so that it isn't something that's fermenting, kind of like a fungus?"

I feel like I've just won a battle when she smiles.

"Fungus, huh? Are you making fun of my dislike of mushrooms?"

"Maybe..."

She leans over and sets her beer on the coffee table, missing the coaster. I reach over and put it on one.

"Thanks."

"I'd just turned nineteen when I went to Nashville to train as a paralegal."

"Why a paralegal?"

"When I was sixteen, the one lawyer in town gave me a job filing for him. Mr. Fortnum's kind of an institution here in Jasper Creek. He's amazing. He's been practicing law for almost fifty years, people from as far away as Kentucky and Alabama try to hire him. But he won't take a case unless he believes in the client. He never did any work for my parents or the old sheriff or my uncle. You've heard about all that, right?"

"A little," I admit.

"Well, that's not the point of this story. Norville, my dad, went to prison when I was fourteen, and all of us kids were ready to lock the prison door behind him. The only shitty part was that Drake had to join the Navy because of trumped-up charges."

I frown. I don't know what she's talking about, but I don't ask questions. She should tell the story her own way. "So, what else happened when you were fourteen?" I ask.

"My youngest sister, Piper, was four. She was still traumatized after Norville broke her arm. The twins were seven, Maddie was ten and Evie? Well Evie was twelve, going on forty."

"What about your mom?"

"You mean Wanda? When she wasn't out chasing dick, she was on the couch passed out. Vodka was her booze of choice." She gives me a considering look. "Is that too much for you?"

I shake my head. "Absolutely not. I want to hear it all." And I do. After the whitewashed, picture-perfect life of

Lizzy, I'm sick of not hearing the truth. Ugly suits me just fine. "How'd y'all survive? Who paid the bills? Bought food?"

"Mom claimed disability from the meat packing plant years ago, and the state was still paying, but it wasn't a lot. Sometimes her *boyfriends*." Trenda put air-quotes around the word. "Sometimes they would contribute to the family coffers, but mostly they wouldn't. We had Granny Laughton, that was Wanda's mom. She was living on social security, and she really *was* disabled. She lived a couple of counties over, but she always sent each of us birthday money, so that helped for school clothes from the secondhand store." Trenda stopped talking.

"What else, Honey?"

"But mostly it was Drake sending half his paycheck to mom that kept the roof over our heads and the lights on. Evie and I never told Drake that Mom would use his money for booze, smokes, and gambling at the Indian casinos down in Mississippi. Sometimes she'd stay there for days. We let him think she was being a good mother to us. He needed something to believe in."

"But didn't you girls need the money?"

"Most of the time Evie and I could catch the mail before Wanda would, then we'd sign the check and then get it cashed at one of those Cash-Your-Check-Here-And-We'll-Rip-You-Off places. They'd charge us a pretty big fee, but would turn a blind eye when Wanda's ID looked nothing like us. Then we'd have the money we needed for rent, electricity, and food. If Wanda got to the mailbox first, she'd never use it for what we needed, and we had to rely on my babysitting and Evie mowing lawns or recycling plastic bottles. Whatever we could think to do to make money. We went to the food bank a lot."

"That's how you grew up?" Looking at the woman in

front of me, I can't square the circle of her growing up in such hardship. I know people said things were rough for the Avery children, but this was fucking heartbreaking.

"I figured you would have heard some talk by now," she sighs.

"Just some, Trenda. Not a lot. And what I did hear is that it was a wonder all of you Avery children turned out so well, considering the parents you had."

She leans in closer. "Really?" She seems really surprised.

"Yeah, Honey. Really. The few people I have talked to in this little town know you or your sisters and think very highly of y'all."

She giggles. "You say y'all wrong."

I know she's deflecting, but I let her. "I do not," I reply in a severe tone. I'll say anything to get her to giggle again.

"I can tell you're not a true Southerner. A true Southerner would have selected sweet tea, not coffee."

"Any Southerner who spent time in the military would have requested coffee," I disagree.

"Drake always asks for sweet tea, and so does Sebastian. He's from Louisiana, and so does—"

I hold up my hand. "Stop already. Fine, I grew up in Ohio and spent the first part of my career in California. But I've been living the last thirteen years in Virginia, which gives me license to use the phrase y'all. So how am I using it wrong?"

"You're missing the rhythm. It's got to sound almost musical."

I smile. "Listen to you, Trenda. Even with the shit start in life, and this supposed big ugly secret, you are one of the loveliest women I've ever met."

She looks down at her plate, totally shutting me out. I put my hand to her cheek and gently guide her face so she's looking at me again. As she looks up, her brown eyes are confused.

"You're not supposed to say something like that."

"Sure I am. I tell the truth, remember? Remember in the truck when I yelled at you?"

She nods.

"You'd told me that you have a phobia when men yell at you. Has someone hurt you in the past?"

"Well, sure, someone has hurt me. Nobody goes through life without getting hurt."

I don't respond. I sit there, waiting for her. At last, the silence gets to her.

"Norville liked to beat on people smaller than him. God forbid he get in a fight with someone his own size. He might actually get hurt."

I look at her. My gut tells me there's more. I push a lock of her hair behind her ear. "Ah, Trenda, I hope you know you can trust me."

Her laugh is weary. "I hope I can. I mean, I think I can. I've been holding this in so long that it's corroding my soul."

Corroding her soul?

I can't stop myself. I reach out and pull her into my arms. It's not as good as it was when she was lying on top of me at my cabin, but it's close. I feel her breath at my neck and press my lips on top of her sweet-smelling hair.

"Let it out, Honey."

"I thought he loved me." I can barely hear her. "I was so dumb, I'd just turned nineteen, and here I was living with a fifty-four-year-old man in his high-rise condominium, not meeting any of his friends, cooking his meals, thinking he's going to pro-pro-propose."

I want to break something. She was just a baby, and some man, three times her age, was defiling her?! It makes me sick just thinking about it.

"How stupid was I? Right?"

"Not stupid."

"It gets worse. He was my first." She pushes back from my shoulder, her shiny brown eyes look up at me. "Do you know what I mean?"

"You were a virgin."

She nods. "After watching my mom, I had planned to wait until I was married. Mr. Fortnum had got me the job at the real estate company in Nashville. Brantley was their biggest customer, and he kept asking me out. He sent me flowers. Then he got me signed sheet music from Miss Dolly Parton for the song "Jolene." He really knew me. So, I finally went out with him. He had a limousine."

Jesus.

"He kept wanting to sleep with me, but I said no. Then he gave me a promise ring, and asked me to move in with him. Again, how stupid was I?"

"Baby, you weren't." I press her face against my chest. She's not crying, but she looks shell-shocked.

"We'd been living together for four months. He was acting strange, so I knew he was getting ready to propose, and the next day was the day his wife showed up."

Trenda's voice was almost robotic as she tells me about Brantley's wife, and the cruel things she'd said to Trenda. How can one woman be so heartless to another?

"It was like she'd poured a bucket of cold water over me, and I woke up from a dream world. I realized what was going on around me, and I realized what was going on with me. My period was late. That was part of what I had not been paying too much attention to. Why bother, because Brantley and I were going to get married, right?"

"Right, Baby." I kiss the top of her head, and stroke her back, willing her to tell me more of the big ugly. Now I know this is going to be truly horrific.

"As soon as his wife leaves, I run to the bathroom, I'm lucky I made it to the toilet, and I puke my guts out. Yet another symptom that I'd been ignoring. That afternoon Brantley calls and says he has to go out of town and won't be back til the next day. I go buy a pregnancy test. Not that I need it. I'd been around Wanda long enough to see what happens when you're pregnant. Of course I was."

She doesn't say anything for a long time, and I don't try to push her. She'll say something when she's ready.

She pushes back a little, so that she can look into my face. "Do you want to know something amazing, Simon?"

"Sure."

Please let it be something good.

"Even with all that scum swirling around me, when I see those lines on the pee stick, I know at that very moment that a miracle is growing inside of me. I know not everyone feels that way; I listened to Wanda bitch about being pregnant the last two times. But for me this was a miracle, and I didn't care that I wasn't going to get my happily ever after with Brantley, because I was going to get one with my child."

Her words wash over me. This. This is how I wanted my wife to feel about us having a child together.

"You're right, Honey. That is amazing. What's even more amazing is that you were nineteen when you were thinking that."

Trenda let out a half laugh. "I kind of wasn't nineteen. I was actually kind of a mother already to my sisters, and I love them to death. But my child? I can't begin to tell you how I felt knowing that I was going to have a baby. I knew I could, and would, survive anything to keep my child safe. I was determined to build a good life for them."

I bent and brushed my lips against hers. How could I not? Yes, Bella is a miracle, but Trenda needed to know that she is a miracle too.

"So did you tell Brantley, or just leave?" I ask.

Trenda's arms sneak around my waist.

"I confront him when he comes home. I tell him I know about his wife and that I'm pregnant." She squeezes me with all of her might. I wait for her to continue. She doesn't.

"Then what happened?" I'm sure I don't want to know, but I have to know.

So softly, in a voice that doesn't sound like hers, "He calls me awful names. He accuses me of sleeping with someone else and says the baby can't be his."

I struggle to hear what she's saying. And when I can make out the words, they make no sense. How could anyone doubt Trenda's integrity?

"He finally tells me it doesn't matter."

Trenda takes in a big gulp of air, and her body quakes. She looks up at me, and now the tears are there.

"Tell me Baby. "Finish, Baby. Finish it, and it will finally be over."

Tears are slowly dripping down her face. "He says that I have to get an a-a-abortion. I have to l-l-leave in th-th-three hours. And…"

Her words trail off. I can't imagine what else she could possibly have to say. I don't want to know what comes after the 'and.'

"Trenda?"

"He tries to give me a lot of money from his wallet. It was a lot. He grabs my hand and tries to force me to hold it, but I can't. I won't. That's when he hits me and I end up on the floor."

The last words she says without tears. In fact, she sounds angry. Not anywhere close to the level of rage that I'm feeling.

She tries to let go of me, tries to wiggle out of my arms, but I refuse to let her go. She's staying right where she is.

"Brantley who?"

She laughs tiredly. "Are you sure we're not related? You're sounding like Evie, and you're doing quite the accurate impression of my big brother."

"Trust me, we're in no way related. Give me a last name."

Chapter Sixteen

I snuggle even closer. He smells like pine, leather, and something else, but the combination soothes me, makes me feel safe.

"Trenda, answer my question."

"He died, Simon."

I feel him kiss the top of my head and draw circles on my back with his big, warm palm. I don't think that I've ever felt safer, but I know this is an illusion. But it is such a wonderful dream, and one I intend to live in a few minutes longer.

Simon lifts my legs, and I find myself straddling him. Now we're chest to breast, core to core. So much nicer. At least it is until he tilts my head up from his shoulder. "Look at me, Baby. All the ugly is on his side. You know that, don't you?"

"Mostly I do." I murmur.

He cups my jaw, his thumb trailing along my bottom lip.

"Mostly?"

I struggle to find the right words. "When I feel like I'm

screwing up in the present, then all this ugly bubbles up and I'm covered in this goo of poison."

"What could you possibly think you're screwing up on? From where I'm sitting, you've got it together. I'm the one acting like a fucking hermit in a cabin in the middle of nowhere."

"About that—"

"Uh-uh, today we're analyzing Trenda's psyche. We'll save Simon's psyche for another day."

I nuzzle against his palm and look into turbulent gray eyes. "Sometimes I catch glimpses of pain in your eyes. It worries me."

"You're seeing it right. Again, that's for another day. Now tell me what's making this all fall down on your head right now? Especially since you were basically a miracle worker just a few days ago."

"Yeah, sure I was. You were the one who did everything. I was the one who fell apart like a loser."

The hand drawing concentric circles on my back slips under the edge of my blouse. The warm heat of his palm lights up my entire body. I feel like an electrical storm is pulsing through my veins.

Looking into his eyes, I can see that he's feeling it, too.

"What do you think you're doing?" I sound like I'm out of breath.

"I'm giving you something else to think about so you're not beating yourself up as much. Now tell me what's going on in the present that has you so upset? Let's see if we can wipe that away, too."

He moves his other hand from my cheek, and instead slips it behind my neck and cradles my skull, his fingers massaging my scalp. That feels good too. I don't ever want him to stop, even if I know what the sneaky man is trying to do. He's trying to befuddle my brain so that I'll tell him all my sorrows.

"So?" Yep, he's a secret-stealer.

"It's Bella."

"What about Bella?" He whispers the question.

"She asked about her father for the first time ever. I've known for a long time that it really isn't normal for a kid not to ask earlier, but I think she instinctively knew that it was a sore spot for me, so she didn't. She's like that. Sometimes I feel like she's the adult and I'm the kid."

"Your daughter is a little spitfire. What did she ask about?"

"She asked me on Saturday if I was ever going to marry her daddy. When I told her no, she said that it was okay, because we're a good enough family."

"Fuck." I see him wince.

His hand goes higher up my top, and he presses me even closer. As he directs my head to rest against his chest, I go there gladly. This time I don't cry, I just breathe him in. There aren't any fireflies fluttering in my stomach, instead I feel like one of God's archangels has gathered me close and his wings are wrapped around me.

"She said that? A good enough family?"

I nod. "Then I had to tell her he's dead."

"A double whammy," he whispers the words into my hair.

When I nod my head, my cheek rubs against his soft sweater and I can feel his pectoral muscles beneath it. I have to force myself to remember what we're talking about.

Double whammy?

Oh yeah.

"I thought her little heart was going to break, and it about killed me, but eventually she calms down. Meanwhile,

I'm still dying about that killer comment. Is that how she's always felt about us, that we're not a good enough family?"

"Trenda, how I saw the two of you interact in that grocery store was magic. Pure magic. In my late twenties and early thirties, when a lot of my friends were having kids, Patsy and I would be invited over to their houses and I'd see how these two-parent families would handle their children and how their children would react. They had nothing on you."

"You don't have to say that." I can hear the hopeful note in my voice, wanting so badly to believe him.

"I'm not 'just saying' any goddamn thing. I'm telling you the truth."

"Yeah? Well, I have one more thing for you to consider. Bella spent yesterday and today telling me what a good family we were. She knew she'd hurt my feelings, so I have a seven-year-old trying to parent me when I had just told her that her father was dead. Could I be more of a shitty mother?"

Simon pulls my right hand away from his sweater. That's when I realize my nails have been biting into his chest.

"I'm sorry."

"Nothing to be sorry about."

"See? I can't do anything right." I hear the dejection in my voice.

"If you kiss it, you'll make me feel better, then you'll have done something right."

I shout out a laugh and jerk back so that I'm looking up at twinkling gray eyes.

"There you are. I knew my girl wouldn't stay down long."

"You're right, I don't want to spend every single time together crying all over you. That would just suck."

He gives me a heated look.

"Trenda, would you do me a favor?"

"Anything."

"Don't use the word *suck* when you're straddling my lap."

I giggle. I giggle some more. Then some more.

"Honey, I have to ask for another favor."

"O-O-Okay."

"Could you please not rock up and down on my cock while you laugh?"

Now I start laughing in earnest. His hand under my blouse now slides all the way around so that it's cupping my breast. His other hand tangled in my hair moves my head so that it's in a perfect position when our lips meet.

The woman is killing me. Not just the story she'd just told me, but her lush body on top of mine, along with her innocence, is a package that sets me on fire.

Slowly, Clark. Take it slow.

She has the most kissable mouth, and I taste salt as I press one soft kiss against them, the first touch, the first brush, the first real meeting of our lips. Trenda lets out a small sigh, just enough to part her lips a little, so that I can trace my tongue along that bottom, plump lip. Under my right hand, she turns so that my entire hand now encompasses her breast.

On the third pass of my tongue, she opens her mouth for a deeper kiss and I hear my groan of satisfaction. I tilt my head and slip my tongue inside the warm cavern of her mouth. I taste mint, and it takes a second for me to realize she must have brushed her teeth after the beer and pizza. This woman, she's such a lady.

Her tongue shies away from mine, so I retreat and go back to kissing the side of her mouth, then the other side. She pushes even closer to me. I know she's not aware that those wonderfully thin yoga pants are pressing even tighter against my raging erection. I swear I can feel her heat.

She lets out a kittenish mewl, her lips parted once more. She's making me crazy, and her lower lip is delectable, so I take it into my mouth, then between my teeth and nibble. I hear her soft cry and I pull back to look at her. Her face is flushed, some of her beautiful hair has fallen across her face, and as I continue to look, she slowly opens her eyes. They're dark with desire, but sparkle with both joy and curiosity. Could there be a better combination?

"More?" I ask.

"Oh, yes."

This time she moves her hands that had been resting on my shoulders, and cups my cheeks. She holds me still as she tries to take over the kiss. I let her. Soul deep, I realize just how meaningful this is. I know in my heart that I am the second man who has kissed Trenda Avery, and I don't want to do anything that might spoil this for her.

She arches closer into my hand and I feel her heartbeat, then I lightly brush my thumb over her nipple. She jolts, and I capture her little cry in my mouth. I pull back.

"Okay?"

Her eyes gleam. "More than okay, it's good. Do it again."

With her eyes watching mine, I brush harder against her turgid nub and she hisses out a breath.

"Do that some more, while we're kissing again," she begs.

"Gladly."

Her lips are a little swollen from the last gentle kisses, and they draw me forward. I clutch her mass of dark hair and tilt her head just right for my hungry mouth to plunder. This time she doesn't balk when my tongue touches hers, instead she softly strokes hers against mine. Everywhere our bodies touch, flames race along my nerves, and I feel on fire.

This moment, with Trenda in my arms, I take my first pain-free breath since Lizzie's death.

Trenda pulls back. "Simon, are you all right?"

Of course, she notices.

"I'm better than I have been for a long time, Baby."

She twines her arms around my neck and cuddles her face in my neck. Even though our kiss has ended, I don't think it will calm down my erection. I withdraw my hand from her blouse.

"Do you have to?"

"Yeah, I do. We haven't gone on a date yet, so we stop at second base," I tease.

She kisses my neck. "Why?"

"Because I was damn close to taking it to third base and rounding to home. I refuse to do that until I know that's what you really want."

She stops kissing my neck. "Thank you," she whispers. "You're right. Second base is all I can handle." She kisses my neck again. "But what exactly do we get to do when we get to third base?"

I bark out a laugh and squeeze her tighter. "After we have a couple of dates, and if you still want to know, I'll give you a demonstration."

Dates? Are you sure, Clark?

"Will visiting Violet, Bernie, and Luther count as a date?" Trenda asks.

"If we grab a meal before or after, then yes."

"I know a great restaurant," she says right before she kisses my neck again. "You're going to love it."

Chapter Seventeen

"Lizzy!"

"Lizzy!"

God! Why can't I get to her? I need to get to her. My hand hits the nightstand and I feel for my gun. My eyes open and I'm hurled into consciousness.

Goddammit, I haven't had the dream in three weeks, not since I'd gone to the grocery store. Why tonight?

I swipe at the wet on my cheeks, blinking until I can see in the dark. I get up and yank the comforter off the bed, then the sweaty sheets. At least I'd done laundry and have a fresh set to put on. I shuffle to the bathroom and turn on the shower, and wait for the small trickle of water to turn warm.

What the fuck is wrong with me?

When will I stop dreaming of Lizzie's death? Shouldn't I start to remember some of the good times we'd had?

I let the water pour over my head and close my eyes. I conjure up that day when Mom and Lizzie had gotten together and baked homemade banana bread and banana cream pie while I was on leave. Two of my favorites. Those ladies sure knew how to bake. It had been a year since my divorce and they were coddling me on my birthday. I was okay with it. As a matter of fact, I was soaking it up.

"Now I know it's my birthday." I rubbed my hands together. *"You've baked banana cream pie and banana bread."* I gave both my mom and my sister hugs. *"Now I want a picture of the two of you, and my birthday will be complete."*

"Come on, Simon Says, blow out the candles. I bought thirty-five of them, and if you don't blow them out, the homemade whipped cream will melt."

I rolled my eyes at my sister. I hated that nickname. She'd used it since she'd heard of the game when she was five years old.

"I'll tell you what, I'll blow out the candles, and even make a wish, if you'll stop calling me Simon Says for the rest of the week."

Lizzie's eyes sparkled as she held up the cake cutter. "Deal. Now hurry."

I blew out the candles, wishing I could spend time with my family more often.

"You got all of them. Your wish will come true! Did you see that, Mom?"

"You are a nut. You realize you are twenty-four years old, but you're acting like you're ten." I grinned at my little sister. God, I missed her brand of nuttiness.

"Take out the candles, birthday boy," Lizzie directed.

"I'm not the one who put them in," I protested.

"No, but you're the one who blew them out. Them's the rules."

I sighed and plucked out all the candles and put them on

the dish Mom provided. I heard Lizzie's phone ding. It was the fifth text message she'd gotten since we'd started eating.

I was getting pretty damned sick of her boyfriend. It was like he had an ankle monitor on her the way she kept having to check in.

She came back into the dining room, holding her phone. "You two start without me. I have to call Ned."

"Surely it can wait, can't it?" Mom asked.

Lizzie shook her head. She looked pale. I wondered if she was coming down with something. "No, he says it's something important, and he needs to talk to me."

"Then you definitely need to call him," Mom said.

As soon as I heard her on the phone in the living room, I turned to Mom. "Is it always like this with Ned? Him trying to control Lizzie?"

"What are you talking about?" she asked.

"Within two hours he texted her five times, and she answered him each time. The Lizzie I knew would have just put her phone on mute."

"You're not understanding how it is. He's not being controlling, he's protective. Why, just last week when she had a flat tire, he left work during a major meeting to find her on the side of the interstate, and he drove her home. He's the one who arranged for her flat to be fixed and her car brought back to her apartment."

I thought about it, and I was slightly mollified. But still. I kept pulling out the candles and putting them on the plate.

Mom must have caught on that I still wasn't satisfied with her answer about Ned, so she continued.

"Simon, he's the one. I'm sure he's going to propose, and Lizzie is head over heels in love with him."

"But they've only been going out a month," I protested.

"Pish, it's been three and a half months. That's plenty of time. What's more, I know Lizzie; she's been keeping a *wedding file for years. It will take a year for her to plan the wedding of her dreams. So, they'll have even longer to get to know one another."*

"You guys haven't cut into Simon's birthday pie. What's the matter with you two?" she asked as she came back into the dining room.

"We were waiting for you, Sis."

Lizzie sat down, and I noticed her smile was strained.

"What's up?" I asked as I cut her a slice of banana cream pie.

"Ned went by my apartment just to make sure everything was okay. He told me that my fridge conked out and the ice has melted all over the kitchen floor, and he could smell rotting fish."

"He has a key to your apartment?" Simon asked.

"Yeah. I have one to his too. I'm so lucky to have someone that will look out for me like he does."

"No wonder you look upset," Mom said as she patted Lizzie's hand.

"I'm going to have to leave tomorrow morning. I need to coordinate with the property manager to get a new fridge installed. Ned says I need to get them to pay for new flooring and all the contents of my fridge that were ruined. I wouldn't have thought of that."

"When am I going to meet this genius?" Mom asked.

"He said we would fly out around Thanksgiving." Lizzie turned to me. "Do you think you could get some leave around then?"

"I'll do my best, Lizzie."

"Okay, everybody, dig in. After that, I've got a treat." Mom said.

"What? Is it a birthday present for Simon?" Lizzie asked.

"Better than that."

"What?" Lizzie was practically bouncing in her chair.

"What, you come home to Mom, and you revert to being a child?" I ask her. Then I turned to Mom. "You better tell her, or we're not going to get any peace to enjoy our dessert."

"Okay." Mom smiles. "I bought two brand new pinochle decks of cards. This time, Lizzie, I expect the two of us to gang up on Simon so he doesn't win, got it?"

"Mom, that's not fair. It's my birthday," I protested.

"All's fair in love and war." Mom gives me a smile.

~

I leave my gun on the nightstand, but I know I'm going to take it with me today. Even in this small town, I feel better just having it with me. I grab my cell phone. Five oh nine. I grimace. Yep, that sounds right. I toss it back down.

I go to the bathroom for a quick shower, knowing that the hot water won't last for long, but I need something to help put the dream behind me. Even when the water runs cold, I stay in, hoping the freezing water will shock my system enough so I'm fully in the present. When my body's blue, I step out of the shower and look in the mirror.

Better.

I no longer look like a man who's being hunted.

I dry off, and go put on warm clothes, even thick socks, though I don't intend to leave the cabin for a while. Walking into the kitchen, I gravitate to my coffee beans and put more than normal into the grinder. I'm going to need extra coffee before I leave, and then some more for my thermos.

While the coffee brews, I walk toward the mantel; it's as if there's a magnetic pull and I have no choice. I stand in front of Mom and Lizzie's picture. They're both beautiful with that same smile. Both of them have a slight overbite that makes it even more precious. I remember afterward mom demanding a picture of Lizzie and me. It's somewhere in the storage unit of Lizzie's stuff in Minneapolis. I need to find that picture and put that on the mantle, too. I remember how Lizzie was laughing in that one because I called her Lizard, like I did when she was five and I was fourteen. She used to write me the funniest letters when I joined the Navy. I'd read them to the other guys in my unit. Even at nine years old, she was a precocious little thing. I'm pretty sure that's why I've taken such a shine to Bella.

Hmmm, this is the first time I even considered going to the storage unit since her death. When I packed and moved all of her shit alongside Ned's cousin, I was a zombie. If someone asked me today what was in that storage unit in Minneapolis, I wouldn't be able to tell them, but I know that picture has to be amongst her belongings.

The coffee is done, so I go to the kitchen and pour myself a cup. After the first sip, I open the fridge and pull out some fresh berries, then I make some oatmeal. I've finished my first cup of coffee just as the oatmeal is finished. I pop a few blueberries in my mouth before dumping a bunch of them on top of my bowl of oatmeal.

I put on my coat and shoes, then come back and pour another cup of coffee, grab my bowl of oatmeal, and head outside. I sit on the front stoop and smile. As much as it's frustrating that I had another nightmare about the night Ned killed Lizzie, this is the first time I follow it up with a joyful memory. It was the last time Lizzie, Mom, and I were together when Mom was healthy. Those few days had been perfect.

Lizzie laughing.

Mom hovering.

My bowl of oatmeal goes flying across the yard, smashing against one of the tall oak trees. I pick up my mug of coffee and let that fly too. How can I possibly be happy when my sister is rotting in the ground?

"Fuck!" I yell out into the dawn.

"Bring her back!" I yell into the sky.

"Take me!" I shout louder.

I grab the rickety railing off its moorings and swing it in circles until I release it into the air. It goes farther than the oatmeal.

I pull at the other railing, satisfied when it's harder to pull off, happy that a nail gouges my palm as I release that one into the air too.

I look around frantically for something else to throw, but I can't find anything. I need to destroy something. I need to hurt something. Anything to make my pain go away.

You don't deserve to have the pain go away, Clark.

I fall to my knees. The voice in my head is right. I don't deserve it. I deserve my pain. When she needed me the most, I failed her. I failed my baby sister. The little girl who used to follow me around and call me Simon Says. I failed her.

I gasp for breath.

I pound the earth with my fists. Hoping for more pain. Anything that will vanquish this brutal ache inside. An ache I created.

Chapter Eighteen

I wake up with a hangover. Dragging my sorry ass out of bed and looking at the half empty bottle of Jack Daniels on the coffee table does not make me feel proud. I pick up the bottle and pour the remaining half down the kitchen sink.

Ugh.

Should have poured it down the toilet and flushed; now I'll be smelling the booze til tomorrow. I find the ibuprofen and take out three and grab a bottle of water out of the fridge. I suck down all the water with the pills. Even though my head still aches, I run the coffee grinder. Have to have coffee, and what the fuck? I deserve the pain after staying drunk all day yesterday.

I'm halfway through my second cup of coffee when my watch alarm goes off. It takes a moment for my synapsis to snap, and I remember that Trenda and I are supposed to meet for lunch after she meets with a client. I better drink a fuck-ton more water.

~

I get to the restaurant in Pigeon Forge before her and wait outside. I'm still feeling the effects of the booze and the Lizzie dream. Part of me had really wanted to cancel, the other part wanted to see Trenda again. The deciding factor was the two hours I'd spent with Trenda on her couch, exploring second base. So often in my world we give out medals for bravery, making that knee-jerk reaction to save your buddies, not caring if you're going to die. But Trenda has a different kind of bravery. She's emotionally brave. Something I'm beginning to think I'm not. I want to be with someone like that today. Besides spending time with a beautiful woman who sets me on fire, I also want to learn some things from her.

I watch her SUV pull up, happy when she takes a spot close to the main entrance of the restaurant. She gets out of the vehicle gracefully. This is the first time I see her dressed up, and the woman rocks it. Wearing a skirt, hair up in a messy bun, red lipstick, and the only thing I have a problem with are the high-heeled boots.

"You should have waited inside," she says as she walks up to me.

"You should have worn safer boots in the slush," I counter.

She grins up at me. "Trust me, I would never wear a spike heel. These are two-inch heels that are really stable. I can barely handle those spindly heels on a rug, let alone in snow." She grabs my shoulder and lifts one leg to show me the bottom of her boot. She starts to lose her balance and I grab her around the waist.

"Color me convinced." I chuckle. "No more acrobatics for you today."

She laughs. "That's probably for the best."

As soon as the hostess leads us to our table, I help her

out of her coat and I get to check out her pencil skirt and white cotton top. Yep, she looks good in business chic.

"Hand me that," she motions to the coat. "I'll put it next to me, with my purse."

A server comes by and hands us the menus and glasses of water. Trenda sets hers aside.

"Do you know what you're going to get?" I ask.

She nods. "I love their hot turkey sandwich. It comes with mashed potatoes. I'll only be able to eat half, but then I can make a salad and share it with Bella tonight."

"If you know the menu so well, is there anything else you would recommend?" I ask.

"The prime rib sandwich. It comes with au jus, and their homemade potato salad. You can't go wrong."

As soon as the server comes back, I place my order.

"So, who was the client?" I ask.

"She's someone I've worked with before. She owns a workout studio here in town and she's opening another one in Knoxville. She's quite the businesswoman."

"I would think that it would be the other way around. You'd start out in Knoxville, then branch out into Pigeon Forge."

Trenda laughed. "That might have been true ten or fifteen years ago, but Pigeon Forge has made its mark here in Tennessee, and a lot of that has to do with Dollywood. Brittany, the studio owner, built her place up from practically nothing. It was a little hole in the wall, but people used to flock to her because she was a former ballet dancer and she worked some of her dance moves into her workouts. It really caught on."

"Good for her. I can't remember who, but one of my lieutenants was telling me that one of his men had taken some ballet training to help him with his coordination."

Trenda giggles. "I'm going to laugh my butt off if it was

Drake." She picks up her glass of water to take a sip, but she starts laughing harder. "As a matter of fact, I'm going to say that I heard a rumor about him doing it, just to give him a hard time. It will be beautiful."

I start laughing. I'd worked with Drake Avery a few times. I admired the man as a SEAL, and as a man. However, he really could trip over his own tongue with some of the bullshit he spewed.

"How is it you and Drake are related? I mean, you're so precise in what you have to say, but Drake seems to..."

"Let it all hang out?" Trenda finishes my sentence for me.

"Precisely."

"He went head-to-head with our father and our uncle a lot. Even at fifteen, Drake was huge for his age. He would protect us, and one way he would do it would be to mouth off so Dad would go after him, instead of coming after us girls. I think always having to run his mouth kind of became part of his personality."

"Why didn't any of you call the authorities?"

This time Trenda's laugh is bitter. "The authorities were working hand in hand with Norville. They turned a blind eye to anything our father did. At least until he tried to kill our baby sister."

"What?" I didn't hear her right. There was no way she had just said that her father had tried to kill one of her younger sisters.

"Here you go." Trenda and I both give our server a smile as she slips our plates and drinks onto the table in front of us.

"Let me know if you need anything else."

We assure her we will.

Trenda picks up the straw for her sweet tea, pulls off the

wrapper, and lays it flat on the table, smoothing it flat again and again.

"Trenda?" I prompt.

"Hmmm?"

"You were going to tell me why, in God's name, would a father try to kill their little girl?"

"Piper was four years old when she witnessed our father kill a man in cold blood. Drake came home and heard Piper crying in the basement, so he witnessed Norville throwing her against the cement wall. There's Drake, seventeen going on eighteen, having to fight two grown men, one with a gun, so he can get his little sister the heck out of the basement to safety."

"What did the cops do?"

Trenda doesn't say anything and I have to tilt my head and wiggle my hand between her eyes and the wrapper. When she looks up, I ask again. "What did the cops do?"

"You have to understand, Jasper Creek is a small town. It was even smaller sixteen years ago. Dad was in cahoots with the judge's son, and the judge was buddies with the sheriff. It was only luck that the sheriff was out fishing that day and the deputies processed the scene and Norville and Frank Comey got arrested for murder. Because the deputies did their job, Frank and Norville got sentenced for second degree murder and ended up at Pikesville. But then Drake got framed by the sheriff and was looking at prison time because the same Frank's dad, the judge, was going to try him. Luckily, another judge stepped in and Drake got to go into the Navy."

"That's a lot."

"Nah, just a typical Southern soap opera," she flicks her hand.

"Eat your lunch before it gets cold," I coax. At least I hope I say it in a coaxing manner.

I watch as she takes a bite and swallows it down with some sweet tea.

"If I have to eat, so do you," she admonishes me.

I give a weak chuckle, but I do what she tells me to do.

"You're right, this is a fantastic sandwich."

"Told you," she says with a smile. She seems a little more like the Trenda I've come to know. We eat in silence a little longer before I ask another question.

"What about you girls after Drake left? You told me that your mom is basically worthless. Why didn't someone in the community contact social services?"

I watch as Trenda struggles to swallow her bite, and then drinks down a large gulp of tea.

"I'm sorry. I'm not trying to make this tough on you. There's a reason I'm asking these questions." She arches an eyebrow my way. "Yeah, there is the fact that I want to get to know you better. But I should explain something to you, but before I do, can you just tell me this? It was you and Evie who were the two in charge when Drake left, right?"

Trenda nods.

"Were you both trying to hide what was going on at home?"

She nods again. Trenda is always pale, but her complexion looks like parchment, and her brown eyes dominate her face. She stops eating, and I watch as she twists the straw wrapper into a knot.

"I gotta think that is a lot of the reason you weren't put into the system, and maybe split up. Am I right?"

"Yeah," she murmurs. "Evie and I were really worried about that. But..." Her eyes drop back down to the table.

She doesn't continue. Now the wrapper has at least five knots in it, and her shoulders are up near her ears.

"Even before that, when Norville was living with you.

When Drake was doing his best to protect you. Nobody called for help. Why?"

Trenda sneaks a peek back up at me, then looks out the window. It's clear she isn't going to answer. If I want to get her to open up again I need to share my story.

"I should have led with this. I'm sorry. Let me tell you about my sister."

She gives me a sideways glance, then looks back out the window. "Sure."

"She died seven months ago. Her husband killed her. It was one of those murder-suicide deals."

Did I really just say that so calmly?

Trenda's entire body turns back to me. Her brown eyes are wide, and they are still filled with pain, but somehow I'm able to tell that some of that pain is on my behalf. Don't ask me how I know, but I do.

I should have asked for a straw.

I sit there mute for over two minutes, and Trenda doesn't pressure me. I'm thankful.

"Lizzie had been married to her bastard of a husband for almost ten years. How could I have not known how abusive he was? I read the autopsy report and the witness statements, looked over all of the crime scene photos."

"They let you do that?"

"No. But I have a friend of a friend, so I got the file." I take a deep breath as my head pounds and continue.

"Trenda, she had broken ribs, and a broken collarbone, a broken jaw. These things had happened and healed over in the ten years she'd been married to him, and those were just the things that they could find, like some hidden treasure map of agony. How could I have been so unaware?"

I suck down a deep breath.

"The police had talked to her friend Dora, who actually knew something about the life that Lizzie had been living.

Dora was going to help Lizzie get away, help her start a new life. Ned would beat her all the time if food wasn't right. If she didn't iron something correctly, or if he was just in a bad fucking mood."

I push my plate to the side of the table and lay my hands flat on the top. I look at them and see scars I've gotten over the years in special forces. I haven't lived an easy life. I wouldn't change a minute of it. I'm proud of having served my country. I know who I am. I know that before I was promoted through the ranks that I was on the front lines in kill or be killed situations. I know I've made a difference, and saved lives. Why couldn't I have saved my sisters?

I look up and see Trenda watching me. I hold up my hands.

"Look at me, Trenda. I'm just as deadly as Drake is."

"I can see that," she agrees as she pulls my hands back down to the table and places hers on top of them.

"If I had been any sort of big brother, I would have known what was going on. I would have gotten her out of there and killed that motherfucker. How could I have missed this? But then again, why didn't she come to me? I don't understand this. Why did she hide this?" I choke out the last few words.

Trenda turns my hands over so that the palms are up, then she places her palms on top of mine.

"I don't know your sister, so I can't speak for her," she says softly. "What I can do is speak for me when our whole family hid what was happening with our father, then when we hid what was going on with Wanda and then later when I hid what had happened with me and Brantley."

I had to strain to hear her words, but her painful laughter comes through clearly.

"You know, Simon, I never looked at this pattern of hiding. I don't much like looking at it now."

"Honey, that's not it at all. Think about everything you've managed to accomplish. You've bragged to me about your sisters. You told me how the four youngest have all made it to college, and that's thanks to you and Drake."

"And Evie. Never forget Evie."

"And Evie," I nod. "The three of you managed to protect those girls and give them a fighting chance at a good life when they had reprehensible parents. You three did that, and if I had to guess, you were the mother to the five of them, and I'm not forgetting Evie this time," I smile.

"But we hid," she says sadly.

"Can you tell me why?"

Now it all makes sense. He had really been getting under my skin with all the questions. But now I get it.

His question is so full of anguish. Yes, there's frustration under it, but mostly just agonizing pain. I think of Chloe and how, even though we have all offered her so much love and support, she is still struggling. I can't imagine how much worse it is for Simon. To be an alpha male who is built to protect, especially his loved ones, and finding out that one of his tribe was being hurt so badly and he failed to protect her. The word devastating doesn't come close to describing it.

"We were scared as kids to say anything, because we knew, we knew down to the bottom of our souls, that the punishment would be hideous if we were to ever tell someone about what went on at home."

He nodded. He was listening with every fiber of his being. "But Simon, that was as a kid. That doesn't begin to explain what was going on with your sister."

"But it hurts so badly for you and your family," Simon

commiserates. "It also opens my eyes to how many other kids are going through the same thing right this very minute."

"So many more than you could ever imagine." I nod.

"And later?" he asks me.

"You were right. After Norville was locked up and Drake was forced into the Navy, Evie and I still took steps to hide what was really going on, like I told you before. Heck, this time we were even hiding it from Drake, so he didn't know how bad it was with Wanda."

"So now you're hiding this untenable situation, not just from the town and CPS, you're hiding it from Drake. Why?"

"Drake is easy to explain. He left still believing in our mother. After helping put our father behind bars, I didn't think he could handle hearing about another parent abusing her children."

Simon nods. "Okay, I get that. How about the town? Somebody could have helped you. They saw you going to the food bank. They had to have known your mother was off drinking and gambling in Mississippi when you'd pick up Piper from school day after day. Why didn't you reach out to somebody like Pearl? You've told me about her, so has Bernie."

"Pearl would have absolutely helped us. I know that now. Back then I didn't. You're absolutely right. I thought people knew what was going on, but Evie and I did the best we could to hide it. We'd sober Wanda up to go to a parent teacher conference, or when one of our little sisters had to go to the doctor's."

"But why? Why not get some help? Some people wouldn't have gone to CPS."

"For me, it was a toxic mixture of pride and shame. I hated the idea of people judging me or my sisters with the same brush as our parents. That's why I applied to work for Mr. Fortnum. If I could work for him, it added an air of respectability to us."

"Why shame? None of this was your fault."

"But it felt like it was. Do you know how many times we hid Wanda's bottles? Do you know how many times I talked to her when she was sober and begged her not to gamble our money away, to think of Piper, Chloe, and Zoe? Sometimes she'd stay sober for a whole month, but then she'd fall back to her old ways. I always failed to find the right words. If only I could have found the right words." My voice trails off.

"So even if I was living right next door, it's possible she wouldn't have reached out for help, she still might have tried to hide things, is that what you're saying?"

"Again, I can't speak for your sister. I'm just wanting you to understand what a toxic brew that shame and pride can be. Especially when she loves and looks up to you so much. You might have been one of the last people she would have told."

Dammit. I look at his face and I feel like I've kicked someone when they've been down for months.

When I say as much, he puts out his hands and I grab them.

"That's not true. You've given me new ways to look at this. I've just been running in the same old circle for months now. Seeing this from another angle really does help."

"Well, that's good."

"Can I ask you a question?" He's so tentative, I know it's going to be a big one. "Why haven't you told anyone else about this bastard? Why only me?"

"That's easy. By the time I came home, there was nothing to tell. It was in the past."

"Didn't your sisters ask?"

"Yeah, when my pregnancy began to show. But that lasted a week, then they respected my privacy."

"Even Evie?"

"Well maybe not Evie. She still asks me about it to this day. She worries that my past is impacting my present?"

"Is it?"

I look into his gleaming gray eyes. "I really hope I've worked it out so I'm finally in the present."

"I hope so too, Trenda. I really do."

Chapter Nineteen

Bella had been bouncing around the kitchen all evening yesterday, and most of the morning. She must have snuck some brownies, or some of the caramel icing, because she was higher than a kite. I wish I had her energy. Even though I'd snuck some of the chocolate icing, I'm still moving slowly.

"Mom, are we going to put them on the unicorn platter? There's so many, we could put them on the unicorn and the kitty platter. Everybody would like that."

"Huh?"

"You're not listening to me. Is something wrong?"

"I'm sorry. Say that again, Sweet Pea."

"Can we put the cupcakes on the unicorn and kitty platters? I think everybody would like that."

"Sure, honey."

I grab another batch of cookies out of the oven while Bella rummages through one of our cupboards for the platters. Maybe I didn't throw out that box I'd gotten from the farmer's market and we could layer some treats in there.

"Found 'em!"

"Honey, do you want to ice the cupcakes or put the last of the cookie dough on the cookie sheet?"

"Ice! Ice! I found the food coloring. Blue and red make purple, right?"

I turn around to see her squirting drops of blue and red food coloring into the vanilla frosting.

"The unicorn platter is purple. This'll be great, Mama."

"It'll be something, all right," I grin back at her. Harvey has a huge gray beard and mustache. I was going to make sure that Bella offered him a purple cupcake.

I put the last batch of cookies into the oven and set the timer, then I help Bella stir the icing until it's a pleasant shade of dark purple. "Hurry and finish icing the cupcakes, because you, my dear, are going to need a bath before we can leave."

"Why?"

Looking down at her caramel-covered lips, and the vanilla icing smeared up and down her arms and covering her legs, I can't help but smile. "Trust me, you look like a giant fingerpainted on you."

She looks down at herself and giggles. "It does! Okay, it has to be a quick bath. We have to feed everybody. You said so."

"You're right, I did. So, finish icing, and get your booty into the bathtub."

The only saving grace is that I had insisted we braid our hair before we started so we wouldn't get any in the batter. Otherwise, I'm sure Bella's hair would be covered in cookie dough. Probably mine, too.

Her cupcakes are heaped with icing before the cookies are ready, and she heads for the bathroom. "Can I wear a dress?" she yells from down the hall.

"No, there's a lot of debris where we're going, so you'll need jeans and your hiking boots."

"'Kay."

When I take out the last batch of chocolate chip, pecan cookies from the oven and put them on the cooling rack, I follow Bella's trail down the hallway. She reminds me of Maddie. I pick up her slippers, then walk another two feet and pick up her pajama top, then another three feet after that, her pajama bottoms. I hear the water running in the bathroom and knock on the door.

"Can I come in?"

"Yeah," she yells.

I open the door. She is just about ready to pour in the bubble bath. "Can I have bubbles?" she asks.

"Nope. And you know you should have asked first. This needs to be a quick bath so we can get going."

She gives me a pout that reminds me of Piper. My girl has all the Avery girl tricks.

"No pouting. You have twenty minutes to get ready, then we're leaving."

"Can we get a latte at the coffee shop?"

"No, we are not getting a latte at the coffee shop. Where do you even come up with these sorts of ideas?"

"Mrs. Richards took Leslie and me for lattes. They're really good. She said she needs her coffee before she can even get started in the mornings."

I sigh. *What in the hell was Vicki thinking? Lattes?*

"Is that something you want to spend your joy money on?" I ask her.

She tilts her head.

"How much is a vanilla latte?"

"I'm guessing about five dollars."

"That's almost as much as what I spent on Chloe's Christmas present. No way, Jose."

I hide my grin. "How about I try to figure out how to make vanilla lattes here at home?"

"Could you?"

"I think so. But now we have a problem. We have only eighteen minutes to get ready. So put a move on."

"Gotcha."

I watch as she picks up her loofah and her favorite strawberry body wash and leave her to it. Now for my shower. I might not have cookie dough and cake batter splattered all over me, but I've been up since five and I need a refresh. I throw my sleep shirt and yoga pants into the hamper, then head for the shower.

I turn the handle to hot so that I'll eventually get warm water and begin my wait while pinning my braid onto the top of my head. I hate having seventeen minutes to think. I really do. Of course, my mind wanders to Simon. Hell, he's the reason I woke Bella up early to bake this morning, so I could get him out of my head.

He kissed me!

Okay, if I'm going to be perfectly honest, we kissed one another. I'd only ever kissed Brantley before, and I thought that with his level of experience that nothing or nobody would ever surpass him. Boy, was I wrong. Simon's kiss took me up to the moon and made me think I could touch the stars.

But I don't want to get involved with someone.

Not ever. And especially not when I'm having my land surveyed so that I can sell it and move. I'd been dead serious with Evie; it was time for Bella and me to make a change.

But that kiss...

I need a distraction. If I get into that shower, all I'll do is relive that kiss and zone out.

I lean down and open the cabinet under the sink. I push back a couple of bottles and boxes until I find the expensive body wash and lotion set that Zoe had given me on my birthday a couple of years back. At the time I thought it had been way too extravagant. Something like that should only be used for special occasions was my thinking.

To hell with it, today was special, and I'm special, so I was going to use deluxe products! Especially after finding out the mascara went bad by not using it. Maybe that could happen to the body wash and lotion too.

So to hell with waiting for a special occasion. why can't my special occasion be that I want to feel good and amazing just because? I finally find it and pull it out. Hell, I haven't even unwrapped the packaging!

Picking up the scissors out of my drawer, I open the package and pull out the body wash. When I twist off the cap, I can't believe the fragrance.

"My God!"

I've been missing out on this? It smells so good. I want to drink it. There was citrus, maybe lemon, or was it orange? Definitely bergamot and something else that makes it pop. I pour just a little on my fingers and rub it into the back of my hand, then breathe it in.

Heavenly.

I look over and see that there is actual steam coming from my shower, so I jump in with my liquid gold and grab my loofah. Just pouring the soap onto my loofah is a transformative experience. I'm no longer in my shower, I'm not even in a spa. I close my eyes and see an endless blue sky, with translucent waters, and pink sand.

"Mama, I'm ready!"

I pull back a bit of the shower curtain and smile at Bella. "You beat me. I need ten more minutes, then I'll be ready."

"Can I use the iPad?"

"Sure can." The water's getting cold, anyway. As soon as my bathroom door closes, I turn off the faucets and step over the lip of the bathtub. I grab the lotion, then wrap the towel around me and walk into my bedroom.

As I go through my drawers, I notice something prettier than my normal white cotton bra and panties. It seems sacrilegious to use that Tender Glow lotion with my normal underwear. I find the ice-mint lace bra and panty set I'd worn with Evie's bridesmaid dress, then throw the set, along with some thick white wool socks to go with my work boots, onto the bed.

It's cold out and normally I would wear a Henley and a flannel shirt that's three sizes too big for me, then pull on an old coat over the top, but not today. Today I'm feeling different thanks to Zoe's gift. I pull on my panties and socks, then slip into black skinny jeans. I look over at my closet. Should I go for it?

Yes. Yes, I should.

What with Bella's school events, and Simon being pulled into helping the town, we've only gone on two lunch dates, one following a visit to Bernie, Luther and Violet, and another lunch date where he told me about his sister. Then him coming over to my house the other night. That was a date wasn't it? Kind of? We kissed a lot, so that had to count as a date. I'd like to count the ride up and down the mountain and the time spent in his cabin as a date, but that was really us just getting to know one another.

Wait! We got to know one another at the grocery store. So, date one was the mountain trip, date two was visiting everybody at the hospital because we had Italian food after that. Then date number three was when we met at Husky's in Pigeon Forge. Then four nights ago was our kissing date. That's four dates. So, wanting to go to third base and slide into home with him is not slutty, it's fine, because it would be our fifth date! Now I just have to figure out a way to arrange this.

"Mama, are you ready now?"

Shit.

"Almost, Sweet Pea. Just need another two minutes."

Quit daydreaming Avery, and get your shit together.

Don't overthink this. You just admitted you wanted to trip the man and beat him to the ground, so hell yes you want to wear the red sweater that hugs all your curves, so go get it out of the back of your closet and put it on.

I go to my closet and pull down a box from the top shelf and start rifling through some clothes that Maddie, Evie and I had bought on a whim when we'd found a sale in Knoxville, one of those kinds that wouldn't allow you to return anything.

Even now, I still wince at some of my purchases that I'd let my sisters talk me into. They were so not me, but I find the one ruby red sweater that I was looking for. It's a thick cable knit turtleneck that fits just a little too well. It covers me from my neck on down to the middle of my butt and it makes it clear that I have curves. This sweater goes with the scent of Tender Glow. I slather some of the lotion on my shoulders, arms, breasts and neck, then slip on the pretty bra and sweater.

I sit on the side of my bed and pull on real work boots, then stand in front of the mirror attached to my closet door. I look different. Even my expression is different. I have a mischievous smile on my face. I recognize it because it's Bella's smile.

"Why not go all out?" I ask myself.

I unwind my braid and shake out my hair, then I go back into the bathroom and even put on some of the new eyeliner and mascara that I'd picked up at the grocery store.

I go back into the bedroom and take another look in the full-length mirror. I really *do* look different. I mean, I look like me, but not like Bella's mom or the oldest Avery girl. I look like Trenda. The inside me.

"Mama, are you ready?" Bella calls from the kitchen.

"Yes, honey. I am."

"I found your letter. It was stuck behind the back of your office table."

"What, Sweet Pea?" I ask as I rush down the hallway so we can get under way.

"Mama, you look beautiful." My little girl reaches out and strokes the arm of my sweater. "It's so soft. Is it warm?"

At over a hundred dollars, it better be!

"It's very warm."

"Don't get any icing on it," Bella warns me as I go into the kitchen and look over all the baked goods we have to bring to the rec center construction site. We've cooked enough to feed an army. I think we're going to need two boxes, along with her kitty and unicorn tray.

"Should we bring them milk?" she asks. "Milk goes good with brownies and cookies."

"You have a good point."

"If we go to the store, can I get a chocolate milk?"

My kid is a trip.

"Bella, look down in that cabinet and see if we have those big, red plastic cups."

"Okay. Here's your letter that you dropped." She hands me an official-looking envelope, then hunkers down in front of the lower cabinet.

It's the dumb lawyer letter. I don't have time for it. I go into my office to shred it, then look a little closer and see that it's addressed to Trenda Avery, personal and confidential. This has to be the first letter that the registered letter had referred to.

"Found the cups, Mama!"

"Good girl. Give me a minute while I open my letter."

Ms. Avery,

. . .

It has come to my firm's attention that you have a vested interest in the estate of the late Brantley T. Harris. Unfortunately, the reading of the will has already taken place, but our due diligence on behalf of our former client compels us to reach out to you so that you and your daughter's interests are seen to as Mr. Harris wanted.

Please get ahold of me immediately at the following email address or telephone number.

Respectfully Yours,

Horace Grant
    Attorney At Law
    Fetterman, Grant and Peterson, LLC

I scowl at the letter. I might not ever want to go to Nashville again, but am I going to let Carla chase me off? No! I'm not that wimpy nineteen-year-old anymore.

I sit down and turn on my computer and open my email. Of course there's another email from the AOL account—this time it's titled *You're Both Dead.* That makes my blood freeze; not so much the threat to me, but that it says *both.*

I open the email. It has a picture of me and Bella making a snowman. It says, *Don't come to Nashville.*

I slam my computer shut.

"Mama, it's time to go."

Don't panic. It's just Carla. She's a bitch, not a killer.

She has a picture of Bella.

"Mama." Bella pats my arm. "We have to leave."

I need to think.

"Honey, can you get me a spoonful of cookie dough from the kitchen? After that, I'll be ready to go."

Bella laughs. "Can I have one too?"

"Absolutely."

There's only one person I can think to show this to, who knows everything.

While Bella is occupied, I open my laptop. The email is still up. Staring at me. I press print. I close the email and shut down my computer this time, then grab the email off the printer. I fold up the printout and the attorney's letter really small and shove them into my pocket.

"Here's your spoon."

Gah.

If I try to eat that, I'll throw up.

"I changed my mind. I'm going to want that for later."

"You're, silly, Mama." Bella eats her treat, then we head out.

Chapter Twenty

"I don't know what's more delicious, this brownie, or how you look," Harvey says with a warm smile.

"Mama looks beautiful," Bella grins up at me.

What a prima donna. I so should have put a coat on before coming out to deliver the treats. Now I'm out here shivering my butt off, all because I wanted to show off in my pretty red sweater. Serves me right.

"Harvey, I think I'm just going to put the cupcakes, brownies, cookies and milk over on that makeshift table you have over there, where you've set up the water and coffee." I point over his shoulder.

"No, Siree. The first three men who get to the table will eat half of your goodies, and put the rest in their pockets." His eyes are twinkling. "You have to pass them around. It's only fair."

"Mama, you promised we could show everyone the unicorn cupcakes."

"Are they the purple ones, Darlin'?"

Harvey has five granddaughters; he knows what's up.

Bella is nodding her head so hard that her hat starts to

come off. "Okay, Sweet Pea, we'll pass out some of the treats to everyone."

"Yay!" Bella says as she shoots her fists in the air. I know she learned that from when Zoe and Chloe had played fastpitch softball. I wasn't sure if Bella was going to be a girly girl, or a full-on competitive jock like my twin sisters. Who knows; maybe she'll end up being a bit of both.

"Head on over to the basketball courts, Trenda. Dave Draper has brought in lumber so that they can start framing out the rec center's gymnasium. I'll catch up with you on your way over there after I've dropped some of the sweets on the coffee table."

Bella is wiggling with delight. She is holding the unicorn platter with unicorn cupcakes and a baggie full of chocolate chip cookies. When Harvey catches up to us, he starts talking where he'd left off. "It's too damn bad that the rec center is almost a total loss. Thanks for setting up the meet with the insurance agent. At least we have an idea on what the payout might be. That's allowing Dave and I to start buying supplies. In the meantime, everybody here is volunteering. We've got the normal suspects, plus two new guys who are quite the find."

Harvey steals another unicorn cupcake off of Bella's tray and she beams. "Reynolds is up their ass, overseeing everything and countermanding everything the guy named Renzo has to say. He's going to make it so all the volunteers leave, and that will be a big loss. I can't bear to watch it. That's why I'm working on the other side. If he tried to direct me, I'd tell him where he could go."

I wince. Arthur Reynolds has been a pain in my side ever since I joined the rec center's Board of Directors. The man is short on brains and long on opinions. Because he was on the Board before me, and his father owns a car dealership in Knoxville that sponsors many of our youth team sports, he feels he has us over a barrel and can have more of a say on how the rec center should be run than any of the rest of us. Half of my job as board secretary is keeping him away from the other members who are ready to kill him.

"You said two people who were new. Besides Renzo, who else?" I know it's stupid, but I hope he's going to say Simon.

"That hermit guy, Simon Clark. Turns out he used to be an officer in the Navy, so he's directing traffic. Dave is laughing up his sleeve because normally he has to go head-to-head with Arthur, but instead it's this guy. I think we finally have someone who'll make Arthur actually shut up."

"What are you and your men doing?"

"While they're doing the framing on that side of the gymnasium, we're still cleaning out some of the debris from the storm that hit the classrooms and auditorium. When we're done with that Dave and his team can come over here and do the framing, then my guys can move over to the already framed side and start doing the mechanical rough-ins."

"Sounds like you have it handled." I turn to my daughter. "You ready to go see Mr. Draper?"

"Do you think Ronnie and Jeff are with him?"

"I don't know, let's go find out."

"Trenda, do you need help juggling that box and two trays?"

My arms are getting tired, but I open my mouth to say no. Harvey raises one eyebrow and I roll my eyes. "You know me so well."

"Yes, I do. You never could ask for help." Harvey shakes his head.

"All right, if you could carry the box, then I can handle the kitty tray with the unicorn cupcakes and the two bags of brownies."

"I could get the bag of brownies," Bella pipes up.

"And I get to keep everything else, right?" Harvey teases.

"No, silly. You have to share," Bella tells him seriously.

"All right. If you say so," Harvey says as he takes the box from me, and I laugh. We start trudging through the mushy, muddy snow. I don't worry about my girl; she is as nimble as a goat. Meanwhile, I am known to fall on my butt if one strand of carpet is higher than another. My reputation must precede me, because Harvey keeps things nice and slow as we round the building. I cringe as I hear Arthur's grating voice spurting out orders. But when I really take a moment to look I see that nobody is doing what he's saying. Arthur is standing on the one remaining bleacher, so he's higher than everybody else and he's sputtering and vainly waving his arms, trying to make his wishes known and followed. It isn't working.

I look at the crew of six men and watch the dynamics. Harvey is right. Dave is calmly doing as directed, and his area is taking shape. I see Aaron from the local nursery; he's humming right along—not as fast as Dave, but getting there. There are the twins who work at their father's garage. Those boys are great, except when Joey had tried to date Piper when he was nineteen and she was sixteen. Not cool.

"Mama, why did you stop?"

"Hold on a minute, Sweet Pea. I want to watch."

She shrugs her shoulders. "Okay."

I can see why Dave is laughing up his sleeve. I see him talking to a man with close-cropped black hair. He's not as tall as Simon, but he's broader in the shoulders. I can't make out his face from where I'm standing, but he looks serious. He must be Renzo. Anyway, as soon as they're done talking, Simon moves to the middle of the site.

"Huddle up," he calls out. Then he notices Bella, Harvey, and me.

"I have cookies!" Bella yells out, waving the bag over her head.

"Guys, we're taking a break," Simon hollers to everyone. I watch as tools are put down and everybody starts to amble our way.

"You can't leave. Get back to work," Arthur yells.

Harvey laughs, and I giggle. I can't help it, Harvey started it. Thank God Bella is hopping up and down shouting about unicorn cupcakes, brownies, and cookies, otherwise Arthur would see I was laughing at him.

"Heya, Mizz Trenda," one of the teenagers yells out from behind the two new men. "You baked?"

"Bella did most of the work," I respond.

"Harvey, let me take that off your hands. Unless of course you want to mingle with all of us and Arthur," Simon says softly as he slips between Harvey and me. How did I miss him coming up on me?

"Hell no. Keep me away from that mealy-mouthed ba —" Harvey looks down at Bella who's looking up at him with a gleam in her eye. "I didn't say it, baby girl, I don't owe you a dime."

"Not this time," she grins. "Wanna take some cookies with you?" she asks as she holds up the bag.

"No way, I'm taking another unicorn cupcake." He steals one as he passes the box to the commander. I watch Harvey wait until Bella is busy handing out cookies to the brothers then he gives his attention to Simon. "At least now you have something to compensate you for having to listen to that weasel-faced asshole. Everybody in town knows that Trenda is the best cook we have."

I know my face is now the color of my sweater.

"Good job dodging Bella," Simon praises Harvey. "I worry that if I stay around her too long I might have to hand over the keys to my car," Simon chuckles.

All three of us look over at Bella to see if she's paying attention. She's not, the Murphy boys are keeping her entertained.

"Uh-oh. Here comes trouble. I'm outta here." I see what Harvey is talking about. Arthur is climbing down off his ivory tower and is heading our way.

"Hi Mr. Reynolds!" Bella shouts. "We brought treats. There's even unicorn cupcakes. Do you want some?"

Arthur is practically on top of all of us before he turns his attention to Bella. "I don't know what a unicorn cupcake is, and it doesn't matter. We have a lot of work to do, and your Mommy knows it. I'm going to have to ask you both to leave."

I see the commander opening his mouth, but this is one I can handle. God knows I've been handling this boy for years as it is.

"Arthur, everybody here is a volunteer, and even if they weren't they'd be entitled to a break. Now I know how important this recreation center is to all of us."

"My daddy in particular," he horns in.

"It means a lot to all of our sponsors, the community, and especially the kids. Bella and I came to provide some well-deserved baked goods to the volunteers working here, and that isn't something that you have any say over."

"But—"

"Arthur," Simon interrupts smoothly. "I know we introduced ourselves a couple of hours ago, but I didn't really go into why I thought I might be a good fit in helping out today. I mentioned I recently retired from the Navy, but what I didn't mention is that I have liaised with the Army Corps of Engineers on a couple different occasions. That means I have some experience dealing with disaster relief. Do you mind me asking what it is you do, and what your qualifications are?"

Jesus. Simon just put it out there. Plain, simple and to the point.

I watch as Arthur, who is already on the short side, slumps down and loses at least two more inches in height as he listens to what Simon has to say. He looks around to the others in the group. Dave. Aaron from the nursery. Even the Murphy brothers. Anybody who might be willing to speak on his behalf. When he looks over at me I just shake my head. I mean, really?

Really?

Harvey is right; he really is a weasel-faced asshole.

"I own and operate two locations of Friendly Dry Cleaners, one here in Jasper Creek and another one in Pigeon Forge," he finally states.

"And?" Simon asks.

"What do you mean, and? I run two successful businesses; I bring a lot to the table."

"So, you helped to build your shops? Renovate the premises?"

"No, I bought them when the last owner wanted to sell."

"With your Daddy's money," Aaron pipes in.

"Shut up, Aaron, nobody was talking to you. I'm also on the recreation center's board of directors, and I have acted as the treasurer for the last four years. I know what I'm talking about. All of you need to start listening to me."

"Arthur, I'm sure they will listen to you, after they have their break," I say in a soothing manner. "But I have to say, you're looking just a little tired. What time did you get up? Have you already put in time at Friendly's before coming here? That's a lot," I commiserate.

He perks up and gives me a grateful smile. "I am a little tired. You're right, Trenda, it is a lot."

"That's what I thought. You're actually the one who

really needs a break. Did you have time to get a thermos of coffee this morning?"

"No, Effy didn't think to make one up for me."

Asshole.

"That's a shame. Why don't you take some of these brownies that I baked? They're the kind with the chocolate chips in them. I've brought them to our meetings, and I know you like them." I see the avarice in his eyes.

"You do?"

"Yep. I thought you'd be here. There's coffee and milk on the other side of the building. Near Harvey."

Harvey will just have to deal.

"Bringing baked goods is right neighborly of you, Trenda," he beams. He stands taller with every line of bullshit I utter and I nudge Simon with my elbow so he can extend the box with the brownies and back-up cupcakes and cookies. He proffers the box but I hear a very low growl that I'm sure nobody else hears. I have to work hard not to laugh as, true to form, Arthur takes three brownies and two cookies. Simon pulls back the box before he can take any more.

"Are Ronnie and Jeff here, Mr. Draper?" Bella asks as she continues to hold out her bag of cookies.

"Just Ronnie. He's at the fire station with his older cousin Ashley. Do you want to go over there with them?"

"Can I, Mama?" Bella asks. "Maybe Uncle Zarek will be there too."

"I don't think he's there, Sweet Pea."

"But Ashley brought her new dog and is showing her off. I'll call her up and she can come back and get you," Dave says.

"I can walk over there by myself." Bella smiles.

Every adult eye looks down at her and frowns. My daughter looks at the ground. "Well, I could," she mutters.

"Bellatrix Star, you would scare the daylights out of me if you were to ever walk that far on your own, you know that don't you?"

"Yes," she says as she looks me in the eye.

"And what else?"

"It's against the rules. I always need your permission before I go anywhere other than our cul-de-sac. But I *was* asking you."

"No, you were telling me, and you knew what my answer was going to be. We'll talk about this later. Let's just wait for Ashley to come get you so you can play with Ronnie and her dog, okay?" I smile as I cup the back of her head. She smiles up at me at the warm touch. I didn't want to embarrass her anymore in front of all the other people, because my gut tells me she was trying to show everyone what a grown-up she is.

She's only seven and a half, what on God's green earth?

"There's Ashley now." Dave points at a cute little blue Honda. He must have texted her the moment he'd mentioned her name.

"How long can I play?"

"Until Ashley brings you back, or until I pick you up."

"I still have half my bag of cookies."

I look around at the ring of men and I see that they've all retrieved cupcakes, brownies or cookies and are beginning to disperse back to work. Before I can say anything to Simon, he starts talking.

"Bella, how about if I put this box into Ashley's trunk, and she can take your unicorn cupcakes to the firemen? What do you think?"

"That'd be great. Then Ronnie will get one too!" She starts towards Ashley's car. "And the dog!"

"You can't give the dog anything chocolate, it's not good for them," Simon warns her.

Bella stops in her tracks. "Is that true, Mama?"

I nod. "Yes, it's true."

She smiles back at Simon. "Okay, Mr. Simon, my Mama agrees with you so it must be true."

He bursts out laughing and I do my best not to join him. I bet he can't remember a time when his authority was questioned, let alone by a seven-year-old.

He looks over at me, a brilliant smile on his face. "I'll be right back. Are you going to be here when I return?" he asks. For that smile, I sure as heck will be. I nod.

He catches up with Bella as they walk over to the part of the parking lot that has been cleared of debris where Ashley has parked her car. He and my daughter seem to be having quite the conversation, God knows what it's about. She's probably giving him advice about something. Simon opens the back door and pulls on her seat belt to make sure it's properly buckled before closing the door and I wonder if he has children because it is such a fatherly thing to do.

Ashley heads back out and Simon makes quick work of walking back to me now that he doesn't have to shorten his steps to match Bella's. As soon as he reaches me, I hand him two brownies that I had purloined, wrapped in a napkin.

"For me?" He smiles. It's that same smile again.

Damn!

"Sure are."

"Well thank you. I'll have to think of something really nice in return." Then he winks at me.

Chapter Twenty-One

"Do you want to go and sit on the bleachers with me? I have a thermos of coffee and we can share."

"I'm coffeed-out for the morning. If I take another hit of caffeine I'll be zooming into the stratosphere. But it'd be nice to sit down for a while," I admit.

"It's tricky around here. We still have debris underneath the slush," he says as he lightly takes my elbow. Where seconds before I had been cold, now I'm warm. Simon towers over me, and once again I feel fireflies flickering around in my stomach.

"Aren't you needed to coordinate things?" I ask as we sit down on the bleachers.

"I was just doing that to help block out Arthur's noise. Dave and Renzo have it covered. What is up with Arthur?"

"He was even like that as a little kid. Luckily, even though we were in the same grade, I didn't go to the same school as him, but we were in the same school district, so I would occasionally brush shoulders with him."

"He's the same age as you? I would have never guessed it with the paunch he has on him and the stooped shoulders.

He looks like he's rounded forty, and you look like you're in your early twenties."

"Are you fishing for more information?"

His silver eyes twinkled. "I guess I am."

"You should have asked my age when we went out to lunch the first time, after we visited with Bernie, Luther and Violet." I don't mention the second lunch; that got really deep.

"I was busy finding out your favorite kind of music, and may I say, I was surprised."

"You were thinking it was going to be all country, weren't you?"

"Yes," he says as he pours himself a cup of coffee. The man seems to live on it. "I was surprised you liked the big band era."

"That was Granny Laughton. She introduced all of us girls to it. Benny Goodman, Louis Armstrong, Glenn Miller, and the Andrew Sisters. They were all great. My sisters and I would go over to Granny's house and would wear some of her old clothes and pretend to be the Andrews sisters. Granny taught Evie, Drake and I how to ballroom dance."

"What about the others?"

"Her arthritis got too bad by then."

"How is your grandmother doing now?"

The question hurts even to this day. "She died six years ago. She left everything to my youngest sister. I want to be like Granny when I grow up."

I watch Simon take another sip of coffee, then he bites into one of the brownies. "My God, woman, what did you put in this thing? It tastes like I'm biting into the world's fluffiest piece of fudge. How did you do this?"

"As soon as I was making a little bit of extra money that didn't have to go to necessities, I asked Pearl to teach me how to bake. She was very kind. She knew we didn't have enough money to buy her desserts, so she taught me, then after I got her recipes down pat, I started to experiment. The girls loved the treats, and I sent care packages to Drake as often as I could."

"You're a caretaker from the word go, aren't you?" Simon's question isn't really a question.

"That's the pot calling the kettle black."

He shrugs.

"What were you talking to Bella about? Or were you able to get a word in edgewise?"

"She wanted to know if I was going to take unicorn cupcakes home. Did I have a dog. How long have I known her Uncle Drake. Why people call me a hermit and if I thought you were beautiful."

"That sounds like my girl. I usually don't have any time to answer before she's onto the next question. Except for the ones about her daddy. Those have been coming in a lot. I'm not surprised, but she wants to know why she'd never met him. Was he handsome? And why I never married him. Unfortunately, she left space between those questions so I had to answer them."

"Damn, Honey, what did you say?"

"I told her the truth. I told her that he was handsome, and that when he and I separated, I knew he didn't want to see me again." I let out a big sigh. "Of course, that took us down another rabbit hole. My daughter is a loyal little thing, and she couldn't comprehend why someone wouldn't want to see me. Fortunately, or unfortunately, there are two kids in her class that have had one of their parents just up and leave. No joint custody, no nothing. They just left. So I was able to use them as examples. She wanted to know how long I was sad about her daddy not wanting to see me. Then she asked if I was mad at him. I told her I was mad because he was missing out on being a daddy to the bestest little girl in the world."

Simon put his arm around my shoulders and hugged me close. "You do that really well."

"What?" I ask.

"Talk to your daughter. I like how you can talk at her level, but you're also a straight shooter. She's lucky to have you."

"You're kidding, right? I'm the one who's blessed. I knew from the moment I saw those two pink lines that I was carrying a miracle."

"Well, I'm happy that she's been asking questions about her father that you can answer, instead of saying that you're a 'good enough' family."

I looked at Simon. "You're right, I kind of forgot about that. That was a killer. Ah, damn, speaking of killers. Well, not really killers, but something really disturbing." How could I have forgotten? I stand up and push up my sweater so I can get to my back pocket. I pull out the folded pieces of paper, then sit back down.

Simon looks at the papers curiously, but I don't hand them to him. Dammit, my hand is trembling again. I put my hands on my thighs to stop the tremors, crushing the papers. Simon covers my trembling hands.

"Hey, whatever it is, it's going to be all right." His voice is laced with concern.

"I hope you're right. I'm just scared. I meant to give this to you first thing. How could I have forgotten?"

Because you distract the hell out of me.

"Do you want me to see it now?"

"Yeah, but let me explain something. This is the third email I've received. I've deleted the first two. This one is the worst." I release the paper and hand it to him.

I watch as he looks at the letter from the lawyer first. He

doesn't say anything, and his face doesn't change expression. He switches to the next page and looks at that one, then looks up at me. Now his expression changes. He looks nothing like the man I've come to know. His jaw looks like it's made of stone, in his eyes I see rage brewing. "You say you deleted the first two emails. Are they in your computer's trash?"

"I empty my trash every day. I need the space on my Mac. It was expensive to buy the Mac with the higher gigabytes of memory so I went—"

He holds up his hand. "I get it. Do you remember what they say?" He clips out the question.

I nod. "One called me a sinner, and told me not to come back to Nashville. The other one called me a whore and told me that Bella and I needed to stay here in Jasper Creek. I was freaking out that they mentioned Bella."

"How long ago did these come in?" Again, his question is abrupt. Is he mad at me?

"The first one came in two weeks ago. The second one came in the day I told Bella about her father, so about a week ago."

"And this one came in today?"

I nod.

"And this letter from the lawyer?"

"See how it's dated three and a half weeks ago?" I point to the date on the letter. "I'm pretty sure I received it three weeks ago when I was making coffee cake for Evie, but it dropped behind my table, so Bella found it and gave it to me today. I got the registered letter the day we kissed and —" He cut me off again. I don't blame him a bit, I'm babbling.

"So really, you started getting the emails, after you received the lawyer's letter," he says, almost to himself. But I nod anyway.

"Do you have any idea what Brantley would leave you in his will?"

"A big old pile of shit?"

Simon gives me a startled look and laughs. I feel a little bit better that I was able to make him laugh.

"Trenda, I think it has to be something else, otherwise his wife wouldn't be sending you these emails."

"*I* think it's Carla, but why do you think it's Carla?"

"From the story you told me. Brantley's wife called you a whore, and one of the emails was titled that. Also it makes sense because she would be a beneficiary, so she wouldn't want somebody else to possibly get a cut of her inheritance."

"But I just told you, Brantley wouldn't give me anything."

"Honey, he obviously did, or the lawyer wouldn't be trying to contact you."

"You just called me Honey; does that mean you're not mad at me?"

His eyes zero in on my face. Again, I can't read his expression. "Why would you think I was mad at you?"

"You looked so angry when you looked at the email, that's why."

He feathers his fingers along my cheek and I nuzzle against his hand. I can't help myself. "Angry? Damn right I'm angry. I'm angry at this bitch for sending you threatening emails. Emails that contain pictures, not just of you, but of your daughter. How dare she do that. How dare she!"

I breathe a sigh of relief when I realize just how mad he is—on my behalf. He sounds like Drake, only he's not my brother. It feels weird. Weird but wonderful.

"So, Honey, can you answer my question?"

"What question?"

"Why did you think I was going to be mad at you?"

"It's just that I'm not used to somebody being mad on my behalf, at least someone who's not family."

Simon stares at me a bit longer than I would have liked. "Trenda, you've got an entire town that has your back. Think of that old lawyer who hired you back when you were pregnant, even though he'd replaced you, just so you'd get benefits while you were pregnant? Look at Harvey, Dave, and his mother Alice. Bernie Faulks thinks the world of you. I think if we were to poll the citizens of Jasper Creek, they would all have something nice to say about you.

"Then there's me. I'm not quite sure what's going on between the two of us, but being with you makes me happier than I ever felt with my ex-wife, and I'm sorry if that scares you. So hell no, I'm not mad at you. I'll always have your back."

I sat there, not with my mouth open, but it was a near thing. I can't believe everything he's just said. It's too much to take in about the town. I'll consider that later. But him? I made Simon happy?

"You make me happy, too," I whisper.

This time he cups my cheek. "I'd kiss you, but I have a reputation to uphold."

"Huh?"

"I told Florence at the diner I was a lousy kisser, and you tend to swoon when I kiss you, so I can't kiss you in public," he grins.

"Simon, what are you talking about?" Now I'm really confused.

"Never mind, Honey. Let's get back to the email and letter. What do you want to do? What's your gut reaction?"

I laugh a little. "Uhm, show them to you."

"I told you, you were a smartass. I mean after that."

"I don't want to do anything. I don't want to call back the attorney, and that way Carla will know I'm not interested, and she can stop sending me threatening emails with pictures of Bella."

"Honey," he says in that low pitched tone that gets to me every time. "The lawyer won't tell her whether he manages to contact you or not, that would be breaking confidentiality. She won't stop."

"Then I'll call her."

Simon rubbed at the silver scruff on his chin. "I don't think that's a good idea, it could just escalate things. What time does Bella go to bed?"

"Eight o'clock. Why?"

"I'm coming over. We can talk about this more after I've had time to think about it."

For the first time since getting the email with Bella's picture, I can take a whole breath. "Really?" I ask.

"Yes, really. What kind of wine do you drink?"

"I'm not picky."

Simon chuckles. "So, you're not a wine drinker."

I duck my head. "How do you know?" I mumble.

"Because a wine drinker would at least say red or white. What can I bring?"

"Are we going to be talking about someone sending me stalkerish emails?"

He nods. "That's the plan."

"You can bring ice cream."

"What kind?"

"Toffee chocolate chip."

"Ahhh, you're an ice cream connoisseur."

I look up and smile. "Yes. Yes I am."

Chapter Twenty-Two

I'd told Dave and Renzo I had some pressing business I had to work on. Dave took it just fine, but Renzo looked at me suspiciously. Great, apparently his brother has been gossiping. Just what I needed. Still, I didn't have time to dwell on petty shit. I need some information, and I need it now.

I have eight men to choose from, four lieutenants and then their team's computer/communications specialists. I didn't want to go to Lieutenant Mason Gault, because his second in command was Trenda's brother. I wanted to let that sleeping dog lie for a while. But I need to find out which teams are out on missions. That leaves me with three lieutenants and three communications specialists.

I press the call command on my truck, and holler out Gray Tyler's name. He usually has a good idea where everybody is, and since he's on the West Coast, I could ask him what was going on with Drake.

"Hey, Commander. It's good to hear from you," Gray answers.

"It's just Simon these days," I respond.

"Okay. Am I going to see you at Nic's wedding? Only six more weeks."

I run my fingers through my hair. God, I need a haircut.

"Josiah has threatened to send Scarlett after me if I don't show up, so yeah, I'm going." I smile when Gray laughs.

"I'm thinking you're not calling to find out what kind of gift to send them, but if you are, they're registered at Pottery Barn."

"Fuck you, Gray."

Gray laughs again. I miss my men.

"How can I help?" Again, I miss my men.

"I need info. It's going to need someone to do some digging into places they probably shouldn't dig."

"You know, Dex was just bitching about not having been able to do anything fun lately. Apparently our little two-month trip in Eastern Europe didn't utilize his skills to their proper potential. Do you need him in Tennessee?"

"So does everybody know my business?" I ask curiously.

"Your four lieutenants do, and Drake does since he's the one who recommended his home town, and I hear from someone on Kostya's team, because Drake also suggested one of his brothers hole up there for a while too. So, what's the deal? Is that town like a spa for men?"

"Yep. That's exactly what it is. My skin has never felt so smooth."

Gray chuckles. "Thought so. I'll let Priya know. So does Dex need to be on site?"

"No, this can be done remotely. Text me with his personal phone number. Tell him to expect my call. Is he available in the next hour?"

"For you? Absolutely."

"I'll send him a couple of pics in the meantime. You're giving me his personal or satellite phone, right?"

"Of course. But it wouldn't matter, Dex has all of our

phones set up so none of them can be traced, or cracked by either the enemy or our friendlies."

"I should have known." I shake my head. The things my men had been doing. It makes a commander proud.

"Good enough. Text me with whatever number you think I should use. Tell him to expect my call within the hour." I have my thumb on the button to hang up when Gray yells out my name.

"Simon!"

"Yeah?"

"Don't be such a stranger. You were never just my boss. You're my friend."

I let that sink in for a second. That was all the time I would allow, for now.

"You're my friend too, Gray. The phone will work both ways from now on. Not only will I call, I'll pick up calls too."

"Good to know."

And that's why I called Gray and not Kostya. Gray was nicer, Kostya is going to bite off my fucking head for not having called or picked up his calls.

I knew I was going to be nervous as hell if I just tried to kill four hours at home before putting Bella to bed and waiting for Simon to show up. I close my eyes and think about how long it will take to clean my kitchen. A half hour, max. How long is it going to take to clean me up? Another half hour since I'm not going to try too hard after having already shown off in the sweater. That means me and my little sidekick have three hours to kill.

Bella's still at the fire station, so I pull out my phone to call over to the hospital in Pigeon Forge where both Violet and Bernie had been admitted. I wasn't going to take Bella to see Luther; he might have been doing pretty well when Simon and I visited, but it was still a crapshoot, so a Bella visit is out of the question.

"Hi, this is Trenda Avery," I say to the operator. "Can I talk to the nurse's station where Bernie Faulks is staying? I'm pretty sure he's in room three oh five."

"Hold on."

I wait.

"I'm sorry, he's been moved to room six thirty-one, let me transfer you to that nurse's station."

Hmmm.

"Hello?" the nurse answers.

"Hi, my name is Trenda Avery. I'm a friend of Bernie Faulks. He was admitted for gout nine days ago. I was hoping to bring my seven-year-old daughter with me to visit him today."

"Let me look at his chart. Are you family?" she asks.

"No, we're neighbors. I don't think he has any family."

There's a pause. "You're right, Mr. Faulks indicated he has no family. I see here that you visited him before. You and your daughter can come, but only for a limited time."

"Why? When I came before I stayed for over an hour."

"You'll need Mr. Faulks to explain. I'm sorry I can't provide you with any information."

"Thank you. My other friend that I want to visit is on your floor as well. Her name is Violet Randolph. May I bring my daughter to visit her?"

"Absolutely, I know she would love to have visitors." The nurse's tone is very different when speaking about Violet, which means something is really wrong with Bernie.

"We have some homemade baked goods." I cross my fingers that the firefighters haven't eaten them all. "Can we bring some?"

"Sure, you can."

"We should be there within the hour."

"That sounds good," the nurse says.

I leave to get Bella. After all the icing and chocolate she had on her from passing around the cupcakes to the men at the construction site, God knew what kind of mess she in was now after being at the firehouse with a dog. She might even need a quick bath before we head over to Pigeon Forge.

I laugh. At least life is never dull with my daughter around.

～

"Hello," Bella says shyly to Violet.

This is the first time I think I've ever seen my daughter shy.

"Hello," Violet replies. "Don't you remember me? You and your Mama came up to visit me last year."

"We did?" Bella asks as she moves closer to Violet's hospital bed.

Violet reaches out with the hand that doesn't have a tube connected to it. I'm happy to see she's even stronger looking than she had been when I visited a few days ago. "Yes, you came to my cabin and went into my yard and picked some pansies, remember?"

Bella's eyes light up. "Oh yeah! You paint pictures. I remember."

"Yes, I do."

"I got to sit on your porch swing with Mr. Luther. Where's he?"

Violet looks up at me. I can see the pain in her eyes.

"He's somewhere else right now," I say. "Mizz Violet's getting better and soon they'll be together and she can paint again."

"Will Mr. Luther swing and plant flowers?" she asks me.

"I don't know, Honey. We're going to try our very best to make that happen."

"How is Luther doing really?" Violet asks me.

I dig in my purse for my wallet and pull out a couple of one-dollar bills. "Bella, can you run to the vending machine that we passed on the way to Mizz Violet's room? What would you like to drink with the cookies that we brought you?"

Her body might not be completely healed, but Violet is sharp as a tack. "Bella, why don't you get me any kind of cola they have."

"R.C.? Pepsi? Coke? Dr. Pepper?" my daughter asks.

"Whatever is your favorite." Violet smiles.

"I like R.C. I'll see if they have that one. I'll be right back." Bella scampers out of the room.

As soon as she's out of sight, I go over to Violet and take her hand. I start talking. "Luther is very anxious to be reunited with you. I'm going to take another video of you, this time with Bella. He'll be relieved to see you on T.V. again."

Violet chuckles.

"Trenda, you don't need to get involved in where we'll stay. We have some money saved up, and a social worker has been in to see me. There's some state housing that will come available that will meet our needs for the time being..." Her voice trails off. I know she's thinking of the time when Luther's dementia will get to the point that he'll need round-the-clock care that Violet will not be able to deliver.

I see her eyes filling with tears, and I grab a tissue out of the box by her bed and give it to her, then take one for myself. The whole thing is killing me.

"Trenda, don't be sad. Luther and I have been together fifty-one years. God willing, we have a few more years of living together." I pull out three more tissues to stop my tears. The last thing Bella needs to see is me crying; she'll have all sorts of questions. I stop crying and blow my nose.

"Do I look okay?" I ask.

"You look blotchy, like you've been crying," she replies.

"Thanks for soft pedaling it," I grin.

"No problem."

We both laugh.

Bella comes in clutching three sodas to her chest.

"What's all this?" Violet asks.

"Mama gave me too much money, so I figured we'd all get sodas with our cookies," she grins proudly.

"That's a great idea," I smile.

"You look blotchy, Mama," Bella scowls at me.

"It's those flowers over there." Violet points to the flowers on the window ledge. "I think your Mama is allergic to the lilies."

"Oh, okay." Bella smiles.

Dammit. I am so going to get busted when Simon comes over tonight.

Chapter Twenty-Three

I like this house more and more each time I walk up to the door. There is just something welcoming about it. I can't understand why Trenda would be thinking about leaving Jasper Creek. Doesn't she understand just what a special place this is? I've never been somewhere where the community will rally around others and pitch in like they do here.

I knock on her door. It immediately opens.

"That was fast." I smile down at the beautiful woman standing in front of me.

"I don't want to wake up Bella. She just got to sleep. It was a rough day for her."

I frown. "It didn't go well at the fire station?"

Trenda ushers me inside and guides me to the sofa. She's gone all out. I see a tray of veggies, fruit, crackers, and cheese.

"I thought we were having ice cream," I tease as I hold up my sack.

"You got the good kind, the kind from the actual ice cream shop."

"Hey, you're a connoisseur, I figured I had to up my game."

She gives me that smooth and smoky laugh that strokes my senses and makes me think of her stroking something else.

Down, boy.

"Let me put this in the refrigerator. I have beer. Didn't you say you liked Samuel Adams?"

"I did. You remembered that?"

"Yeah." She came out with a Heineken for her and a Samuel Adams for me.

"So, sit down and tell me what has you and Bella upset." She sits down beside me.

"I just said Bella is upset. What makes you think that I'm upset too?"

"There's just a tiny bit of red around your eyes. I think, possibly, maybe, you've been crying."

"Damned pasty complexion. It gives me away every damned time."

"You better keep your voice down or you'll wake up your daughter with your swearing and she'll be here with her hand out," I tease.

Trenda sighs. "No, I think she is down for the count. I took her to the hospital to visit Bernie and Violet. I thought that would be an okay thing to do. I figured Violet's on the mend and so is Bernie."

"And?"

"Bernie's now up on the floor where they have people with lung problems. He has something called pleural effusion, and they just did a procedure where they took out fluid between his chest wall and his heart."

"Fuck. Doesn't that go hand in hand with congestive heart failure."

She ducks her head and nods.

"Hey, hey. Trenda, that's not a death sentence. I know it sounds bad, but I've had friends with that diagnosis who have done really well, they've just had to..."

"Exactly. Bernie was in a tizzy, bitching about what they wanted him to do. Things like exercise, eating healthy, no drinking and he has to quit smoking." She's sounding sadder with each doctor directive she's telling me. It's with the last phrase that I lose it.

I pull her into my arms and swipe her tears with my thumbs.

She pulls back. "Uh-uh, no way."

"Huh?"

"No more crying in your arms for me. I'm sick of that mess."

I look down at her, totally confused.

"Honey, what are you talking about?"

"I am not a crier, ask anybody. People cry on *my* shoulder. That's the way it is. If someone needs to cry, they come to me. If I were to cry tonight, that would be the third time, and three strikes and you're out. I don't want to be out, so no crying. I want to go to third base, not three strikes, do you—"

I press two fingers against her mouth. "Do you know that sometimes you talk a lot when you're scared or upset?"

She nods her head.

"Can I talk now?"

She nods her head.

"Good." I take my fingers away.

"But, I don't want to—"

"Uh-uh, my turn to talk."

"Oh, right." She stops talking and I chuckle.

"Trenda, I told you about my sister, remember?"

She nods. My lips twitch. I can't help it; she's so cute when she's trying not to say anything.

"Can you understand why it's a huge deal for you to be open and honest with me with your feelings? I'm not turned off by your crying, I celebrate it."

Her mouth opens, but nothing comes out.

"Talking to you has also opened my eyes on why things didn't work with my ex-wife. I always thought I was to blame. My job. The way I couldn't tell her what I was doing. But I see now that she never opened up with me either. Hell, Trenda, you and I have been together a total of what, twenty-two, maybe twenty-five hours, and we've hit a lot of emotions, both low and high. I feel like I know you better than I ever knew my wife, and that's on her. I look back on things and I know I tried to get her to open up, but she didn't. I realize now, that was part of the reason she married me, knowing the job I had and the fact that I couldn't tell her about things made it okay for her not to have to open up to me, and that's the way she wanted it."

Shit, did I just say all that?

Trenda's eyes are shining as she looks at me.

"My God, did you just say that? Do you mean it?"

"Yeah, I said it and I meant it. I don't want to live in an emotional vacuum. I kind of like this kooky little town, with all these people." I press my fingers against her lips again. "And before you say anything, let me qualify that statement. I like the Bernies of this town who say they're loners but want to take care of a whole damn mountain. I like Florence who is still looking for a good kisser after thirty years. I like the fact that we've got Bertha who is ready to shoot people on sight if she doesn't like them. Hell, even Arthur cracks me the hell up, and I absolutely adore how well you can manipulate that man. And the biggest character in this town has to be your daughter who is going to grow up to be either mayor of this place or President of the United States."

Trenda pulls my hand away from her lips as she starts to giggle.

"You are not wrong," she agrees.

"I know this. And I haven't even met your sisters, and that out-and-out scares me, God knows what they're like. So. Can I ask you something seriously?"

Her eyes are shining with mirth. "Shoot."

"I want to know, why would you ever think about leaving this place?"

"After the sales job you just did, I have no earthly idea."

"Seriously, Trenda. Why?"

She looks up at the ceiling as she thinks. "I think part of it, I was lonely with so many members of my family having moved on with their lives." She looks back at me. "Then there's the fact that everybody does know me, and sometimes it feels like I don't have a chance to meet new people, like it's all the same, all the time."

"Is it really? I mean, you'll have to tell me. But this place seems like it's always got something going on. And I hear there's going to be some kind of Spring Festival."

She sighs. "I know. I'm kind of in charge of the picnic baskets this year."

"Picnic baskets?"

"It's a long story. Florence has been in charge for years, but last year somebody caught her cheating because she arranged to have one of the John Deere men select her basket, even though he hadn't put in a ticket for her basket."

"Huh?"

"Let's not go there, okay?"

"That's what I'm telling you, this place is kooky. But in a good way." I pull her closer to me. "So are you still thinking about leaving?"

"I'm still waiting for them to start the survey on my

land. They think they can fit me in four months from now. It's pretty expensive to get it done."

"So don't do it," I coax. "Stay here."

She gives me a shy smile. "Have you been trying to make me feel better about the lawyer's letter and the email?"

"You caught me. I need you to do me a favor. Before we dig into the ice cream, can you forward the email to a friend of mine? He's really good at ferreting out information when it comes to things like this. He can probably backtrack the email and find out who it's coming from for sure."

"Absolutely."

She starts to get up, but I grab her wrist in a light hold. "You know this is going to be all right, don't you?"

She bites her lower lip. "Simon, my life right now is good. But there have been a lot of 'not all rights' that I've had to live through. So what I guess I'm saying is that if this turns to shit, I'll deal." Then she bends forward so we're eye to eye. "What I'm not good with, what I'll never be good with, is something happening to my daughter. You commanded SEALs, you were a SEAL, my brother is a SEAL, I know his team. There's another Navy SEAL who lives here some of the time. I will call in every single one of y'all to protect my daughter. Do you hear?" The last words were said in a growl.

"Okay, okay, now I *know* you're related to Drake."

"No. Now you know I'm a *mother*. Simon, I'm trusting you with the most precious thing in my world. I really don't want to bring my brother into this. My gut is saying don't, that he'll just muddy the water."

I coax her to sit back down beside me. "What else is your gut telling you?"

"To trust you. That you are the man who will handle this. That if you can't, you will not let your ego stop you from bringing in other people if you need them."

"You're reading me right. Right now, you don't have enough to go to the police. This might be a threatening email, but until you've been accosted, their hands are tied. With Dex looking into this, we can most likely find out what's in the will and find out Carla's motive for sending you these threatening emails. I wouldn't be surprised if he finds out what's in the will tonight, okay?"

She slumps against me, like her bones have turned to water.

"That's more than okay. That's perfect."

"Now why don't we get you to forward the email to Dex, and then finish the beer and this platter of food."

"Do we have to?"

"Forward the email?"

"No. Of course I'm forwarding the email. Can we get rid of the beers and put this platter in the fridge and concentrate on the ice-cream, or will your hard body go into some kind of toxic shock?"

"Lady, you make me laugh. Thank you for that."

"That's not an answer," she pouts.

"Definitely ice cream."

"Hallelujah."

Chapter Twenty-Four

While I'm booting up my Mac computer I realize I don't want him to go home.

Ever.

When he told me that he liked me sharing my emotions, and how his wife didn't share? Well, I felt like I had won the relationship jackpot.

I mean, he wasn't Jeffrey Dahmer! He is one of life's good guys, and he likes me! Me! Trenda Avery. And I have chosen correctly. My brother respects him, and says he's a 'good guy.'

Then there's the fact that he's off-the-charts gorgeous. That salt-and-pepper head of hair, with the silver scruff. I want to scrape my fingers through his hair for days. And, he is a good kisser, despite what Pearl said. How in the hell Pearl got that piece of information was beyond me. This town *is* kooky!

"I think it's turned on," he whispers.

His arms are on either side of me, resting on the table as I move my mouse to open my email. I scroll through the normal business emails as well as the shoe advertisements until I get to the evil email. I click it open.

Simon tells me the email address and I forward it to his friend.

"Okay, done. Now you get some ice cream," he says as he strokes his hand over my hair. I'd worn it down again tonight. I had noticed him noticing it. Apparently, he likes my hair as much as I like his hair.

I get up from the kitchen chair that I use as an office chair, and head to the freezer. I pull out the bag and feel that there are two quarts of ice cream in the bag. "So, what all did you get?" I ask.

"Real ice cream," he answers.

I open the bag and find rocky road.

Of course.

"We need to set them out for a few minutes to let them thaw so we can scoop them out easier," I explain.

He raises his eyebrow. "Allow me."

"I will never oppose someone if he can get me ice cream faster. Scoop away." I hand him the ice cream scoop and take down two bowls.

"How much do you want?" he asks as he starts putting my chocolate chip toffee into one bowl.

"How long will it take Dex to get back to us?" I ask.

He gives me a long look. "Do you have a bigger bowl?"

I get out the smallest stainless steel mixing bowl I have. It's twice the size of my regular cereal bowl. "Fill 'er up," I tell him.

He chuckles and proceeds to put darn near the entire quart of ice cream in the bowl. How am I going to eat all of that? I don't know, but I'll try my best.

Simon takes the two bowls and puts them back in the cupboard.

"Hey, what are you doing? Aren't you going to have any ice cream?"

"Which one is your silverware drawer?" he asks as he puts the ice cream scoop into the sink.

I open the drawer. He pulls out two spoons, one he hands to me, the other he puts right into his quart of rocky road ice cream.

"Have I told you how much I like you?" I ask.

"You've intimated it, but you haven't come right out and said it."

I set my bowl down on the counter and stretch up on my toes and kiss his cheek. "I like you very much."

"Enough to trade tastes of ice cream on your couch, and risk cooties?"

I nod. "Yep, I like you that much."

It's easy talking to Trenda. She knows what she can and can't ask about my job, and because of it, I realize just how much I *can* actually talk about. We both commiserate about having to do paperwork, but she agrees that government paperwork has to be the worst, so she gives me extra bites of her ice cream. I tell her that the best part of my job, the actual juice, came from mentoring. I asked her what she liked and didn't like in her job.

"I hate having to sell myself. The best thing in the world is when one of my current clients recommends me to one of their friends and they just want to hire me. Then I don't have to convince them that I'm the right person for the job, they just give me the job. Sending back RFQs is the worst." She takes another dainty bite of ice cream. She is never going to finish that bowl at the rate she's going.

"I can see that," I nod.

"If you like the mentoring so much, why didn't you have kids?"

She really knows how to hit the nail on the head. "Patsy didn't want kids, but that's not what she said before we got married. Before we married, she said she wanted a big family. After we got married, she said she didn't want to have kids with an absentee husband."

Trenda frowns. "Didn't she know about your job? Hadn't you explained it to her?"

"Hell, Trenda, she and I lived together for a year before we got engaged. She knew what she was in for. She just flat-out lied so she could get a ring on her finger."

"Simon, I try very hard not to judge people. I mean, God knows I'm not perfect, and I can be a raging bitch, at least in my head, so I really can't point fingers. But I don't like your ex-wife very much. As a matter of fact, I think I could go as far as to say, I dislike her."

"Pull in those claws, Tiger."

I wipe off the little bit of ice cream on the corner of her mouth and then lick my finger.

Her eyes darken and she shivers. God, she's so responsive.

I want to ask when Bella's next sleepover is when my cellphone buzzes, dammit, and I pick it up. It's Dex Evan's number, and I smile.

"It looks like we only needed to eat a third of a quart of ice cream," I tell Trenda.

"That's your friend? The one like Clint Archer from Drake's team?"

I nod, then answer the phone.

"Hello."

"Hi, Commander."

"It's just Simon these days."

"Okay, just Simon. I want to thank you for giving me

something to work on. The first part was way too simple so I did a little extra digging which was actually fun."

I would put the phone on speaker, but I don't want to do anything that might wake up Bella.

"Do you have information you can email to us? I have Trenda Avery sitting right next to me. I'd put you on speaker, but her daughter is asleep down the hall."

"I know how that goes," Dex laughs. "Yeah, I'll forward everything to her email. It's clear as day that the email came from the widow, but based on what I'm seeing on the will? I'm going to do a couple more checks. The widow isn't the only one with skin in the game. You'll see what I mean. I just hate leaving things unfinished."

"Okay, Dex. Do what you think is best."

"I will probably have something for you in forty-eight to seventy-two hours. I'm going to dive deep."

"Thanks."

"No problem. Like I said, I've been bored."

I don't understand. I read the words on the screen for a fourth time, then turn to Simon.

"Why would he word it that way? How many illegitimate children does he think he has?"

"By the way you described how he reacted when you told him you were pregnant, I think you're the only probable candidate."

"But he hated me. He didn't want me to have the baby. Why would he add that clause into his will? It reads clear as day. Carla gets two hundred and fifty thousand dollars and then the rest of his estate is to be distributed equally amongst all of his remaining children. He doesn't name any names. That's just odd. Seriously, Simon, I might not have finished my paralegal training, but I got close, and leaving that open-ended like that is just not done. Plus, he must have told his lawyer about me or how would he know to contact me otherwise?" Which means Brantley looked me up at some point. I shiver.

Simon is still looking down at the printout.

"What? What are you thinking?" I ask.

"Dex confirmed that Carla sent the emails. But tell me, was she the type of woman who would be coming to Jasper Creek to take pictures of you and Bella?"

I think about it. "Absolutely not. It might ruin her manicure to press a button on her camera."

"Thought so. So, she arranged to have someone take pictures of you. I want Dex to track that down. There's something else I want to tell you. Dex said there were a couple of other things he wanted to check out. If he found anything, he'd let me know."

"What are they?"

"He didn't say. It sounded like he wasn't sure they would pan out, so he was just going to wait to give us something if it did."

I nod. It feels good to have Simon and this Dex guy on my side. "Thanks for calling your friend. I was thinking I'd have to go talk to Mr. Fortnum. I mean, I trust him, but I really didn't want to talk to him about all my dirty laundry. But he might have been somebody who could..." Simon's smiling at me. "I'm babbling again, aren't I?"

"Just a little bit. It's really cute."

"I have never babbled in my life until I met you. You have brought out the babbler in me, and I'm not happy about it."

He bends over me and puts a hand on each of the arms of the kitchen chair. When he opens his mouth to talk, I smell rocky road ice cream. "How about the pouter? Have I brought the pouter out in you? Because if you stick your lower lip out like that, I'm duty bound to kiss it."

"In that case, I'm going to be pouting a lot."

"Hmmm," he hums right before he kisses me. This isn't a soft, getting-to-know-you kiss. This is a kiss that electrifies and sensitizes every nerve and synapse in my brain and body. I yank at his beautiful head of hair, trying to get the kiss to go deeper. I moan when I realize we're not close enough. I try to stand up without losing his mouth.

He takes a nip of my lower lip.

"Ow." That hurt. I pout again.

Simon laughs, then licks over my bottom lip where he gave me a tiny love bite. "What were you trying to do?" he asks.

"You looming over me while I'm sitting in this chair is not conducive to good kissing."

"I know. That's the point. When your daughter comes out of her bedroom because her highly honed daughter senses tell her that her Mama is up to no good, I want us to be able to easily break apart."

"I don't like that." Damn, now I'm whining. Crying, babbling, and whining. This is so not a winning combination.

"Hey, what has you frowning?"

"Nothing."

"Wrong answer," he says as he taps the end of my nose. "Something has you upset, now tell me."

"I am not showing you my best side."

"Like I have?" he asks. "I think I had a meltdown at a restaurant as I told you about my sister, and you had to handle me like you handled Arthur. Does that ring a bell?"

I frown. "No, that doesn't ring a bell in the slightest. You talked about your sister and I listened. I might have asked a question. But you didn't have a meltdown."

"I did, Trenda," he insists.

My hands are still in his hair, and now I move them, kneading the back of his tight neck. I want to say the next words just right. I don't want to hurt his feelings, but I need to be his mirror, too. "Simon, Honey, you just showed some emotion. Some of the uncomfortable ones. You were sad and angry. I promise, it wasn't over the top. But did it feel like that?" I ask quietly.

"Yeah," he whispers.

"Take it from someone who has felt very comfortable having meltdowns in front of you. I'm talking Chernobyl-sized meltdowns. You are just sharing a little bit of your hurt, and I think it is a good thing."

"Mama, can I have a drink of water?"

Simon stands up as he holds back his laughter. I get out of my chair and meet my daughter at the end of the hall.

"Sure you can, Sweet Pea. Come on in the kitchen, and I'll get you one."

Even with tired eyes, she doesn't miss a trick. "Is that a chocolate ice cream spill?"

This time Simon laughs out loud.

Bella turns around. "Oh, hi, Mr. Simon. What are you doing here?"

"I was helping your Mama with some work."

"I thought you were in the Navy. You build websites?"

"I do a lot of things. Your Mama needed my expertise on some other developments."

I watch her forehead scrunch, then smooth out. I hand her a half full glass of water. "Here you go, Love."

She gulps it all down. She *had* been thirsty. "I really needed that. Thank you, Mama." She turns to Simon. "Good luck with the 'velopments. You should come over more often. I think Mama needs lots of help."

I'm afraid to glance over at him, but I do anyway. He

looks about ready to bust a gut, but he restrains from laughing. I roll my eyes.

"Let's get you tucked in." I put my hand on the back of Bella's head and we walk back to her bedroom and I tuck her in for a second time.

"Mr. Simon is really nice. And he knows about dogs. And he knows Uncle Drake. And he's really strong, I saw him lifting things at the rec center. And he's—"

"Enough, Bella. Say goodnight, Sweetheart."

She gives me a huge put-upon sigh.

"Good night, Mama."

I kiss her forehead. At least I know that she comes by her babbling honestly.

Chapter Twenty-Five

"His truck was in your driveway until almost midnight last night. What is that all about?"

I smile. It is the most animated my sister, Chloe, has been since her miscarriage.

"He and I were just talking about Bernie. You know that he's now going to have to be in the hospital longer, don't you?"

"Is it the gout? Zarek told me something about that."

"No, the last round of meds cleared that up. It's his heart. From what I've read up on it, he can do okay with his diagnosis, but according to him, with all he has to give up, there's no point in living."

I wince as soon as those words leave my mouth.

"But I talked to him about everyone who is depending on him. I told him what it was like visiting Azariah. And Bertha giving him the hot and spicy apple chutney. Of course, that just put him into another round of bitching, saying how he couldn't have her preserves anymore."

"Trenda, stop."

"But I'm not done talking about the trip down the

mountain." I want to keep talking. Anything to cover-up my faux pas by bringing up death to Chloe. She's been deeply depressed since her baby's death, and my mouth actually says that some man says there's no point in living.

I am such a dumbass!

"Trenda, I can hear you beating yourself up. You need to stop it."

"Chloe, I can't believe what I just said, it was so thoughtless," I whisper.

"It's okay." Her voice is emphatic. "I'm no longer just trying to pull myself up by my bootstraps. I realized that I needed help, and I started seeing my old counselor, and my physician has put me back on a low dose antidepressant. I've got a ways to go. But at least I'm pretty sure I'm in a tunnel, even though I don't see light, yet."

"What made you change your mind?"

"Zarek." She laughs softly. "Of course, Zarek. It's always Zarek."

"Do you mind me asking what he said?"

"It wasn't what he said, it was how he was doing. I realized that my depression, and me refusing to open up about the miscarriage, was really hurting him. Some of the sessions I'll be setting up will be for both of us, some he'll have on his own."

Chloe makes a choking sound.

"Honey, what is it?"

"It's just that it's tough to realize I hurt him so badly."

"You didn't. It's just that you were both affected by this, and you needed one another's support to heal."

"Yeah, that's what Zoe said. She stopped by. I was kind of scared she might hit me upside my head."

"That's what twins are for," I chuckle.

"She's scary when she's riled," Chloe laughs too. "Of course, nobody has anything on Evie."

"You got that right."

"So back down to business. Zarek told me that Simon isn't a good kisser. And before you make a snarky comment, Zarek heard it from Aaron, who heard it from Pearl who heard it from Florence who heard it from Simon. So, can I squelch the rumor?"

I think about it for a moment. "He must have had a reason for telling Florence he wasn't a good kisser. I would hate to say differently if that's the word he wants out there."

"Ah ha! I knew it. You have empirical evidence that tells you the rumor is *not* true! Ever since the truck sighting I've called Drake every other hour, and he hasn't called me back. I've left a message every time—I have to be annoying the hell out of him—but I don't care. I want to find out what he knows about Simon. Since Simon's Navy, I'm praying Drake knows him."

"That's good thinking, Sis, and everybody in California knows one another too."

"Hey, cut the sarcasm. This is important. My big sister is interested in a man. And, she kissed him. I need to know that he is good enough for her. Zoe wants to know too."

"So, Zoe came all the way from ETSU, and didn't come by to say hi? She even dissed her niece?"

"Yep, she drove the whole half hour over to my place and failed to drop by your place. What are you talking about? You see her all the time."

I sigh. "I guess so. It just feels like besides you, everybody has left."

"And I'm chopped liver?"

"My God, is this the same woman I've been talking to for the last four months?"

There is a long pause. "It is, Trenda, but I'm doing better. Far from good, but better."

I feel tears well in my eyes. "Well, that's good, Chloe."

I'm not going to dwell on it or make a big deal out of it if she's making the right steps. Teasing, however? Teasing is always acceptable if it's kind, and it gets me what I need. "So, if you're doing so much better, do you feel up to doing a sister a solid?"

"Does it involve a truck and getting laid?"

"You *are* back! I'm not sure about the laid part, but I have been promised a trip to third base."

"Then you are definitely getting laid. Is it true he's hot with gray hair?"

"Ooooh yeah."

"So do you want me to pick up Bella from school?"

"Is today too short of notice?"

"Pish. You know it's not. I've been practicing not swearing, but I also have been squirreling away all the one-dollar bills I get in change, just in case."

I laugh. "I don't know why everybody still puts up with her schtick."

"Because she's adorable and we love her. Now go call your man."

"He's not my man."

"Anybody you're rounding bases with better be your man. It is unacceptable for anyone to be just fooling around with my sister; he needs to be thinking for keeps. If he's not, he'll have five angry women on his ass."

I frown. "Seriously, Chloe, we're not getting serious. I'm not sure he even knows what his plans are for the future. So please don't have any expectations. I don't."

Chloe's voice was gentle when she replied. "Okay, I won't. I won't even tell the others about me babysitting so my big sister can get herself some. But Honey, I don't want you to get hurt. You deserve only good things in this life."

"Simon is one of life's good things, even if all I get out of this is one night, okay?"

Liar.

"Okay. Just take care of my big sister's heart for me. Will you?"

"I will."

I cross my fingers.

"I'm going to stop by and pick up what Bella needs for school tomorrow, so that I don't have to interrupt you in the morning, either. Sound good?"

"That sounds great."

"Dex, I let it slide on Saturday because I was with Trenda but tell me who or what you're checking into."

"The older of the two sons, as well as Brantley Harris Sr. I'm checking into the whole clan. I just need another day and I should have what I need."

"I don't want to wait another day. I've thought about it, and I can buy that this woman might call Trenda a sinner, and say something like, stay away, or you'll regret it. I can even believe she'd call her a whore on the next one, but I'm having a tough time believing she'd say that Trenda and her daughter would die if they don't stay away."

"You'd be surprised, Simon. I have to troll the internet, it's part of my job. When people get behind their screen they feel both anonymous, and free and inflated enough to say whatever the hell they want without repercussions. That's a lot of the reason we have such a vile stew out there."

I consider what he's saying.

"Okay, I see your point, but there isn't any damn way that she took a picture of Trenda and Bella when they're here in Jasper Creek and she lives in Nashville."

"She's rich, she pays to have it done," Dex answers.

Again, I consider it. But it still doesn't feel right.

"Why are you checking out the other two sons?" I ask.

"Because they have as much motive as the widow to not want Bella to get her share. I want to find out what kind of life they live, and if anything pops up that makes them plausible suspects for sending the emails."

I relax. "Dex, that's excellent."

"And that's precisely why you're calling, isn't it, Commander? You were going to tell me to do that exact same thing, weren't you?"

I grin. "Yes, I was."

"Captain Hale is going to have a hell of a time finding a replacement for you, Sir."

"Cut that out, I told you to call me Simon."

"Got it. I'll get back to you as fast as I can."

"I appreciate it."

When I get to the rec center, Harvey Sadowski grabs me before I can get to the gymnasium.

"Yeah? Is Arthur acting up? I thought if I got here at six a.m. I'd have three hours of peace," I laugh.

"I wanted to talk to you about Renzo Drakos. Do you have any pull with him?"

"Nope. Why?"

"The man is a machine. Not only does he put in the effort, he can run circles around me when it comes to planning. You know that normally for something like this we should have called in architects and engineers, instead we're going off the original plans. Renzo is making changes on the fly that are genius, and he's doing it in such a way that the inspectors won't notice, but will make the structure stronger."

I frown. This is not good. "Harvey, you should be

getting the plans modified and stamped off by the engineer and then approved by the city."

"Jerry, over at city planning, is going through a divorce. We'd be lucky to get those plans approved by next fall. Renzo has a degree in architectural engineering from University College London. Back in Texas he was working on getting certified to work here in the US, but something sidetracked him, he's not saying what."

"Harvey, get to the point."

"I want to hire him."

"Let me get this straight. You have a guy who has a master's in architectural engineering from a school in London and you think you can tempt him to go to work for you in Jasper Creek, Tennessee?" I can't stop the sarcasm coloring my words.

"Hey, I know it's a bit of a longshot. But my construction company is three generations old, same as Dave Draper's hardware store. I do business all the way into Knoxville, and Nashville is knocking on my door. I can meet or exceed anything Texas might want to pay him; I just need a hook to get him to move to Jasper Creek. That's where you come in. You're looking hooked into this town, so how can we hook *him*?"

"Harvey, I've only had two cups of coffee this morning. Trying to figure out a way to convince a guy I really don't know all that well to change his life's trajectory is too much for me right now. Talk to me tomorrow morning, maybe I might have an idea."

He gives me a toothy grin that I can somehow see underneath the gray beard and mustache. He claps me on the shoulder. "That's the only thing I can ask, Clark. The only thing."

~

I'm dreading turning on my Mac's Safari program, but I need it to pick up some clipart for the final pieces to the website so I need to access the internet. I don't want to see the little envelope icon on my email. I just can't bear to see it. No, no, no. Not today. Today is all Simon.

Today is also about paying bills.

I need to finish this website so I can present it to my client.

I click on the Safari icon. There's mail.

I *have* to open it.

"You don't have to open anything from the AOL user," I tell myself firmly.

I can show restraint...

I can look up the word restraint in the dictionary and start living my life under that definition....yeah, sure, that'll work.

I scan my inbox. The worst email in there is a sale on shoes by my favorite designer. I click on it so the pretty pictures can soothe me.

After I can breathe again, I pull up the stock art catalogue, purchase the clipart that I need, and pump my fist as I complete the website.

I go through every page, making sure that every single hyperlink works, and they do. I keep it in my testbed, so that the customer can't have it go live until payment. I forward them a link to the website in the testbed so they can review.

Normally at a time like this, I would be planning a fancy dinner at the local Burger Barn with Bella. The place has the curly fries that she likes, and peanut shells on the floor, which always makes her giggle. But tonight I'm up for a different kind of celebration.

I get up from my chair and stretch. I really should invest in a chair that doesn't make my back and butt ache. Maybe after the dentist's website is done. That job came in two days ago, and it's a big one.

I pick my phone up off the table and go to the living room and curl up into the corner of my couch. I can't help the smile that must cover half of my face, but I shiver as I remember this is the exact spot where Simon had kissed me when we were on my couch.

I press his number.

"Trenda, hello. How are you?"

"I'm doing really well. No emails and I finished that website I told you about. How about you? Are you making progress on the gymnasium?"

"Yeah, we are. Harvey and his team are doing a great job. So is Renzo."

"I imagine everything is coming together with Arthur coordinating things."

"Oh, I forgot to tell you, we had to send him into Knoxville to find some specific types of hinges that we need right away. If he can't find them there, he'll probably have to go into Nashville."

I bite my lip. "Now it's not like I'm an expert at building things, but I've done my fair share of repairs around the house. Aren't you still at the foundation, framing, and roof point?"

"Yeah," Simon answers me slowly.

"So you're a long way before you're going to get to doors or cabinets, am I right?"

"That's true."

"So, you basically sent him out on a snipe hunt."

"Now, Trenda, a snipe hunt is when you send someone out to hunt for something that doesn't exist. This hinge exists, but you've got to order it from Italy."

"And you have no need of it, right?"

"Maybe." I like the way he answers me, slow and sexy-like.

"Was this your idea?"

"It depends." Again with the sexy sound.

"On what?"

"Whether you will be mad or not."

"Nope, not mad, impressed. I'm going to tuck this little tidbit away for future use."

"So why did you call?" he asks.

"I wanted to invite you over for dinner tonight. Bella is spending the night with her aunt. And Chloe is taking her straight to school tomorrow morning."

There is a long pause. Why?

"How about if I take you to dinner tonight?"

I don't like that idea at all. I want as much alone time with Simon as I can possibly get. How do I say that without sounding like I want his body?

"That's a long pause, Honey. How about if I bring dinner over to your house tonight, so you don't have to cook? And it won't be pizza."

"That would be great." I grin.

"What time do you want me there?"

"The sooner the better."

Shit, I said that out loud!

Simon just chuckles. It's a nice chuckle. It doesn't stop me from turning red as a tomato.

"How about six tonight?" he suggests. "That way I'll be able to place a to-go order and pick it up."

"Okay."

I manage to keep my answer to one word.

"I'll see you tonight, Honey."

"Okay."

His chuckle feels warm and soothing.

"Good-bye Trenda."

Chapter Twenty-Six

I cannot get into the book I'm reading, even though it's one of my favorites. Every time a car drives into our cul-de-sac, I peek out the window. I've been doing that since five-thirty. Since when have my neighbors had such an active social life? I turn on my stereo and start my playlist of soothing and romantic forties music, trying to drown them out.

Another loud car comes into the cul-de-sac and my nails try to draw blood from my e-reader.

It's Monday, they're coming home from work, Girl.

I roll my eyes at myself.

Really, Trenda? You forgot that? Is your mind perhaps on a six-foot-two hunk of man?

I look back down at my reader. Ah, shit, I just turned to the sex part. I can't read this part; I'll jump Simon the moment he comes through the door! I page past the sex, and get to the place where the big misunderstanding happens and they're close to breaking up. If he would only just listen to her. Why won't he let her talk? I'm about ready to throw my e-reader across the room.

I jump when Simon knocks on the door.

I quickly close it down; he doesn't need to see the type of reading material I like. I shove it into the side table drawer, then I rush to the door. I fling it open and smile.

"Trenda, did you even look through your peephole?" He's frowning.

"No. Come on in."

He walks in and looks at my door.

"You need a deadbolt on your front door. Don't you have a sliding glass door to your backyard? What kind of—"

I put two fingers against his lips like he has done to me.

"I did tell you that Bella is sleeping over at my sister's tonight, didn't I?"

Simon looks sheepish. "Yeah, you did."

He turns and closes the door, then holds up bags from my favorite seafood restaurant. "How'd you know about Topmate Fish?"

"I asked Zarek."

"Let's take this into the dining room." The dining room is a little bigger than the kitchen nook, and it's prettier. I'd put out the good plates that my friend Lilah had bought for me when she'd had a bumper crop, along with the tablecloth that I'd picked out with Bella two years ago. That's why it had daisies at the edges. I'd *also* put out the pretty crystal candlesticks that Piper had given me when she'd been twelve, but I had *not* put any candles in them' that would have been too over the top.

"Since you bought the food, let me plate it." I offer.

"How about we both do it?" he suggests as he walks with me to the kitchen.

We were soon in the dining room eating jumbo tempura prawns with asparagus and wild mushrooms along with jasmine fried rice. That was after finishing off the mussels roasted with orange tarragon butter. It was all succulent.

"You have good taste, Trenda Avery. This is really good food, and I live in Virginia, where we get fresh seafood."

"Yeah, the brothers who own this place have things flown in fresh every day. That's why you had to sell a kidney to purchase this meal. You actually are looking pretty good for someone who's missing an organ," I tease.

"I'm willing to give them part of my liver for their Australian lobster tail," he teases in return.

I laugh. "I tell you what. Next time, I'll buy."

"You can try," he says, but even though he's smiling I get the feeling I'll always lose this argument.

"What kind of wine would have gone well with this?" I ask, even thought we'd both had beer with dinner.

"Actually I'm more of a beer guy. I did live in California for a while, so I can tell you it would be a white, maybe a Sauvignon Blanc, but I prefer a beer."

"I'm a beer or a sweet tea kind of girl. Emphasis on the sweet. That's why wine has never really done it for me."

I lean over to pick up his empty plate, but he stills my hand. "I've got it."

"No, the rule is, he who cooks gets to sit out while the other person does the dishes."

"I get that, but what you don't understand is, I want to spend as much time, and as close to you, as possible."

My hand trembles as I pull it back to rest in my lap.

"Isn't that how you feel, Trenda?"

I nod. He picks up his plate, and I pick up mine. He follows me into my kitchen. It's like I'm sleepwalking as I rinse the plate then put it into the dishwasher. He does the same thing. Our bodies are so close in front of the sink I'm worried I'll never be able to breathe again.

Simon closes the dishwasher and cocks his head.

"I like this song."

I listen. It's Ella singing.

Bewitched, Bothered and Bewildered.

He turns off the overhead light, so that only the light above the stove is shining. I give him a funny look, until he puts his right hand on my waist and holds up his left hand. I put my hand into Simon's and he smiles down at me.

He steps forward, and I step back in perfect harmony. Suddenly I'm transported back to Granny Laughton's parlor, but with Simon. This is not the kind of dancing I've seen when I've volunteered as a chaperone at the high school dances, this is proper ballroom dancing, where he twirls me out and I grin, and then he pulls me back in close and we're breast to chest. Now *that* was never done at Granny's.

As he's bewitching me around my kitchen in the semi-darkness I admit to myself that even though I told Chloe I don't have any expectations, I sure have wants and dreams. I've fallen for this man, and this dance has clenched it.

He spins me out, and we whirl around. My linoleum floor becomes a marble ballroom, the moonlight from the kitchen window tints his face in magic. Another revolution around the room and I'm bewitched. We are pressed against one another so my head rests against his heart and I'm beguiled. Every move he makes has me shivering like a child again. When he dips me over his arm as the song finishes and smiles down at me, I can barely breathe.

"I want nothing to shatter this moment. Nothing will ever be better than this."

"Yes, it will, Baby."

Simon pulls me up and kisses me and once again I'm floating on clouds. He gives me no choice but to follow him wherever he wants to take me. He lifts me up. "Are you sure about this?" he asks me.

"If you don't," I kiss him on his chin.

"Intend to make," I kiss him under his ear.

"A homerun after all this," I kiss him on the side of his mouth.

"Then get the hell out of my house," I kiss him on his mouth and linger.

I taste his laughter.

~

I swiftly look around her bedroom. She'd left the bedside lamp on. I would bet my bottom dollar that's the only light she wants on tonight. She blew me away tonight when she opened the door and was wearing a dress. Trenda has the curves to carry off a sweater dress more than any woman I have ever met.

Am I biased?

Maybe.

Do I give a damn?

Hell no!

She's in front of me and she starts toward the bed. That's another hell no. Two strides and I'm in front of her.

"I forgot something," I say.

She looks up at me, confused.

"At the end of the dance, the guy gets a kiss. It's a rule."

Her lips twitch. "I chaperone high school dances. That is not a rule, trust me."

"Ahhh," I pull both of her arms up and wrap them around my neck. "That's the problem. You're basing your rules on the wrong sources. You need to be basing them off of some of the dance clubs in Paris, then you'd know they end in a kiss."

"Paris?" Her voice is breathless.

"Paris." I nod. I put my knuckles under her chin and start with a soft and fleeting kiss. Then lift my head back up to look at her beautiful face. She opens her eyes and frowns.

I wait. She smiles, then drives her fingers through my hair, and I even feel the sting of her nails in my scalp. She thinks she's forcing me to kiss her, when in actuality she's fallen into my trap.

Kissing Trenda is like a journey. There is the physical pleasure of feeling her plump lips against mine, tangling my tongue with hers, the euphoria I get when I feel her melt into my arms. And then I can feel her breasts, soft and full, pillowed against my chest. My hand roams upwards and encircles her neck so that I can feel the hummingbird flutter of her pulse.

But there's more than that. I am no longer part of the here and now; I'm in the past where she and I have met before, and in the future where Trenda and I will live again.

When she moans, I gather her even closer, and then she shudders. I feel her knees give out as her weight shifts to me.

Perfect.

I lift her up and place her on top of the blue comforter with the mandala designs and stroke the back of my knuckles against her jaw.

"You look beautiful, Trenda. Your hair strewn across your pillow, your arms reaching for me. I want to savor this moment."

She blinks rapidly, and I realize she's holding back tears.

"Trenda?"

"I'm fine," she assures me. "What you said, it made me happy. It's because of you. You make me feel beautiful."

I want to be the man who is in her life every single day, telling her that she is beautiful, making sure she feels it, knows it, believes it.

I've travelled the world enough, and lately I've been in my own head and heart enough to know that I'm in love with Trenda Avery. And I'm in love with her daughter.

Who wouldn't be?

But until I know for damn sure what my plans are, where I'm going to land and what I'm going to do, I am not going to make any commitments to this woman, and telling her I love her is a commitment.

"Simon?"

"Hmm?"

"It seemed like I lost you for a minute."

"Just trying to figure out how to get you out of this dress. I didn't see a zipper on the back."

She grins. It's a temptress's smile. "This is one you pull over your head and shimmy it on down until it's kind of plastered on your body."

"Does it come in other colors?" I ask.

"I'm pretty sure," she answers. "Why?"

"I'm going to go to the store and get all the other colors and watch you shimmy into each one of them. Instead of a fashion show, it'll be a shimmy show."

She giggles.

I lie down beside her, propping myself up on my elbow so that we're nose to nose. My other hand is resting at the hem of her dress. I watch as she bites her lower lip. I'd noticed at dinner that the nails on both of her thumbs were bitten down to the quick. She's had a lot of shit piled on her lately. Is this really the right time for—

"Stop it," she whispers loudly. "I can almost hear the gears grinding in your head right now."

I frown at her. "Oh yeah? What are my gears grinding about?"

"You're thinking, for some unknown reason only known to men who are uber overprotective, that you might be taking advantage of me."

Am I blushing?

"Maybe," I mutter.

"Well stop it. I'm the one who told you I wanted third

base the other night. I'm the one who, less than twenty minutes ago told you I wanted a home run, and now you think you're taking advantage of me? What is it about me that's made you think I don't know my own mind?"

I chuckle. "Point taken." I gather her up so that she's now lying on top of me. One of my hands is under her dress and cupping her ass, the other is tangled in her hair.

Trenda's eyes are closed with a blissful smile on her face. She's happy.

I pull her down and kiss her for long moments, then slowly roll us over and laugh as she starts the shimmy process and her skirt is now above her hips. I kneel up.

"You want this off?"

"Only if you take off your shirt off first," she murmurs.

I pull my shirt off over my head, not bothering to unbutton it. I watch as her hands reach for me, but I stop her. Instead, I tug at her dress and pull her up into a sitting position.

Swoosh.

I throw her dress over my shoulder so that it lands somewhere next to my forgotten shirt. Who cares where, because now I'm looking at black lace adorning lush, creamy skin. She reaches for me again, and I love the thought of her wanting me so badly, but she doesn't get a turn quite yet. I gently grab her wrists and hold them on either side of her head, intending to kiss and nibble my way down to her breasts, but when I see her shining, parted lips, I have to kiss her again.

As she parts her lips and thrusts her tongue into my mouth, my cock feels like it's going to hammer its way out of my jeans. I pull away just enough to nip her bottom lip. Based on her low moan, I'd say she likes it.

I kiss her chin, then continue down until I finally get to

suckle that rapidly beating pulse on her neck, and feel it flutter against my tongue. She arches against me.

I continue my journey down her body, until I arrive at her sumptuous breasts that are displayed just for me, in the black lace and satin. I lick along the ribbon of satin, and she shivers. I do it again on the other side. Back and forth, she smells so good, and her skin is as soft as the petal of a flower.

I let one of her hands go so I can pull back the cups of her bra and mold her breast in my hand. So warm. Her nipple is a tight velvet nub that scrapes against my palm, and I look at its twin, and can't resist suckling it.

"Simon," she cries out as my mouth tightens around the taut tip, my tongue swirling around and around, bringing her deeper into my mouth. If my mouth weren't so busy, I would have grinned as I feel her fingernails digging into my scalp. Her legs are restless, until they finally find the right position, lying on either side of my thighs.

I let go of her other hand, and mold both breasts so that I can more easily see her naked beauty on display, just for me. She jolts, and I look up, wanting to see her expression. Even with both hands now tangled in my too-long hair, she gives me only a fleeting, shy glance.

Words.

She needs words, Clark.

"You are gorgeous, Trenda." Her eyes meet mine. "I don't know why I've been so blessed to get this moment with you, but I thank God for it."

It's true.

I can't remember a more sublime moment in my life.

She opens her mouth to say something, but I cut her off with a kiss. When I'm done, I continue to talk. "There's never been a woman that I've wanted more than you."

She stills beneath me. Her brown eyes dominate her face. I know her question before she asks it.

"It's the truth. I'm never going to lie to you when we're in our bed together. And whenever we're together it is *our* bed."

Those words popped out without my permission. I'm still not ready to tell her I love her. I want to be sure I can follow through on the level of commitment that those words would imply. But I needed her to know—soul deep—how much this moment means to me.

"Do you understand?" I ask.

"You're right, Simon. This is our bed." She tries to twine her arms around my neck, but I don't let her; instead I move downward. I kiss her sternum, then her belly button, and soon am licking above the satin ribbon along the top of her panties.

I hook my fingers and pull the panties off her hips, down her legs, then throw them over my shoulder onto an ever-increasing pile of clothes. I push her legs wider and look at her glistening sex. Seeing her pink folds part open for me makes me feel powerful and weak. I'm the conqueror and the conquered.

"Are you—"

"I need you, Trenda," I interrupt whatever she was going to say. "Give me this," I sigh right before my thumbs part her flesh even more, so that my tongue can gently swipe from her entrance that beckons me, upwards to that little bundle of nerves that invites me to play.

Again, I feel another jolt go through her body as I lick, suckle, feast and nibble. Now Trenda is digging her nails into my scalp again and her heel is pressing deeply into my back.

"Too much," she gasps.

If she can still form words, it's not enough.

I thrust a finger inside her sheath. She wails softly. I release her swollen bud so I can look up at her.

Is she okay?

Her head is shaking back and forth on her pillow, a radiant expression on her face. She's more than okay. I dip back down and start my very serious play, a smile on my lips right before I suckle her clitoris. This time when she wails, I know to keep going.

I thrust two fingers inside her body and curve them, rasping them within her tight channel until she shrieks. Then I lightly scrape my teeth against her swollen knot and she arches up against my face and hands, yelling for me to stop. Yelling for me to keep going. Then not yelling at all.

I kiss my way up her body, until we are side by side. We are both breathing hard.

I look at her beautiful face, trace the line and dips, then smile as I feel her fingernails scrape against the front of my jeans.

"Are you looking for trouble?" I ask.

"Oh yeah."

Chapter Twenty-Seven

I am wiped out. Part of me feels like I'll never be able to move again, but the other part of me feels like I could party all night during Mardi Gras. I go with the part that feels energetic, because there isn't a chance in hell I'm not going to make love with Simon Clark.

Simon grabs my wandering hand. "What kind of trouble are you looking for?" he asks.

"The kind that gets you out of your jeans and underwear."

"I'm not wearing underwear."

I look at him and remember the 'no lying in bed' promise.

"Prove it," I purr.

He gets up off the bed and reaches into his pocket. He pulls out condoms and puts them onto my nightstand. Then he unbuttons his jeans and I get the first look at his cock. My heart starts beating faster. I can feel it. If they ever had beauty pageants for penises, his would win.

So long.

So thick.

So straight.

He must have taken off his shoes when he'd come into the bedroom earlier, because when he takes off his jeans he is completely naked. He gives me a little bit of a gloating look, but I don't blame him. The man has a whole hell of a lot to gloat about.

He kneels on the bed and I wrap my fingers around the stalk of his erection. He feels hard, yet velvety smooth.

"Baby, don't. I don't have the control right now."

When I can bring myself to stop looking at his penis and look into his face I can see him gritting his teeth. I let go and kneel up so I can put my hands on his shoulders. "Can we fuck now?"

"Trenda, we're never going to fuck, we're always going to be making love."

I'd heard Chloe and Evie talking and I know some things. I lift up, my breasts scraping against his chest hair as I whisper into his ear. "I definitely want to make love with you..." I just barely stop myself from saying forever.

"Good," he whispers back.

"But," I start talking again with a smile in my voice. "I definitely want to try the whole fucking thing at least once."

Simon bursts out laughing and hauls me even tighter to his body. "You are something else, Trenda Avery."

He lowers me back down onto the bed, and pulls a condom off the nightstand. My mouth goes dry just watching as he covers himself. At that moment I realize his fingers had been a tight fit, and I try to picture his cock inside me.

He gives me an indulgent smile, and caresses me, shoulder to hip. I undulate under his touch, every part of my body seeking him, wanting that connection. He stretches down on top of me, and I breathe a sigh of relief. So good. His weight feels so good. It's as if his body has me enclosed and sheltered. Even as all of my nerve endings are crying out for release, I also feel safer than I have ever felt in my life.

I wrap my arms around his waist. He pulls up, placing one hand against my jaw, his thumb brushing my lower lip.

"The things you make me feel." He shakes his head. "You're beyond my wildest dreams."

It's then I realize that his hand is shaking just the slightest little bit.

"You're the dream I didn't know I had," I whisper back.

I feel his cock begin to press against my entrance. Stretching me. It stings just a little, but there are a lot more good feelings to offset the slight bit of pain as he delves deeper. He pauses. I see him searching my face and that has to stop. I pull up my knees and arch my pelvis. Simon shudders and plunges even deeper. So deep that soon our hips meet. I have never felt so full in my life. Again, he stays still.

"Move, dammit," I demand.

"Give it time, Love."

The word love barely registers, I'm too immersed in sensation. If he doesn't start moving and assuage the ache he has created I'm going to go up in flames.

"Please, Simon. I need you to move." I lift up and bite his shoulder.

Hard.

His laugh is sharp and hoarse. Is he mad? I don't care, because now he's started to move. He thrusts, and I arch. Is it moments, or is it an eternity that we move in a rhythm that only nature understands?

On and on I breathe and feel Simon. I let myself drown in the flashes of pleasure as he takes me to a place I've never felt before. Then everything narrows to an urgent pinpoint as I try to grasp something great. Something momentous.

"It's okay, I've got you," I hear him whisper.

His hand moves between us.

I'm flying.

I soar.

I roll over, trying to block out the sun so I can burrow in for a little bit more sleep with Trenda in my arms.

The sun?

Wait a damn minute.

I move slowly so that I don't disturb Trenda, then reach over to the nightstand that is now empty of condoms but does have my phone. I pick it up.

Holy fuck!

It's oh seven hundred.

How in the hell did that happen? Even after I'd tried to drink my weight in Jack Daniels the other night I'd gotten up at oh five hundred, but this morning I've slept in two hours? I roll over and look at Trenda who, even now, is snuggling back up against me. I pull her close and sigh with contentment.

That's another thing. I'd been married for seven years and I did *not* do snuggling. I'd tried it in the beginning, but I liked my space. I'd always figured it was because I'd gotten married in my late twenties so having my space in bed was just ingrained in me.

Guess not.

With Trenda Avery, I was all onboard with snuggling.

An old dog can learn new tricks.

The sunlight brings out the auburn highlights in her hair, and I trace my fingers over her soft cheek, careful not to wake her. I have never met any woman who I connect with on so many different levels. I stroke her cheek again and she smiles in her sleep.

I'm going to need to get my head screwed on straight mighty quick. First, I need to make sure that she isn't serious about leaving town. Then I have to figure out what in the hell I'm going to do with myself if I stay here in town. Working for Harvey or Dave don't sound like good options, nor does finding a cabin up on the mountain. Granted, I am enjoying time getting the rec center rebuilt, but that's not something that is really using a lot of my brain cells. It might if I have to do the plumbing, but I'm going to be too smart to get involved with that shit. That's a new trick I don't want to learn.

I feel Trenda's breathing change.

"You waking up?" I ask.

"You have a good reason for me to wake up?" she responds.

"I made dinner. I was hoping you would offer to make breakfast."

"You like breakfast? I thought you lived on coffee," she teases.

She starts to roll out of my arms, but I'm not having any of it. "Where do you think you're going?"

"I'm going to get up and start the coffee."

"I just thought of something better for us to do with our time."

I grin as I read the glowing response from my client. He's thrilled with everything I've done. There is not one single change that he wants to make on the website. He tells me to bill him an extra fifteen percent since I was done two weeks earlier than anticipated and he wants to sign a two-year maintenance contract with me. Normally this would have me walking on cloud nine, but that's hard to do when you start out the day walking on cloud number four hundred.

It was hard seeing Simon go, but I need to get back to things before Bella comes home. Of course, he'd stayed with me as I'd opened my email to make sure there was nothing more from the evil AOL account. He was going to go visit Bernie again, give him updates on Vincent Marsh and Adelaide Winters, since he'd had to give them their supplies three days after the ice storm.

I'm pretty sure he's visiting Bernie just to keep his spirits up. I want him to find out who the lady friend is that took Bernie into the doctor for his gout in the first place. It seems to me she's fallen off the face of the earth. I want to know if Bernie kicked her to the curb as soon as he got a scary diagnosis because he didn't want to burden the little lady.

Such a typical man thing to do.

My phone rings. I look down and see it's Chloe again. Sometimes it sucks having another sister with flexible work hours—it means they can stalk you. I pick up this time, otherwise she'll be coming over, probably in Zarek's Jeep with Slayer riding shotgun.

"Hello," I answer. "Don't you have a patient you need to be bending in some godawful way to make them feel better?"

"I've told you a thousand times, that's not how physical therapy works. But even if I did have a patient, I would have called you before the session or after the session." There was a pause. "Oh wait. I did. You didn't answer."

"I've been busy. I finished that big job I told you about, the client is real—"

"Horsefeathers. If you think I'm calling about your job —or my job—you are out of your mind. You tell me in minute details exactly how it went with you and the silver-haired God last night. I mean, this man even went to the trouble of finding out what your favorite restaurant was."

My eyes glaze over just thinking about it.

"I don't think I can possibly ever explain it, Chloe."

She doesn't say anything for a long time.

"Does he make you happy?"

"He makes me feel beautiful. He makes me feel…" I have to stop talking. I'd been so happy this morning. I still am. But my emotions are overwhelming. "Chloe, it feels like I'm safe with him."

"And for an Avery girl, that's the best praise in the world," she whispers.

"Yeah," I sigh. "But I don't know what he's planning to do with his life. I'm trying to be logical."

Again, I was met by silence.

"Chloe? You there?"

"Trenda? Can I give you some advice that you once gave me years ago?"

I think back to when Zarek first stormed back into her life, and how much she resisted.

"Yeah, hit me with it."

"Take the good moments God gives you, and hold them tight. It's all you can do."

"God, I sounded really sanctimonious."

"No, you sounded like my wise big sister. I love you, Trenda."

"Love you, Chloe."

∼

I can't wait to pick up Bella. She encompasses so many of my life's precious moments, and it always kills me to be away from her overnight, even to be with Simon. Today was gerbil day, which had a big red circle on our calendar for the last month. Bella is going to be able to take Apollo, the gerbil from school, home tonight and babysit him. I've already been given all of the instructions by her teacher on what I need to make Apollo comfortable.

When Ronnie's mom, Georgia Draper, found out it was Bella's day with the gerbil, she told me that if there were any problems to not worry. She had an *in* at the pet store. They'd replaced Apollo three times already this school year, so all I had to do was call her, and she would have them open up the pet store early so I could get a replacement Apollo.

I know I should probably be appalled, but instead I am very grateful to have a back-up if needed. Not that I wouldn't be willing to step up and say there was a problem, but I don't want Bella to go through elementary school known as the gerbil killer.

When I get to the school, I park my SUV instead of waiting up front like I normally would. I head to her classroom. Bella is one of the last kids in the class. She's talking to her teacher, Mrs. Stapleton.

"Mama! Look, it's Apollo! He's coming home with us."

I weave between the desks and stand next to her as her teacher puts Apollo into his 'travelling' cage.

"Do you have any other questions, Bella?"

"Are you sure he won't want ice cream? I mean, if he eats all of his salad, I think he deserves dessert."

"It's not good for his digestive system. Just give him the food on the list."

Mrs. Stapleton explains things really well for Bella. She puts up with my girl's flights of fancy, and never gets impatient.

"How are you doing?" Mrs. Stapleton asks me. "I hear you had quite the adventure."

"Uhhh."

She frowns at me when I don't answer her.

"Getting Luther and Violet to the hospital during that ice storm couldn't have been easy."

That *adventure. Get a grip, Trenda.*

"Yeah, that was something else," I agree, trying to keep the amusement out of my voice. "Is there anything else we need to know before we take Apollo home with us?"

"Do you have any pets?"

"No. Mama said not right now, maybe when I'm older. I want a dog like Aunt Chloe's and Uncle Zarek's. His name is Slayer."

"I think a gerbil is enough for now, Sweet Pea." I look up at her teacher. "So, anything else?"

"Did you talk to Georgia Draper?" she asks with a twinkle in her eye.

"Uhm," I look down at Bella who is looking up at the two of us with her big ears wide open. "I did talk to her, but hopefully her instructions won't be necessary."

"Unfortunately, they've been more helpful than I would have thought. This is my last year having gerbil sleepovers. I've heard turtles are a much better way to go."

"Good to know."

She hands me Apollo's travelling cage, and Bella and I head out to the parking lot.

"Why did you have to talk to Ronnie's mom?" Bella asks.

"She had an interesting idea she wanted to run by me." Before she could get in a follow-up question, I ask her if she would like to get a vanilla latte. It's worth going against my better judgement just so I don't have to lie about my conversation with Georgia.

By the time Bella and Apollo are buckled in, I'm ready to head to town. The streets are clear now, which makes driving so much easier. I hit my blinker to go right down the two-lane highway that will take me into Jasper Creek proper.

"Hey, Mama?"

I look in the rearview mirror and see Bella swinging her legs in her booster seat. Then I quickly look back at the road.

"Yes, Baby?"

"Could Slayer have a sleepover at our house some time, like Apollo is?"

"I think it's best if we go visit him. He'd miss Chloe and Zarek too much if we brought him to our house."

"But Mooommmm," Bella starts to whine.

I glance in the rearview mirror again and see her face getting flushed. I look back at the road. I have lucked out with my kid; she's normally so upbeat, but if she gets overtired, or wound-up she can have a meltdown just like her mother.

"Bella, let's talk about this when we get home. We need to make sure that Apollo is co—"

"No!" I scream, as I slam on my brakes and wrench the wheel to the right.

I hear my baby's screams as metal shrieks and my car buckles and lurches to a stop.

"Apollo!"

"Bella!"

"Mama, Apollo's dead."

The airbag has deployed and I can't see anything. I fight against it, desperate to get to my baby. "Are you all right?"

"Help me!" my baby cries.

I have to get to her.

My brain starts spinning at supersonic speed, and I reach over to the middle console and dig for my nail file. I stab and stab and stab at the airbag until it starts deflating.

"Mama! I have to help Apollo."

I can see a car coming up behind me and another one coming at us. It looks like one of Aaron's nursery trucks.

Who hit us?

I glance over at Bella. She's messing with her seatbelt.

The car from behind isn't slowing down to help us. They're speeding up, and heading directly for us!

"Don't touch your seatbelt!" I yell. "Leave it on!"

I hear someone laying on their horn. I struggle to get over the seat to protect Bella as the car behind us comes closer but I can't move. At the last moment, it turns and whizzes by.

Gravel flies as Aaron's truck screeches to a stop in front of my SUV.

"Trenda!"

I hear the yelling, but I ignore it as I start crying. I can't get unhooked from my seatbelt. The airbag and steering wheel have me locked in place. I try to keep my shit together, even though all I want to do is sob.

"It's okay, Bella."

"Mama! I need you."

My heart is breaking.

Get your shit together!

"It's going to be fine, Baby."

Someone yanks my door open.

"Trenda. My God, are you okay?"

I don't recognize the voice, or the face. I fumble with my fingernail file.

"It's me, Renzo Drakos, Simon's friend."

I slump with relief.

"Renzo, get Bella out of the backseat. Make sure she's okay, then we can worry about me."

I watch as Bella's door is opened and Renzo's concerned expression turns into a smile for my daughter. "Well hello, Miss Bella," he says, exaggerating his Spanish accent. "How are you today? You sure seem to have gotten into a fix. Did your mom let you try to drive the car today?"

Bless the man's heart, I hear my daughter give a giggle.

"It's gerbil day today," she whispers. "Can you get Apollo? He's over there." I watch her point to someplace I can't see. Renzo leans past Bella and lifts the gerbil's cage up high. "Your mom let him drive?" he asked incredulously.

"You're silly." Bella really giggled.

"Why don't you stay right here, and I'll get your mom unstuck. How does that sound?" He puts the cage in Bella's lap.

"Okay. Thank you, Sir."

"No problem Cariña."

I watch as he carefully shuts her door as best he can. He can't close it all the way because of the damage that has been done to my vehicle. Thank God I always have her sit on the opposite side as me so I can see her easier, otherwise she could have been badly injured. I start to shake.

"Trenda?"

Renzo's by my side. "Let's get you out of here, okay?"

"Did you see what happened?" I ask him.

"Yeah, I did. They were aiming to run you off the road into that tree over there." He points to the big black oak.

My teeth are chattering, and even as he gets me standing by the side of the road, I feel like my knees are made of water.

"I need to get to Bella."

"You sit in the backseat with her. I'm going to call the sheriff. I'll also call your brother-in-law."

"Can you grab my cell phone too?" I ask as I pull open the door to the back seat.

"Look, Mama, Apollo had fun. Even though it was really, really, scary, he wasn't scared at all." She puts down his cage and reaches for me. "Were you scared, Mama?"

"I was so scared. I'm always scared when I think something could hurt you. I love you all the way to the stars."

"I love you too, Mama. You don't have to be scared, cause I'm here."

I feel the cool air as Renzo opens the door. "Here's your purse, Trenda."

"Thanks, Renzo."

He shuts the door.

I rifle through my purse until I find my cell phone. I press Simon's number.

"Hello, Trenda." His voice sounds so warm and safe. I bite my lip so hard that I taste blood.

"Trenda?"

"I was driving Bella home from school. Someone drove us off the road. Renzo thinks the driver was trying to make us hit a big black oak. When that didn't work, they turned around to try again."

"Is Renzo with you now?"

"Yes."

"Anyone else?"

"He's calling the sheriff and Zarek."

"Good. I'll be there as soon as I can. Are you on LaMars Hwy?"

"Just after the turnoff from Brookline."

"Got it."

Chapter Twenty-Eight

I lean against the fireplace mantle, next to Renzo with the big dog, watching everything that is going on.

"It's called the Avery Avalanche," Zarek says as he offers me and Renzo bottles of water. Then he puts a bowl of water down for his dog named Slayer. None of us are drinking anything that might impair our cognitive abilities. Trenda's front door opens, and two more people enter her house without knocking. I go over and lock the door after they step in. The dog follows me.

I recognize another Avery sister, even though I haven't met her before. She's smaller than Trenda, and Chloe and Zoe who are already here. When I see the tall blond man who follows her into the house, I know this must be Evie Avery O'Malley.

Aiden O'Malley does a swift scan around the room, his eyes missing nothing. It surprises me that he's here, but Drake isn't, since they're both stationed in Southern California. I look at my watch. Actually, it makes no sense that Evie and Aiden could have made it here from Southern

California in the three and a half hours since Trenda and Bella were run off the road.

"Uncle Aiden!" Bella screeches as she launches herself off the couch into his arms. The hard-eyed operator I had just watched walk in the door is gone, and in his place is a doting uncle. Soon Bella is hanging down his back as he holds her by her knees, causing her to laugh uproariously.

Zarek, Renzo, and I look at one another and smile. Bella has been acting rather subdued since coming home, so this is good to see.

We're close enough to see and hear the action, but far enough away that we're not drawn into the mix, which makes both of us very happy.

"What do you mean she hasn't told you what's going on?" Evie practically roars. She might be little, but nobody could miss the anger rolling off her.

"Evie. Stop it this instant. What right do you have to come barging in here and yelling at Zoe and Chloe because I, apparently, have not provided them with enough information to tell you? That's just rude. So, calm your ass down, and have a seat."

The woman continues to stand over the other three sisters, her hands crossed over her chest. "I am not going to calm my ass down. You tell me what is going on, right now. I have been on a small plane from Texas for the last two and a half hours, and you know I hate small planes. So, tell me what's going on, and when Drake is going to be here."

Again, Zarek, Renzo, and I trade glances. This is not sounding good. Talk about too many chefs in the kitchen. As soon as I think that, I realize Bella is no longer laughing. I turn around and see that even though she's on her uncle's shoulders, her attention is riveted on her Aunt Evie.

"Why are you mad at my Mama, Aunt Evie?"

"I need a kiss, Baby Girl." Evie walks over to where Aiden is holding Bella and he stoops down so that Evie can kiss her niece. "Now, that's better. I'm not mad at your Mama, I'm just worried because you were in an accident. You know I get scared."

"Mama says that the louder you yell, the more scareder you are."

Bella starts bouncing on Aiden's shoulders because he's laughing. Evie glares at her husband, then turns around and gives her older sister the evil eye.

"Just telling it the way I see it." Trenda shrugs.

"And the way I see it, you're keeping us in the dark. Now tell us what is going on. According to what you said to the police, you don't think this is an accident. Who do you think is trying to kill you?"

"Evie!"

"Evie!"

"Evalyn Lavender! You come with me into the kitchen right this minute," Trenda said as she shot up off the sofa.

"Mama, where are you going? You're not going to leave me, are you?"

I watch Trenda's distress as she tries to figure out how to take Evie to task, and comfort Bella at the same time.

"Zarek," I say quietly. "Do you think you, Chloe, and Slayer can entertain Bella in the yard, where she can still see her mom here in the living room?"

"Done deal. Let me get Chloe and Trenda onboard."

He weaves between Zoe and Chloe and then puts his hand on Trenda's shoulder. He whispers into her ear. She nods. She gives Evie a glare, then walks over to Aiden. "Bella, I'm not going to leave you, I promise."

The little spitfire's lower lip is trembling. I can see her trying to be stoic, she's been through too much.

"Can you go get Apollo for me?" Trenda asks her daughter.

Sneaky. My woman is sneaky.

Bella gives her a wobbly smile, then runs down the hall.

She comes running back, that damn cage banging back and forth against her knee as she runs. Poor little guy has to be getting motion sick.

"I've got 'im."

"I think he needs some playtime outside. But, you can't take him out of his cage, else he'll run away."

"He needs a treat like we had, Mama. We got ice cream. What should Apollo get?"

"I'll go find something in the fridge, Bella." Zoe shoots up off the couch.

"In the meantime, I need you to be a big girl for me. I promise I won't go someplace you can't see me, but I need you to go out into the yard with Aunt Chloe and Uncle Zarek and Slayer and Apollo. You know how Slayer needs his outside time, well so does Apollo."

Bella gives her a long look, then she turns her head and looks at her Aunt Evie. She turns back to look at Trenda. "You don't want me to listen, right?"

Trenda crouches down and looks her daughter in the eye. "You're right, I want to talk to Aunt Evie about some things that I'll tell you about when you're older. But right now it's private between me and her. Can you respect that?"

Bella looks back over at Evie. "She's wrong, isn't she, Mama? Nobody's trying to kill you are they?"

"She is wrong. She—"

"Of course I'm wrong," Evie says as she kneels down in front of the little girl. "I just get so crazy scared about things that my mouth runs away with itself, and then I make everybody else around me scared."

"Is that why you had to marry Uncle Aiden, so you wouldn't be scared no more?"

I hear soft giggles, and watch Zoe and Chloe doing their best not to burst out laughing.

"That's right, Bella. Your aunt gets scared really easy, so she needs me to protect her." Aiden smiles down at the little girl.

Oh, he's not getting any for at least a week if Evie's expression is anything to go by.

"Okay, Mama, I'll go play outside, but you promise I can see you?"

"Yes, I promise."

~

"I'm so sorry, Trenda. I can't believe that came out of my mouth in front of Bella. Please forgive me."

"You're forgiven... for that. I know you weren't thinking. But you're not forgiven for coming into my home and acting like you can demand answers about something you know nothing about, and treat me and your other two sisters like crap. That is not acceptable. What the hell, Evie?"

My armor-plated sister's eyes well with tears.

Holy hell.

"You're so right. I was so out of line."

I watch as Aiden's arms come around her and pull her back against his front. She melts into him, allowing him to give her comfort.

Zoe is to the right of me, and I can feel her befuddlement as well. I normally would not come on as strong to any of my other sisters, but full-on force is usually needed to get through Evie's thick skull. Now I feel like I've just kicked a kitten.

"Trenda, can you tell us what's going on?" Aiden asks.

I can feel Simon coming up behind me, I don't know how, but I can. "I can't prove anything, but I've had some threatening emails, and Simon has been doing what he can to have them checked out."

"Threatening how?" Zoe asks.

"Why?" Evie's question comes at the same time Zoe's does.

"Bella's father recently passed away. She's been named as a beneficiary. It looks like one of the other beneficiaries does not want to share."

"Who are they?" Evie demands to know. She's no longer leaning on Aiden; now he's holding her back. "Have you talked to them?"

"When was the reading of the will?" Zoe queries. "What did they say then? How did they seem?"

I look over my shoulder to Simon for help. I didn't want to tell my sisters everything. I just didn't. He steps closer and puts his hand around my waist and I immediately breathe easier. "Evie, this is Simon Clark. He's retired from the Navy. He used to be Aiden and Drake's commander. He's been living here for almost four months now, and he's been helping me with this."

Evie's gaze switches from me, to Simon, to his hand, to Simon, to me again. "What have you found out?" she asks Simon. "Are they going to come after Trenda and Bella again?"

"I should be getting a call from Dex Evans in another couple of hours. He's checking into the other beneficiaries. He's been investigating them for the last seventy-two hours."

"What's taking him so long?" Evie demands again. "You should have talked to Clint."

I wince. My sister is not known for her tact and diplomacy.

"Dex will get the job done," Simon says. His tone is velvet-covered steel. By the look on Evie's face, even she knows enough to back down.

"In the meantime, until this is all settled, Trenda and Bella need a new place to stay."

"She can stay with us," Evie immediately states. "Our place is a fortress."

"It can also be traced to you. I don't want any place that can be connected to a member of Trenda's family." He squeezes my waist and I look up to meet his gaze.

"What?" I ask.

"Bella can't go to school until this is settled. They knew your schedule; they knew that you were picking her up from school and they struck when they could."

"Okay." I nod in agreement.

"I have another idea of where Trenda can stay. We can hide with her, and she'll be protected."

Evie's excluding Simon. I peek up at Aiden's face and I see a flash of laughter before his expression is, once again, placid.

"If you're here, why isn't Drake?" Zoe asked.

"Aiden and I took a long weekend and were at Jack and Beth's ranch," Evie answers. "As soon as we heard what happened, Jack loaned us a plane to get out here. Drake's still with the rest of the team at Coronado."

I shake my head. I always think of Aiden being as rich as they come, but he doesn't hold a candle to his teammate, Jack Preston.

I jerk as Simon moves me out of the way. He and Aiden turn toward the front door, their guns drawn The front door pushes open.

"I surrender," Maddie says with her hands up and a grin on her face.

"Dammit, Trenda. I thought we discussed you locking your front door," Simon growls as he turns back to me. He puts his gun away and shakes his head in disgust.

Chapter Twenty-Nine

I watch as more of the Avery Avalanche comes crashing in. The sisters all pull together, but even as they all rally around Trenda, she still only shares the bare bones of what's going on. Aiden tips his chin and I follow him into the hallway.

"What's the real deal, Commander? I don't want or need to know any of the particulars of Trenda's past. I just want to know what we're up against."

"Call me Simon."

Aiden nods.

I go on to explain, "Renzo saw the whole thing. Not only did they try to run her off the road so that she would hit a huge old tree head on, when they missed they turned around and were making another run for her when Renzo chased them away."

"Do we know who?"

"I texted Dex to let him know how things have escalated. He's going to call within the hour. I want Trenda and Bella out of this house within the hour as well."

"If Evie can score it, there's a chalet that will do nicely. Hard to get to, and when you get there, the road to the place is hard to find. Then it's gated with lots of electronic security."

I grin. "Sounds perfect."

"That's because it is."

When I look up and see Renzo, I motion for him to come and join us. When I was speeding to make it to Trenda after her call, I'd called Renzo's brother Jase. I needed to get a handle on Renzo. Was he only a construction guy or was there more than met the eye?

There was more.

As he ambles over, my phone buzzes with an incoming call. I see it's Dex.

I answer. "I'll call you right back."

"Good." He hangs up.

As Renzo joins us, I speak. "I've got some information that will help us. Let's go."

The two men follow me out the front door—which is actually locked, a minor miracle that I will celebrate some other time. We got into my truck. I turn it on and start up the heater and my Bluetooth, then called Dex.

"Hey, Simon."

"Hi, Dex. You have Aiden O'Malley on the phone with you. You probably know him, right?"

"Vaguely." There was laughter in Dex's voice. At his laughter, I remember that Aiden had once been on the Black Dawn SEAL team before transferring over to Midnight Delta. "It's good you're there with Simon," Dex says. "This could turn even uglier."

"You also have Renzo Drakos in the car with us," I say. "He's Jase Drakos' brother. According to Jase he's a good man to have on your side during a fight."

I look over at Renzo. "Are you armed?"

He nods.

"Good." I turn my attention to the cars' speakers. "Okay, Dex, what do you have for us?"

"I've triple-checked. The emails are coming from Carla Harris' IP address, but I can't find any payments coming from her account or her joint account with Brantley to anybody that seems like they would be doing work taking pictures of Trenda and Bella in Tennessee."

"Maybe it was a cash deal?" Aiden guesses.

"No cash has been withdrawn in the last year. Woman has a black Amex and she uses the shit out of it. The woman sure can shop."

"Have you checked to see if she's returned anything and asked for the money back in cash?" I ask.

"I did that very thing, Simon. She does return a shit-ton of what she purchases, but the returns always go back onto her card. If it's her, she either asked a favor off someone, or did it herself."

After Trenda gave me even more details about her encounter with Carla and how she'd acted, I just don't see her driving her Botoxed ass down to Jasper Creek.

"From what Trenda has said, it's highly unlikely she would have made the drive," is all I say. "What have you got on the older sons from the previous marriage?" I ask.

"Oh, one other thing. Brantley insisted that all three of his sons get DNA tested in order to receive their inheritance."

"What are the results of the DNA testing?"

"All three of them check out as Brantley's kids." Dex says. "I've emailed photos of the widow, her twelve-year-old son, Kevin, and the other two sons, twenty-nine-year-old Richard and thirty-five-year-old Brantley Jr."

"Did you email them to Trenda?"

"Yeah."

"Text them to me," I tell him.

"Is there a reason I can't send them to her? I thought you said she was okay," Dex swiftly replies.

"She is, she's just occupied with all of her sisters."

"I'm texting the information now," Dex says. "I've got more information. Richard used to be a big fish, not quite a whale, over at the Gold Strike Casino in Tunica, Mississippi. His game was poker. He abruptly stopped playing four months ago. All of his accounts were zeroed out, but I noticed that he was getting advances from Harris Developments. My guess is he had found private games."

"So besides just wanting the money, he has a *need* for the money," I say.

"Probably thinks that whatever his cut is, he can't afford to have another person cutting into his piece of the pie," Renzo agrees.

"Same deal with Carla. The house she and her son have been living in for the last fourteen years is going to be sold and split three ways. She's getting a quarter of a mil from the reading of the will, but with her spending habits, that'll last her no more than two years. The house she's living in has a mortgage of twenty-five thousand a month. Yeah, she needs her son to get his share of the money. And she would probably think she needs as much as she could get."

"Sounds like that's true," I snort. "Dex, how much of this information can you feed to the Jasper Creek sheriff?"

"I can give him everything as an anonymous source. Is the sheriff worth a damn?"

I turn to Aiden. "I haven't been here long enough to hear about the sheriff; what's your take?" I ask.

"He's honest. But you have to remember, this isn't a job you're promoted into, it's one you're voted into. It's basically a popularity contest. He likes wearing the uniform, and because this will be a high-profile case, he won't do the smart thing and leave it to his deputies who have years on the job. He'll want to handle it himself, he'll definitely run with it. It'll get fucked up for sure."

"Don't bother giving it to the sheriff." I tell Dex.

"That there is one of the reasons I would never move to a small town," Dex says. I can practically hear his shudder through my truck's speaker.

"I'm okay with this being just us," Renzo says.

"Yeah, I'm in," Dex agrees.

"Drake's going to prefer not having to deal with the sheriff. We take care of our own," Aiden says.

"SEALs don't operate on US soil," I remind Aiden.

"Currently I'm a member of the Navy who is on leave, Simon. I'm here with my wife, staying at our second home here in Jasper Creek, and we're visiting with her family. I'm lucky enough to find out one of the men I used to work with, Simon Clark, has retired and is living here. When my sister-in-law gets run off the road, I naturally feel protective."

"How come I think you've said damn near this same spiel many times before?" I ask the big blond SEAL.

"Because he has," Dex pipes up. "Our women tend to get in trouble. Welcome to the club, Simon."

"What club?" I ask.

"The club where I saw you stake claim on Trenda inside the house, or were my eyes deceiving me?" Aiden gives me a hard look. I return it.

"When I'm here, I will always be Trenda's protector," I say slowly. Clearly. Again, I'm not making a long-term commitment to this man, until I've made one to myself, and then to Trenda.

Fuck, I need to get my head screwed on straight, as of yesterday.

"You had best get that sorted," Aiden says. "I think very highly of Trenda, I don't want to see her hurt."

"Point taken," I reply.

"And this is why I'm single," Renzo quips. I know he's horning in to cut through the tension in the truck.

"Do you have anything else to give us?" I ask Dex.

"That about does it. Call if there's anything else you need me to run down."

"Will do."

When we walk back inside, I see that Bella, Zarek, Slayer and Chloe are back inside. Bella is lying on the floor poking her fingers through the cage to get her gerbil's attention. Evie motions the three of us over.

"Bad news, Larry has rented the Chalet out. I think the best course of action is to get Trenda and Bella over to our house," she says looking up at Aiden.

I shake my head. "No." I stand by what I said earlier. "That can be traced back to an Avery." A lightbulb flashes. "I'm going to call Bernie."

"Your cabin is too small," Evie says.

"No, *his* cabin. He has a good-sized A-frame that we might be able to borrow if he's still in the hospital. I checked on him a few days ago. His place isn't the easiest to find, and it'll be large enough for Trenda, Bella, and I to hang until we get shit sorted."

"What are we doing?" Trenda asks as she walks up to our little huddle.

"We're trying to think of a place for us to go until things blow over. Maybe Bernie's place," I explain.

She nods. "Sounds good. I'm going to start packing."

"I'll help," Maddie says.

"So will I," Zoe and Chloe say in unison. I look at them and stare. They see my stare and giggle.

Trenda looks at me and pats my shoulder. "You'll get used to hearing them talk in stereo," she smiles. "This way, ladies."

They all go down the hall.

I call Bernie.

~

"Hi Mr. Bernie, have you met Gerry?" Bella runs to the sliding glass door to show off her gerbil, Slayer running right behind her. He lets out some ferocious barking. She turns around and points her finger at him.

"Down!"

Slayer immediately stops barking and sits down. She goes over and pets him. "Mr. Bernie is a friend."

I go over and pet Slayer. "Go. Lie down." I point over at the oversized pet bed that Zarek had given us to take for Slayer. He ambles over and drops on his side, happy as a clam. Simon is in the hallway watching everything.

"Damn, that's one heck of a dog, you got there. I'm not sure that I need to show Simon the contents of my safe."

"I think you do," I disagree.

Simon ambles over and shakes Bernie's hand. "It's great to see you out of the hospital. Are you following the doctor's orders?"

"Don't have no choice. My lady friend is forcing me too."

"Tell me about your lady friend," Trenda invites.

"How about I bring Mora around some time, and you can meet her for yourself?"

"That'd be great."

"Now, let's go see about that safe," Bernie smiles at Simon.

Of course, the first smile I see on Simon's face since he hugged me and Bella on the side of the road is when Bernie shows him his gun safe.

We go to the room that Bernie had been using as a study, and I find Simon there with his laptop open.

"What's the deal, Bernie? Are you a prepper?" Simon asks.

"Funny you should ask that, Simon." Bernie looks over at me. "Trenda, do you remember Ralph Gunderson?"

I shake my head.

"Yeah, he would have been before you started coming up on the mountain. He died of cancer twelve years ago. He left his gun safe and all of his guns and rifles to me. I haven't known what to do with them, so here they've sat."

"Is there ammunition?" Simon asks.

Bernie goes over to an armoire in the study and opens the doors. There is box after box after box of ammunition. Simon walks over and starts examining things. "Good, there are even cleaning supplies. Yep, the man was certainly prepared."

I walk away and go to my favorite place in Bernie's modest house, the kitchen. Evie had put away the nine bags of groceries. I might have overbought at the supermarket, but I don't think so. I have the sneaking suspicion that Simon will not be letting Bella and me leave until things are sorted, which is fine by me. I don't want Bella in harm's way.

Evie walks into the kitchen as I'm reorganizing the pantry. She starts laughing.

"I don't know why I bothered putting the groceries away. I should have known you would have moved them all around anyway."

"I'm not moving them around, I'm organizing them. The oatmeal and the peanut butter can't be on the same shelf. One is for lunch, the other is for breakfast. And you put the cookies right next to the crackers. They need to be separated by the potato chips."

Evie launches herself at me, and pulls me close for a big hug.

"Please don't be mad at me," she whispers into my neck.

"I'm not. I promise. It's done. You know those are the Avery girl rules."

She doesn't let go, just sniffles for a moment. Then two.

"I hate that I scared Bella," she whispers.

"Bella is resilient. You had to shell out twelve dollars for your swearing, she's fine now."

Evie pulls away from me and looks me in the eye. My shoulders slump. "Okay, not entirely fine, but she'll get there. She has a gerbil for today, but her teacher is eventually going to stop by and pick him up. And Zarek is letting us have Slayer for her to play with."

Evie snorts. "Yeah, sure, he's here to play. I would never want to be on that dog's bad side."

"Isn't that the truth."

He must have heard his name because I hear his nails on the hardwood heading toward the kitchen. I pull down the dog treats and hold one out for him. He gently nips it out of my hand with his big white teeth.

"He does have a massive jaw and sharp teeth," I admit to Evie.

"Zarek has Slayer trained to be one hell of a guard dog, and he is devoted to Bella."

Slayer looks up and gives me his version of a doggy smile. He doesn't have to look up far, since he's so tall.

"I love that picture of Bella riding him, remember?" I say.

"When she was little, he was horse-sized in comparison. Hell, he still almost is. Aiden is looking at getting a couple of dogs for us when he retires. He's considering Russian Terriers because of Slayer."

Woof.

"Yeah, you know when you're being complimented, don't you?" I rub his massive head.

Woof.

"Oh, I hope he doesn't wake Bella."

"That's why I came down," Evie said. "She woke up and was heading to the bathroom. That's the only reason I left to come down here. She said she's hungry."

"Are you?"

"I could eat," Evie grins.

"Let me get something started. Take Slayer with you and go find something on TV that will keep Bella occupied, will you?"

"Sure thing."

I turn on the oven. I already know what we're having. I usually like cooking from scratch, but I knew I wasn't going to be up for it tonight, so I'd bought a couple of family-size lasagnas and two loaves of French bread.

"Hi, Mama," Bella yawns as she walks into the kitchen, Slayer following behind her. Why doesn't that surprise me? "I'm hungry."

"So I heard." I reach into the fridge and pull out a bundle of grapes. I grab a colander and dump them in so I can rinse them. The kitchen is a good size. I pick up my baby and plant her on the counter next to the sink. When I'm done rinsing the grapes, I pull off a stem with ten or twelve grapes and hand it to her. "Try this to begin with. If it's not enough, I'll get you something else."

"What's for dinner?"

I look over at the oven and see it has reached three-hundred-and-fifty-degrees. "Lasagna." I answer her as I pull the two boxes out of the freezer.

"Not the freezer kind," Bella whines. "I like your kind."

"Sweet Pea, I didn't have time to make homemade

lasagna today. It's freezer lasagna." I open the boxes and slip the casseroles into the oven.

"B-b-but I want *your* lasagna," Bella whimpers.

I was waiting for this. Even having one of her aunts sleeping with her, even with her favorite dog following her around, and the class gerbil here to entertain her, I was waiting for this meltdown.

I go over and put my arms around her. "Do you know what?" I ask.

She doesn't respond to my question. She's definitely cranky and sad.

"Bella? Do you know what I think?"

"No," she whispers into my chest.

"I think you and I were both really scared today."

"The big balloon hit you, and your face is scraped. Aunt Evie said someone was trying to kill you. I don't want you in heaven like my d-d-daddy."

She bursts into tears.

Slayer whines.

I pull her off the counter and she wraps her arms around my neck and her legs around my waist. She's getting to the point where we won't be able to do this much longer, and I'm going to mourn that day.

"You cry all you need to, Bella. I've got you. I'm not leaving."

"You're hurted. Mama, I don't want you to die. I want Uncle Dwake, he'll save you."

I wince. When her language skills regress, she's really worked up. I rock her back and forth. According to Aiden, after going to Coronado, his team had to take off on a sudden mission without him and Jack. So, Drake is out of the country.

"He can't be here, Bella. But Uncle Aiden's here, and so is Simon."

"I want Uncle Dwake," she sobs. "He can do anything."

"Uncle Aiden works with Uncle Drake," I say, trying to reason with her.

"Uncle Dwake is bigger and louder."

He is that.

"Simon was Uncle Drake's boss. Did you know he taught Uncle Drake how to be a SEAL?" I fib. I don't know if Simon was involved with Drake's actual training, but he had trained SEALs.

"He was his teacher?" she hiccups.

"Yes."

She looks past me. "Can you do what Uncle Drake does?"

I look over my shoulder and see Simon standing at the kitchen entrance.

"I can," he answers, solemnly.

"He throws really far. Can you?"

"I can."

"He runs really fast. Can you?"

"I can do that too."

"You don't swear a lot like Uncle Drake."

Simon walks closer to us. "That's one of the things I've failed at teaching your uncle. He's not supposed to swear in front of ladies."

"We not ladies, we family."

Simon rests his hand in the middle of my back, above Bella's ankles, offering me the support I didn't even know I needed.

"Why do you have gray hair?" Bella asks.

"Because I'm older than your Uncle Drake, so I know more and that will help me take care of you and your Mama. The bad guys won't get you. I promise."

I feel my daughter's body relax. "You do? Cross your heart?"

I look over my shoulder just in time to see Simon crossing his heart.

"That's good," she says in a happier tone of voice. She reaches over and drops the uneaten grapes back into the colander. "Mama, I want ice cream."

"Not before dinner. You can have a slice of bread and some juice, how does that sound?"

She looks up at me, her eyes no longer wet with tears. "It doesn't sound as good as ice cream."

I hear Simon start to laugh behind me.

It seems there are two people in this kitchen that I love.

Chapter Thirty

"Your reading glasses are sexy," Trenda says to me.

I glance over the top of my computer to look at her. She's been saying silly things all morning, ever since she got a lesson plan from Mrs. Stapleton to print out and give to Bella so she can start working on it. Now she's in the process of driving me insane.

"Thank you. I'm glad you think so."

I look back down at my laptop and try to figure out why I've got a shut-off notice for my gas at the La Mesa residence, when my on-line account shows it's paid in full.

"You have this adorable little frown when you're concentrating. Are you having to deal with a spreadsheet?"

I take off my glasses and toss them on the desk. We've been working across from one another in this head-to-head office setup for the last six days. I've been so goddamned bored waiting for mine and Dex's plans to bear fruit, that I'm even ready to start going through my Navy mail today. Not only am I bored, I'm horny. But there isn't a chance in hell I'm going to do anything about it when we have Bella in the house with us, and therein lies the problem.

Trenda disagrees with me.

She thinks we can finesse this if we have sex in the upstairs master, then she goes down to her room downstairs. While that is a wonderful suggestion, I don't want the slightest chance of her impressionable girl finding us in bed together. Not that I think it will scar her. Nope, not that. I just think that any man who is in her mother's bed better damn well be either her husband or her soon-to-be-husband.

And I've decided that's what I want to be, her soon-to-be-husband. I want to be her husband here in Jasper Creek, but Arthur has bought up all the dry-cleaning franchises, so I have no fucking clue what I'm going to do for a living.

I bring this up to Josiah when I'm on the phone with him. It's oh eight hundred and I'm freezing my motherfucking ass off outside calling him on my satellite phone, explaining my problems, when he suggests that I retire.

"I *have* retired, remember? I draw a pension from the Navy and everything. I'm talking, what is my job going to be every day?"

"Shit, Simon, not only do you have savings, you *do* have your pension, and those rental properties bringing in money every month. So, sit back and enjoy life. Maybe get her pregnant and become a house husband."

"Not that childrearing isn't a full-time job, but I've been missing the *job*. Not the fucking politics, but the puzzles, the strategizing, the juice. I always planned to stay until I got my forty in. By then I planned to have a plan. But I don't have a fucking *plan*!"

I am so pissed at myself for not having had more foresight.

"The way I see it, you're one of the lucky ones. Not everybody ends up with their soulmate."

I rock back on my heels. *Soulmate.* That word has never passed my lips, but as soon as Josiah says it, it fits. That's what she is to me. I think all the way back to that first moment she sidled up beside me at the check-out line, all smart-ass like, and even at that moment I knew she was pretty damned special.

"You with me, Simon, or did I just rock your world? I know that you'd prefer a root canal without anesthesia to discussing feelings." Josiah laughed.

"Fuck you," I said without heat. "I'm thinking."

"Think faster. You have the makings of a beautiful life right there in your hands. Grab hold and don't let it go because you can't figure out what you want to be when you grow up. You've found the most important thing; the other shit will work itself out."

"You're right," I say. I'm still in shock. The man is totally right.

"I know I am. Now I want to meet her, so you better be bringing her to the wedding. You've got three weeks to get a ring on her finger. I want to see that girl of hers too. She sounds like a little firebrand."

"I have to go, Josiah."

I hear him laughing before I end the call.

When I get back into the house, I smell something delicious coming from the kitchen, so I follow my nose. Trenda has stir-fry sizzling in the wok. I come up behind her and move her hair so I can kiss her behind her ear.

"What's that for?" she asks.

"Just because."

"That's a good reason," she responds.

～

"I've been monitoring the attorney's office. They are executors of Harris' will and they're dragging their feet distributing assets because they haven't heard back from Trenda. According to the notes taken by Horace Grant's assistant, there are two very pissed-off people. They demand to be told who is holding up the process, and they're threatening to sue the law firm. I've forwarded this to *your* email this time," Dex said.

I look over to where Trenda is helping Bella with the homework she received from her schoolteacher.

"What else you got?" I ask.

"Junior and Richard are running the business since Daddy's death and it's not going well. The board of directors is pissed. I got ahold of the notes to the last board meeting, and they're not happy with how things are being run, especially about the lawsuit they are supposed to be handling."

"The company is being sued?"

"Yeah. I'm sending the filing over to you, as well as the board of directors' notes. Here's what's been bothering me, Simon. Whereas Carla didn't have any cash lying around to pay someone to take pictures, the boys have access to the company coffers so I think they do, even Richard, who's broke."

"Enough for a hit?" I whisper my question. I press my fingers against the bridge of my nose. Trenda had told me how her parents had actually tried to kill her youngest sister for the land her grandmother had bequeathed her. It's possible that it has come around full circle and this time one of Bella's half-brothers is trying to kill her.

"Dex, I don't have the heart to tell her anything until we know something for sure. But we've got to do something. As much as I enjoy being holed up with a beautiful woman and her kick of a kid, I need to shake the tree to get things moving so I can put this thing to bed."

"I have an idea," Dex says.

"Actually, so do I," I respond.

"Why are you packing?" she asks.

"It's just for one night," I assure her.

"That wasn't what I asked," Trenda says firmly.

Uh-oh, I'm getting the mother voice.

I turn to look at her. She's in the yoga pants I love so much. It's great living with her and seeing how she dresses when it's just around the house. I get to see the cropped tank tops when we're close to the fire. Those are the best nights.

"Simon, concentrate. Tell me where you're going and what you're planning on doing. Or should I tell you? You're impatient, so you're going to Nashville, and that's why Aiden and Evie are downstairs."

I cross the bedroom and take her into my arms. "You're perfect for me. You can even read my mind."

She pushes at my chest so we're not quite as close. "Yeah, well, I still don't know what you're going to be doing, so please enlighten me."

"I'm going to visit with all the beneficiaries, and see what bad apples fall out of the tree. Not Kevin of course, I'll be talking to his delightful mother, Carla."

She bites her lip as she looks up at me. "I don't like this. I don't like it at all. I've been thinking about that car crash. I don't think that was just a warning. I think they were actually trying to kill us."

I do too, but I don't say it aloud.

"Trenda, us just sitting around waiting is accomplishing nothing. We need to end this."

"Why not wait for the police?"

I raise my eyebrow.

She bangs her forehead against my chest. "Oh yeah, the *sheriff* is working the case. We're so screwed."

"I'll be back tomorrow at the latest. You can call me any time," I promise.

"You promise?"

"I just did."

I get a call from Dex as I'm driving to Nashville.

"You there yet?"

"Nope. I've got another hour before I hit the outskirts, then thirty before I hit the hotel. I need two hours before the meeting to buy something besides jeans and a t-shirt. All three of them have agreed to meet me. Richard and Carla were falling all over themselves to meet somebody who represented the other beneficiary. Not one of them gave it away on the phone that they knew I was representing Trenda. I want to see if they do when we're in person."

"That'll give our guys time to get the GPS tracking and Bluetooth listening set up."

"And Evie and Aiden can afford this?" I question again.

"Aiden is loaded; trust me, ten or twenty grand won't be missed. He even probably has one of those black American Express cards." Dex chuckled.

"And why did this guy we're working with decide on this hotel?"

"It's all valet express. They don't park any cars in front of the hotel, and the parking is all underground. He knows

his shit around Nashville. He was also able to get you a
meeting room at the last minute."

"Okay."

Chapter Thirty-One

I'd met the type before. The two Harris boys are just like a lot of the lobbyists and politicians that I would occasionally have to deal with up on Capitol Hill. All tan and teeth with no honor. And Carla was another easy one to read. She fit right into the Beverly Hills types who occasionally accompanied their husbands down to San Diego while they golfed. They would drink, eat a lettuce leaf, and gossip at some country club.

I came in wearing chinos, an expensive button-down shirt, and nice loafers. I throw a leather portfolio and pen onto the conference room table as if I own it, then I sit down.

"Can I have your card?" Junior asks.

"Let's cut with the niceties, shall we?" I pick up my pen and open the binder to a blank page. "The way I hear it, you need my... shall we say, *friend,* to come forward. Because every day they don't, you're burning money. Doesn't that about sum it up?"

"All I know is your name. What company do you work for?" Junior persists.

"I'm me, Simon Clark. I'm retired. I'm here in the best interests of my friend, and I'm not sure you have their best interests at heart."

"Cut the crap. Your friend is that back-woods trollop, Linda Avery."

"Who?" I ask.

"Linda, Minda, Trenda, whatever her name is. She spit out some brat, and now thinks she's entitled to tens of millions. Well she can think again."

"Mrs. Harris," I say calmly. "I don't know who this Linda person is. I'm representing my friend."

"Are you saying there could be more than Trenda's kid?" Richard gasps.

"Shut up, Richard," Junior says calmly. Richard shuts up. "Mr. Clark, what I don't quite understand is how you or your friend think it is a problem for us if they don't come forward. We didn't have this money when our father was alive, so why is it important that we have it now?"

"Speak for yourself, Brant," Carla snarls. "Your father paid all my bills. Now that he's gone, I'm left hanging in the breeze. You two might be fine because you can siphon off money from the business, but I don't have that luxury."

"We're not siphoning off anything, we're taking our salaries and all other compensation like bonuses and expenses that are due to us," Richard says smugly.

Junior slaps the table. "I said, shut up, Richard!"

I chuckle. "Quite the little duo you have to handle, Junior."

"I prefer to be called Brant."

I pick up my pen and write down Junior, large enough for everybody to see.

Junior flushes.

"So, as I was saying, you have—"

"Who are you representing? I demand to know!" Carla's voice could shatter glass.

I look at my watch. We've been dicking around for twenty minutes. Dex's guy needs at least twenty, he'd prefer thirty. Then he's got people who are hitting each of these losers' residences while they're here, so forty minutes would be best.

"Lady, and I use the phrase loosely, you are not in a position to demand shit."

She stands up and grabs her purse. "Then I'm leaving."

I look over at Junior.

"Sit down, Carla," he says in a tired voice.

"But, Brant, he's not being helpful. You said he was going to ask for a cut, then make the other heir go away."

I chuckle. "Is that how you saw it going down, Junior? How do you figure that? For all you know, I'm representing my wife. Seriously, for such a so-called high-powered businessman, you're not too smart."

"Don't lie to me. You called this meeting. You want something to feather your own nest."

"I've got a question that I want all three of you to answer individually. Is that possible, or is Junior your mouthpiece?"

"He doesn't speak for me," Richard said.

"Me neither," Carla squawked.

"You heard them," Junior sighed. "What's your question?"

"Just how far are you willing to go to get rid of other heirs? Murder?"

I watch each of them closely.

Junior looks bored. "That'd be a no."

Richard looks over-the-top offended. "Good God, no. Have you lost your mind, Clark?"

"How could you even ask someone like me a question like that?" Carla clutches an actual strand of pearls.

"Now tell me the reason for such an offensive question," Junior asks. His boredom is shot after hearing his brother and his father's second wife's over-the-top responses.

"I've been doing a little digging to see just how financially sound this purported fortune is, and how the split is going to come down. First, with the lawsuit, I'm not sure that the company's in as good of shape as everyone thinks. Second, I'm thinking that things might need to be split five ways after hearing about Minda. Still a decent amount, but not as much as my friend was expecting. What's Trenda's last name?"

"Go fuck yourself," Carla shrieks. "I don't care what you say, Brant. I'm not listening to this a moment longer. I'm leaving." She grabs her purse and sweeps out of the room.

"How about you two? Do you know Linda's last name?"

"I'm sorry Mr. Clark. We can't help you," Junior stands up, having to yank at his brother's arm.

"Ah, but Richard, it really seemed like you knew something."

"I agree with Carla, go fuck yourself." He wrenches away from Junior's hold and storms out of the room.

I hold my hand out to Junior so we can shake.

"I think I'll decline."

I grin.

~

I continue to grin as I drive my GTO back to Nashville. I'm surrounded by trucks on the freeway, but I don't care, it's nice to be in a car that can *move*. I hit my Bluetooth.

"Hey Dex, how'd it go?"

"According to Mitch, everything went perfectly at the hotel. He was able to hack into all of the cars' GPS and Bluetooth devices. We'll be able to hear everything and track them anywhere. Two of the three agents that hit the houses have reported back successfully. He's waiting to hear back from his last person."

"Sounds good. I just want to get back to Jasper Creek. I won't feel better until all of this is over."

"I can't say that I blame you."

"I've got to go. I have another call coming in."

I switch over to the other line.

"It's about damn time you called," I say to Bernie Faulks. "Do you know how much grief I've been getting about you from Trenda?"

He chuckles. "Yeah, the settings on the dryer are a might touchy. She can't use the fluff cycle; she'll have to use the gentle cycle instead."

"Fuck that noise. She wants to know where you've been. You were discharged from the hospital four days ago, and then you haven't been answering your phone. I keep telling her you're a big boy and can take care of yourself, but she will not let this drop."

"Yep, she's a caretaker of the first order. You do realize, no matter how many kids you have, she's still going to be up your ass to take care of yourself, don't you? You better not start smoking cigars or anything like that."

"Bernie," I growl. "Tell me where you are so that I can ease Trenda's mind."

"How about if me and my lady friend come over for a visit?"

"When?"

"In the next hour."

I relax. "That would be perfect. I'll call her and tell her you're coming."

"Where are you?"

"I'm finishing up some things in Nashville. I should be there in two hours."

"Gotcha. We'll still be around when you show up. I'll barbeque."

"Sounds good."

I smile when we disconnect. Bernie sneaked away for a bootie call and that makes me happy.

I hit the Bluetooth again and call Trenda's number. It goes straight to voicemail.

That's odd.

I call Aiden.

"Hey, Simon," he answers.

"Trenda isn't answering her phone, is everything okay?" I ask.

"She's down with a migraine. According to Evie, it's a bad one."

"Did she take her medicine?" I ask.

"That's another thing, she's never been in to see a doctor about them, so she doesn't have any medication beyond ibuprofen."

My hands hurt, and I realize I've got my steering wheel in a death grip.

"What do you mean she's never been to a doctor about them?"

"Don't shoot the messenger," he chuckles. "Protective much?"

I relax my fingers. "Aren't there shots for them?"

"Pretty sure," Aiden says.

"Let me call you back."

I call Bernie back. Even being a mountain man, the man

is hooked into the town network. If anyone would know a doctor who does house calls, he would be the one.

I moan as I roll over.

"Hold on, let me get you some water."

I'm pretty sure I'll have to pull a wad of cotton out of my mouth before I can drink any water.

"Here, Honey, drink this."

Simon lifts me up just a little, and a spike goes through my head. I moan again.

"Ah, shit. Do you want me to lie you down again?"

"Water," I say. I hear how I'm slurring my words.

Simon puts the glass up to my mouth and a little bit of water trickles in. I want to see Simon. He's been gone, but I know opening my eyes will hurt too much.

The water is gone, which is good because I want to lie down again. I don't know if I said it out loud, or Simon just read my mind, but he lowers me back to a pillow that no longer feels like cement. Now it feels like it's filled with oranges. I guess that's an improvement.

"Baby, the doctor said it might make you feel better if I massage your head. Can I do that for you?"

I'm not quite sure what he's asking, but it's Simon so I say, "Yes."

He moves my body, which makes me moan. I should not have said yes. Then I'm still again. At least I didn't throw up. I feel his fingers slide through my hair as he holds my head up a little from the uncomfortable pillow. I relax the tiniest amount because his hands feel good. Then his fingers press in just a little bit and stroke upward from the base of my skull to the top of my scalp. One hand always supporting me, as the other hand does that same rhythm.

"Ahhh."

I feel my body begin to relax a tiny bit instead of holding itself rigid, trying to brace against the pain.

"What day is it?" I ask.

"Wednesday."

"You left this morning?" I remember.

"Yes."

"What time is it?"

"A little before midnight."

I should not be feeling this good. I should still be racked with pain, and I say so.

"Bernie had Dr. Evans follow him up and he gave you a shot that he said might help on the duration and pain level of your migraine. It sounds like it did. Nice guy. He stayed for the barbeque."

"I don't remember Doc Evans giving me a shot."

Simon continues with the massage.

After the pain I've been in, this massage is almost, not quite, but it's up there, on par with an orgasm.

"You'll have to give me a massage some time," Simon chuckles.

"Ah, damn, did I say that out loud?"

He chuckles a little louder. "Sure did. I like Trenda unfiltered. You're always so cautious about what you say, never wanting to hurt anyone's feelings. I like that you feel like you can be your real self with me. Let me get you some more water, then we can work on the massage again."

"Okay."

I'm careful not to think that I don't want water, because that means he has to stop. I wait. He doesn't chuckle. Okay, I'm in the clear. I'm thinking things and not saying them. That's a relief.

He continues to hold my head with one hand and brings

the water to my lips. I take a longer sip this time. It tastes *so* good.

"Do you want some more?"

"Yes please."

He tips the glass and I greedily take some more. Then he goes back to massaging my head for long moments, until I start to finally feel human.

"Where's Bella?"

"She's in the bedroom beside the one where Evie and Aiden are sleeping. Slayer's in there with her."

"Of course, he is. And the gerbil?"

"Mrs. Stapleton came and took the gerbil. Apparently, another lucky parent has to walk the tightrope of keeping Gerry the Gerbil alive." I can hear the smile in Simon's voice. "Do you feel good enough to sit up and really drink a glass of water?"

"Oh yeah. I've never felt this good so fast after a headache."

"Migraine," Simon says.

"No, it's only a headache," I protest.

"Trenda, I saw you. You were in severe pain. The doctor diagnosed it; it was—is—a migraine."

"It *was* a headache," I stress.

"Why are you so against having migraines?" he asks softly.

"Because I've read up on them, they're debilitating. You're out of control. You can't do anything. I need to be in control and be able to take care of Bella. I can't have migraines. Did you know sometimes they come monthly for people? My headaches don't come monthly. They happen occasionally."

"How often?" he asks.

"Maybe every other month."

"The shot the doctor gave you is specifically for migraines. Why did it help your supposed headache?"

I feel like I'm going to cry. My eyes have been open for a while. I look at Simon. "What if they *are* migraines? How am I going to cope with Bella?"

"You're going to cope how you always do. With help."

"I guess I will." I stir. "I want to get up now. I need a shower."

He helps me to the bathroom.

"Honey, I'm going to close the door almost all the way shut, then I'm going to turn the light on here in the bedroom so you have a little light in there, but not too much, okay?"

"Okay," I say softly.

I watch as he closes the door, then I take off my clothes and get into the shower. It would be so nice if he would be here all the time to take care of Bella and me.

Stop with your wishful thinking.

Chapter Thirty-Two

She seems sad. I don't like that. And I really don't think it was because of the migraine. I go downstairs to bring up a tray for her.

There's some of the grilled chicken breasts that Mora had brought for Bernie to eat. There wasn't any potato salad, but there was still macaroni salad, and there was still some of the homemade red velvet cake that Trenda made yesterday.

By the time I get up there, Trenda's in her bathrobe, sitting on the side of the bed in the dark, finishing the glass of water.

"You okay?" I ask as I put the tray of food on the bed.

"Sure. Why do you ask?"

"You seemed sad. You're still not over your headache, are you?"

My phone buzzes on the nightstand. I head for it.

"I'm fine now that there's food." She gives me a half smile. "Don't worry about me. Midnight calls are never good."

She's right about that.

It's Dex.

I don't put it on speakerphone.

"It's Junior," he says. "He's talking to a hitman who's already in Jasper Creek. He's pissed off because the guy is squeezing him for more money because he has to take out a kid. Fucking A, Simon, that's how he put it, *take out a kid*. What kind of animal talks like that?"

There's disgust, sorrow, and rage in Dex's voice.

"Did you get any idea whether the hitman knows where we're at?"

"He said he has an idea on how to find out. You better call everyone Trenda knows and make sure they're on the lookout. My guess is that he's going to look for a soft target to find out information."

"Fuck!"

"What? What is it?" Trenda is at my elbow asking.

"Anything else, Dex?"

"That's it. Take care."

The phone goes dead. I look up at Trenda.

"Where are all of your sisters? The ones here in Jasper Creek?"

"Not Evie, cause she's downstairs, right?"

"Yeah, not her."

"I'm pretty sure that Zoe and Maddie are at Evie's house and Chloe and Zarek are at their house. Are they in trouble?"

"I'm not sure, but I don't want to take any chances. I'll call Zarek, you get Maddie or Zoe on the phone. When you get them, put it on speaker."

Zarek answered on the first ring. "Yeah?"

"We've got a problem. It's possible a hitman will be coming to you and Chloe to find out where Trenda and Bella are."

"Jesus, I'm at the firehouse. Chloe's alone and you have Slayer. Gotta go." Zarek hung up.

I turn to Trenda. Her fingers are trembling as she's going through her contacts.

"Zoe didn't answer," she said. "It's possible she has her phone on do not disturb. I heard what you said to Zarek."

"It's okay, Aiden said his house is a fortress. I'm going to go get Aiden so he can explain to them how to arm the house. Just keep calling the girls."

I brush a kiss on top of her hair, then race out of the room and down the stairs. Aiden must have heard me because his bedroom door is open. He's holding his cargo pants and a gun.

"What?"

"Come upstairs."

"Okay."

He follows me back upstairs.

Trenda is smiling.

"Put it on speaker," I say. She does.

"It's Maddie," she tells us. "Maddie, Simon, and Aiden are here. Listen to them and do what they say."

"Maddie, this is Simon. I think somebody could be coming there to harm you. I need you to get ready."

I look to Aiden.

"Lock yourself into the safe room," he said. "You'll have everything you need."

"Aiden, are you sure we need—"

"If Simon says somebody might be on his way to harm you, don't do anything else, get your asses into the safe room. Are we clear?"

"What's going on?" Evie asks from the door. "Why does Maddie need—"

I point at her, and she shuts up.

My phone buzzes; it's Zarek. "I've got a deputy a minute

from my house. I called Chloe; she's going with them to the sheriff's department."

I'm not satisfied. Not until we've got a call from Chloe actually in the back seat of the patrol car.

"Aiden, is there a way for them to call out of the safe room?" I demand to know.

"There's a landline set up in there," he assures me.

I nod.

Trenda starts talking. "Maddie said she and Zoe were heading in, then the line went dead." I nod, knowing the girls will be smart enough to call. The hitman isn't wanting to kill any of the women, he just wants to get Trenda and Bella's location.

A call comes through on Trenda's phone. "I don't recognize the number," she hands her phone to Aiden.

"Yep, this is the safe room." He answers the call. "This is Aiden. Did you lock the door?" he asks as he puts the phone on speaker.

"Oh shit, were we supposed to do that?" Maddie asks. "That never fucking occurred to us.

"Those are really bad words, Aunt Maddie. You should owe me more than two dollars," Bella yawned.

Slayer pushes his way over to me. Bella sidles up to her mother. How had I missed her entrance into the room?

"Sweetheart, Uncle Aiden and Simon will both pay you ten dollars," Maddie promises. "They've been saying a lot of bad words."

She looks over at me from her mother's side. "Really?"

She looks adorable, all rumpled from bed, wearing pajamas with little unicorns on them.

My phone buzzes again. It's Zarek. "Well?" I ask.

"They have her. I'm headed to the station right now." I hear the relief in his voice.

"Chloe's headed to the sheriff's station," I tell everybody.

"Is she in trouble?" Bella asks.

"No, Sweet Pea," Trenda answers. "She's meeting Uncle Zarek there."

"What's the deal with Maddie and Zoe?" Zarek asks. Again, I haven't put him on speaker phone.

"They're in the safe room in Aiden and Evie's house," I answer him with a satisfied smile.

"Sweet. I remember him telling me about that, and thinking he'd gone way over the top."

"I'd put one in my house," I say.

"Yeah, well after tonight, I'm considering it. These Avery girls," Zarek sighs. "After I get Chloe, I'm taking her to the Whispering Pines Hotel."

As soon as he says that, I remember Renzo. Why it took me so long, I have no idea. "Sounds good, Zarek."

"Aiden, I'm thinking you and Evie should get back to your house, get the girls out of the safe room, then arm your house like the fortress you say it is. In the meantime, I'll have Renzo come up here for backup. I think it's overkill, but I like to have a contingency to my contingency plan."

"That's why both Gray and Mason have always had good things to say about you," Aiden says with a smile. "Evie and I will wait here until Renzo gets here."

I give him a grim smile.

"What about Maddie and Zoe? Shouldn't they be let out of the safe room as soon as possible?" Trenda asks.

"Hell no," Evie answers. "I have that room setup sweet. I always check the battery on the laptop, it has plenty of movies stored. It has sugar and salty treats in a cute little basket and all the prices listed. Just kidding, it has a mini-fridge. I've got two recliners in there that recline all the way back for sleeping. I thought that was better than cots. Plus, I have books in there. They're set."

"Shit, how big is that thing?" I ask Aiden.

"Too big, but Evie insisted. She's the one who wanted us to have a planet-killer of a house. And there she is barely five feet tall. Doesn't make any sense to me," he grins indulgently down at his wife.

"Asshole."

"Aunt Evie. I get two dollars from you. And Mr. Simon, I get eleven dollars now from you."

I look over at Trenda. "She must ace all of her math classes."

I hang up the phone, still laughing.

"It's not nice to laugh when Aiden is five minutes away from locking himself into the safe room," Simon says to me.

"Your sisters are loco," Renzo says, then goes back to reading his book.

"No wonder Drake is the way he is," Simon says from the dining room table, "if it's that bad when just three of you get together."

"Hey, he didn't have it that bad. When he left, the twins were just seven years old. He missed them as teenagers, so he has nothing to complain about."

"How about Evie, did he suffer through her teenage years?" Simon asks me.

"Nope." I answer. I look over at Bella sitting on the couch, missing her gerbil, and try to form my question without alerting her to what I'm asking. "How much longer do we all need to housesit for Bernie? Do you think that your trip to Nashville worked?"

He looks over at Bella as well. "Forty-eight to seventy-two hours is my guess." He looks like he wants to say more, so he mouths the word 'later.'

"Thanks for the info, Simon. So, what do you gentlemen want for dinner?" I ask Renzo and Simon.

"Your kind of lasagna, Mama."

I raise my eyebrow at my daughter, and she sits back down on the sofa. She knows better than to answer when I've asked someone else.

Renzo looks over at Bella. "Are you telling me that your mom makes homemade lasagna, Cariña?"

"Sweet Pea, Bernie doesn't have a pasta maker here, so I can't do homemade pasta."

"You actually make homemade pasta?" Simon asks. He looks at me with an impressed expression and I feel my chest swelling with pride.

I give him a big smile and nod.

"That's too bad," Renzo says. "Do you have store-bought noodles? That's what my mom used to use, and I still thought that was the sh—" He stops himself before he has to owe any money to Bella. He and Simon have a bet to see who can last the longest without owing Bella money. I think it's cute.

I go to Bernie's cupboard to see if he has lasagna pasta shells, and he does. "Okay, lasagna it is. We still have a head of lettuce that looked good, for a Caesar salad."

"Sweet," Renzo says. "Anything I can do to help?"

"Not right now."

"Mama, can we have ice cream for dessert?"

"I already have something else planned."

"Okay. I guess that'll be okay."

The men laugh at her over-the-top sigh of despondency.

❧

After Bella's bath, I put her to bed, then I go back out to the living room. I look at the pillows and blankets folded at the end of the couch and they kind of piss me off. I haven't argued with Simon since he told me how he feels about us sleeping together with Bella in the house. It is gallant, but annoying. Renzo offers to sleep on the couch. I think he should since he's shorter, but Simon says he will since he's already used to it.

I pull out my laptop and sit cross-legged on the couch and start getting some work done on the dentist's website. His is one of the most complicated that I've ever worked on. He has a lot of locations, and each one has a different specialization. Plus, each of the different dentists from each location have been emailing me their requests and updates.

I look over at Simon. He's at the dining room table with still a mountain of mail that I've offered to go through for him, but he says he can take care of it himself. There is definitely something going on, as to why he isn't opening it. The man has a passive-aggressive relationship with his mail.

Renzo is so silent and still I wouldn't even know he is in the recliner in the corner except I see him touch the screen of his e-reader out of the corner of my eye every so often. He's been glued to his e-reader for hours. I finally can't stand it.

"What book are you reading?" I ask him.

"*How Difficult It Is To Be a God*. It's about the revolutionary war in Peru."

"When was that?" I ask.

"In the eighties and nineties. My dad was killed in it, and so were three of his brothers. I had always heard my grandmother's side of things, even though I was pretty young to comprehend it. I was looking around and saw this book and it seems pretty unbiased. I thought it would be good for me to read."

"So Drakos is a Peruvian last name?"

Renzo laughed. "No, it's Greek. I was adopted by the Drakos' when I was six or seven. When some of the other kids were being adopted by them and getting their names changed, I wanted my name changed too."

I must have looked confused because Renzo explained further. "My grandmother raised me until I was three or four, who knows. She died and I was put into an orphanage. I hated it there. Never enough to eat, and you were hit by the jailers with sticks. I was one of the lucky ones who spent a few years in a better situation and knew better, so when some older boys said they were breaking out, I got them to take me with them."

"When we ended up living in abandoned buildings, I was happy. It was better than the orphanage. I learned how to steal; I was usually the one who would be the decoy since I was the youngest. I would keep the mark busy talking while one of the older boys would try to pickpocket, or just out and out steal some lady's purse. One time I didn't get away. The man was pissed. But the woman was worried about me. Said I was too skinny."

"That was Sharon Drakos. Her husband was a construction project manager, and he worked on big projects like dams, bridges, and airports all over the world. Their family would stay in a country for a year or two. According to her husband, my adopted dad, for every place they stayed, he ended up with at least one more kid. I was their Peruvian kid."

My eyes must be twice their normal size. I look over at Simon. He's not looking at his computer; he's as riveted by Renzo's story as I am.

"How many brothers and sisters do you have?" I ask.

"I was one of the older kids, so when I lived with them, there were thirteen of us. By the time I moved out, Sharon was bringing more in. They have fostered and adopted a total of seventeen children. You should see the family group texts."

I adore his smile. You can see how much he loves his family. Which makes it strange that Simon had to go make him call his mother.

"I'm going to stretch my legs. I'll be back in about forty-five minutes or so."

"You covered?" Simon asks.

"Yeah, got what I need with me," Renzo answered.

I don't ask, I don't want to know.

Chapter Thirty-Three

My phone buzzes with an incoming text from Renzo, forty-five minutes after he takes patrol.

Not good.

> Renzo: Smelled cigarette smoke. Two miles south of house.

> Me: You tracking it?

> Renzo: He's thirty feet to the east of the road. Found tracks coming from the south. So this guy is headed to you.

> Me: If he's smoking he's not moving fast.

> Renzo: Agreed.

> Me: Do you see a weapon?

> Renzo: He's carrying a good-sized duffle bag.

> Me: Sniper rifle.

> Renzo: Yep.

> Me: Can you get back here without being spotted?

> Renzo: Yep.

> Me: Get here fast. I've got an M4A1 that I can use. I'm going hunting.

> Renzo: Coming in back window, Trenda's room.

> Me: I'll open the window and take off the screen.

Trenda is standing beside me. She'd got off the couch the moment I'd started texting.

"What is it?" she asks when I get up from the table.

"We've got trouble. Can you go unlock the window in your room and take out the screen? I'll be upstairs changing, then meet me at the gun safe."

"Okay."

We go our separate ways. As soon as I'm upstairs I turn on the bedroom light and look at all my clothes, all clean and nicely folded, in Bernie's dresser. I pull out a long-sleeved dark green shirt and a pair of green cargo pants and quickly change into them.

"You're changed already?" Trenda says when I meet her at the gun safe holding my boots that I'd picked up from the living room.

"Yep," I say as I go to the gun safe and unlock it. I had spent the first two days cleaning and making sure the guns and rifles I would need were in good working order. I pull out the M4A1, and Glock and keep the safe open for Renzo to choose his weapon of choice. I go to the armoire, where I had put the extra bullets for my SIG Sauer, the M4A1, and Trenda's Glock in an easy to reach place. I strap my knife to my cargo pants. I am set up pretty good, all things considered.

I hear something, I pull out my SIG, and rush to the doorway.

"Renzo here," he whispers from Trenda's room.

I proceed to Trenda's room in time to see Renzo pulling himself through the window.

"You should have texted, first," I say.

"You're right, sorry."

Trenda has followed me. "Get Bella and take her upstairs to the master bedroom." I turn to Renzo. "The gun safe is open; take what you need and extra, then lock it up."

Trenda leaves the room to wake up Bella.

I climb out the window.

The moon is waning, so it's only a quarter full, which is to my advantage. I head fifty yards south of the road; that will be far enough from his position thirty feet from the road for me to spot him without him noticing me if I fuck up and make a sound.

I go slowly, with my rifle raised, so I can use the scope. My watch says I've gone a quarter of a mile. Still no sign of him.

I continue to walk silently through the woods, until I get to a mile and a half.

Shit, I missed him.

Had Renzo been inaccurate about the distance? Not likely, the man is an architectural engineer, he's good with spatial analysis. Could he have switched sides of the road? It'd make sense. If he has a GPS and he's looking at terrain view, he'd see that the forest comes in a lot thicker and closer on the west side of the house.

I hustle to the west side of the road, and then start hustling north, not using my scope, just my eyes to avoid stepping on anything that will make noise.

I get out my phone.

> Me: Get all of you into the master bathroom. Every place else in the bedroom has that big window and a sniper can make a shot if he's in a tree.

> My phone buzzes.

> Renzo: In the bathroom.

> Me: Good.

Then I hear:

Crack.

The fucker is shooting at me.

The bullet hits a rotten tree four trees in front of me and the trunk explodes wide open. It begins to topple to the right.

I duck down and go left, I'd stayed too long in one place to text. That's how he got the shot. Now I go forward in a zig-zag pattern. Don't need to check my GPS, I'm close.

Crack.

Another tree to my left explodes. I hide behind a tree to my right and look up with my scope. I slowly scan the treetops. I can't find him. I start forward.

Ping.

Another shot, this one from a pistol. It's coming from the East, probably the road.

Dammit, there's two men.

Ping. Ping.

I duck and roll. I need to get rid of this joker before I can handle the sniper. Both of them have to have night vision goggles.

I zig zag south, neither of them should be expecting that. If I can get behind the one with a pistol, I can take him out.

I go, what I hope is far enough, then go slowly to the road. There he is, right there at the edge. Dumbass, at least get into the brush. I don't want to alert the sniper that I've got his friend, so I pull out my knife and come in slow behind him.

When I'm within reaching distance, I pull his head back, and slit his throat. He doesn't have a chance to radio his buddy. I toss his comm system, but I grab the night vision goggles. They'll come in handy.

I get back into the trees and move in that same zig zag pattern, this time with the night vision goggles, and I'm going faster. I see a little bit of the house through the trees. I've got to be close to where the sniper is.

I smell cigarette smoke. The tree rustles above me, just in time for me to see the rifle start to point down. I spray the area with bullets from my M4A1.

I hear one muffled scream before a body falls partway down the tree, landing twenty feet from the ground. Dead as a doornail.

Now I can take my time to text.

> Me: Got him. Keep Bella and Trenda in bathroom, then come help me hide the body from their view. We can call the Sheriff after that.

> Renzo: Will do.

~

"Mama I'm scared. Why do we have to stay in the bathroom?"

Bella has sat on the small bathroom counter for almost an hour. She hasn't talked at all. Not even when Renzo tries to talk to her in Spanish while he made funny faces.

"Okay, ladies," Renzo says. "We're safe now. Simon took care of our problem. You two need to stay in the bathroom a little bit longer, and then you can come back out. Okay?"

Bella just nods and so do I. I want to ask if Simon is hurt, but I can't ask that in front of my daughter.

Renzo leaves the bathroom with a jaunty wave.

"Is it true? Did Mr. Simon save us?"

"Yes, he did. He's going to come here and tell us that the bad guy is taken care of and we don't have to worry about him ever again?"

"You promise?"

"I do."

"I'm going to ask Mr. Simon." Bella said.

"I think you should,"

The wait seems to take forever, but finally there's a knock on the door.

"Can I come in?"

"Yes," as I scramble to the door and open it for Simon. I look him over in a millisecond and he looks fine, then I throw my arms around him and give him a passionate kiss. In just a moment, his arms are around my waist and the kiss starts to get carnal. My breasts are tight, and I feel an ache in my core.

"Mama?"

I reluctantly release Simon.

"Are you all right?" I ask, as I pet his chest and look into his eyes.

"I'm fine, Honey." He looks over my shoulder. "Hey there, Bella. Do you want to get out of the bathroom now?"

"No, I have to tinkle. But I didn't want to do it in front of Mr. Renzo."

Simon and I chuckle. "That makes sense," Simon says with a smile.

"You like my Mama a whole lot, don't you?"

"Yes, I do. I love your Mama."

My knees go weak, but Simon clutches me tighter so I don't fall. He looks into my eyes. "Trenda, I am so in love with you." His gray eyes look almost black, they are so filled with emotion.

"I love you too, Simon."

"Do you love me, Mr. Simon?"

Simon releases me carefully, making sure I can stand on my own. Then he turns us both so that we are facing Bella who is sitting on the counter with a worried expression on her face. Simon bends down so that Bella and he are eye to eye. "I love you very much. I think I started loving you when you helped me bag groceries."

Her eyes get wide. "That was a long, long time ago. You must love me lots, Mr. Simon."

He lifts her off the vanity and brings her in for a hug. "I do love you lots, just like I love your Mama lots."

"We all love each other, that's really good." She smiles.

Back at my house, Simon is doing his best to get me to smile. I am practically burrowing into him on my couch. But even being in his arms can't bring me to smile. It was my visit to Mrs. Stapleton today that did it. Seeing all her bruising tore me up. Knowing that she had been beaten in her home to find out where Bella was staying, leaves me heartbroken.

"I can't believe he'd staked out the school and followed her, hoping she would give homework to Bella. He was evil, Simon."

"But she's getting better. That's why she asked you to come over today."

"I know. She was so nice. She said it wasn't my fault. It was out of my control, and I shouldn't feel bad. It was the person who hired the man. That's another thing that I can't believe, that one of Bella's half-brothers was trying to kill her. How could a man do that to a little girl?"

"The Nashville police arrested him."

Now the tears started. "Of course they did." I was in Simon's arms. I always cried all over him. "But why? You told me that Richard and Carla have motives, but Brantley didn't."

"I know, Baby. That's why they gave him bail. The D.A. doesn't have a motive. Dex has brought in Lydia Archer to figure out what his motive is. Apparently, Lydia is as good as her husband Clint."

"Do you have any idea when the Midnight Delta team is going to be back?"

"Even if I was the Commander, with a lot of those missions we won't know the duration. They'll last as long as they need to last. I'm sorry, Honey. Are you missing Drake?"

"Yeah. But not nearly as much, because I have you,"

His eyelids lower, and his silver eyes get dark with passion.

"I feel the same way, Baby. Having you in my life has pushed away the darkness and let in the sun."

Hearing those words, it feels like at last my heart has burst open. This man is my soulmate. I reach up and give him a slow, warm, wet kiss and I feel him shudder.

I lean back and give him a sultry smile. "You're the miracle worker in this relationship. You've freed me from my past. I feel like I can fly."

"Trenda, let's agree to disagree, and we can both be right, shall we?" I love it when he laughs.

"All right."

He lifts me off the couch and carries me down the hall to my bedroom. He stands me up beside the bed and we both slowly undress. I've come to learn that watching like this is part of the build-up. Part of foreplay.

I lie down on the bed, and he kneels beside me. He strokes his hands down my ribs, down my hips then down the outside of my thighs.

"Quit teasing," I beg. I begin to open my legs.

"You're beautiful. I love it when you spread yourself for me. Only ever for me."

"Yes," I sigh. "Only for you."

He brushes his hands up the insides of my legs but avoids my sex. *The tease*. I moan.

His hands span my waist, then move to caress my stomach, his thumb tracing my belly button. I arch up. "Simon. Enough," I wail.

He bends and then he kisses me as magic flows between us. It feels like I'm caught in a whirlwind of want. Then finally he grasps a condom from off the nightstand.

"Finally," I sigh.

∾

After I'm sheathed, I stay still. I soak in her beauty. I smile as she wraps her heels around my ass, but I press her thighs back onto the bed.

"Easy. We're taking this slow."

"No," she wails.

I bend down and give her a long, wet, kiss that leaves me dizzy. She tastes so good, I can't get enough of her. When she bites my lower lip, I laugh.

"Bad girl."

"Now," she growls.

I kneel back up and peruse her body, her flushed face, her beautiful breasts, her wet folds. I can't hold on any longer.

I sink into her tight depths, and she moans. I look at her beautiful eyes as I rest against her and hold her head in my hands. I see nothing but passion and pleasure.

"So good." She gives me a decadent smile.

"I desperately need to feel her smile, so I rub my cheek against hers, and then blow in her ear. I thrust harder and Trenda wraps her legs around me, pulling me close, but she's no match for my strength.

I pull out and then push in. Our rhythm is a dance that is like no other. I nip her earlobe, and she wails my name.

I feel sweat trickling down my back as I hear her panting, so close. She's so close. I feel the tingling and I can't hold on much longer.

I push upwards.

"There. Yes, there again," she yells.

I grin harshly. I give two more thrusts and her channel squeezes my cock, tight.

"Yes, yes, yes," Trenda screams. She grips me like a fist. I see her smile as she starts to whisper my name.

Fire surrounds me and I feel my head exploding.

"I love you, Trenda."

Chapter Thirty-Four

Knoxville and Pigeon Forge don't have anything that I like. When did I turn into such a picky bastard for an engagement ring? For Patsy's, it took me ten minutes. I trudge back out to my GTO after crossing off the last jeweler in the Knoxville area. This is ridiculous. Gray Tyler was the only man I ever heard of who had this kind of problem and he finally had one made. That's out of the question because Nic's wedding is next weekend.

I get in my car and head to Nashville, with the music on a normal volume. Don't want to do anything that might fuck up my hearing. I can't believe that Trenda made me a country music playlist that I actually like, but I boot it up and start with that.

It's not until I'm halfway to Nashville that Trenda calls. I've been expecting it, because she was due to get a courier over to her about Bella's inheritance.

"Hello there, Beautiful Lady."

"Simon, have you found the wedding present that you wanted to give them?"

"Not yet. Still looking."

"I think it's wonderful that you're not just going to their online registry. I think they'll treasure whatever you end up finding."

"I sure hope it ends up being treasured," I say. "Why are you calling? Did you get the papers?"

"Yes I did, and there are a lot more than I expected. Not only does Bella get a payout of Brantley's estate, she also gets shares in his business. Those were equally distributed amongst the four children."

"Seems straightforward."

"It isn't. Mr. Grant, the attorney, also sent me this big box full of paper that's this ongoing lawsuit between Harris Development and the homeowners of his largest residential project. Mr. Grant gave me a cover letter explaining that if they win, that Harris Development could go bankrupt paying out to the claimants, and that they could go after the assets from the estate."

"That sounds like a bunch of bullshit to me."

"I don't know, I keep thinking this is too good to be true. What's more, taking something—anything from Brantley has just felt ucky."

"Even if it's for Bella?"

There is a long pause.

"Trust me, that's the only reason I stepped forward, is because this is money that Bella is entitled to."

"So what are you going to do?"

"I'm going to take the box over to Mr. Fortnum and see what he has to say."

"I think that's a good move."

"Good luck finding a gift."

"Thank you. Good luck with Mr. Fortnum."

As soon as I get off the phone with Trenda, I call Dex. It goes to voicemail. I don't have Lydia's number, and Clint is part of Mason's team and they're out of the country. Gray should have it.

"Hi, Simon. Am I going to see you at the wedding?"

"Absolutely. Hey, I need a favor."

"Anything."

"I need to talk to Lydia Archer; do you know how to get to her? I can't get ahold of Dex."

"Dex is on the obstacle course right now. I don't know Lydia's number, but I can pull Dex off the course and call you back."

"That would be great."

Now I have to put on some music that will truly soothe me, so I put on the Foo Fighters and wait for Dex's call. It comes through in twenty minutes.

"Hey Simon, you called?"

"Yeah. Got a call from Trenda. She got a letter from Horace Grant. It says that if Harris Development loses this lawsuit, that the claimants could end up bankrupting Harris Development and go after the heirs for their money. Sounds like Junior has a motive now for wanting as much money as possible.

"Whoa there, Simon. Remember, even if it's divided into thirds instead of quarters, he would still lose it if they go after their inheritance money," Dex says.

"Yeah but, if they end up not losing everything, he has a cushion with Bella's portion."

"You're right. I'll update the Nashville police."

"How's the ring hunt going?"

"Terrible."

"Don't forget to pick-up a gift for Nic and Cami."

"I keep forgetting that. Thanks."

"You're welcome."

∽

"This is a lot of information, Trenda. It seems like the claimants have a good case that their houses are being contaminated with ammonia and methane gas buildup. This would account for the health problems they're experiencing. The fact that Harris Development built on this land could go one of two ways. Were they unaware, and therefore they're not liable, or were they aware of the potential problems and they built anyway?"

I sit down hard in one of the chairs in front of Mr. Fortnum's desk.

"He knew. Brantley knew."

"My dear, can you explain yourself?"

"When I was living with Brantley, somebody delivered a file to him, but he wasn't home. It was a thick file, and when I went to put it on his desk, some of the papers spilled out. One was something that was a gas probe test with big bold letters, *not suitable for build*, written on it. I can't remember the other one but it had the word *shallow* in it. It had big red letters that said *fail*."

"So your boyfriend knew about this problem ahead of time. That puts a whole new light on this case. But now we just have your word on this."

I thought back to the guy who gave me the files. He was icky, actually he made me feel icky. "Mr. Fortnum, a man came to the door and gave them to me to give to Brantley. I remember he was rude."

"Can you remember anything about him?"

I shook my head. "No, nothing."

"Give it some time my dear. Maybe you will."

I will.

"I must congratulate you, Trenda. I have always felt that you and all of the Avery children have a very strong moral compass and I see I'm not wrong. By trying to remember all of this, you could very well be walking away from millions."

"Yes, but I read just how badly the children have been affected by the methane gas. Some of them will never recover. This just isn't right."

"I agree with you."

"Can I have the box back? Maybe something in it will have the guy's name on it, and I'll remember."

"Of course, it's your box."

"Please send me a bill for your time this afternoon." I say.

"This was just time spent between old friends, my dear. There will certainly not be a bill." The old gentleman smiles.

"Thank you, Sir."

After all of that, I need something happy to do. I leave the box in the back of my SUV and head over to the Mid Lake Retirement Community.

"Ooops."

I turn right at the next stop sign. Need to go by Roger's. Can't visit someone without a gift.

When I get there, Roger is up near the cash registers.

"Trenda, how are you?" he gushes as he practically runs to me.

"I'm fine," I smile. This is the kind of reception I've been getting in a lot of places in town. It's pretty big gossip when you have a hitman out after you, and the deputies aren't known for their discretion.

"We here at Roger's were worried about you. That had to be a traumatic experience."

"I feel terrible about Bella's teacher, but it could have been worse. She's recovering nicely. I dropped off some of my homemade lasagna when I went to see her."

"And your situation could have been worse as well."

"Luckily, I had some very experienced help. Simon Clark has been trained like my brother, so he was able to protect Bella and me."

"He's a SEAL?"

I thought Roger's eyes would pop out of his head.

"I said he had the same training, Roger."

"Oh, okay." He was real disappointed, which is what I wanted.

"The important thing is that you and Bella are safe. I don't know what we would've all done if something had happened to you two. Our town would have been devastated."

What do I say to that?

"Hmmm. Roger, I'm looking for some really good baked goods that I can bring to Violet and Luther Randolph. I'm going to go visit them. Oh, and a flower arrangement, already in a vase, in case Violet doesn't have one."

"That is exceptionally nice of you, Trenda. See what I mean? That's why the town loves you. You pay for the food, the flowers will be on me."

"I'll be sure to tell Violet," I squeeze his arm and he blushes.

"You head on over to the bakery. I'm pretty sure that Anna just took some cherry pies out of the oven. You can't go wrong with that." I give him a grateful smile.

"Maybe I'll buy two. One for Violet and Luther, and one for home."

"That's the ticket." He puts two fingers to his forehead in a salute then turns to go to the floral department.

By the time I get to the front of the line at the check-out aisle, Roger is waiting with a gorgeous display of tulips.

"Those are perfect."

Roger takes the flowers and puts them on the floor of

my front seat. They have a box around them so they won't slip.

"They'll love your tulips, Roger. My guess is you'll get a thank you card from Violet."

"I wouldn't be surprised," he says as I start my car.

Now I can go to the Mid Lake Retirement Community.

"Trenda, what a nice surprise! Luther, look, it's Trenda."

Luther comes to the door and smiles. "Let me take those flowers from you, they look heavy." He takes the box and proceeds to put it on the coffee table.

"This is one of his really good days. You came at a wonderful time," she whispers. In a louder voice she says, "Come on in."

"Those flowers are from Roger Clemmons, over at the grocery store. Isn't that nice?"

"I'll have to send him a thank you card," Violet smiles.

"Thank you. I also brought cherry pie."

"I like cherry pie," Luther says as he puts his arm around Violet and looks down at her with a loving glance. I melt seeing that, after my last visit with him. This is beautiful.

"So how are you liking it here?" I ask, after we all settle down on the sofa and chair.

"I like it a lot." Luther smiles, with his arm still around Violet. "I get to go in the..." He pauses for a long time. "Where do I go, Violet? I like it."

"You go to the garden and plant flowers."

He turns to me. "I plant flowers."

"That is so nice. How's the food?"

He turns to Violet again. She bites her lip and looks at me. I can see some of his concentration has slipped. "Remember the restaurant, Luther?"

He turns back to me and smiles. "We go to a restaurant every day with friends. We get to eat good food most of the time. Sometimes it's bad food."

I laugh. "I can always depend on you to tell the truth, Luther."

"You should never tell a lie," Luther says.

"That's right, my Love." Violet reaches up and smooths her hand down his jaw and he grabs it and gives her a kiss in the middle of her palm.

I would have never forgiven myself if Violet hadn't made it down the mountain alive. She looks at me and smiles. It's as if she can read my mind.

"You take on too much, Trenda. You can't control everything in life. When you learn to let go and let others take care of you, you'll be a happier woman."

As we continue to talk for the rest of the afternoon, I ruminate on what she says. Violet Randolph is a wise woman.

Chapter Thirty-Five

"So, Bella doesn't inherit anything?" Evie asks.

"Everything is up in the air. But from what Mr. Fortnum had to say, she won't get anything. It will go to all those poor people who bought houses in the housing development."

"And it's all because you remembered some guy's name from almost ten years ago and the company Ryker. You've got quite the memory. I have to say, Trenda, I'm not sure I would have done what you did if I were in your shoes."

"Yes, you would have."

"Sure, now I would; Aiden's loaded. But before that? Knowing I could have set up my kid for life?"

"What's more important—money or teaching Bella values?"

Evie sighs. "As a future mother, I take your point."

I scream as she jumps up from the couch. Then she jumps up in the air and promptly drops her cellphone. I bend down and scoop it up.

"Are you telling me you're pregnant?"

"I shouldn't be telling you this. The rule is, don't tell

anybody until you're twelve weeks along, but I peed on a stick today, and...*I'm pregnant*!" Evie screams the last two words.

"Oh my God. This is so wonderful. What did Aiden say?"

"He's not answering his cellphone. I waited three whole hours for him to call me back and then I couldn't wait any longer. So, you got a call."

I laugh. That's typical Evie.

"I'm worried about Chloe," Evie says softly.

"She's doing better. I promise. She'll be able to handle you being pregnant." I say softly.

"I hope so—"

"Hang up your phone."

My head whips around to my front door and I see Carla there, holding a gun.

"Evie—"

She shoots the gun and a bullet rips into the couch right beside me. I drop my phone, and she shoots at it, misses, shoots at it again. I lunge for her. She backs up and holds the gun steady, pointed right at me. She's wearing gloves.

"Go hang up the phone. I might not be able to hit the phone, but I'll be able to hit you," she whispers. I hang up the phone.

"I've hated you for years, you whore."

I turn back toward her. "You're never going to get away with this."

"You live at the end of the cul-de-sac, nobody to the back or the sides. I will. I have an unregistered gun. So easy to get. But I'm going to do one of the movie things where you have to listen to all the reasons I hate your bitch ass."

"Evie was recording you, she heard your voice," I protest.

"Stupid cow, I whispered to you. A recording can't pick

that up."

"Sure they can." Then I try to reason with her. "Think of your son."

"I have. That's all I've thought about. He's going to be out on his ass, right beside me, because of you. You've ruined his life, just like you've ruined mine."

I want to keep her talking as long as possible, just like she said, in the movies. Evie heard the gunshot. I'll have Simon, Zarek, and better not be Evie on their way.

"Do you know how you ruined my marriage?" she continues. "Brant started comparing me to you after I got rid of you. How pretty and young you were. I had to go and get plastic surgery, but it was never good enough. After you, he was blatant with his affairs. He'd take them to our country club and I was a laughingstock. Did you know that? Some backwoods trash like you, ruined my life."

"I'm sorry," I whisper.

"Sorry doesn't mean anything."

"It was Brantley, he fooled me too. I was taken for a ride just like you were. Coming back home with an illegitimate child. Do you know how hard it was for me?"

"I don't care about your sob story. It was nothing like what I had to put up with."

"Did he hit you? He hit me," I commiserate.

"Twice."

"No man, who's really a man, should ever hit a woman. He was a pig." I say.

"He gave me a black eye. I couldn't go out in public for two weeks. I had to miss a charity luncheon."

"How about your son? How was he to Kevin?"

"He was awful. He only cared about his two older boys. He treated Kevin like garbage. Never talked to him. He didn't care that he got all A's in school. He never complimented him."

"He is lucky he has you."

"He was, but you ruined it all!" she screeches. "Now we have nothing!"

She shoots the gun again. Her aim is off, and she hits the couch again.

"I meant to do that," she says. "I'm going to make you kneel in front of me, just like in those mafia movies."

Fat chance that's ever happening.

"I'm going to shoot you right between the eyes. Now march to your backyard."

This I like. It gives me more room to move. Hopefully, it gives the guys a better shot. I look at the clock over the stove. It's one thirty-five. I had looked at my phone when I picked it up after I dropped it when Evie told me she was pregnant. It wasn't quite one-fifteen. Shouldn't the guys be here by now?

"Open the door. Do it slowly."

I do.

As soon as I'm out of the door, Simon yanks my arm, and I'm out of the doorway. Carla screams as she starts shooting at the empty yard straight in front of her. Simon hits her in the jaw with his right fist as he yanks the gun out of her hand with his left hand. Carla crumples to the ground. Unconscious.

He turns to me.

"Baby, are you all right?"

"No injuries, just scared."

He hauls me into his arms and kisses me.

"You are never allowed to leave me. You got that?" He says.

"I promise. Never ever."

Then I reach up and kiss him. He tastes like a warrior, like a man, like my man.

Epilogue

I don't check the P.O. box I've set up in Jasper Creek all that often. When I finally do, I see a letter from Dora Mathews of Minneapolis that's about four months old and has been forwarded from the Department of the Navy. I drive my GTO back to my cabin, even though I had planned to go Trenda's.

I sit down on the crappy brown couch that came with the place and see that my hand is actually trembling as I look at the letter. It's a legal-sized envelope, and when I open it, I see a letter addressed to me, written on one sheet of yellow paper.

Dear Commander Clark, I'm going to call you Simon because Liz did,

My name is Dora and I was the only friend that your sister had here in Minneapolis. I did her nails at Finest Nails on Fifth Street. She came once every

three weeks, because she had to look good for her husband.

I started noticing things weren't good right off. My ex used to beat me too. I know Liz wore all the fancy stuff, but even if you got money, doesn't mean you can't get beat. You know? It started to get real bad, but the worse it got the more she thought it was her fault. I tried to tell her it wasn't.

I even had the police come one time, and she denied everything. It was so sad, they couldn't do nothing. She didn't come to me for three months, but then she came back, because she said I was her only friend.

About six months before she died she started talking about you. I got excited because I thought that meant she would ask you for help. She just talked about how great it was having you as a big brother when she was little. I asked her why she wouldn't go to you for help if you were such a big guy and all. She said she never wanted you to see her like this. It was just like with the police, she had pride and she had shame.

But the reason I'm writing you this letter is to tell you that in the end she was getting out of there. She was saving money, and I had a friend in El Paso she could stay with for a while. She just kept wanting to save a little bit more.

So I want you to know in the end she died brave.

Dora Mathews

I sit there until it's dark. My phone rings a few times, but I ignore it. I need to process. I finally get up and walk over to the mantel and pick up the picture of Mom and Lizzie. What beautiful smiles they had. I wipe away the two tears that mar the glass.

"Rest in peace, Lizzie. Mom, take care of our girl. I love you, Lizard."

I look at my watch. I've missed dinner time, but Trenda will understand.

I pick up the letter, my keys, and my phone, then head out.

"You may now kiss the bride."

Nic and Cami kiss, and everybody claps. Actually there's a lot of stomping as well as many of the Night Storm team hollering 'Hooyah.' I look down and Bella is squeezing the life out of both mine and Trenda's hands.

"Are they married?" she asks in a very soft whisper. Trenda has taught her well.

Trenda nods.

"Now what?"

Nic and Cami walk down the aisle, grinning wide as can be.

"Now we're going to eat and have cake and dance," I tell her.

"I know how to dance," she tells me proudly.

"Then let's go."

We take a cab from the church back to the hotel, Trenda looking gorgeous in her lavender dress, and Bella wearing a green and lavender dress. They both have lavender shoes. Trenda's have been driving me insane all night.

When we get to the hotel, I ask them if they want to go straight to the reception hall or go up to their room for anything.

"I have to go to the bathroom."

"Then let's go up to our rooms," I suggest.

As soon as we get into Bella and Trenda's room and Bella is in the bathroom, I pounce.

"You have been driving me crazy, woman."

"Back at you, in that uniform." She pulls my head down for a ravenous kiss.

I pull her closer. The silk of her dress feels good, but not as good as naked skin would.

I hear the toilet flush, and reluctantly release her.

She smiles up at me. "I have to redo my lipstick, don't I?"

"Do I have to redo mine?" I ask.

"Perhaps you might want to check it out," she chuckles.

"Bella is having a ball," I whisper to Simon.

He looks over his shoulder so he can see what I'm seeing. Right now, Cullen Lyons is holding her up in one arm, with his other arm sticking out, holding her hand. They are twirling around the dance floor. I hadn't met him until tonight. He was seated at our table and is a member of Nic's team. He told the funniest stories.

"She couldn't be having as much fun as I am," Simon says as he kisses the top of my head and pulls me even closer. We've danced at least five songs in a row, and we both continue to keep watch for Bella, who is constantly entertained.

I'm sorry to see the party about to end, but I know the venue is closing at midnight.

"Ladies and Gentlemen, I would like to have your attention."

On the dais with the disc jockey is Josiah Hale.

"The servers are coming around with new glasses of champagne. I've talked to Nic and Cami and they think this is a fabulous idea. So we're going to have one more little thing to toast tonight."

I look around and watch as Bella does a fist pump as a server gives her a glass of sparkling cider. I can't remember the name of the man who is currently dancing with Bella now, but he has a son about her age.

"Let's hear a hooyah, if you all have your champagne."

The crowd goes wild with the sound of men crying hooyah. Josiah grins.

"Well okay then. I need the following people to come up here on the stage. Commander Simon Clark."

I feel Simon tense in my arms. I know he doesn't like being called Commander, because he feels that there were politics with the way he retired. But men like his former captain, Josiah Hale have said, they will always think of him as—and call him—Commander.

"I would also like to have one of the infamous Avery sisters take the stage."

Simon grips my waist just a little tighter for a moment as he looks up at the ceiling as if he were looking for strength.

"And last but not least, the little spitfire, Bella Avery. Will she come up to the stage?"

I watch as Max Hogan—I finally remember his name—starts walking forward with Bella in his arms.

≈

"Honey, we better go on up there. Max is taking Bella; I don't want her up there all by herself."

"Okay." I smile down at Trenda. We start weaving our way to the stage, me shooting killer looks at Josiah the entire way. He knows damn good and well I have Trenda's ring in my pocket; he asked to see it.

Bastard. He's going to make me propose in front of everybody.

As I help Trenda up on the stage, I look at her baffled expression and think that if anybody deserves an over-the-top proposal with a hundred people toasting her, it is Trenda Avery. I look at Josiah again. He smirks, cause he knows I am now down with the program.

I had been intending to propose underneath one of the pretty lit trees in the lobby, with an abundance of flowers. This is going to be so much better.

Bella is still standing next to Max and holding her cider. Trenda is standing in front of me looking bewildered.

"Bella, can you come stand next to your Mama for a minute?"

"Sure," she smiles.

"I'll take this for awhile," Max says as he plucks the flute of cider out of her hands. When Trenda sees that happen, she gives me a suspicious look, and I take her flute of champagne and hand it to the D.J.

When my two girls are in front of me, I smile, and they smile back at me.

"Mr. Simon, what's going on?"

I get down on one knee and look at the little girl who has captured my heart. "I'll tell you what's going on, I'm going to ask you and your Mama to be my family."

She gasps in a deep breath and for the first time is left speechless.

I turn to Trenda and pull out the perfect ring for her. It's a square cut topaz ring to match her eyes, with a two-carat diamond on either side, set in platinum.

"Simon. My God, it's beautiful."

"You are my soulmate, Trenda Avery. Will you marry me?"

"Yes. My God, yes. Because of you, I can touch the stars."

I put the ring on her ring finger, and it fits perfectly.

Now I turn to Bella and take out another box. In it is a pretty gold necklace with three circles intertwined, and a ruby at each connection point.

"Bella, will you allow me to be part of your family? I want to love you and your Mama forever. Will you let me do that?"

She touches the necklace, then looks at me.

"Can I call you Daddy?"

Dear God, I think I'm going to cry.

Out of the corner of my eye, I see that Trenda *is* crying.

"Yes, you can."

"I wished for us to be a family."

She throws her arms around my neck.

"I did too." I pick her up, and pull Trenda close in my other arm.

I'm holding miracles in my arms. True miracles.

About the Author

Caitlyn O'Leary is a USA Bestselling Author, #1 Amazon Bestselling Author and a Golden Quill Recipient from Book Viral in 2015. Hampered with a mild form of dyslexia she began memorizing books at an early age until her grandmother, the English teacher, took the time to teach her to read -- then she never stopped. She began re-writing alternate endings for her Trixie Belden books into happily-ever-afters with Trixie's platonic friend Jim. When she was home with pneumonia at twelve, she read the entire set of World Book Encyclopedias -- a little more challenging to end those happily.

Caitlyn loves writing about Alpha males with strong heroines who keep the men on their toes. There is plenty of action, suspense and humor in her books. She is never shy about tackling some of today's tough and relevant issues.

In addition to being an award-winning author of romantic suspense novels, she is a devoted aunt, an avid reader, a former corporate executive for a Fortune 100 company, and totally in love with her husband of soon-to-be twenty years.

She recently moved back home to the Pacific Northwest from Southern California. She is so happy to see the seasons again; rain, rain and more rain. She has a large fan group on Facebook and through her e-mail list. Caitlyn is known for telling her "Caitlyn Factors", where she relates her little and big life's screw-ups. The list is long. She loves hearing and connecting with her fans on a daily basis.

Keep up with Caitlyn O'Leary:

Website: www.caitlynoleary.com
FB Reader Group: http://bit.ly/2NUZVjF
Email: caitlyn@caitlynoleary.com
Newsletter: http://bit.ly/1WIhRup

facebook.com/Caitlyn-OLeary-Author-638771522866740

twitter.com/CaitlynOLearyNA

instagram.com/caitlynoleary_author

amazon.com/author/caitlynoleary

bookbub.com/authors/caitlyn-o-leary

goodreads.com/CaitlynOLeary

pinterest.com/caitlynoleary35

Also by Caitlyn O'Leary

PROTECTORS OF JASPER CREEK SERIES

His Wounded Heart (Book 1)

Her Hidden Smile (Book 2)

OMEGA SKY SERIES

Her Selfless Warrior (Book #1)

Her Unflinching Warrior (Book #2)

Her Wild Warrior (Book #3)

Her Fearless Warrior (Book 4)

Her Defiant Warrior (Book 5)

NIGHT STORM SERIES

Her Ruthless Protector (Book #1)

Her Tempting Protector (Book #2)

Her Chosen Protector (Book #3)

Her Intense Protector (Book #4)

Her Sensual Protector (Book #5)

Her Faithful Protector (Book #6)

Her Noble Protector (Book #7)

Her Righteous Protector (Book #8)

NIGHT STORM LEGACY SERIES

Lawson & Jill (Book 1)

THE MIDNIGHT DELTA SERIES

Her Vigilant Seal (Book #1)

Her Loyal Seal (Book #2)

Her Adoring Seal (Book #3)

Sealed with a Kiss (Book #4)

Her Daring Seal (Book #5)

Her Fierce Seal (Book #6)

A Seals Vigilant Heart (Book #7)

Her Dominant Seal (Book #8)

Her Relentless Seal (Book #9)

Her Treasured Seal (Book #10)

Her Unbroken Seal (Book #11)

BLACK DAWN SERIES

Her Steadfast Hero (Book #1)

Her Devoted Hero (Book #2)

Her Passionate Hero (Book #3)

Her Wicked Hero (Book #4)

Her Guarded Hero (Book #5)

Her Captivated Hero (Book #6)

Her Honorable Hero (Book #7)

Her Loving Hero (Book #8)

THE FOUND SERIES

Revealed (Book #1)

Forsaken (Book #2)

Healed (Book #3)

SHADOWS ALLIANCE SERIES

Declan

Made in the USA
Columbia, SC
26 June 2023

19408287R00200